The curtain sprang aside
and his eyes were dazzled
by the light of diamonds.

KING—*of*
THE KHYBER RIFLES

A ROMANCE OF ADVENTURE

By TALBOT MUNDY
Author of Rung Ho!

ILLUSTRATED BY
J. CLEMENT COLL

WILDSIDE PRESS

www.wildsidepress.com

KING—OF THE KHYBER RIFLES

Suckled were we in a school unkind
On suddenly snatched deduction,
And ever ahead of you (never behind!)
Over the border our tracks you'll find,
Wherever some idiot feels inclined
To scatter the seeds of ruction.

For eyes we be, of Empire, we!
Skinned and puckered and quick to see!
And nobody guesses how wise we be.
Unwilling to advertise we be.
But, hot on the trail of lies, we be
The pullers of roots of ruction!

——Song of the Indian Secret
Service.

King—
Of The Khyber Rifles

CHAPTER I

THE men who govern India—more power to them and her!—are few. Those who stand in their way and pretend to help them with a flood of words are a host. And from the host goes up an endless cry that India is the home of thugs, and of three hundred million hungry ones.

The men who know—and Athelstan King might claim to know a little—answer that she is the original home of chivalry and the modern mistress of as many decent, gallant, native gentlemen as ever graced a page of history.

The charge has seen the light in print that India—well-spring of plague and sudden death and money-lenders—has sold her soul to twenty succeeding conquerors in turn.

1

Athelstan King and a hundred like him whom India has picked from British stock and taught, can answer truly that she has won it back again from each by very purity of purpose.

So when the world war broke the world was destined to be surprised on India's account. The Red Sea, full of racing transports crowded with dark-skinned gentlemen, whose one prayer was that the war might not be over before they should have struck a blow for Britain, was the Indian army's answer to the press.

The rest of India paid its taxes and contributed and muzzled itself and set to work to make supplies. For they understand in India, almost as nowhere else, the meaning of such old-fashioned words as gratitude and honor; and of such platitudes as, "Give and it shall be given unto you."

More than one nation was deeply shocked by India's answer to "practises" that had extended over years. But there were men in India who learned to love India long ago with that love that casts out fear, who knew exactly what was going to happen and could therefore afford to wait for orders instead of running round in rings.

Athelstan King, for instance, nothing yet but a captain unattached, sat in meagerly furnished quarters with his heels on a table. He is not a doctor, yet he read a book on surgery; and when he went over to the club he carried the book under his arm and continued to read it there. He is considered a rotten conversationalist, and he did nothing at the club to improve his reputation.

"Man alive—get a move on!" gasped a wondering senior, accepting a cigar. Nobody knows where he gets those long, strong, black cheroots, and nobody ever refuses one.

"Thanks—got a book to read," said King.

"You ass! Wake up and grab the best thing in sight, as a stepping stone to something better! Wake up and worry!"

King grinned. You have to when you don't agree with a senior officer, for the army is like a school in many more ways than one.

"Help yourself, sir! I'll take the job that's left when the scramble's over. Something good's sure to be overlooked."

"White feather? Laziness? Dark Horse?" the major wondered. Then he hurried away to write telegrams, because a belief thrives in the early days of any war that influence can make or break a man's chances. In the other room where the telegraph blanks were littered in confusion all about the floor, he ran into a crony whose chief sore point was Athelstan King, loathing him as some men loathe pickles or sardines, for no real reason whatever, except that they are what they are.

"Saw you talking to King," he said.

"Yes. Can't make him out. Rum fellow!"

"Rum? Huh! Trouble is he's seventh of his family in succession to serve in India. She has seeped into him and pickled his heritage. He's a believer in Kismet crossed on to Opportunity. Not sure he doesn't pray to Allah on the sly! Hopeless case."

"Are you sure?"

"Quite!"

So they all sent telegrams and forgot King who sat and smoked and read about surgery; and before he had nearly finished one box of cheroots a general at Peshawur wiped a bald red skull and sent him an urgent telegram.

"Come at once!" it said simply.

King was at Lahore, but miles don't matter when the dogs of war are loosed. The right man goes to the right place at the exact right time then, and the fool goes to the wall. In that one respect war is better than some kinds of peace.

In the train on the way to Peshawur he did not talk any more volubly, and a fellow traveler, studying him from the opposite corner of the stifling compartment, catalogued him as "quite an ordinary man." But *he* was of the Public Works Department, which is sorrowfully underpaid and wears emotions on its sleeve for policy's sake, believing of course that all the rest of the world should do the same.

"Don't you think we're bound in honor to go to Belgium's aid?" he asked. "Can you see any way out of it?"

"Haven't looked for one," said King.

"But don't you think—"

"No," said King. "I hardly ever think. I'm in the army, don't you know, and don't have to. What's the use of doing somebody else's work?"

"Rotter!" thought the P. W. D. man, almost aloud; but King was not troubled by any further forced conversation. Consequently he reached Peshawur comfortable, in spite of the heat. And his genial manner of saluting the full-general who met him with a dog-cart at Peshawur station was something scandalous.

"Is he a lunatic or a relative or royalty?" the P. W. D. man wondered.

Full-generals, particularly in the early days of war, do not drive to the station to meet captains very often; yet King climbed into the dog-cart unexcitedly, after keeping the general waiting while he checked a trunk! The general cracked his whip without any other comment than a smile. A blood mare tore sparks out of the macadam, and a dusty military road began to ribbon out between the wheels. Sentries in unexpected places announced themselves with a ring of shaken steel as their rifles came to the "present," which courtesies the general noticed with a raised whip. Then a fox-terrier resumed his chase of squirrels between the planted shade-trees, and Peshawur became normal, shimmering in light and heat reflected from the "Hills."

(The P. W. D. man, who would have giggled if a general mentioned him by name, walked because no conveyance could be hired. Judgment was in the wind.)

On the dog-cart's high front seat, staring straight ahead of him between the horse's ears, King listened. The general did nearly all the talking.

"The North's the danger."

King grunted with the lids half-lowered over full dark eyes. He did not look especially handsome in that attitude. Some men swear he looks like a Roman, and others liken him to a gargoyle, all of them choosing to ignore the smile that can transform his whole face instantly.

"We're denuding India of troops—not keeping back more than a mere handful to hold the tribes in check."

King nodded. There has never been peace along the northwest border. It did not need vision to foresee trouble from that quarter. In fact it must have been partly on the strength of some of King's reports that the general was planning now.

"That was a very small handful of Sikhs you named as likely to give trouble. Did you do that job thoroughly?"

King grunted.

"Well—Delhi's chock-full of spies, all listening to stories made in Germany for them to take back to the 'Hills' with 'em. The tribes'll know presently how many men we're sending oversea. There've been rumors about Khinjan by the hundred lately. They're cooking something. Can you imagine 'em keeping quiet now?"

"That depends, sir. Yes, I can imagine it."

The general laughed. "That's why I sent for you. I need a man with imagination! There's a woman you've got to work with on this occasion who can imagine a shade or two too much. What's worse, she's ambitious. So I chose you to work with her."

King's lips stiffened under his mustache, and the corners of his eyes wrinkled into crow's-feet to correspond. Eyes are never coal-black, of course, but his looked it at that minute.

"You know we've sent men to Khinjan who are said to have entered the Caves. Not one of 'em has ever returned."

King frowned.

"She claims she can enter the Caves and come out again at pleasure. She has offered to do it, and I have accepted."

It would not have been polite to look incredulous, so King's expression changed to one of intense interest a little overdone, as the general did not fail to notice.

"If she hadn't given proof of devotion and ability, I'd have turned her down. But she has. Only the other day she uncovered a plot in Delhi—about a million dynamite bombs in a ruined temple in charge of a German agent for use by mutineers supposed to be ready to rise against us. Fact! Can you guess who she is?"

"Not Yasmini?" King hazarded, and the general nodded and flicked his whip. The horse mistook it for a signal, and it was two minutes before the speed was reduced to mere recklessness.

The helmet-strap mark, printed indelibly on King's jaw and cheek by the Indian sun, tightened and grew whiter—as the general noted out of the corner of his eye.

"Know her?"

"Know *of* her, of course, sir. Everybody does Never met her to my knowledge."

"Um-m-m! Whose fault was that? Somebody ought to have seen to that. Go to Delhi now and meet her. I'll send her a wire to say you're coming. She knows I've chosen you. She tried to insist on full discretion, but I overruled her. Between us two, she'll *have* discretion once she gets beyond Jamrud. The 'Hills' are full of our spies, of course, but none of 'em dare try Khinjan Caves any more and you'll be the only check we shall have on her."

King's tongue licked his lips, and his eyes wrinkled. The general's voice became the least shade more authoritative.

"When you see her, get a pass from her that'll take you into Khinjan Caves! Ask her for it! For the

sake of appearances I'll gazette you Seconded to the
Khyber Rifles. For the sake of success, get a pass
from her!"

"Very well, sir."

"You've a brother in the Khyber Rifles, haven't
you? Was it you or your brother who visited Khinjan
once and sent in a report?"

"I did, sir."

He spoke without pride. Even the brigade of
British-Indian cavalry that went to Khinjan on the
strength of his report and leveled its defenses with
the ground, had not been able to find the famous Caves.
Yet the Caves themselves are a by-word.

"There's talk of a jihad (holy war). There's worse
than that! When you went to Khinjan, what was your
chief object?"

"To find the source of the everlasting rumors about
the so-called 'Heart of the Hills,' sir."

"Yes, yes. I remember. I read your report. You
didn't find anything, did you? Well. The story is
now that the 'Heart of the Hills' has come to life. So
the spies say."

King whistled softly.

"There's no guessing what it means," said the general. "Go and find out. Go and work with Yasmini. I
shall have enough men here to attack instantly and
smash any small force as soon as it begins to gather
anywhere near the border. But Khinjan is another
story. We can't prove anything, but the spies keep
bringing in rumors of ten thousand men in Khinjan
Caves, and of another large lashkar not far away from
Khinjan. There must be no jihad, King! India is
all but defenseless! We can tackle sporadic raids.

We can even handle an ordinary raid in force. But this story about a 'Heart of the Hills' coming to life may presage unity of action and a holy war such as the world has not seen. Go up there and stop it if you can. At least, let me know the facts."

King grunted. To stop a holy war single-handed would be rather like stopping the wind—possibly easy enough, if one knew the way. Yet he knew no general would throw away a man like himself on a useless venture. He began to look happy.

The general clucked to the mare and the big beast sank an inch between the shafts. The sais behind set his feet against the drop-board and clung with both hands to the seat. One wheel ceased to touch the gravel as they whirled along a semicircular drive. Suddenly the mare drew up on her haunches, under the porch of a pretentious residence. Sentries saluted. The sais swung down. In less than sixty seconds King was following the general through a wide entrance into a crowded hall. The instant the general's fat figure darkened the doorway twenty men of higher rank than King, native and English, rose from lined-up chairs and pressed forward.

"Sorry—have to keep you all waiting—busy!" He waved them aside with a little apologetic gesture. "Come in here, King."

King followed him through a door that slammed tight behind them on rubber jambs.

"Sit down!"

The general unlocked a steel drawer and began to rummage among the papers in it. In a minute he produced a package, bound in rubber bands, with a faded photograph face-upward on the top.

"That's the woman! How d'you like the look of her?"

King took the package and for a minute stared hard at the likeness of a woman whose fame has traveled up and down India, until her witchery has become a proverb. She was dressed as a dancing woman, yet very few dancing women could afford to be dressed as she was.

King's service uses whom it may, and he had met and talked with many dancing women in the course of duty; but as he stared at Yasmini's likeness he did not think he had ever met one who so measured up to rumor. The nautch he knew for a delusion. Yet—!

The general watched his face with eyes that missed nothing.

"Remember—I said work *with* her!"

King looked up and nodded.

"They say she's three parts Russian," said the general. "To my own knowledge she speaks Russian like a native, and about twenty other tongues as well, including English. She speaks English as well as you or I. She was the girl-widow of a rascally Hill-rajah. There's a story I've heard, to the effect that Russia arranged her marriage in the days when India was Russia's objective—and that's how long ago?—seems like weeks, not years! I've heard she loved her rajah. And I've heard she didn't! There's another story that she poisoned him. I know she got away with his money—and that's proof enough of brains! Some say she's a she-devil. I think that's an exaggeration, but bear in mind she's dangerous!"

King grinned. A man who trusts Eastern women over readily does not rise far in the Secret Service.

"If you've got *nous* enough to keep on her soft side and use her—not let her use you—you can keep the 'Hills' quiet and the Khyber safe! If you can contrive that—now—in this pinch—there's no limit for you! Commander-in-chief shall be your job before you're sixty!"

King pocketed the photograph and papers. "I'm well enough content, sir, as things are," he said quietly.

"Well, remember *she's* ambitious, even if you're not! I'm not preaching ambition, mind—I'm warning you! Ambition's bad! Study those papers on your way down to Delhi and see that I get them back."

The general paced once across the room and once back again, with hands behind him. Then he stopped in front of King.

"No man in India has a stiffer task than you have now! It may encourage you to know that I realize that! She's the key to the puzzle, and she happens to be in Delhi. Go to Delhi, then. A jihad launched from the 'Hills' would mean anarchy in the plains. That would entail sending back from France an army that can't be spared. There must be no jihad, King! —There must—not—be—one! Keep that in your head!"

"What arrangements have been made with her, sir?"

"Practically none! She's watching the spies in Delhi, but they're likely to break for the 'Hills' any minute. Then they'll be arrested. When that happens the fate of India may be in your hands and hers! Get out of my way now, until tiffin-time!"

In a way that some men never learn, King proceeded to efface himself entirely among the crowd in the hall, contriving to say nothing of any account to anybody

until the great gong boomed and the general led them
all in to his long dining table. Yet he did not look
furtive or secretive. Nobody noticed him, and he
noticed everybody. There is nothing whatever secretive about that.

The fare was plain, and the meal a perfunctory
affair. The general and his guests were there for no
other reason than to eat food, and only the man who
happened to seat himself next to King—a major by
the name of Hyde—spoke to him at all.

"Why aren't you with your regiment?" he asked.

"Because the general asked me to lunch, sir!"

"I suppose you've been pestering him for an appoint-
ment!"

King, with his mouth full of curry, did not answer,
but his eyes smiled.

"It's astonishing to me," said the major, "that a captain should leave his company when war has begun!
When I was captain I'd have been driven out of the
service if I'd asked for leave of absence at such a
time!"

King made no comment, but his expression denoted
belief.

"Are you bound for the front, sir?" he asked presently. But Hyde did not answer. They finished the
meal in silence.

After lunch he was closeted with the general again
for twenty minutes. Then one of the general's carriages took him to the station; and it did not appear to
trouble him at all that the other occupant of the carriage was the self-same Major Hyde who had sat next
him at lunch. In fact, he smiled so pleasantly that
Hyde grew exasperated. Neither of them spoke. At

the station Hyde lost his temper openly, and King left him abusing an unhappy native servant.

The station was crammed to suffocation by a crowd that roared and writhed and smelt to high heaven. At one end of the platform, in the midst of a human eddy, a frenzied horse resisted with his teeth and all four feet at once the efforts of six natives and a British sergeant to force him into a loose-box. At the back of the same platform the little dark-brown mules of a mountain battery twitched their flanks in line, jingling chains and stamping when the flies bit home.

Flies buzzed everywhere. Fat native merchants vied with lean and timid ones in noisy effort to secure accommodation on a train already crowded to the limit. Twenty British officers hunted up and down for the places supposed to have been reserved for them, and sweating servants hurried after them with arms full of heterogeneous baggage, swearing at the crowd that swore back ungrudgingly. But the general himself had telephoned for King's reservation, so he took his time.

There were din and stink and dust beneath a savage sun, shaken into reverberations by the scream of an engine's safety valve. It was India in essence and awake!—India arising out of lethargy!—India as she is more often nowadays—and it made King, for the time being of the Khyber Rifles, happier than some other men can be in ballrooms.

Any one who watched him—and there was at least one man who did—must have noticed his strange ability, almost like that of water, to reach the point he aimed for, through, and not around, the crowd.

He neither shoved nor argued. Orders and blows

would have been equally useless, for had it tried the crowd could not have obeyed, and it was in no mind to try. Without the least apparent effort he arrived—and there is no other word that quite describes it—he arrived, through the densest part of the sweating throng of humans, at the door of the luggage office.

There, though a *bunnia's* sharp elbow nagged his ribs, and the *bunnia's* servant dropped a heavy package on his foot, he smiled so genially that he melted the wrath of the frantic luggage clerk. But not at once. Even the sun needs seconds to melt ice.

"Am I God?" the babu wailed. "Can I do all the-e things in all the-e world at once if not sooner?"

King's smile began to get its work in. The man ceased gesticulating to wipe sweat from his stubbly jowl with the end of a Punjabi head-dress. He actually smiled back. Who was he, that he should suspect new outrage or guess he was about to be used in a game he did not understand? He would have stopped all work to beg for extra pay at the merest suggestion of such a thing; but as it was he raised both fists and lapsed into his own tongue to apostrophize the ruffian who dared jostle King. A Northerner who did not seem to understand Punjabi almost cost King his balance as he thrust broad shoulders between him and the *bunnia*.

The *bunnia* chattered like an outraged ape; but King, the person most entitled to be angry, actually apologized! That being a miracle, the babu forthwith wrought another one, and within a minute King's one trunk was checked through to Delhi.

"Delhi is right, sahib?" he asked, to make doubly sure; for in India where the milk of human kindness is not hawked in the market-place, men will pay over-measure for a smile.

"Yes. Delhi is right. Thank you, babuji."

He made more room for the Hillman, beaming amusement at the man's impatience; but the Hillman had no luggage and turned away, making an unexpected effort to hide his face with a turban end. He who had forced his way to the front with so much violence and haste now burst back again toward the train like a football forward tearing through the thick of his opponents. He scattered a swath a yard wide, for he had shoulders like a bull. King saw him leap into a third-class carriage. He saw, too, that he was not wanted in the carriage. There was a storm of protest from tight-packed native passengers, but the fellow had his way.

The swath through the crowd closed up like water in a ship's wake, but it opened again for King. He smiled so humorously that the angry jostled ones smiled too and were appeased, forgetting haste and bruises and indignity merely because understanding looked at them through merry eyes. All crowds are that way, but an Indian crowd more so than all.

Taking his time, and falling foul of nobody, King marked down a native constable—hot and unhappy, leaning with his back against the train. He touched him on the shoulder and the fellow jumped.

"Nay, sahib! I am only constabeel—I know nothing —I can do nothing! The teerain goes when it goes, and then perhaps we will beat these people from the platform and make room again! But there is no authority—no law any more—they are all gone mad!"

King wrote on a pad, tore off a sheet, folded it and gave it to him.

"That is for the Superintendent of Police at the office. Carriage number 1181, eleven doors from here —the one with the shut door and a big Hillman inside sitting three places from the door, facing the engine. Get the Hillman! No, there is only one Hillman in the carriage. No, the others are not his friends; they will not help him. He will fight, but he has no friends in that carriage."

The "constabeel" obeyed, not very cheerfully. King stood to watch him with a foot on the step of a first-class coach. Another constable passed him, elbowing a snail's progress between the train and the crowd. He seized the man's arm.

"Go and help that man!" he ordered. "Hurry!"

Then he climbed into the carriage and leaned from the window. He grinned as he saw both constables pounce on a third-class carriage door and, with the yell of good huntsmen who have viewed, seize the protesting Northerner by the leg and begin to drag him forth. There was a fight, that lasted three minutes, in the course of which a long knife flashed. But there were plenty to help take the knife away, and the Hillman stood handcuffed and sullen at last, while one of his captors bound a cut forearm. Then they dragged him away; but not before he had seen King at the window, and had lipped a silent threat.

"I believe you, my son!" King chuckled, half aloud. "I surely believe you! I'll watch! *Ham dekta hai!*"

"Why was that man arrested?" asked an acid voice behind him; and without troubling to turn his head, he knew that Major Hyde was to be his carriage mate again. To be vindictive, on duty or off it, is foolishness; but to let opportunity slip by one is a crime. He looked glad, not sorry, as he faced about—pleased, not disappointed—like a man on a desert island who has found a tool.

"Why was that man arrested?" the major asked again.

"I ordered it," said King.

"So I imagined. I asked you why."

King stared at him and then turned to watch the prisoner being dragged away; he was fighting again, striking at his captors' heads with handcuffed wrists.

"Does he *look* innocent?" asked King.

"Is that your answer?" asked the major. Balked ambition is an ugly horse to ride. He had tried for a command but had been shelved.

"I have sufficient authority," said King, unruffled. He spoke as if he were thinking of something entirely different. His eyes were as if they saw the major from a very long way off and rather approved of him on the whole.

"Show me your authority, please!"

King dived into an inner pocket and produced a card that had about ten words written on its face, above a general's signature. Hyde read it and passed it back.

"So you're one of those, are you!" he said in a tone of voice that would start a fight in some parts of the world and in some services. But King nodded cheerfully, and that annoyed the major more than ever; he snorted, closed his mouth with a snap and turned to rearrange the sheet and pillow on his berth.

Then the train pulled out, amid a din of voices from

the left-behind that nearly drowned the panting of the overloaded engine. There was a roar of joy from two coaches full of soldiers in the rear—a shriek from a woman who had missed the train—a babel of farewells tossed back and forth between the platform and the third-class carriages—and Peshawur fell away behind.

King settled down on his side of the compartment, after a struggle with the thermantidote that refused to work. There was heat enough below the roof to have roasted meat, so that the physical atmosphere became as turgid as the mental after a little while.

Hyde all but stripped himself and drew on striped pajamas. King was content to lie in shirt-sleeves on the other berth, with knees raised, so that Hyde could not overlook the general's papers. At his ease he studied them one by one, memorizing a string of names, with details as to their owners' antecedents and probable present whereabouts. There were several photographs in the packet, and he studied them very carefully indeed.

But much most carefully of all he examined Yasmini's portrait, returning to it again and again. He reached the conclusion in the end that when it was taken she had been cunningly disguised.

"This was intended for purpose of identification at a given time and place," he told himself.

"Were you muttering at me?" asked Hyde.

"No, sir."

"It looked extremely like it!"

"My mistake, sir. Nothing of the sort intended."

"H-rrrrr-ummmmmmph!"

Hyde turned an indignant back on him, and King studied the back as if he found it interesting. On the

whole he looked sympathetic, so it was as well that
Hyde did not look around. Balked ambition as a
rule loathes sympathy.

After many prickly-hot, interminable, jolting hours
the train drew up at Rawal-Pindi station. Instantly
King was on his feet with his tunic on, and he was out
on the blazing hot platform before the train's motion
had quite ceased.

He began to walk up and down, not elbowing but
percolating through the crowd, missing nothing worth
noticing in all the hot kaleidoscope and seeming to find
new amusement at every turn. It was not in the least
astonishing that a well-dressed native should address
him presently, for he looked genial enough to be asked
to hold a baby. King himself did not seem surprised
at all. Far from it; he looked pleased.

"Excuse me, sir," said the man in glib babu English.
"I am seeking Captain King sahib, for whom my
brother is ver*ee* anxious to be servant. Can you
kind*lee* tell me, sir, where I could find Captain King
sahib?"

"Certainly," King answered him. He looked glad
to be of help. "Are you traveling on this train?"

The question sounded like politeness welling from
the lips of unsuspicion.

"Yes, sir. I am traveling from this place where I
have spent a few days, to Bombay, where my business
is."

"How did you know King sahib is on the train?"
King asked him, smiling so genially that even the police
could not have charged him with more than curiosity.

"By telegram, sir. My brother had the misfortune
to miss Captain King sahib at Peshawur and therefore

sent a telegram to me asking me to do what I can at
an interview."

"I see," said King. "I see." And judging by the
sparkle in his eyes as he looked away, he could see a
lot. But the native could not see his eyes at that instant, although he tried to.

He looked back at the train, giving the man a good
chance to study his face in profile.

"See that carriage?" he asked, pointing. "The fourth
first-class carriage from this end? Well—there are
only two of us in there; I'm Major Hyde, and the
other is Captain King. I'll tell Captain King to look
out for you."

"Oh, thank you, sir!" said the native oilily. "You
are most kind! I am your humble servant, sir!"

King nodded good-by to him, his dark eyes in the
shadow of the khaki helmet seeming scarcely interested
any longer.

"Couldn't you find another berth?" Hyde asked him
angrily when he stepped back into the compartment.
"What were you out there looking for?"

King smiled back at him blandly.

"I think there are railway thieves on the train," he
announced without any effort at relevance. He might
not have heard the question.

"What makes you think so?"

"Observation, sir."

"Oh! Then if you've seen thieves, why didn't you
have 'em arrested? You were precious free with that
authority of yours on Peshawur platform!"

"Perhaps you'd care to take the responsibility, sir?
Let me point out one of them."

Full of grudging curiosity Hyde came to stand by

him, and King stepped back just as the train began to move.

"That man, sir—over there—no, beyond him—there!"

Hyde thrust head and shoulders through the window, and a well-dressed native with one foot on the running-board at the back end of the train took a long steady stare at him before jumping in and slamming the door of a third-class carriage.

"Which one?" demanded Hyde impatiently.

"I don't see him now, sir!"

Hyde snorted and returned to his seat in the silence of unspeakable scorn. But presently he opened a suit-case and drew out a repeating pistol which he cocked carefully and stowed beneath his pillow; not at all a contemptible move, because the Indian railway thief is the most resourceful specialist in the world. But King took no overt precautions of any kind.

After more interminable hours night shut down on them, red-hot, black-dark, mesmerically subdivided into seconds by the thump of carriage wheels and lit at intervals by showers of sparks from the gasping engine. The din of Babel rode behind the first-class carriages, for all the natives in the packed third-class talked all together. (In India, when one has spent a fortune on a third-class ticket, one proceeds to enjoy the ride.) The train was a Beast out of Revelation, wallowing in noise.

But after other, hotter hours the talking ceased. Then King, strangely without kicking off his shoes, drew a sheet up over his shoulders. On the opposite berth Hyde covered his head, to keep dust out of his hair, and presently King heard him begin to snore

gently. Then, very carefully he adjusted his own position so that his profile lay outlined in the dim light
from the gas lamp in the roof. He might almost have
been waiting to be shaved.

The stuffiness increased to a degree that is sometimes
preached in Christian churches as belonging to a sul-
phurous sphere beyond the grave. Yet he did not move
a muscle. It was long after midnight when his vigil
was rewarded by a slight sound at the door. From
that instant his eyes were on the watch, under dark
closed lashes; but his even breathing was that of the
seventh stage of sleep that knows no dreams.

A click of the door-latch heralded the appearance of
a hand. With skill, of the sort that only special train-
ing can develop, a man in native dress insinuated
himself into the carriage without making another
sound of any kind. King's ears are part of the equip-
ment for his exacting business, but he could not hear
the door click shut again.

For about five minutes, while the train swayed head-
long into Indian darkness, the man stood listening and
watching King's face. He stood so near that King
recognized him for the one who had accosted him on
Rawal-Pindi platform. And he could see the outline
of the knife-hilt that the man's fingers clutched underneath his shirt.

"He'll either strike first, so as to kill us both and do
the looting afterward—and in that case I think it will
be easier to break his neck than his arm—yes, decidedly his neck; it's long and thin;—or—"

His eyes feigned sleep so successfully that the native
turned away at last.

"Thought so!" He dared open his eyes a mite

wider. "He's pukka—true to type! Rob first and *then* kill! Rule number one with his sort, run when you've stabbed! Not a bad rule either, from their point of view!"

As he watched, the thief drew the sheet back from Hyde's face, with trained fingers that could have taken spectacles from the victims' nose without his knowledge. Then as fish glide in and out among the reeds without touching them, swift and soft and unseen, his fingers searched Hyde's body. They found nothing. So they dived under the pillow and brought out the pistol and a gold watch.

After that he began to search the clothes that hung on a hook beside Hyde's berth. He brought forth papers and a pocketbook—then money. Money went into one bag—papers and pocketbook into another. And that was evidence enough as well as risk enough. The knife would be due in a minute.

King moved in his sleep, rather noisily, and the movement knocked a book to the floor from the foot of his berth. The noise of that awoke Hyde, and King pretended to begin to wake, yawning and rolling on his back (that being much the safest position an unarmed man can take and much the most awkward for his enemy).

"Thieves!" Hyde yelled at the top of his lungs, groping wildly for his pistol and not finding it.

King sat up and rubbed his eyes. The native drew the knife, and—believing himself in command of the situation—hesitated for one priceless second. He saw his error and darted for the door too late. With a movement unbelievably swift King was there ahead of him; and with another movement not so swift, but

much more disconcerting, he threw his sheet as the
retiarius used to throw a net in ancient Rome. It
wrapped round the native's head and arms, and the two
went together to the floor in a twisted stranglehold.

In another half-minute the native was groaning, for
King had his knife-wrist in two hands and was bending
it backward while he pressed the man's stomach with
his knees.

"Get his loot!" he panted between efforts.

The knife fell to the floor, and the thief made a
gallant effort to recover it, but King was too strong
for him. He seized the knife himself, slipped it in his
own bosom and resumed his hold before the native
guessed what he was after. Then he kept a tight grip
while Hyde knelt to grope for his missing property.
The major found both the thief's bags, and held
them up.

"I expect that's all," said King, loosening his grip
very gradually. The native noticed—as Hyde did not
—that King had begun to seem almost absent-minded;
the thief lay quite still, looking up, trying to divine
his next intention. Suddenly the brakes went on, but
King's grip did not tighten. The train began to scream
itself to a standstill at a wayside station, and King (the
absent-minded) very nearly grinned.

"If I weren't in such an infernal hurry to reach
Bombay—" Hyde grumbled; and King nearly laughed
aloud then, for the thief knew English, and was listening with all his ears, "—may I be damned if I wouldn't
get off at this station and wait to see that scoundrel
brought to justice!"

The train jerked itself to a standstill, and a man with
a lantern began to chant the station's name.

"Damn it!—I'm going to Bombay to act censor. I can't wait—they want me there."

The instant the train's motion altogether ceased the heat shut in on them as if the lid of Tophet had been slammed. The prickly heat burst out all over Hyde's skin and King's too.

"Almighty God!" gasped Hyde, beginning to fan himself.

There was plenty of excuse for relaxing hold still further, and King made full use of it. A second later he gave a very good pretense of pain in his finger-ends as the thief burst free. The native made a dive at his bosom for the knife, but he frustrated that. Then he made a prodigious effort, just too late, to clutch the man again, and he did succeed in tearing loose a piece of shirt; but the fleeing robber must have wondered, as he bolted into the blacker shadows of the station building, why such an iron-fingered, wide-awake sahib should have made such a truly feeble showing at the end.

"Damn it!—couldn't you hold him? Were you afraid of him, or what?" demanded Hyde, beginning to dress himself. Instead of answering, King leaned out into the lamp-lit gloom, and in a minute he caught sight of a sergeant of native infantry passing down the train. He made a sign that brought the man to him on the run.

"Did you see that runaway?" he asked.

"Ha, sahib. I saw one running. Shall I follow?"

"No. This piece of his shirt will identify him. Take it. Hide it! When a man with a torn shirt, into which that piece fits, makes for the telegraph office after this train has gone on, see that he is allowed to send any

telegrams he wants to! Only, have copies of every one
of them wired to Captain King, care of the station-
master, Delhi. Have you understood?"

"Ha, sahib."

"Grab him, and lock him up tight afterward—but
not until he has sent his telegrams!"

"Atcha, sahib."

"Make yourself scarce, then!"

Major Hyde was dressed, having performed that
military evolution in something less than record time

"Who was that you were talking to?" he demanded
But King continued to look out the door.

Hyde came and tapped on his shoulder impatiently,
but King did not seem to understand until the native
sergeant had quite vanished into the shadows.

"Let me pass, will you!" Hyde demanded. "I'll have
that thief caught if the train has to wait a week while
they do it!"

He pushed past, but he was scarcely on the step
when the station-master blew his whistle, and his
colored minion waved a lantern back and forth. The
engine shrieked forthwith of death and torment; carriage doors slammed shut in staccato series; the heat
relaxed as the engine moved—loosened—let go—
lifted at last, and a trainload of hot passengers sighed
thanks to an unresponsive sky as the train gained
speed and wind crept in through the thermantidotes.

Only through the broken thermantidote in King's
compartment no wet air came. Hyde knelt on King's
berth and wrestled with it like a caged animal, but
with no result except that the sweat poured out all over
him and he was more uncomfortable than before.

"What are you looking at?" he demanded at last, sitting on King's berth. His head swam. He had to wait a few seconds before he could step across to his own side.

"Only a knife," said King. He was standing under the dim gas lamp that helped make the darkness more unbearable.

"Not that robber's knife? Did he drop it?"

"It's my knife," said King.

"Strange time to stand staring at it, if it's yours! Didn't you ever see it before?"

King stowed the knife away in his bosom, and the major crossed to his own side.

"I'm thinking I'll know it again, at all events!" King answered, sitting down. "Good night, sir."

"Good night."

Within ten minutes Hyde was asleep, snoring prodigiously. Then King pulled out the knife again and studied it for half an hour. The blade was of bronze, with an edge hammered to the keenness of a razor. The hilt was of nearly pure gold, in the form of a woman dancing.

The whole thing was so exquisitely wrought that age had only softened the lines, without in the least impairing them. It looked like one of those Grecian toys with which Roman women of Nero's day stabbed their lovers. But that was not why he began to whistle very softly to himself.

Presently he drew out the general's package of papers, with the photograph on the top. He stood up, to hold both knife and papers close to the light in the roof.

It needed no great stretch of imagination to suggest a likeness between the woman of the photograph and the other, of the golden knife-hilt. And nobody, looking at him then, would have dared suggest he lacked imagination.

If the knife had not been so ancient they might have been portraits of the same woman, in the same disguise, taken at the same time.

"She knew I had been chosen to work with her. The general sent her word that I am coming," he muttered to himself. "Man number one had a try for me, but I had him pinched too soon. There must have been a spy watching at Peshawur, who wired to Rawal-Pindi for this man to jump the train and go on with the job. She must have had him planted at Rawal-Pindi in case of accidents. She seems thorough! Why should she give the man a knife with her own portrait on it? Is she queen of a secret society? Well —we shall see!"

He sat down on his berth again and sighed, not discontentedly. Then he lit one of his great black cigars and blew rings for five or six minutes. Then he lay back with his head on the pillow, and before five minutes more had gone he was asleep, with the cold cigar still clutched between his fingers.

He looked as interesting in his sleep as when awake. His mobile face in repose looked Roman, for the sun had tanned his skin and his nose was aquiline. In museums, where sculptured heads of Roman generals and emperors stand around the wall on pedestals, it would not be difficult to pick several that bore more than a faint resemblance to him. He had breadth and depth of forehead and a jowl that lent itself to smiles

as well as sternness, and a throat that expressed manly
determination in every molded line.

He slept like a boy until dawn; and he and Hyde
had scarcely exchanged another dozen words when the
train screamed next day into Delhi station. Then he
saluted stiffly and was gone.

"Young jackanapes!" Hyde muttered after him.
"Lazy young devil! He ought to be with his regiment,
marching and setting a good example to his men!
We'll have our work cut out to win this war, if there
are many of his stamp! And I'm afraid there are—
I'm afraid so—far too many of 'em! Pity! Such a
pity! If the right men were at the top the youngsters
at the foot of the ladder would mind their P's and
Q's. As it is, I'm afraid we shall get beaten in this
show. Dear, oh, dear!"

Being what he was, and consistent before all things,
Major Hyde drew out his writing materials there and
then and wrote a report against Athelstan King, which
he signed, addressed to headquarters and mailed at
the first opportunity. There some future historian
may find it and draw from it unkind deductions on the
morale of the British army.

The only things which can not be explained are facts. So, use 'em.

A riddle is proof there is a key to it. Nor is it a riddle when you've got the key.

Life is as simple as all that.—COCKER.

CHAPTER II

DELHI boasts a round half-dozen railway stations, all of them designed with regard to war, so that to King there was nothing unexpected in the fact that the train had brought him to an unexpected station. He plunged into its crowd much as a man in the mood might plunge into a whirlpool,—laughing as he plunged, for it was the most intoxicating splurge of color, din and smell that even India, the many-peopled—even Delhi, mother of dynasties—ever had evolved.

The station echoed—reverberated—hummed. A roar went up of human voices, babbling in twenty tongues, and above that rose in differing degrees the ear-splitting shriek of locomotives, the blare of bugles, the neigh of led horses, the bray of mules, the jingle of gun-chains and the thundering cadence of drilled feet.

At one minute the whole building shook to the thunder of a grinning regiment; an instant later it clattered to the wrought-steel hammer of a thousand hoofs, as led troop-horses danced into formation to

31

invade the waiting trucks. Loaded trucks banged into one another and thunderclapped their way into the sidings. And soldiers of nearly every Indian military caste stood about everywhere, in what was picturesque confusion to the uninitiated, yet like the letters of an index to a man who knew. And King knew. Down the back of each platform Tommy Atkins stood in long straight lines, talking or munching great sandwiches or smoking.

The heat smelt and felt of another world. The din was from the same sphere. Yet everywhere was hope and geniality and by-your-leave as if weddings were in the wind and not the overture to death.

Threading his way in and out among the motley swarm with a great black cheroot between his teeth and sweat running into his eyes from his helmet-band, Athelstan King strode at ease—at home—intent— amused—awake—and almost awfully happy. He was not in the least less happy because perfectly aware that a native was following him at a distance, although he did wonder how the native had contrived to pass within the lines.

The general at Peshawur had compressed about a ton of miscellaneous information into fifteen hurried minutes, but mostly he had given him leave and orders to inform himself; so the fun was under way of winning exact knowledge in spite of officers, not one of whom would not have grown instantly suspicious at the first asked question. At the end of fifteen minutes there was not a glib staff-officer there who could have deceived him as to the numbers and destination of the force entraining.

"Kerachi !" he told himself, chewing the butt of his

cigar and keeping well ahead of the shadowing native.
Always keep a "shadow" moving until you're ready
to deal with him is one of Cocker's very soundest rules.
"Turkey hasn't taken a hand yet—the general said
so. No holy war yet. These'll be held in readiness
to cross to Basra in case the Turks begin. While they
wait for that at Kerachi the tribes won't dare begin
anything. One or two spies are sure to break North
and tell them what this force is for—but the tribes
won't believe. They'll wait until the force *has* moved
to Basra before they take chances. Good! That means
no especial hurry for me!"

He did not have to return salutes, because he did
not look for them. Very few people noticed him at
all, although he was recognized once or twice by former
messmates, and one officer stopped him with an outstretched hand.

"Shake hands, you old tramp! Where are you bound
for next? Tibet by any chance—or is it Samarkand
this time?"

"Oh, hullo, Carmichel!" he answered, beaming instant good-fellowship. "Where are you bound for?"
And the other did not notice that his own question had
not been answered.

"Bombay! Bombay—Marseilles—Brussels—Berlin!"

"Wish you luck!" laughed King, passing on. Every
living man there, with the exception of a few staff-
officers, believed himself en route for Europe; their
faces said as much. Yet King took another look at
the piles of stores and at the kits the men carried.

"Who'd take all that stuff to Europe, where they
make it?" he reflected. "And what 'u'd they use camel
harness for in France?"

At his leisure—in his own way, that was devious and like a string of miracles—he filtered toward the telegraph office. The native who had followed him all this time drew closer, but he did not let himself be troubled by that.

He whispered proof of his identity to the telegraph clerk, who was a Royal Engineer, new to that job that morning, and a sealed telegram was handed to him at once. The "shadow" came very close indeed, presumably to try and read over his shoulder from behind, but he side-stepped into a corner and read the telegram with his back to the wall.

It was in English, no doubt to escape suspicion; and because it was war-time, and the censorship had closed on India like a throttling string, it was not in code. So the wording, all things considered, had to be ingenius, for the Mirza Ali, of the Fort, Bombay, to whom it was addressed, could scarcely be expected to read more than between the lines. The lines had to be there to read between.

"Cattle intended for slaughter," it ran, "despatched Bombay on Fourteen down. Meet train. Will be inspected en route, but should be dealt with carefully on arrival. Cattle inclined to stampede owing to bad scare received to North of Delhi. Take all precautions and notify Abdul." It was signed "Suliman."

"Good!" he chuckled. "Let's hope we get Abdul too. I wonder who he is!"

Still uninterested in the man who shadowed him, he walked back to the office window and wrote two telegrams; one to Bombay, ordering the arrest of Ali Mirza of the Fort, with an urgent admonition to discover who his man Abdul might be, and to seize him as soon as found; the other to the station in the north, insisting on close confinement for Suliman.

"Don't let him out on any terms at all!" he wired.

That being all the urgent business, he turned leisurely to face his shadow, and the native met his eyes with the engaging frankness of an old friend, coming forward with outstretched hand. They did not shake hands, for King knew better than to fall into the first trap offered him. But the man made a signal with his fingers that is known to not more than a dozen men in all the world, and that changed the situation altogether.

"Walk with me," said King, and the man fell into stride beside him.

He was a Rangar,—which is to say a Rajput who, or whose ancestors had turned Muhammadan. Like many Rajputs he was not a big man, but he looked fit and wiry; his head scarcely came above the level of King's chin, although his turban distracted attention from the fact. The turban was of silk and unusually large.

The whitest of well-kept teeth, gleaming regularly under a little black waxed mustache betrayed no trace of betel-nut or other nastiness, and neither his fine features nor his eyes suggested vice of the sort that often undermines the character of Rajput youth.

On second thoughts, and at the next opportunity to see them, King was not so sure that the eyes were brown, and he changed his opinion about their color a dozen times within the hour. Once he would even have sworn they were green.

The man was well-to-do, for his turban was of costly silk, and he was clad in expensive Jodpur riding breeches and spurred black riding boots, all perfectly

immaculate. The breeches, baggy above and tight
below, suggested the clean lines of cat-like agility and
strength.

The upper part of his costume was semi-European.
He was a regular Rangar dandy, of the type that can
be seen playing polo almost any day at Mount Abu—
that gets into mischief with a grace due to practise and
heredity—but that does not manage its estates too well,
as a rule, nor pay its debts in a hurry.

"My name is Rewa Gunga," he said in a low voice,
looking up sidewise at King a shade too guilelessly.
Between Cape Comorin and the Northern Ice guile is
normal, and its absence makes the wise suspicious.

"I am Captain King."

"I have a message for you."

"From whom?"

"From her!" said the Rangar, and without exactly
knowing why, or being pleased with himself, King felt
excited.

They were walking toward the station exit. King
had a trunk check in his hand, but returned it to his
pocket, not proposing just yet to let the Rangar overhear instructions regarding the trunk's destination; he
was too good-looking and too overbrimming with personal charm to be trusted thus early in the game.
Besides, there was that captured knife, that hinted at
lies and treachery. Secret signs as well as loot have
been stolen before now.

"I'd like to walk through the streets and see the
crowd."

He smiled as he said that, knowing well that the
average young Rajput of good birth would rather fight

a tiger with cold steel than walk a mile or two. He
drew fire at once.

"Why walk, King sahib? Are we animals? There
is a carriage waiting—*her* carriage—and a coachman
whose ears were born dead. We might be overheard
in the street. Are you and I children, tossing stones
into a pool to watch the rings widen!"

"Lead on, then," answered King.

Outside the station was a luxuriously modern vic-
toria, with C springs and rubber tires, with horses
that would have done credit to a viceroy. The Rangar
motioned King to get in first, and the moment they
were both seated the Rajput coachman set the horses
to going like the wind. Rewa Gunga opened a jeweled
cigarette case.

"Will you have one?" he asked with the air of
royalty entertaining a blood-equal.

King accepted a cigarette for politeness' sake and
took occasion to admire the man's slender wrist, that
was doubtless hard and strong as woven steel, but was
not much more than half the thickness of his own.

The Rajputs as a race are proud of their wrists and
hands. Their swords are made with a hilt so small
that none save a Rajput of the blood could possibly
use one; yet there is no race in all warring India, nor
any in the world, that bears a finer record for hard
fighting and sheer derring-do. One of the questions
that occurred to King that minute was why this well-
bred youngster whose age he guessed at twenty-two or
so had not turned his attention to the army.

"My height!"

The man had read his thoughts!

"Not quite tall enough. Besides—you are a soldier, are you not? And do you fight?"

He nodded toward a dozen water-buffaloes, that slouched along the street with wet goatskin *mussuks* slung on their blue flanks.

"*They* can fight," he said smiling. "So can any other fool!" Then, after a minute of rather strained silence ı "My message is from *her*."

"From Yasmini?"

"Who else?"

King accepted the rebuke with a little inclination ⟨f the head. He spoke as little as possible, because he was puzzled. He had become conscious of a puzzled look in the Rangar's eyes—of a subtle wonderment that might be intentional flattery (for Art and the East are one). Whenever the East is doubtful, and recognizes doubt, it is as dangerous as a hillside in the rains, and it only added to his problem if the Rangar found in him something inexplicable. The West can only get the better of the East when the East is too cock-sure.

"She has jolly well gone North!" said the Rangar suddenly, and King shut his teeth with a snap. He sat bolt upright, and the Rangar allowed himself to look amused.

"When? Why?"

"She was too jolly well excited to wait, sahib! She is of the North, you know. She loves the North, and the men of the 'Hills'; and she knows them because she loves them. There came a *tar* (telegram) from Peshawur, from a general, to say King sahib comes to Delhi; but already she had completed all arrangements here. She was in a great stew, I can assure you.

Finally she said, 'Why should I wait?' Nobody could answer her."

He spoke English well enough. Few educated foreign gentlemen could have spoken it better, although there was the tendency to use slang that well-bred natives insist on picking up from British officers; and as he went on, here and there the native idiom crept through, translated. King said nothing, but listened and watched, puzzled more than he would have cared to admit by the look in the Rangar's eyes. It was not suspicion—nor respect. Yet there was a suggestion of both.

"At last she said, 'It is well; I will not wait! I know of this sahib. He is a man whose feet stand under him and he will not tread my growing flowers into garbage! He will be clever enough to pick up the end of the thread that I shall leave behind and follow it and me! He is a true hound, with a nose that reads the wind, or the general sahib never would have sent him!'—So she left me behind, sahib, to—to present to you the end of the thread of which she spoke."

King tossed away the stump of the cigarette and rolled his tongue round the butt of a fresh cheroot. The word "hound" is not necessarily a compliment in any of a thousand Eastern tongues and gains little by translation. It might have been a slip, but the East takes advantage of its own slips as well as of other peoples' unless watched.

The carriage swayed at high speed round three sharp corners in succession before the Rangar spoke again.

"She has often heard of you," he said then. That was not unlikely, but not necessarily true either. If it were true, it did not help to account for the puzzled

look in the Rangar's eyes, that increased rather than
diminished.

"I've heard of her," said King.

"Of course! Who has not? She has desired to
meet you, sahib, ever since she was told you are the
best man in your service."

King grunted, thinking of the knife beneath his shirt.

"She is very glad that you and she are on the same
errand." He leaned forward for the sake of emphasis
and laid a finger on King's hand. It was a delicate,
dainty finger with an almond nail. "She is very glad.
She is far more glad than you imagine, or than you
would believe. King sahib, she is all bucked up about
it! Listen—her web is wide! Her agents are here—
there—everywhere, and she is obeyed as few kings
have ever been! Those agents shall all be held answer-
able for your life, sahib,—for she has said so! They
are one and all your bodyguard, from now forward!"

King inclined his head politely, but the weight of the
knife inside his shirt did not encourage credulity.
True, it might not be Yasmini's knife, and the Rangar's
emphatic assurance might not be an unintentional admission that the man who had tried to use it was
Yasmini's man. But when a man has formed the habit
of deduction, he deduces as he goes along, and is prone
to believe what his instinct tells him.

Again, it was as if the Rangar read a part of his
thoughts, if not all of them. It is not difficult to
counter that trick, but to do it a man must be on his
guard, or the East will know what he has thought and
what he is going to think, as many have discovered
when it was too late.

"Her men are able to protect anybody's life from any

God's number of assassins, whatever may lead you to think the contrary. From now forward your life is in her men's keeping!"

"Very good of her, I'm sure," King murmured. He was thinking of the general's express order to apply for a "passport" that would take him into Khinjan Caves—mentally cursing the necessity for asking any kind of favor,—and wondering whether to ask this man for it or wait until he should meet Yasmini. He had about made up his mind that to wait would be quite within a strict interpretation of his orders, as well as infinitely more agreeable to himself, when the Rangar answered his thoughts again as if he had spoken them aloud.

"She left this with me, saying I am to give it to you! I am to say that wherever you wear it, between here and Afghanistan, your life shall be safe and you may come and go!"

King stared. The Rangar drew a bracelet from an inner pocket and held it out. It was a wonderful, barbaric thing of pure gold, big enough for a grown man's wrist, and old enough to have been hammered out in the very womb of time. It looked almost like ancient Greek, and it fastened with a hinge and clasp that looked as if they did not belong to it and might have been made by a not very skilful modern jeweler.

"Won't you wear it?" asked Rewa Gunga, watching him. "It will prove a true talisman! What was the name of the Johnny who had a lamp to rub? Aladdin? It will be better than what he had! He could only command a lot of bogies. This will give you authority over flesh and blood! Take it, sahib!"

So King put it on, letting it slip up his sleeve out of

sight,—with a sensation as the snap closed of putting
handcuffs on himself. But the Rangar looked relieved.
"That is your passport, sahib! Show it to a Hill-
man whenever you suppose yourself in danger. The
Raj might go to pieces, but while Yasmini lives—"
"Her friends will boast about her, I suppose!"

King finished the sentence for him because it is not
considered good form for natives to hint at possible
dissolution of the Anglo-Indian Government. Everybody knows that the British will not govern India
forever, but the British—who know it best of all, and
work to that end most fervently—are the only ones
encouraged to talk about it.

For a few minutes after that Rewa Gunga held his
peace, while the carriage swayed at breakneck speed
through the swarming streets. They had to drive
slower in the Chandni Chowk, for the ancient Street
of the Silversmiths that is now the mart of Delhi was
ablaze with crude colors, and was thronged with more
people than ever since '57. There were a thousand
signs worth studying by a man who could read them.

King, watching and saying nothing, reached the conclusion that Delhi was in hand—excited undoubtedly,
more than a bit bewildered, watchful, but in hand.
Without exactly knowing how he did it, he grew aware
of a certain confidence that underlay the surface fuss.
After that the sea of changing patterns and raised
voices ceased to have any particular interest for him
and he lay back against the cushions to pay stricter
attention to his own immediate affairs.

He did not believe for a second the lame explanation
Yasmini had left behind. She must have some good
reason for wishing to be first up the Khyber, and he

was very sorry indeed she had slipped away. It might
be only jealousy, yet why should she be jealous? It
might be fear—yet why should she be afraid?

It was the next remark of the Rangar's that set him
entirely on his guard, and thenceforward whoever
could have read his thoughts would have been more
than human. Perhaps it is the most dominant char-
acteristic of the British race that it will not defend
itself until it must. He had known of that thought-
reading trick ever since his ayah (native nurse) taught
him to lisp Hindustanee; just as surely he knew that
its impudent, repeated use was intended to sap his
belief in himself. There is not much to choose between
the native impudence that dares intrude on a man's
thoughts, and the insolence that understands it, and is
rather too proud to care.

"I'll bet you a hundred dibs," said the Rangar, "that
she jolly well didn't fancy your being on the scene
ahead of her! I'll bet you she decided to be there first
and get control of the situation! Take me? You'd
lose if you did! She's slippery, and quick, and like all
women, she's jealous!"

The Rangar's eyes were on his, but King was not to
be caught again. It is quite easy to think behind a
fence, so to speak, if one gives attention to it.

"She will be busy presently fooling those Afridis,"
he continued, waving his cigarette. "She has fooled
them always, to the limit of their bally bent. They all
believe she is their best friend in the world—oh, dear
yes, you bet they do! And so she is—so she is—but
not in the way they think! They believe she plots with
them against the Raj! Poor silly devils! Yet Yasmini
loves them! They want war—blood—loot! It is all

they think about! They are seldom satisfied unless
their wrists and elbows are bally well red with other
peoples' gore! And while they are picturing the loot,
and the slaughter of unbelievers—(as if *they* believed
anything but foolishness themselves!)—Yasmini plays
her own game, for amusement and power—a good
game—a deep game! You have seen already how
India has to ask her aid in the 'Hills'! She loves
power, power, power—not for its name, for names are
nothing, but to use it. She loves the feel of it! Fighting is not power! Blood-letting is foolishness. If
there is any blood spilt it is none of her doing—unless—"

"Unless what?" asked King.

"Oh—sometimes there were fools who interfered.
You can not blame her for that."

"You seem to be a champion of hers! How long
have you known her?"

The Rangar eyed him sharply.

"A long time. She and I played together when we
were children. I know her whole history—and that is
something nobody else in the world knows but she
herself. You see, I am favored. It is because she
knows me very well that she chose me to travel North
with you, when you start to find her in the 'Hills'!"

King cleared his throat, and the Rangar nodded,
looking into his eyes with the engaging confidence of a
child who never has been refused anything, in or out
of reason. King made no effort to look pleased, so
the Rangar drew on his resources.

"I have a letter from her," he stated blandly.

From a pocket in the carriage cushions he brought
out a silver tube, richly carved in the Kashmiri style

and closed at either end with a tightly fitting silver cap.
King accepted it and drew the cap from one end.   A
roll of scented paper fell on his lap, and a puff of hot
wind combined with a lurch of the carriage springs
came near to lose it for him; he snatched it just
in time and unrolled it to find a letter written to himself in Urdu, in a beautiful flowing hand.

Urdu is perhaps the politest of written tongues and
lends itself most readily to indirectness; but since he
did not expect to read a catalogue of exact facts, he
was not disappointed.

Translated, the letter ran:

"To Athelstan King sahib, by the hand of Rewa
Gunga.   Greeting.   The bearer is my well-trusted
servant, whom I have chosen to be the sahib's guide
until Heaven shall be propitious and we meet.   He is
instructed in all that he need know concerning what is
now in hand, and he will tell by word of mouth such
things as ought not to be written.   By all means let
Rewa Gunga travel with you, for he is of royal blood,
of the House of Ketchwaha and will not fail you.
His honor and mine are one.   Praying that the many
gods of India may heap honors on your honor's head,
providing each his proper attribute toward entire ability to succeed in all things, but especially in the present
undertaking,

"I am Your Excellency's humble servant,

"YASMINI."

He had barely finished reading it when the coachman
took a last corner at a gallop and drew the horses up
on their haunches at a door in a high white wall.
Rewa Gunga sprang out of the carriage before the
horses were quite at a standstill.

"Here we are!" he said, and King, gathering up the

letter and the silver tube, noticed that the street curved
here so that no other door and no window overlooked
this one.

He followed the Rangar, and he was no sooner into
the shadow of the door than the coachman lashed the
horses and the carriage swung out of view.

"This way," said the Rangar over his shoulder.
"Come!"

Lie to a liar, for lies are his coin.
Steal from a thief, for that is easy.
Set a trap for a trickster, and catch him at the first attempt.
But beware of the man who has no axe to grind.

—EASTERN PROVERB.

CHAPTER III

IT was a musty smelling entrance, so dark that to see was scarcely possible after the hot glare outside. Dimly King made out Rewa Gunga mounting stairs to the left and followed him. The stairs wound backward and forward on themselves four times, growing scarcely any lighter as they ascended, until, when he guessed himself two stories at least above road level, there was a sudden blaze of reflected light and he blinked at more mirrors than he could count. They had been swung on hinges suddenly to throw the light full in his face.

There were curtains reflected in each mirror, and little glowing lamps, so cunningly arranged that it was not possible to guess which were real and which were not. Rewa Gunga offered no explanation, but stood watching with quiet amusement. He seemed to expect King to take a chance and go forward, but if he did he reckoned without his guest. King stood still.

Then suddenly, as if she had done it a thousand times before and surprised a thousand people, a little nut-brown maid parted the middle pair of curtains and

49

said "Salaam!" smiling with teeth that were as white
as porcelain. All the other curtains parted too, so that
the whereabouts of the door might still have been in
doubt had she not spoken and so distinguished herself
from her reflections. King looked scarcely interested
and not at all disturbed.

Balked of his amusement, Rewa Gunga hurried past
him, thrusting the little maid aside, and led the way.
King followed him into a long room, whose walls were
hung with richer silks than any he remembered to have
seen. In a great wide window to one side some twenty
women began at once to make flute music. Silken
punkahs swung from chains, wafting back and forth a
cloud of sandalwood smoke that veiled the whole scene
in mysterious, scented mist. Through the open window came the splash of a fountain and the chattering
of birds, and the branch of a feathery tree drooped
near by. It seemed that the long white wall below was
that of Yasmini's garden.

"Be welcome!" laughed Rewa Gunga; "I am to do
the honors, since she is not here. Be seated, sahib."

King chose a divan at the room's farthest end, near
tall curtains that led into rooms beyond. He turned his
back toward the reason for his choice. On a little
ivory-inlaid ebony table about ten feet away lay a
knife, that was almost the exact duplicate of the one
inside his shirt. Bronze knives of ancient date, with
golden handles carved to represent a woman dancing,
are rare. The ability to seem not to notice incriminat-
ing evidence is rarer still—rarest of all when under
the eyes of a native of India, for cats and hawks are
dullards by comparison to them. But King saw the
knife, yet did not seem to see it.

There was nothing there calculated to set an Englishman at ease. In spite of the Rangar's casual manner,
Yasmini's reception room felt like the antechamber to
another world, where mystery is atmosphere and ordinary air to breathe is not at all. He could sense hushed
expectancy on every side—could feel the eyes of many
women fixed on him—and began to draw on his guard
as a fighting man draws on armor. There and then
he deliberately set himself to resist mesmerism, which
is the East's chief weapon.

Rewa Gunga, perfectly at home, sprawled leisurely
along a cushioned couch with a grace that the West
has not learned yet; but King did not make the mistake
of trusting him any better for his easy manners, and
his eyes sought swiftly for some unrhythmic, un-
planned thing on which to rest, that he might save
himself by a sort of mental leverage.

Glancing along the wall that faced the big window,
he noticed for the first time a huge Afridi, who sat
on a stool and leaned back against the silken hangings
with arms folded.

"Who is that man?" he asked.

"He? Oh, he is a savage—just a big savage," said
Rewa Gunga, looking vaguely annoyed.

"Why is he here?"

He did not dare let go of this chance side-issue. He
knew that Rewa Gunga wished him to talk of Yasmini
and to ask questions about her, and that if he suc-
cumbed to that temptation all his self-control would
be cunningly sapped away from him until his secrets,
and his very senses, belonged to some one else.

"What is he doing here?" he insisted.

"He? Oh, he does nothing. He waits," purred the

Rangar. "He is to be your body-servant on your journey to the North. He is nothing—nobody at all! —except that he is to be trusted utterly because he loves Yasmini. He is Obedience! A big obedient fool! Let him be!"

"No," said King. "If he's to be my man I'll speak to him!"

He felt himself winning. Already the spell of the room was lifting, and he no longer felt the cloud of sandalwood smoke like a veil across his brain.

"Won't you tell him to come here to me?"

Rewa Gunga laughed, resting his silk turban against the wall hangings and clasping both hands about his knee. It was as a man might laugh who has been touched in a bout with foils.

"Oh!—Ismail!" he called, with a voice like a bell, that made King stare.

The Afridi seemed to come out of a deep sleep and looked bewildered, rubbing his eyes and feeling whether his turban was on straight. He combed his beard with nervous fingers as he gazed about him and caught Rewa Gunga's eye. Then he sprang to his feet.

"Come!" ordered Rewa Gunga.

The man obeyed.

"Did you see?" Rewa Gunga chuckled. "He rose from his place like a buffalo, rump first and then shoulder after shoulder! Such men are safe! Such men have no guile beyond what will help them to obey! Such men think too slowly to invent deceit for its own sake!"

The Afridi came and towered above them, standing with gnarled hands knotted into clubs.

"What is thy name?" King asked him.

"Ismail!" he boomed.

"Thou art to be my servant?"

"Aye! So said she. I am her man. I obey!"

"When did she say so?" King asked him blandly, asking unexpected questions being half the art of Secret Service, although the other half is harder to achieve.

The Hillman stroked his great beard and stood considering the question. One could almost imagine the click of slow machinery revolving in his mind, although King entertained a shrewd suspicion that he was not so stupid as he chose to seem. His eyes were too hawk-bright to be a stupid man's.

"Before she went away," he answered at last.

"When did she go away?"

He thought again, then "Yesterday," he said.

"Why did you wait before you answered?"

The Afridi's eyes furtively sought Rewa Gunga's and found no aid there. Watching the Rangar less furtively, but even less obviously, King was aware that his eyes were nearly closed, as if they were not interested. The fingers that clasped his knee drummed on it indifferently, seeing which King allowed himself to smile.

"Never mind," he told Ismail. "It is no matter. It is ever well to think twice before speaking once, for thus mistakes die stillborn. Only the monkey-folk thrive on quick answers—is it not so? Thou art a man of many inches—of thew and sinew—Hey, but thou art a man! If the heart within those great ribs of thine is true as thine arms are strong I shall be fortunate to have thee for a servant!"

"Aye!" said the Afridi. "But what are words?

She has said I am thy servant, and to hear her is to obey !"

"Then from now thou art my servant?"

"Nay, but from yesterday when she gave the order !"

"Good !" said King.

"Aye, good for thee ! May Allah do more to me if I fail !"

"Then, take me a telegram !" said King.

He began to write at once on a half-sheet of paper that he tore from a letter he had in his pocket, setting down a row of figures at the top and transposing ·into cypher as he went along.

"Yasmini has gone North. Is there any reason at your end why I should not follow her at once ?"

He addressed it in plain English to his friend the general at Peshawur, taking great care lest the Rangar read it through those sleepy, half-closed eyes of his. Then he tore the cypher from the top, struck a match and burned the strip of paper and handed the code telegram to Ismail, directing him carefully to a government office where the cypher signature would be recognized and the telegram given precedence.

Ismail stalked off with it, striding like Moses down from Sinai—hook-nose—hawk-eye—flowing beard— dignity and all, and King settled down to guard himself against the next attempt on his sovereign self-command.

Now he chose to notice the knife on the ebony table as if he had not seen it before. He got up and reached for it and brought it back, turning it over and over in his hand.

"A strange knife," he said.

"Yes,—from Khinjan," said Rewa Gunga, and King eyed him as one wolf eyes another.

"What makes you say it is from Khinjan?"

"She brought it from Khinjan Caves herself! There is another knife that matches it, but that is not here. That bracelet you now wear, sahib, is from Khinjan Caves too! She has the secret of the Caves!"

"I have heard that the 'Heart of the Hills' is there," King answered. "Is the 'Heart of the Hills' a treasure house?"

Rewa Gunga laughed.

"Ask her, sahib! Perhaps she will tell you! Perhaps she will let you see! Who knows? She is a woman of resource and unexpectedness—Let her women dance for you a while."

King nodded. Then he got up and laid the knife back on the little table. A minute or so later he noticed that at a sign from Rewa Gunga a woman left the great window place and spirited the knife away.

"May I have a sheet of paper?" he asked, for he knew that another fight for his self-command was due.

Rewa Gunga gave an order, and a maid brought him scented paper on a silver tray. He drew out his own fountain pen then and made ready.

In spite of the great silken punkah that swung rhythmically across the full breadth of the room the heat was so great that the pen slipped round and round between his fingers. Yet he contrived to write, and since his one object was to give his brain employment, he wrote down a list of the names he had memorized in the train on the journey from Peshawur, not thinking of a use for the list until he had finished. Then, though, a real use occurred to him.

While he began to write more than a dozen dancing women swept into the room from behind the silk hangings in a concerted movement that was all lithe slumberous grace. Wood-wind music called to them from the great deep window as snakes are summoned from their holes, and as cobras answer the charmer's call the women glided to the center and stood poised beneath the punkah.

There they began to chant, still dreamily, and with the chant the dance began, in and out, round and round, lazily, ever so lazily, wreathed in buoyant gossamer that was scarcely more solid than the sandalwood smoke they wafted into rings.

King watched them and listened to their chant until he began to recognize the strain on the eye-muscles that precedes the mesmeric spell. Then he wrote and read what he had written and wrote again. And after that, for the sake of mental exercise, he switched his thoughts into another channel altogether. He reverted to Delhi railway station.

"The Turks can spy as well as anybody.—They know those men are going to Kerachi to be ready for them.—*Therefore,* having cut his eye-teeth B. C. several hundred, the Unspeakable Turk will take care not to misbehave UNTIL he's ready. And I suppose our government, being ours and we being us, will let him do it! All of which will take time.—And that again means no trouble in the 'Hills'—probably—until the Turks really do feel ready to begin. They'll preach a holy war just ahead of the date. The tribes will keep quiet because an army at Kerachi *might* be meant for their benefit. Oh, yes, I'm quite sure they were entraining for Kerachi in readiness to move on Basra.

Trucks ready for camels—and camel drivers—and food for camels—and Eresby, who's just come from taking a special camel course. Not a doubt of it!— And then, Corrigan—Elwright—Doby—Gould—all on the platform in a bunch, and all down on the Army List as Turkish interpreters! Not a doubt left!"

"What have you written?" asked a quiet voice at his ear; and he turned to look straight in the eyes of Rewa Gunga, who had leaned forward to read over his shoulder. Just for one second he hovered on the brink of quick defeat. Having escaped the Scylla of the dancing women, Charybdis waited for him in the shape of eyes that were pools of hot mystery. It was the sound of his own voice that brought him back to the world again and saved his will for him unbound.

"Read it, won't you?" he laughed. "If you know, take this pen and mark the names of whichever of those men are still in Delhi."

Rewa Gunga took pen and paper and set a mark against some thirty of the names, for King had a manner that disarmed refusal.

"Where are the others?" he asked him, after a glance at it.

"In jail, or else over the border."

"Already?"

The Rangar nodded. "Trust Yasmini! She saw to that jolly well before she left Delhi! She would have stayed had there been anything more to do!"

King began to watch the dance again, for it did not feel safe to look too long into the Rangar's eyes. It was not wise just then to look too long at anything, or to think too long on any one subject.

"Ismail is slow about returning," said the Rangar.

"I wrote at the foot of the *tar,*" said King, "that they are to detain him there until the answer comes."

The Rangar's eyes blazed for a second and then grew cold again (as King did not fail to observe). He knew as well as the Rangar that not many men would have kept their will so unfettered in that room as to be able to give independent orders. He recognized resignation, temporary at least, in the Rangar's attitude of leaning back again to watch from under lowered eyelids. It was like being watched by a cat.

All this while the women danced on, in time to wailing flute-music, until, it seemed from nowhere, a lovelier woman than any of them appeared in their midst, sitting cross-legged with a flat basket at her knees. She sat with arms raised and swayed from the waist as if in a delirium. Her arms moved in narrowing circles, higher and higher above the basket lid, and the lid began to rise. Nobody touched it, nor was there any string, but as it rose it swayed with sickening monotony.

It was minutes before the bodies of two great king-cobras could be made out, moving against the woman's spangled dress. The basket lid was resting on their heads, and as the music and the chanting rose to a wild weird shriek the lid rose too, until suddenly the woman snatched the lid away and the snakes were revealed, with hoods raised, hissing the cobra's hate-song that is prelude to the poison-death.

They struck at the woman, one after the other, and she leaped out of their range, swift and as supple as they. Instantly then she joined in the dance, with the snakes striking right and left at her. Left and right she swayed to avoid them, far more gracefully than a matador avoids the bull and courting a deadlier peril than he—poisonous, two to his one. As she danced she whirled both arms above her head and cried as the were-wolves are said to do on stormy nights.

Some unseen hand drew a blind over the great window and an eerie green-and-golden light began to play from one end of the room, throwing the dancers into half-relief and deepening the mystery.

Sweet strange scents were wafted in from under the silken hangings. The room grew cooler by unguessed means. Every sense was treacherously wooed. And ever, in the middle of the moving light among the languorous dancers, the snakes pursued the woman!

"Do you do this often?" wondered King, in a calm aside to Rewa Gunga, turning half toward him and taking his eyes off the dance without any very great effort.

Rewa Gunga clapped his hands and the dance ceased. The woman spirited her snakes away. The blind was drawn upward and in a moment all was normal again with the punkah swinging slowly overhead, except that the seductive smell remained, that was like the early-morning breath of all the different flowers of India.

"If *she* were here," said the Rangar, a little grimly—with a trace of disappointment in his tone—"you would not snatch your eyes away like that! You would have been jolly well transfixed, my friend! These—she—that woman—they are but clumsy amateurs! If *she* were here, to dance with her snakes for you, you would have been jolly well dancing with her, if she had wished it! Perhaps you shall see her dance some day! 'Ah,—here is Ismail," he added in an altered tone of voice. He seemed relieved at sight of the Afridi.

Bursting through the glass-bead curtains at the door, the great savage strode down the room, holding out a telegram. Rewa Gunga looked as if he would have snatched it, but King's hand was held out first and Ismail gave it to him. With a murmur of conventional apology King tore the envelope and in a second his eyes were ablaze with something more than wonder. A mystery, added to a mystery, stirred all the zeal in him. But in a second he had sweated his excitement down.

"Read that, will you?" he said, passing it to Rewa Gunga. It was not in cypher, but in plain every-day English.

"She has not gone North," it ran. "She is still in Delhi. Suit your own movements to your plans."

"Can you explain?" asked King in a level voice. He was watching the Rangar narrowly, yet he could not detect the slightest symptom of emotion.

"Explain?" said the Rangar. "Who can explain foolishness? It means that another fat general has made another fat mistake!"

"What makes *you* so certain she went North?" King asked.

Instead of answering, Rewa Gunga beckoned Ismail, who had stepped back out of hearing. The giant came and loomed over them like the Spirit of the Lamp of the *Arabian Nights*.

"Whither went *she?*" asked the Rangar.

"To the North!" he boomed.

"How knowest thou?"

"I saw her go!"

"When went she?"

"Yesterday, when a telegram came."

The word "came" was the only clue to his meaning, for in the language he used "yesterday" and "to-morrow" are the same word; such is the East's esti-mate of time.

"By what route did she go?" asked Rewa Gunga.

"By the terrrain from the isstation."

"How knowest thou that?"

"I was there, bearing her box of jewels."

"Didst thou see her buy the tikkut?"

"Nay, I bought it, for she ordered me."

"For what destination was the tikkut?"

"Peshawur!" said Ismail, filling his mouth with the word as if he loved it.

"Yet"—it was King who spoke now, pointing an accusing finger at him—"a burra sahib sends a *tar* to me—this is it!—to say she is in Delhi still! Who told thee to answer those questions with those words?"

"She!" the big man answered.

"Yasmini?"

"Aye! May Allah cover her with blessings!"

"Ah!" said King. "You have my leave to depart out of earshot."

Then he turned on Rewa Gunga.

"Whatever the truth of all this," he said quietly, "I suppose it means she has done what there was to do in Delhi?"

"Sahib,—trust her! Does a tigress hunt where no watercourses are, and where no game goes to drink? She follows the sambur!"

"You are positive she has started for the North?"

"Sahib, when she speaks it is best to believe! She

told me she will go. Therefore I am ready to lead
King sahib up the Khyber to her!"

"Are you certain you can find her?"

"Aye, sahib,—in the dark!"

"There's a train leaves for the North to-night," said
King.

The Rangar nodded.

"You'll want a pass up the line. How many servants? Three—four—how many?"

"One," said the Rangar, and King was instantly
suspicious of the modesty of that allowance; however
he wrote out a pass for Rewa Gunga and one servant
and gave it to him.

"Be there on time and see about your own reservation," he said. "I'll attend to Ismail's pass myself."

He folded the list of names that the Rangar had
marked and wrote something on the back. Then he
begged an envelope, and Rewa Gunga had one brought
to him. He sealed the list in the envelope, addressed it
and beckoned Ismail again.

"Take this to Saunders sahib!" he ordered. "Go
first to the telegraph office, where you were before,
and the babu there will tell you where Saunders sahib
may be found. Having found him, deliver the letter
to him. Then come and find me at the Star of India
Hotel and help me to bathe and change my clothes."

"To hear is to obey!" boomed Ismail, bowing; but
his last glance was for Rewa Gunga, and he did not
turn to go until he had met the Rangar's eyes.

When Ismail had gone striding down the room, with
no glance to spare for the whispering women in the
window, and with dignity like an aura exuding from

him, King looked into the Rangar's eyes with that engaging frankness of his that disarms so many people.

"Then you'll be on the train to-night?" he asked.

"To hear is to obey! With pleasure, sahib!"

"Then good-by until this evening."

King bowed very civilly and walked out, rather unsteadily because his head ached. Probably nobody else, except the Rangar, could have guessed what an ordeal he had passed through or how near he had been to losing self-command.

But as he felt his way down the stairs, that were dimly lighted now, he knew he had all his senses with him, for he "spotted" and admired the lurking places that had been designed for undoing of the unwary, or even the overwary. Yasmini's Delhi nest was like a hundred traps in one.

"Almost like a pool table," he reflected. "Pocket 'em at both ends and the middle!"

In the street he found a gharry after a while and drove to his hotel. And before Ismail came he took a stroll through a bazaar, where he made a few strange purchases. In the hotel lobby he invested in a leather bag with a good lock, in which to put them. Later on Ismail came and proved himself an efficient bodyservant.

That evening Ismail carried the leather bag and found his place on the train, and that was not so difficult, because the trains running North were nearly empty, although the platforms were all crowded. As he stood at the carriage door with Ismail near him, a man named Saunders slipped through the crowd and sought him out.

"Arrested 'em all!" he grinned.

"Good."

"Seen anything of *her?* I recognized Yasmini's scent on your envelope. It's peculiar to her—one of her monopolies!"

"No. I'm told she went North yesterday."

"Not by train, she didn't! It's my business to know that!"

King did not answer; nor did he look surprised. He was watching Rewa Gunga, followed by a servant, hurrying to a reserved compartment at the front end of the train. The Rangar waved to him and he waved back.

"I'd know her in a million!" vowed Saunders. "I can take oath she hasn't gone anywhere by train! Unless she has walked, or taken a carriage, she's in Delhi!"

The engine gave a preliminary shriek and the giant Ismail nudged King's elbow in impatient warning. There was no more sign of Rewa Gunga, who had evidently settled down in his compartment for the night.

"Get my bag out again!" King ordered, and Ismail stared.

"Get out my bag, I said!"

"To hear is to obey!" Ismail grumbled, reaching with his long arm through the window.

The engine shrieked again, somebody whistled, and the train began to move.

"You've missed it!" said Saunders, amused at Ismail's frantic disappointment. The giant was tugging at his beard. "How about your trunk? Better wire ahead and have it spotted for you."

"No," said King; "it's still in the baggage room at the other station. I didn't intend to go by this train. Came down here to see another fellow off, that's all! Have a cigar and then let's go together and look those prisoners over!"

Men boast in the Hills, when they ought to pray;
For the wind blows lusty, and the blood runs red,
And Law lies belly upwards for a man to wreak his
*   fancy on it.*
Down in the plains, in the dust of the plains
Where law is master and a good man ought to boast,
They all lie belly downwards praying for their Hills
*   again!*

CHAPTER IV

THE rear lights of the train he had not taken swayed out of Delhi station and King grinned as he wiped the sweat from his face with a dripping handkerchief. Behind him towered the hook-nosed Ismail, resentful of the unexpected. In front of him Saunders eyed the proffered black cheroots suspiciously, accepted one with an air of curiosity and passed the case back. Around them the clatter of the station crowd began to die, and Parsimony in a shabby uniform went round to lower lights.

"Are you sure—"

King's merry eyes looked into Saunders' as if there were no world war really and they two were puppets in a comedy.

"—are you absolutely certain Yasmini is in Delhi?"

"No," said Saunders. "What I swear to is that she has not left by train. It's my business to know who leaves by train."

"What can you suggest?" asked King, twisting at his scrubby little mustache. But if he wished to convey the impression of a man at his wits' end, he failed signally.

"I? Nothing! She's the most elusive individual in Asia! One person in the world knows where she is, unless she has an accomplice. My information's negative. I know she has not gone by—"

King struck a match and held it out, so the sentence was unfinished; the first few puffs of the astonishing cigar wiped out all memory of the missing word. And then King changed the subject.

"Those men I asked you to arrest—?"

"Nabbed"—puff—"every one of 'em!"—puff-puff—"all under"—puff-puff—"lock and key,—best smoke I ever tasted—where d'you get 'em?"

"Had they been in communication with her?"

Puff-puff—"You bet they had! Where d'you get these things?"

"Not her special men by any chance?"

Puff—"Gad, what smoke!—couldn't say, of course, but"—puff-puff—"shouldn't think so."

"Well—I'll go along with you if you like and look them over."

Both tone and manner gave Saunders credit for the suggestion, and Saunders seemed to like it. There is nothing like following up, in football, war or courtship.

"I see you're a judge of a cigar," said King, and Saunders purred, all men being fools to some extent, and the only trouble being to demonstrate the fact.

They had started for the station entrance when a nasal voice began intoning, "Cap-teen King sahib— Cap-teen King sahib!" and a telegraph messenger passed them with his book under his arm. King whistled him. A moment later he was tearing open an official urgent telegram and writing a string of figures in pencil across the top. Then he de-coded swiftly

"Advices are Yasmini was in Delhi as recently as six this evening. Fail to understand your inability to get in touch. Have you tried at her house? Matters in Khyber district much less satisfactory. Word from O-C Khyber Rifles to effect that lashkar is collecting. Better sweep up in Delhi and proceed northward as quickly as compatible with caution. L. M. L."

The three letters at the end were the general's coded signature. The wording of the telegram was such that as he read King saw a mental picture of the general's bald red skull and could almost hear him say the "fail to understand." The three words "much less satisfactory" were a bookful of information. So, as he folded up the telegram, tore the penciled strip of figures from the top and burned it with a match, he was at pains to look pleased.

"Good news?" asked Saunders, blowing smoke through his nose.

"Excellent. Where's my man? Here—you—Ismail!"

The giant came and towered above him.

"You swore *she* went North!"

"Ha, sahib! To Peshawur she went!"

"Did she start from this station?"

"From where else, sahib?"

But this was too much for Saunders, who stepped forward and thrust in an oar. King on the other hand stepped back a pace so as to watch both faces.

"Then, when did she go?"

"I saw her go!" said Ismail, affronted.

"When? When, confound you! When?"

"Yesterday."

"I expect he means to-morrow," said King. With

the advantage of looker-on and a very deep experience
of Northerners, he had noted that Ismail was lying
and that Saunders was growing doubtful, although
both men concealed the truth with what was very close
to being art.

"I have a telegram here," he said, "that says she is
in Delhi!"

He patted his coat, where the inner pocket bulged.

"Nay, then the *tar* lies, for I saw her go with these
two eyes of mine!"

"It is not wise to lie to me, my friend," King assured
him, so pleasantly that none could doubt he was telling
truth.

"If I lie may I eat dirt!" Ismail answered him.

Inches lent the Afridi dignity, but dignity has often
been used as a stalking horse for untruth. King
nodded, and it was not possible to judge by his expression whether he believed or not.

"Let's make a move," he said, turning to Saunders.
"She seems at any rate to wish it believed she has gone
North. I can't stay here indefinitely. If she's here
she's on the watch here, and there's no need of me.
If she has gone North, then that is where the kites are
wheeling! I'll take the early morning train. Where
are the prisoners?"

"In the old Mir Khan Palace. We were short of
jail room and had to improvise. The horse-stalls
there have come in handy more than once before.
Shall we take this gharry?"

With Ismail up beside the driver nursing King's bag
and looking like a great grim vulture about to eat the
horse, they drove back through swarming streets in

the direction of the river. King seemed to have lost
all interest in crowds. He scarcely even troubled to
watch when they were held up at a cross-roads by a
marching regiment that tramped as if it were herald
of the Last Trump, with bayonets glistening in the
street lights. He sat staring ahead in silence, although
Saunders made more than one effort to engage him in
conversation.

"No!" he said at last suddenly—so that Saunders
jumped.

"No what?"

"No need to stay here. I've got what I came for!"

"What was that?" asked Saunders, but King was
silent again. Conscious of the unaccustomed weight
on his left wrist, he moved his arm so that the sleeve
drew and he could see the edge of the great gold
bracelet Rewa Gunga had given him in Yasmini's name.

"Know anything of Rewa Gunga?" he asked suddenly again.

"The Rangar?"

"Yes, the Rangar. Yasmini's man."

"Not much. I've seen him. I've spoken with him,
and I've had to stand impudence from him—twice.
I've been tipped off more than once to let him alone
because he's her man. He does ticklish errands for
her, or so they say. He's what you might call 'known
to the police' all right."

They began to approach an age-old palace near the
river, and Saunders whispered a pass-word when an
armed guard halted them. They were halted again at
a gloomy gateway where an officer came out to look
them over; by his leave they left the gharry and fol-

lowed him ander the arch until their heels rang on
stone paving in a big ill-lighted courtyard surrounded
by high walls.

There, after a little talk, they left Ismail squatting
beside King's bag, and Saunders led the way through a
modern iron door, into what had once been a royal
prince's stables.

In gloom that was only thrown into contrast by a
wide-spaced row of electric lights, a long line of barred
and locked converted horse-stalls ran down one side
of a lean-to building. The upper half of each locked
door was a grating of steel rods, so that there was
some ventilation for the prisoners; but very little light
filtered between the bars, and all that King could see
of the men within was the whites of their eyes. And
they did not look friendly.

He had to pass between them and the light, and they
could see more of him than he could of them. At the
first cell he raised his left hand and made the gold
bracelet on his wrist clink against the steel bars.

A moment later he cursed himself, and felt the
bracelet with his finger-nail. He had made a deep nick
in the soft gold. A second later yet he smiled.

"May God be with thee!" boomed a prisoner's voice
in Pashtu.

"Didn't know that fellow was handcuffed," said
Saunders. "Did you hear the ring? They should have
been taken off. Leaving his irons on has made him
polite, though."

He passed on, and King followed him, saying nothing. But at the next cell he repeated what he had done
at the first, taking better care of the gold but letting
his wrist stay longer in the light.

"May God be with thee !" said a voice within.

"Gettin' a shade less arrogant, what ?" said Saunders.

"May God be with thee !" said a man in the third stall as King passed.

"They seem to be anxious for your morals !" laughed Saunders, keeping a pace or two ahead to do the honors of the place.

"May God be with thee !" said a fourth man, and King desisted for the present, because Saunders looked as if he were growing inquisitive.

"Where did you arrest them ?" he asked when Saunders came to a stand under a light.

"All in one place. At Ali's."

"Who and what is Ali ?"

"Pimp—crimp—procurer—Prussian spy and any other evil thing that takes his fancy ! Runs a combination gambling hell and boarding house. Lets 'em run into debt and blackmails 'em. Ali's in the kaiser's pay —that's known ! 'Musing thing about it is he keeps a photo of Wilhelm in his pocket and tries to make himself believe the kaiser knows him by name. Suffers from swelled head, which is part of their plan, of course. We'll get *him* when we want him, but at present he's useful 'as is' for a decoy. Ali was very much upset at the arrest—asked in the name of Heaven— seems to be familiar with God, too, and all the angels ! —how he shall collect all the money these men owe him !"

"You wouldn't call these men prosperous, then ?"

"Not exactly ! Ali is the only spy out of the North who prospers much at present, and even he gets most of his money out of his private business. Why, man, the real Germans we have pounced on are all as poor

as church mice. That's another part of the plan, of
course, which is sweet in all its workings. They're
paid less than driven by threats of exposure to us—
comes cheaper, and serves to ginger up the spies! The
Germans pay Ali a little, and he traps the Hillmen
when they come South—lets 'em gamble—gets 'em
into debt—plays on their fear of jail and their
ignorance of the Indian Penal Code, which altereth
every afternoon—and spends a lot of time telling 'em
stories to take back with 'em to the Hills when they
can get away. They can get away when they've paid
him what they owe. He makes that clear, and of
course that's the fly in the amber. Yasmini sends and
pays their board and gambling debts, and she's our
man, so to speak. When they get back to the 'Hills'—"

"Thanks," said King, "I know what happens in the
'Hills.' Tell me about the Delhi end of it."

"Well, when the wander-fever grabs 'em again they
come down once more from their 'Hills' to drink and
gamble,—and first they go to Yasmini's. But she
won't let 'em drink at her place. Have to give her
credit for that, y'know; her place has never been a
stews. Sooner or later they grow tired of virtue,
'specially with so much intrigue goin' on under their
noses, and back they all drift to Ali's and tell him tales
to tell the Germans—and the round begins again.
Yasmini coaxes all their stories out of 'em and primes
'em with a few extra good ones into the bargain.
Everybody's fooled—'specially the Germans—and
exceptin', of course, Yasmini and the Raj. Nobody
ever fooled that woman, nor ever will if my belief
goes for anything!"

"Sounds simple!" said King.

"Simple and sordid!" agreed Saunders.

King looked up and down the line of locked doors and then straight into Saunders' eyes in a friendly, yet rather disconcerting way. One could not judge whether he were laughing or just thinking.

"D'you suppose it's as simple as all that?"

"How d'you mean?"

"D'you suppose the Germans aren't in directer touch with the tribes?"

"Why should they be? The simpler the better, I expect, from their point of view; and the cheaper the better, too!"

"Um-m-m!" King rubbed his chin. "On what charge did you get these men?"

"Defense of the Realm—suspicious characters— charge to be entered later."

"Good! That's simple at all events! Know anything of my man Ismail?"

"Sure! He's one of Yasmini's pets. She bailed him out of Ali's three years ago and he worships her. It was he who broke the leg and ribs of a pup-rajah a month or two ago for putting on too much dog in her reception room! He's Ursus out of *Quo Vadis!* He's dog, desperado, stalking horse and Keeper of the Queen's secrets!"

"Then why d'you suppose she passed him along to me?" asked King.

"Dunno! This is your little mystery, not mine!"

"Glad you appreciate that! Do me a favor, will you?"

"Anything in reason."

"Get the keys to all these cells—send 'em in here to me by Ismail—and leave me in here alone!"

Saunders whistled and wiped sweat from his glistening face, for in spite of windows open to the courtyard it was hotter than a furnace room.

"Mayn't I have you thrown into a den of tigers?" he asked. "Or a nest of cobras? Or get the fiery furnace ready? You'll find 'em sore—and dangerous! That man at the end with handcuffs on has probably been violent! That 'God be with thee' stuff is habit—they say it with unction before they knife a man!"

"I'll be careful, then," King chuckled; and it is a fact that few men can argue with him when he laughs quietly in that way. "Send me in the keys, like a good chap."

So Saunders went, glad enough to get into the outer air. He slammed the great iron door behind him as if he were glad, too, to disassociate himself from King and all foolishness. Like many another first-class man, King sheds friends as a cat sheds fur going under a gate. They grow again and quit again and don't seem to make much difference.

The instant the door slammed King continued down the line with his left wrist held high so that the occupant of each cell in turn could see the bracelet.

"May God be with thee!" came the instant greeting from each cell until down toward the farther end. The occupants of the last six cells were silent.

Numbers had been chalked roughly on the doors. With wetted fingers he rubbed out the chalk marks on the last six doors, and he had scarcely finished doing that when Ismail strode in, slamming the great iron door behind him, jangling a bunch of keys and looking more than ever like somebody out of the Old Testament.

"Open every door except those whose numbers I have rubbed out!" King ordered him.

Ismail proceeded to obey as if that were the least improbable order in all the world. It took him two minutes to select the pass-key and determine how it worked, then the doors flew open one after another in quick succession.

"Come out!" he growled. "Come out!—Come out!" although King had not ordered that.

King went and stood under the center light with his left arm bared. The prisoners, emerging like dead men out of tombs, blinked at the bright light—saw him—then the bracelet—and saluted.

"May God be with thee!" growled each of them.

They stood still then, awaiting fresh developments. It did not seem to occur to any one of them as strange that a British officer in khaki uniform should be sporting Yasmini's talisman; the thing was apparently sufficient explanation in itself.

"Ye all know this?" he asked, holding up his wrist. "Whose is this?"

"*Hers!*"

The answer was monosyllabic and instant from all thirty throats. "May Allah guard her, sleeping and awake!" added one or two of them.

King lit a cheroot and made mental note of the wisdom of referring to her by pronoun, not by name.

"And I? Who am I?" he asked, since it saves worlds of trouble to have the other side state the case. The Secret Service was not designed for giving information, but discovering it.

"Her messenger! Who else? Thou art he who shall take us to the 'Hills'! She promised!"

"How did she know ye were in this jail?" he asked
them, and one of the Hillmen laughed like a jackal,
showing yellow eye-teeth. The others cackled in
chorus after him.

"Answer that riddle thyself—or else ask her! Who
are we? Bats, that can see in the night? Spirits, who
can hear through walls? Nay, we be plain men of the
mountains!"

"But where were ye when she promised?"

"At Ali's. All of us at Ali's—held for debt. We
sent and begged of her. She sent word back by a
woman that one of the sirkar's men shall free us and
send us home. So we waited, eating shame and little
else, at Ali's. At last came a sahib in a great rage, who
ordered irons put on our wrists and us marched hither.
Only when each was pushed into a separate cell were
the irons taken off again. Yet we were patient, for
we knew this is part of her cunning, to get us away
from Ali without paying him. 'May Ali die of want,'
said we, with one voice all together in these cells! And
now we be ready! They fed us before we had been
in here an hour. Our bellies be full, but we be hungry
for the 'Hills'!"

King thought of the gold-hilted knife, that still rested
under his shirt. He was tempted to show it to them
and find out surely whose it was and what it meant.
But wisdom and curiosity seldom mingle. He thought
of Ismail—"Ursus, of *Quo Vadis*—dog, desperado,
stalking-horse and Keeper of the Queen's secrets." It
was not time yet to run risks with Ismail. The knife
stayed where it was.

"I shall start for the Hills at dawn," he said slowly,
and he watched their eyes gleam at the news. **No**

caged tiger is as wretched as a prisoned Hillman. No
freed bird wings more wildly for the open. No moth
comes more foolishly back to the flame again. It was
easy to take pity on them—probably not one of whom
knew pity's meaning.

"Is there any among you who would care to
come—?"

"Ah-h-h-h!"

"—at the price of strict obedience?"

"Eh-h-h-h-h!"

It seemed there was no word in Pashtu that could
express their willingness.

"We be very, very weary for our Hills!" explained
the nearest man.

"Aye!" King answered. "And ye all owe Ali!"

"Uh-h-h-h-h!"

But he knew better than to browbeat them on that
account just then, for the men of the North are easier
led than driven—up to a certain point. Yet it is no
bad plan to remind them of the fundamentals to begin
with.

"Will ye obey me, and him?" he asked, laying his
hand on Ismail's shoulder, as much to let them see the
bracelet again as for any other reason.

"Aye! If we fail, Allah do more to us!"

King laughed. "Ye shall leave this place as my
prisoners. Here ye have no friends. Here ye *must*
obey. But what when ye come to your 'Hills' at last?
Can one man hold thirty men prisoners then? In the
'Hills' will ye still obey me?"

They answered him in chorus. Every man of the
thirty, and Ismail into the bargain, threw his right
hand in the air.

"Allah witness that we will obey!"

"Ah-h-h!" said King. "I have heard Hillmen swear by Allah many a time! Many a time!"

The answer to that was unexpected. Ismail knelt—seized his hand—and pressed the gold bracelet to his lips!

In turn, every one of them filed by, knelt reverently and kissed the bracelet!

"Saw ye ever a Hillman do that before?" asked Ismail. "They will obey thee! Have no fear!"

"Kutch dar nahin hai!" King answered. "There is no such thing as fear!" and Ismail grinned at him, not knowing that King was feeling as Aladdin must have done.

"I have heard you swear," said King; "be ye true men!"

"Ah-h-h!"

"Have they belongings that ought to be collected first?" he asked, and Ismail laughed.

"No more than the dead have! A shroud apiece! Ali gave them bitterness to eat and picked their teeth afterward for gleanings! They stand in what they own!"

"Then, come!" ordered King, turning his back confidently on thirty savages whom Saunders, for instance, would have preferred to drive in front of him, after first seeing them handcuffed. But when he is not pressed for time neither pistols, nor yet handcuffs, are included in King's method.

"Each lock has a key, but some keys fit all locks," says the Eastern proverb. King has been chosen for many ticklish errands in his time, and Saunders is still in Delhi.

Through the great iron door into dim outer darkness King led them and presently made them squat in a close-huddled semicircle on the paving stones, like night-birds waiting for a meal.

"I want blankets for them—two good ones apiece— and food for a week's journey!" he told the astonished Saunders; and he spoke so decidedly that the other man's questions and argument died stillborn. "While you attend to that for me, I'll be seeing his dibs and making explanations. You look full of news. What do you know?"

"I've telephoned all the other stations, and my men swear Yasmini has not left Delhi by train!"

King smiled at him.

"If I leave by train d'you suppose she'll hear of it?"

"You bet! Bet your boots! Man alive—if she's interested in you by so much,"—he measured off a fraction of his little finger end—"she knows your next two moves ahead, to say nothing of your past half-dozen! I crossed her bows once and thought I had her at a disadvantage. She laughed at me. On my honor, my spine tingles yet at the mere thought of it! You've never met her? Never heard her laugh? Never seen her eyes? You've a treat in store for you—and a *mauvais quat' d'heure!* What'll you bet me she doesn't laugh you out of countenance the very first time you meet? Come now—what'll you bet?"

"Not in the habit," King answered, glancing at his watch. "Will you see about their rations, please, and the blankets? Thanks!"

They went then in opposite directions and the prisoners were left squatting under the eyes and bayonets of a very suspicious prison guard, who made no secret of

being ready for all conceivable emergencies. One en-
thusiast drew the cartridge out of his breech-chamber
and licked it at intervals of a minute or two, to the
very great interest of the Hillmen, who memorized
every detail that by any stretch of imagination might
be expected to improve their own shooting when they
should get home again.

King found his way on foot through a maze of
streets to a palace where he was admitted through one
door after another by sentries who saluted when he
had whispered to them. He ended by sitting on the
end of the bed of a gray-headed man who owns three
titles and whose word is law between the borders of
a province. To him he talked as one schoolboy to a
bigger one, because the gray-haired man had understanding, and hence sympathy.

"I don't envy you!" said he under the sheet. "There
was an American here not long ago—most amusing
man I ever talked to. He had the right expression.
'I do not desiderate that pie!' was his way of putting
it. Good, don't you think?"

All the while he talked the older man was writing
on a pad that he held propped by his knees beneath the
bedclothes, holding the paper tight to keep it from
fluttering in the breeze of a big electric fan.

"There's the release for your prisoners. Take it—
and take them! Whatever possessed you to want such
a gift?"

"Orders, sir."

"Whose?"

"His. He sent for me to Peshawur and gave me
strict orders to work *with*, not against her. This was
obvious."

"How obvious? It seems bewildering!"

"Well, sir,—first place, she doesn't want to seem to be connected with me. Otherwise she'd have been more in evidence. Second place, she has left Delhi— his telegram and Saunders' men on oath notwithstanding—and she did not mean to leave those men. I imagine her best way to manage Hillmen is to keep promises, and they say she promised them. Third place, if those thirty men had been anything but her particular pet gang they'd either have been over the border or else in jail before now,—just like all the others. For some reason that I don't pretend to understand, she promised 'em more than she has been able to perform. So I provide performance. She gets the credit for it. I get a pretty good personal following at least as far as up the Khyber! Q. E. D., sir!"

The man in bed nodded. "Not bad," he said.

"Didn't she make some effort to get those men away from Ali's?" King asked him. "I mean, didn't she try to get them dry-nursed by the sirkar in some way?"

"Yes. She did. But it was difficult. In the first place, there didn't seem to be any particular hurry. They were eating Ali's substance. The scoundrel had to feed them as long as he kept them there, and we wanted that. We forbade her to pay their debts to Ali, because he has too urgent need of money just now. He is being pressed on account of debts of his own, and the pressure is making him take risks. He has been begging for money from the German agents. We know who they are, and we expect to make a big haul within a few hours now."

"Hope I didn't spoil things by butting in, sir?"

"No. This is different. She wanted them arrested

and locked up at a moment when the jails were all crowded. And then she wanted us to put 'em into trucks and railroad 'em up North out of harm's way as she put it, and we happened to be too busy. The railway staff was overworked. Now things are getting straightened out. I felt it keenly not being able to oblige her, but she asked too much at the wrong moment! I would have done it if I could out of gratitude; it was she who tipped off for us most of the really dangerous men, and it was not her fault a few of them escaped. But we've all been working both tides under, King. Take me; this is my first night in bed in three, and here I am awake! No—nothing personal—glad to see you, but please understand. And I'm a leisured dilettante compared to most of the others. She must have known our fix. She shouldn't have asked."

King smiled. "Perfectly good opportunity for me, sir!" he said cheerfully.

"So you seem to think. But look out for that woman, King—she's dangerous. She's got the brains of Asia coupled with Western energy! I think she's on our side, and I know *he* believes it; but *watch* her!"

"*Ham dekta hai!*" King grinned. But the older man continued to look as if he pitied him.

"If you get through alive, come and tell me about it afterward. Now, mind you do! I'm awfully interested, but as for envying you—"

"Envy!" King almost squealed. He made the bedsprings rattle as he jumped. "I wouldn't swap jobs with General French, sir!"

"Nor with me, I suppose!"

"Nor with you, sir!"

'Good-by, then. Good-by, King, my boy. Good-by, Athelstan. Your brother's up the Khyber, isn't he? Give him my regards. Good-by!"

Long before dawn the thirty prisoners and Ismail squatted in a little herd on the up-platform of a railway station, shepherded by King, who smoked a cheroot some twenty paces away, sitting on an unmarked chest of medicines. He seemed absorbed in a book on surgery that he had borrowed from a chance-met acquaintance in the go-down where he drew the medical supplies. Ismail sat on the one trunk that had been fetched from the other station and nursed the new hand-bag on his knees, picking everlastingly at the lock and wondering audibly what the bag contained to an accompaniment of low-growled sympathy.

"I am his servant—for she said so—and he said so. As the custom is he gave me the key of the great bag on which I sit—as he said himself, for safe-keeping. Then why—why in Allah's name—am I not to have the key of this bag too? Of this little bag that holds so little and is so light?"

"It might be money in it?" hazarded one of the herd.

"Nay, for that it is too light."

"Paper money!" suggested another man. "Hundies, with printing on the face that sahibs accept instead of gold."

"Nay, I know where his money is," said Ismail. "He has but little with him."

"A razor would slit the leather easily," suggested another man. "Then with a hand inserted carefully through the slit, so as not to widen it more than need-

ful, a man could soon discover the contents. And
later, the bag might be dropped or pushed violently
against some sharp thing, to explain the cut."

Ismail shook his head.

"Why? What could he do to thee?"

"It is because I know not what he would do to me
that I will do nothing!" answered Ismail. "He is not
at all like other sahibs I have had dealings with. This
man does unexpected things. This man is not mad, he
has a devil. I have it in my heart to love this man.
But such talk is foolishness. We are all her men!"

"Aye! We are *her* men!" came the chorus, so that
King looked up and watched them over the open book.

At dawn, when the train pulled out, the thirty prisoners sat safely locked in third-class compartments.
King lay lazily on the cushions of a first-class carriage
in the rear, utterly absorbed in the principles of anti-
septic dressing, as if that had anything to do with
Prussians and the Khyber Pass; and Ismail attended
to the careful packing of soda water bottles in the ice-
box on the floor.

"Shall I open the little bag, sahib?" he asked.

King shook his head.

Ismail shook the bag.

"The sound is as of things of much importance all
disordered," he said sagely. "It might be well to rearrange."

"Put it over there!" King ordered. "Set it down!"

Ismail obeyed and King laid his book down to light
another of his black cheroots. The theme of anti-
septics ceased to exercise its charm over him. He
peeled off his tunic, changed his shirt and lay back in
sweet contentment. Headed for the "Hills," who

would not be contented, who had been born in their
very shadow?—in their shadow, of a line of Britons
who have all been buried there!

"The day after to-morrow I'll see snow!" he
promised himself. And Ismail, grinning with yellow
teeth through a gap in his wayward beard, understood
and sympathized.

Forward in the third-class carriages the prisoners
hugged themselves and crooned as they met old land-
marks and recognized the changing scenery. There
was a new cleaner tang in the hot wind that spoke of
the "Hills" and home!

Delhi had drawn them as Monte Carlo attracts the
gamblers of all Europe. But Delhi had spewed them
out again, and oh! how exquisite the promise of the
"Hills" was, and the thunder of the train that hurried
—the bumping wheels that sang *Himahlyas—Himahlyas!*—the air that blew in on them unscented—the
reawakened memory—the heart's desire for the cold
and the snow and the cruelty—the dark nights and the
shrieking storms and the savagery of the Land of the
Knife ahead!

The journey to Peshawur, that ought to have been
wearisome because they were everlastingly shunted
into sidings to make way for roaring south-bound
troop trains and kept waiting at every wayside station
because the trains ahead of them were blocked three
deep, was no less than a jubilee progress!

Not a packed-in regiment went by that was not
howled at by King's prisoners as if they were blood-
brothers of every man in it. Many an officer whom
King knew waved to him from a passing train.

"Meet you in Berlin!" was a favorite greeting. And

after that they would shout to him for news and be
gone before King could answer.

Many a man, at stations where the sidings were all
full and nothing less than miracles seemed able to
release the wedged-in trains, came and paced up and
down a platform side by side with King. From them
he received opinions, but no sympathy to speak of.

"Got to stay in India? Hard lines!" Then the
conversation would be bluntly changed, for in the
height of one's enthusiasm it is not decent to hurt another fellow's feelings. Simple, simple as a little child
is the clean-clipped British officer. "Look at that babu,
now. Don't you think he's a marvel? Don't you think
the Indian babu's a marvel? Sixty a month is more
than the beggar gets, and there he goes, doing two jobs
and straightening out tangled trains into the bargain!
Isn't he a wonder, King?"

"India's a wonderful country," King would answer,
that being one of his stock remarks. And to his credit
be it written that he never laughed at one of them. He
let them think they were more fortunate than he, with
manlier, bloodier work to do.

Peshawur, when they reached it at last, looked dusty
and bleak in the comfortless light of Northern dawn.
But the prisoners crowed and crooned it a greeting, and
there was not much grumbling when King refused to
unlock their compartment doors. Having waited thus
long, they could endure a few more hours in patience,
now that they could see and smell their "Hills" at last.

And there was the general again, not in a dog-cart
this time, but furiously driven in a motor-car, roaring
and clattering into the station less than two minutes
after the train arrived. He was out of the car, for all

his age and weight, before it had come to a stand. He took one steady look at King and then at the prisoners before he returned King's salute.

"Good!" he said. And then, as if that were not enough: "Excellent! Don't let 'em out, though, to chew the rag with people on the platform. Keep 'em in!"

"They're locked in, sir."

"Excellent! Come and walk up and down with me."

Death roosts in the Khyber while he preens his wings!
    —NATIVE PROVERB.

CHAPTER V

"SEEN *her?*" asked the general, with his hands behind him.

"No," said King, looking sharply sidewise at him and walking stride for stride. His hands were behind him, too, and one of them covered the gold bracelet on his other wrist.

The general looked equally sharply sidewise.

"Nor've I," he said. "She called me up over the phone yesterday to ask for facilities for her man Rewa Gunga, and he was in here later. He's waiting for you at the foot of the Pass—camped near the fort at Jamrud with your bandobast all ready. She's on ahead —wouldn't wait."

King listened in silence, and his prisoners, watching him through the barred compartment windows, formed new and golden opinions of him, for it is common knowledge in the "Hills" that when a burra sahib speaks to a chota sahib, the chota sahib ought to say, "Yes, sir, oh, yes!" at very short intervals. Therefore King could not be a chota sahib after all. So much the

better. The "Hills" ever loved to deal with men in
authority, just as they ever despised underlings.

"What made you go back for the prisoners?" the
general asked. "Who gave you that cue?"

"It's a safe rule never to do what the other man
expects, sir, and Rewa Gunga expected me to travel
by his train."

"Was that your only reason?"

"No, sir. I had general reasons. None of 'em specific. Where natives have a finger in the pie there's
always something left undone at the last minute."

"But what made you investigate those prisoners?"

"Couldn't imagine why thirty men should be singled
out for special treatment. Rewa Gunga told me they
were still at large in Delhi. Couldn't guess why. Had
'em arrested so's to be able to question 'em. That's
all, sir."

"Not nearly all!" said the general. "You realize
by now, I suppose, that they're her special men—special
personal following?"

"Guessed something of that sort."

"Well—she's clever. It occurred to her that the
safest way to get 'em up North was to have 'em
arrested and deported. That would avoid interference
and delay and would give her a chance to act deliverer
at this end, and so make 'em grateful to her—you see?
Rewa Gunga told me all this, you understand. He
seems to think she's semi-divine. He was full of her
cleverness in having thought of letting 'em all get
into debt at a house of ill repute, so as to have 'em at
hand when she wanted 'em."

"She must have learned that trick from our mer-
chant marine." said King.

"Maybe. She's clever. She asked me over the phone whether her thirty men had started North. I sent a telegram in cypher to find out. The answer was that you had found 'em and rounded 'em up and were bringing 'em with you. When she called me up on the phone the second time I told her so, and I heard her chuckle with delight. So I emphasized the point of your having discovered 'em and saved 'em every wit whole and all that kind of thing. I asked her to come and see me, but she wouldn't;—said she was disguised and particularly did not want to be recognized, which was reasonable enough. She sent Rewa Gunga instead. Now, this seems important:

"Before I sent you down to Delhi—before I sent for you at all—I told her what I meant to do, and I never in my life knew a woman raise such terrific objections to working with a man. As it happened her objections only confirmed my determination to send for you, and before she went down to Delhi to clean up I told her flatly she would either have to work with you or else stay in India for the duration of the war."

The general did not notice that King was licking his lips. Nor, if he had noticed King's hand that now was in front of him pressing on something under his shirt, could he have guessed that the something was a gold-hilted knife with a bronze blade. King grunted in token of attention, and the general continued.

"She gave in finally, but I felt nervous about it. Now, without your getting sight of her—you say you haven't seen her?—her whole attitude has changed! What have you done? Bringing up her thirty men seems a little enough thing. Yet, she swears by you! Used to swear *at* you, and now says you're the only

officer in the British army with enough brains to fill a
helmet! Says she wouldn't go up the Khyber without
you! Says you're indispensable! Sent Rewa Gunga
round to me with orders to make sure I don't change
my mind about you! What have you done to her—
bewitched her?"

"Done nothing," said King.

"Well, keep on doing nothing in the same style and
the world shall render you its best jobs, one after the
other, in sequence! You've made a good beginning!"

"Know anything of Rewa Gunga, sir?"

"Nothing, except that he's her man. She trusts him,
so we've got to, and you've got to take him up the
Khyber with you. What she orders, he'll do, or you
may take it from me she would never have left him
behind. As long as she is on our side you will be pretty
safe in trusting Rewa Gunga. And she has *got* to be
on our side. *Got* to be! She's the only key we've got
to Khinjan, and hell is brewing there this minute! She
dare unlock the gates and ride the devil down the
Khyber if she thought it worth her while! You're to
go up the Khyber after her to convince her that there
are better mounts than the devil and better fun than
playing with hell-fire! The Rangar told me he had
given you her passport—that right?"

As they turned at the end of the platform King
bared his wrist and showed the gold bracelet.

"Good!" said the general, but King thought his face
clouded. "That thing is worth more than a hundred
men. Jack Allison wore that same bracelet, unless
I'm much mistaken, on his way down in disguise from
Bukhara. So did another man we both knew; but he

died. Be sure not to forget to give it back to her when
the show's over, King."

King nodded and grunted. "What's the news from
Khinjan, sir?"

"Nothing specific, except that the place is filling up.
You remember what I told you about the 'Heart of
the Hills' being in Khinjan? Well, they say now that
the 'Heart of the Hills' has been awake for a long time,
and that when the heart stirs the body does not lie
quiet long. No use trying to guess what they mean;
go and find out. And remember—the whole armed
force at my disposal in this Province isn't more than
enough to tempt the tribes to conclusions! It's a case
for diplomacy. It's a case where diplomacy *must not
fail*."

King said nothing, but the chin-strap mark on his
cheek and chin grew slightly whiter, as it always does
under the stress of emotion. He can not control it,
and he has dyed it more than once on the eve of hap-
penings, there being no more wisdom in wearing feelings on one's face than on a sleeve.

"Here comes your engine," said the general. "Well
—there are two battalions of Khyber Rifles up the Pass
and they're about at full strength. They've got word
already that you are gazetted to them. They'll expect
you. By the way, you've a brother in the K. R.,
haven't you?"

"At Ali Masjid, sir."

"Give him my regards when you see him, will you?"

"Thank you, sir."

"There's your engine whistling. You'd better hurry.
Good-by, my boy. Get word to me whenever pos-

sible. Good luck to you! Regards to your brother?
Good-by !"

King saluted and stood watching while the general
hurried to the waiting motor-car. When the car
whirled away in a din of dust he returned leisurely
to the train that had been shortened to three coaches.
Then he gave the signal to start up the spur-track, that
leads to Jamrud, where a fort cowers in the very throat
of the dreadfulest gorge in Asia—the Khyber Pass.

It was not a long journey, nor a very slow one, for
there was nothing to block the way except occasional
men with flags, who guarded culverts and little bridges.
The Germans would know better than to waste time
or effort on blowing up that track, but there might be
Northern gentlemen at large, out to do damage for the
sport of it, and the sepoys all along the line were posted
in twos, and awake.

It was low-tide under the Himalayas. The flood that
was draining India of her armed men had left Jamrud
high and dry with a little nondescript force stranded
there, as it were, under a British major and some native officers.

There were no more pomp and circumstance; no
more of the reassuring thunder of gathering regiments,
nor for that matter any more of that unarmed native
helplessness that so stiffens the backs of the official
English.

Frowning over Jamrud were the lean "Hills,"
peopled by the fiercest fighting men on earth, and the
clouds that hung over the Khyber's course were an
accent to the savagery.

But King smiled merrily as he jumped out of the
train, and Rewa Gunga, who was there to meet him,

advanced with outstretched hand and a smile that
would have melted snow on the distant peaks if he had
only looked the other way.

"Welcome, King sahib!" he laughed, with the air
of a skilled fencer who admires another, better one.
"I shall know better another time and let you keep in
front of me! No more getting first into a train and
settling down for the night! It may not be easy to
follow you, and I suspect it isn't, but at least it jolly
well can't be such a job as leading you! I trust you
had a comfortable journey?"

"Thanks," said King, shaking hands with him, and
then turning away to unlock the carriage doors that
held his prisoners in. They were baying now like
wolves to be free, and they surged out, like wolves
from a cage, to clamor round the Rangar, pawing him
and struggling to be first to ask him questions.

"Nay, ye mountain people; nay!" he laughed. "I,
too, am from the plains! What do I know of your
families or of your feuds? Am I to be torn to pieces
to make a meal?"

At that Ismail interfered, with the aid of an ash
pick-handle, chance-found beside the track.

"Hill-bastards!" he howled at them, beating at them
as if they were sheaves and his cudgel were a flail.
"Sons of nameless mothers! Forgotten of God!
Shameless! Brood of the evil one! Hands off!"

King had to stop him, not that he feared trouble,
for they did not seem to resent either abuse or cudgel-
ing in the least—and that in itself was food for
thought; but broken shoulders are no use for carrying
loads.

Laughing as if the whole thing was the greatest joke

imaginable, Rewa Gunga fell into stride beside King
and led him away in the direction of some tents.

"She is up the Pass ahead of us," he announced.
"She was in the deuce of a hurry, I can assure you.
She wanted to wait and meet you, but matters were too
jolly well urgent, and we shall have our bally work
cut out to catch her, you can bet! But I have everything ready—tents and beds and stores—everything!"

King looked over his shoulder to make sure that
Ismail was bringing the little leather bag along.

"So have I," he said quietly.

"I have horses," said Rewa Gunga, "and mules
and—"

"How did she travel up the Khyber?" King asked
him, and the Rangar spared him a curious sidewise
glance.

"On a horse. You should have seen the horse!"

"What escort had she?"

"She?"

Rewa Gunga chuckled and then suddenly grew
serious.

"The 'Hills' are her escort, King sahib. She is
mistress in the 'Hills.' There isn't a murdering ruffian
who would not lie down and let her walk on him! She
rode away alone on a thoroughbred mare and she jolly
well left me the mare's double on which to follow her.
Come and look."

Not far from where the tents had been pitched in a
cluster a string of horses whinnied at a picket rope.
King saw the two good horses ready for himself, and
ten mules beside them that would have done credit to
any outfit. But at the end of the line, pawing at the
trampled grass, was a black mare that made his eyes

open wide. Once in a hundred years or so a viceroy's cup, or a Derby is won by an animal that can stand and look and move as that mare did.

"Just watch!" the Rangar boasted, hooking up the bit and throwing off the blanket. And as he mounted into the native-made rough-hide saddle a shout went up from the fort and native officers and half the soldiery came out to watch the poetry of motion.

The mare was not the only one worth watching; her rider shared the praise. There was something unexpected, although not in the least ungainly, about the Rangar's seat in the saddle that was not the ordinary, graceful native balance and yet was full of grace. King ascribed the difference to the fact that the Rangar had seen no military service, and before the inadequacy of that explanation had asserted itself he had already forgotten to criticize in sheer admiration.

There was none of the spurring and back-reining that some native bloods of India mistake for horsemanship. The Rangar rode with sympathy and most consummate skill, and the result was that the mare behaved as if she were part of him, responding to his thoughts, putting a foot where he wished her to put it and showing her wildest turn of speed along a level stretch in instant response to his mood.

"Never saw anything better," King admitted ungrudgingly, as the mare came back at a walk to her picket rope.

"There is only one mare like this one," laughed the Rangar. "She has her."

"What'll you take for this one?" King asked him. "Name your price!"

"The mare is *hers*. You must ask *her*. Who

knows? She is generous. There is nobody on earth
more generous than she when she cares to be. See
what you wear on your wrist!"

"That is a loan," said King, uncovering the bracelet.
"I shall give it back to her when we meet."

"See what she says when you meet!" laughed the
Rangar, taking a cigarette from his jeweled case with
an air and smiling as he lighted it. "There is your
tent, sahib."

He motioned with the cigarette toward a tent pitched
quite a hundred yards away from the others and from
the Rangar's own; with the Rangar's and the cluster
of tents for the men it made an equilateral triangle,
so that both he and the Rangar had privacy.

With a nod of dismissal, King walked over to inspect
the bandobast, and finding it much more extravagant
than he would have dreamed of providing for himself,
he lit one of his black cheroots, and with hands clasped
behind him strolled over to the fort to interview
Courtenay, the officer commanding.

It so happened that Courtenay had gone up the Pass
that morning with his shotgun after quail. He came
back into view, followed by his little ten-man escort
just as King neared the fort, and King timed his approach so as to meet him. The men of the escort were
heavily burdened; he could see that from a distance.

"Hello!" he said by the fort gate, cheerily, after he
had saluted and the salute had been returned.

"Oh, hello, King! Glad to see you. Heard you
were coming, of course. Anything I can do?"

"Tell me anything you know," said King, offering
him a cheroot which the other accepted. As he bit off
the end they stood facing each other, so that King

could see the oncoming escort and what it carried.
Courtenay read his eyes.

"Two of my men!" he said. "Found 'em up the Pass.
Gazi work I think. They were cut all to pieces.
There's a big lashkar gathering somewhere in the
'Hills,' and it might have been done by their skirmish-
ers, but I don't think so."

"A lashkar besides the crowd at Khinjan?"

"Yes."

"Who's supposed to be leading it?"

"Can't find out," said Courtenay. Then he stepped
aside to give orders to the escort. They carried the
dead bodies into the fort.

"Know anything of Yasmini?" King asked, when
the major stood in front of him again.

"By reputation, of course, yes. Famous person—
sings like a bulbul—dances like the devil—lives in
Delhi—mean her?"

King nodded. "When did she start up the Pass?"
he asked.

"How d'ye mean?" Courtenay demanded sharply.

"To-day or yesterday?"

"She didn't start! I know who goes up and who
comes down. Would you care to glance over the list?"

"Know anything of Rewa Gunga?" King asked him.

"Not much. Tried to buy his mare. Seen the
animal? Gad! I'd give a year's pay for that beast!
He wouldn't sell and I don't blame him."

"He goes up the Khyber with me," said King. "He's
what the Turks would call my youldash."

"And the Persians a hamrah, eh? There was an
American here lately—merry fellow—and I was learn-
ing his language. Side partner's the word in the

States. I can imagine a worse side partner than that
same man Rewa Gunga—much worse."

"He told me just now," said King, "that Yasmini
went up the Pass unescorted, mounted on a mare the
very dead spit of the black one you say you wanted to
buy."

Courtenay whistled.

"I'm sorry, King. I'm sorry to say he lied."

"Will you come and listen while I have it out with
him?"

"Certainly."

King threw away his less-than-half-consumed
cheroot and they started to walk together toward
King's camp. After a few minutes they arrived at a
point from which they could see the prisoners lined up
in a row facing Rewa Gunga. A less experienced eye
than King's or Courtenay's could have recognized their
attitude of reverent obedience.

"He'll make a good adjutant for you, that man,"
said Courtenay; but King only grunted.

At sight of them Ismail left the line and came hurrying toward them with long mountainman's strides.

"Tell Rewa Gunga sahib that I wish to speak to
him!" King called, and Ismail hurried back again.

Within two minutes the Rangar stood facing them,
looking more at ease than they.

"I was cautioning those savages!" he explained.
"They're an escort, but they need a reminder of the
fact, else they might jolly well imagine themselves
mountain goats and scatter among the 'Hills'!"

He drew out his wonderful cigarette case and offered
it open to Courtenay, who hesitated, and then helped
himself. King refused.

"Major Courtenay has just told me," said King, "that nobody resembling Yasmini has gone up the Pass recently. Can you explain?"

"You see, I've been watching the Pass," explained Courtenay.

The Rangar shook his head, blew smoke through his nose and laughed.

"And you did not see her go?" he said, as if he were very much amused.

"No," said Courtenay. "She didn't go."

"Can you explain?" asked King rather stiffly.

"Do you mean, can I explain why the major failed to see her? 'Pon my soul, King sahib, d'you want me to insult the man? Yasmini is too jolly clever for me, or for any other man I ever met; and the major's a man, isn't he? He may pack the Khyber so full of men that there's only standing room and still she'll go up without his leave if she chooses! There is nobody like Yasmini in all the world!"

The Rangar was looking past them, facing the great gorge that lets the North of Asia trickle down into India and back again when weather and the tribes permit. His eyes had become interested in the distance. King wondered why—and looked—and saw. Courtenay saw, too.

"Hail that man and bring him here!" he ordered.

Ismail, keeping his distance with ears and eyes peeled, heard instantly and hurried off. He went like the wind and all three watched in silence for ten minutes while he headed off a man near the mouth of the Pass, stopped him, spoke to him and brought him along. Fifteen minutes later an Afridi stood scowling in front of them with a little letter in a cleft stick in

his hand. He held it out and Courtenay took it and
sniffed.

"Well—I'll be blessed! A note"—sniff-sniff—"on
scented paper!" Sniff-sniff! "Carried down the
Khyber in a split stick! Take it, King—it's addressed
to you."

King obeyed and sniffed too. It smelt of something
far more subtle than musk. He recognized the same
strange scent that had been wafted from behind
Yasmini's silken hangings in her room in Delhi. As
he unfolded the note—it was not sealed—he found
time for a swift glance at Rewa Gunga's face. The
Rangar seemed interested and amused.

"Dear Captain King," the note ran, in English.
"Kindly be quick to follow me, because there is much
talk of a lashkar getting ready for a raid. I shall wait
for you in Khinjan, whither my messenger shall show
the way. Please let him keep his rifle. Trust him, and
Rewa Gunga and my thirty whom you brought with
you. The messenger's name is Darya Khan.
"Your servant,
"YASMINI."

He passed the note to Courtenay, who read it and
passed it back.

"Are you the messenger who is to show this sahib
the road to Khinjan?" he asked.

"Aye!"

"But you are one of three who left here and went
up the Pass at dawn! I recognize you."

"Aye!" said the man. "She met me and gave me this
letter and sent me back."

"How great is the lashkar that is forming?" asked
Courtenay.

"Some say three thousand men. They speak truth. They who say five thousand are liars. There *is* a lashkar."

"And *she* went up alone?" King murmured aloud in Pashtu.

"Is the moon alone in the sky?" the fellow asked, and King smiled at him.

"Let us hurry after her, sahib!" urged Rewa Gunga, and King looked straight into his eyes, that were like pools of fire, just as they had been that night in the room in Delhi. He nodded and the Rangar grinned.

"Better wait until dawn," advised Courtenay. "The Pass is supposed to be closed at dusk."

"I shall have to ask for special permission, sir."

"Granted, of course."

"Then, we'll start at eight to-night!" said King, glancing at his watch and snapping the gold case shut.

"Dine with me," said Courtenay.

"Yes, please. Got to pack first. Daren't trust anybody else."

"Very well. We'll dine in my tent at six-thirty," said Courtenay. "So long!"

"So long, sir," said King, and each went about his own business, King with the Rangar, and Ismail and all thirty prisoners at his heels, and Courtenay alone, but that much more determined.

"I'll find out," the major muttered, "how she got up the Pass without my knowing it. Somebody's tail shall be twisted for this!"

But he did not find out until King told him, and that was many days later, when a terrible cloud no longer threatened India from the North.

Oh, a broken blade,
And an empty bag,
And a sodden kit,
And a foundered nag,
And a whimpering wind
Are more or less
Ground for a gentleman's distress.
Yet the blade will cut,
(He should swing with a will!)
And the emptiest bag
He may readiest fill;
And the nag will trot
If the man has a mind,
So the kit he may dry
In the whimpering wind.
Shades of a gallant past—confess!
How many fights were won with less?

CHAPTER VI

"**I** THINK I envy you!" said Courtenay.

They were seated in Courtenay's tent, face to face across the low table, with guttering lights between and Ismail outside the tent handing plates and things to Courtenay's servant inside.

"You're about the first who has admitted it," said King.

Not far from them a herd of pack-camels grunted and bubbled after the evening meal. The evening breeze brought the smoke of dung fires down to them, and an Afghan—one of the little crowd of traders who had come down with the camels three hours ago—sang a wailing song about his lady-love. Overhead the sky was like black velvet, pierced with silver holes.

"You see, you can't call our end of this business war —it's sport," said Courtenay. "Two battalions of Khyber Rifles, hired to hold the Pass against their own relations. Against them a couple of hundred thousand tribesmen, very hungry for loot, armed with up-to-date rifles, thanks to Russia yesterday and Germany to day, and all perfectly well aware that a world war is in progress. That's sport, you know—not the 'image

107

and likeness of war' that Jorrocks called it, but the real
red root. And you've got a mystery thrown in to give
it piquancy. I haven't found out yet how Yasmini got
up the Pass without my knowledge. I thought it was
a trick. Didn't believe she'd gone. Yet all my men
swear they know she has gone, and not one of them
will own to having seen her go! What d'you think of
that?"

"Tell you later," said King, "when I've been in the
'Hills' a while."

"What d'you suppose I'm going to say, eh? Shall
I enter in my diary that a *chit* came down the Pass
from a woman who never went up it? Or shall I say
she went up while I was looking the other way?"

"Help yourself!" laughed King.

"Laugh on! I envy you! If the worst comes to the
worst, you'll have had the best end of it. If you fail
up there in the 'Hills' you'll get scoughed and be done
with you. You'll at least have had a show. All we
shall know of your failure will be the arrival of the
flood! We'll be swamped ingloriously—shot, skinned
alive and crucified without a chance of doing anything
but wait for it! You're in luck—you can move about
and keep off the fidgets!"

For a while, as he ate Courtenay's broiled quail,
King did not answer. But the merry smile had left his
eyes and he seemed for once to be letting his mind
dwell on conditions as they concerned himself.

"How many men have you at the fort?" he asked at
last.

"Two hundred. Why?"

"All natives?"

"To a man."

"Like 'em?"

"What's the use of talking?" answered Courtenay. "You know what it means when men of an alien race stand up to you and grin when they salute. They're my own."

King nodded. "Die with you, eh?"

"To the last man," said Courtenay quietly with that conviction that can only be arrived at in one way, and that not the easiest.

"I'd die alone," said King. "It'll be lonely in the 'Hills.' Got any more quail?"

And that was all he ever did say on that subject, then or at any other time.

"Here's to her!" laughed Courtenay at last, rising and holding up his glass. "We can't explain her, so let's drink to her! No heel-taps! Here's to Rewa Gunga's mistress, Yasmini!"

"May she show good hunting!" answered King, draining his glass; and it was his first that day. "If it weren't for that note of hers that came down the Pass, and for one or two other things, I'd almost believe her a myth—one of those supposititious people who are supposed to express some ideal or other. Not an hallucination, you understand—nor exactly an embodied spirit, either. Perhaps the spirit of a problem. Let y be the Khyber district, z the tribes, and x the spirit of the rumpus. Find x. Get me?"

"Not exactly. Got quinine in your kit, by the way?"

"Plenty, thanks."

"What shall you do first after you get up the Pass? Call on your brother at Ali Masjid? He's likely to know a lot by the time you get there."

"Not sure," said King. "May and may not. I'd

like to see him. Haven't seen the old chap in a don-
key's age. How is he?"

"Well two days ago," said Courtenay. "What's your
general plan?"

"Hunt!" said King. "Hunt for x and report. Hunt
for the spirit of the coming ruction and try to scrag it!
Live in the open when I can, sleep with the lice when it
rains or snows, eat dead goat and bad bread, I expect;
scratch myself when I'm not looking, and take a tub at
the first opportunity. When you see me on my way
back, have a bath made ready for me, will you—and
keep to windward!"

"Certainly!" said Courtenay. "What's the Rangar
going to do with that mare of his? Suppose he'll leave
her at Ali Masjid? He'll have to leave her somewhere
on the way. She'll get stolen. Gad! That's the
brightest notion yet! I'll make a point of buying her
from the first horse-thief who comes traipsing down
the Pass!"

"Here's wishing you luck!" said King. "It's time
to go, sir."

He rose, and Courtenay walked with him to where
his party waited in the dark, chilled by the cold wind
whistling down the Khyber. Rewa Gunga sat,
mounted, at their head, and close to him his personal
servant rode another horse. Behind them were the
mules, and then in a cluster, each with a load of some
sort on his head, were the thirty prisoners, and Ismail
took charge of them officiously. Darya Khan, the man
who had brought the letter down the Pass, kept close
to Ismail.

"Are you armed?" King asked, as soon as he could
see the whites of the Rangar's eyes through the gloom.

"You jolly well bet I am!" the Rangar laughed.

King mounted, and Courtenay shook hands; then he went to Rewa Gunga's side and shook hands with him, too.

"Good-by!" called King.

"Good-by and good luck!"

"Forward! March!" King ordered, and the little procession started.

"Oh, men of the 'Hills,' ye look like ghosts—like graveyard ghosts!" jeered Courtenay, as they all filed past him. "Ye look like dead men, going to be judged!"

Nobody answered. They strode behind the horses, with the swift silent strides of men who are going home to the "Hills"; but even they, born in the "Hills" and knowing them as a wolf-pack knows its hunting-ground, were awed by the gloom of Khyber-mouth ahead. King's voice was the first to break the silence, and he did not speak until Courtenay was out of ear-shot. Then:

"Men of the 'Hills'!" he called. *"Kuch dar nahin hai!"*

"Nahin hai! Hah!" shouted Ismail. "So speaks a man! Hear that, ye mountain folk! He says, 'There is no such thing as fear!' "

In his place in the lead, King whistled softly to himself; but he drew an automatic pistol from its place beneath his armpit and transferred it to a readier position.

Fear or no fear, Khyber-mouth is haunted after dark by the men whose blood-feuds are too reeking raw to let them dare go home and for whom the British hangman very likely waits a mile or two farther south. It is one of the few places in the world where a pistol is better than a thick stick.

Boulder, crag and loose rock faded into gloom behind; in front on both hands ragged hillsides were beginning to close in; and the wind, whose home is in
Allah's refuse heap, whistled as it searched busily
among the black ravines. Then presently the shadow
of the thousand-foot-high Khyber walls began to cover
them, and King drew rein to count them all and let
them close up. To have let them straggle after that
point would be tantamount to murder probably.

"Ride last!" he ordered Rewa Gunga. "You've got
the only other pistol, haven't you?"

Darya Khan, who had brought the letter, had a rifle;
so King gave him a roving commission on the right
flank.

They moved off again after five minutes, in the same
deep silence, looking like ghosts in search of somebody
to ferry them across the Styx. Only the glow of King's
cheroot, and the lesser, quicker fire of Rewa Gunga's
cigarette, betrayed humanity, except that once or twice
King's horse would put a foot wrong and be spoken to.

"Hold up!"

But from five or ten yards away that might have
been a new note in the gaining wind or even nothing.

After a while King's cheroot went out, and he threw
it away. A little later Rewa Gunga threw away his
cigarette. After that, the veriest five-year-old among
the Zakka Khels, watching sleepless over the rim of
some stone watch-tower, could have taken oath that
the Khyber's unburied dead were prowling in search
of empty graves. Probably their uncanny silence was
their best protection; but Rewa Gunga chose to break
it after a time.

"King sahib!" he called softly, repeating it louder

and more loudly until King heard him. "Slowly! Not
so fast!"

"Why?"

King did not check speed by a fraction, but the Rangar legged his mare into a canter and forced him to
pull out to the left of the track and make room.

"Because, sahib, there are men among those boulders, and to go too fast is to make them think you are
afraid! To seem afraid is to invite attack! Can we
defend ourselves, with three firearms between us?
Look! What was that?"

They were at the point where the road begins to lead
up-hill, westward, leaving the bed of a ravine and ascending to join the highway built by British engineers
Below, to left and right, was pit-mouth gloom, shadows
amid shadows, full of eerie whisperings, and King
felt the short hair on his neck begin to rise.

So he urged his horse forward, because what Rewa
Gunga said is true. There is only one surer key to
trouble in the Khyber than to seem afraid—and that is
to be afraid. And to have sat his horse there listening
to the Rangar's whisperings and trying to see through
shadows would have been to invite fear, of the sort
that grows into panic.

The Rangar followed him, close up, and both horse
and mare sensed excitement. The mare's steel shoes
sent up a shower of sparks, and King turned to rebuke
the Rangar. Yet he did not speak. Never, in all the
years he had known India and the borderland beyond,
had he seen eyes so suggestive of a tiger's in the dark!
Yet they were not the same color as a tiger's, nor the
same size, nor the same shape!

"Look, sahib!"

"Look at what?"

"Look!"

After a second or two he caught a glimpse of bluish flame that flashed suddenly and died again, somewhere below to the right. Then all at once the flame burned brighter and steadier and began to move and to grow.

"Halt!" King thundered; and his voice was as sharp and unexpected as a pistol-crack. This was something tangible, that a man could tackle—a perfect antidote for nerves.

The blue light continued on a zigzag course, as if a man were running among boulders with an unusual sort of torch; and as there was no answer King drew his pistol, took about thirty seconds' aim and fired. He fired straight at the blue light.

It vanished instantly, into measureless black silence.

"Now you've jolly well done it, haven't you!" the Rangar laughed in his ear. "That was *her* blue light—Yasmini's!"

It was a minute before King answered, for both animals were all but frantic with their sense of their riders' state of mind; it needed horsemanship to get them back under control.

"How do you know whose light it was?" King demanded, when the horse and mare were head to head again.

"It was prearranged. She promised me a signal at the point where I am to leave the track!"

"Where's that guide?" demanded King; and Darya Khan came forward out of the night, with his rifle cocked and ready.

"Did *she* not say Khinjan is the destination?"

"Aye!" the fellow answered.

"I know the way to Khinjan. That is not it. Get down there and find out what that light was. Shout back what you find!"

The man obeyed instantly and sprang down into darkness. But King had hardly given the order when shame told him he had sent a native on an errand he had no liking for himself.

"Come back!" he shouted. "I'll go."

But the man had gone, slipping noiselessly in the dark from rock to rock.

So King drove both spurs home, and set his unwilling horse to scrambling downward at an angle he could not guess, into blackness he could feel, trusting the animal to find a footing where his own eyes could make out nothing.

To his disgust he heard the Rangar follow immediately. To his even greater disgust the black mare overtook him. And even then, with his own mount stumbling and nearly pitching him headforemost at each lurch, he was forced to admire the mare's goatlike agility, for she descended into the gorge in running leaps, never setting a wrong foot. When he and his horse reached the bottom at last he found the Rangar waiting for him.

"This way, sahib!"

The next he knew sparks from the black mare's heels were kicking up in front of him, and a wild ride had begun such as he had never yet dreamed of. There was no catching up, for the black mare could gallop two to his horse's one; but he set his teeth and followed into solid night, trusting ear, eye, guesswork and the God of Secret Service men who loves the reckless.

Once in a minute or so he would see a spark, or a shower of them, where the mare took a turn in a hurry.

Once in every two or three minutes he caught sight for a second of the same blue siren light that had started the race. He suspected that there were many torches placed at intervals. It could not be one man running. More than once it occurred to him to draw and shoot, but that thought died into the darkness whence it came. Never once while he rode did he forget to admire the Rangar's courage or the black mare's speed.

His own horse developed a speed and stamina he had not suspected, and probably the Rangar did not dare extend the mare to her limit in the dark; at all events, for ten, perhaps fifteen, minutes of breathless galloping he almost made a race of it, keeping the Rangar either within sight or sound.

But then the mare swerved suddenly behind a boulder and was gone. He spurred round the same great rock a minute later, and was faced by a blank wall of shale that brought his horse up all standing. It led steep up for a thousand feet to the sky-line. There was not so much as a goat-track to show in which direction the mare had gone, nor a sound of any kind to guide him.

He dismounted and stumbled about on foot for about ten minutes with his eyes two feet from the earth, trying to find some trace of hoof. Then he listened, with his ear to the ground. There was no result.

He knew better than to shout, for that would sound like a cry of distress, and there is no mercy whatever in the "Hills" for lost wanderers, or for men who seem lost. He had not a doubt there were men with long jezails lurking not far away, to say nothing of those responsible for the blue torchlight.

After some thought he mounted and began to hunt the way back, remembering turns and twists with a gift

for direction that natives might well have envied him.
He found his way back to the foot of the road at a trot,
where ninety-nine men out of almost any hundred
would have been lost hopelessly; and close to the road
he overtook Darya Khan, hugging his rifle and staring
about like a scorpion at bay.

"Did you expect that blue light, and this galloping
away?" he asked.

"Nay, sahib; I knew nothing of it! I was told to
lead the way to Khinjan."

"Come on, then!"

He set his horse at the boulder-strewn slope and
had to dismount to lead him at the end of half a minute. At the end of a minute both he and the messenger were hauling at the reins and the horse had grown
frantic from fear of falling backward. He shouted
for help, and Ismail and another man came leaping
down, looking like the devils of the rocks, to lend their
strength. Ismail tightened his long girdle and stung
the other two with whiplash words, so that Darya
Khan overcame prejudice to the point of stowing his
rifle between some rocks and lending a hand. Then it
took all four of them fifteen minutes to heave and haul
the struggling animal to the level road above.

There, with eyes long grown used to the dark, King
stared about him, recovering his breath and feeling in
his pockets for a fresh cheroot and matches. He
struck a match and watched it to be sure his hand did
not shake before he spoke, because one of Cocker's
rules is that a man must command himself before trying it on others.

"Where are the others?" he asked, when he was certain of himself.

"Gone!" boomed Ismail, still panting, for he had

heaved and dragged more stoutly than had all the rest together.

King took a dozen pulls at the cheroot and stared about again. In the middle of the road stood his second horse, and three mules with his baggage, including the unmarked medicine chest. Close to them were three men, making the party now only six all told, including Darya Khan, himself and Ismail.

"Gone whither?" he asked.

"Whither?"

Ismail's voice was eloquent of shocked surprise.

"They followed! Was it then thy baggage on the other mules? Were they *thy* men? They led the mules and went!"

"Who ordered them?"

"Allah! Need the night be ordered to follow the day?"

"Who told them whither to go?"

"Who told the moon where the night was?" Ismail answered.

"And thou?"

"I am *thy* man! She bade me be thy man!"

"And these?"

"Try them!"

King bethought him of his wrist, that was heavy with the weight of gold on it. He drew back his sleeve and held it up.

"May God be with thee!" boomed all five men at once, and the Khyber night gave back their voices, like the echoing of a well.

King took his reins and mounted.

"What now?" asked Ismail, picking up the leather bag that he regarded as his own particular charge.

"Forward!" said King. "Come along!"

He began to set a fairly fast pace, Ismail leading the spare horse and the others towing the mules along. Except for King, who was modern and out of the picture, they looked like Old Testament patriarchs, hurrying out of Egypt, as depicted in the illustrated Bibles of a generation ago—all leaning forward—each man carrying a staff—and none looking to the right or left.

After a time the moon rose and looked at them from over a distant ridge that was thousands of feet higher than the ragged fringe of Khyber wall. The little mangy jackals threw up their heads to howl at it; and after that there was pale light diffused along the track, and they could see so well that King set a faster pace, and they breathed hard in the effort to keep up. He did not draw rein until it was nearly time for the Pass to begin narrowing and humping upward to the narrow gut at Ali Masjid. But then he halted suddenly. The jackalls had ceased howling, and the very spirit of the Khyber seemed to hold its breath and listen.

In that shuddersome ravine unusual sounds will rattle along sometimes from wall to wall and gully to gully, multiplying as they go, until night grows full of thunder. So it was now that they heard a staccato cannonade—not very loud yet, but so quick, so pulsating, so filling to the ears that he could judge nothing about the sound at all, except that whatever caused it must be round a corner out of sight.

At first, for a few minutes King suspected it was Rewa Gunga's mare, galloping over hard rock away ahead of him. Then he knew it was a horse approaching. After that he became nearly sure he was mistaken altogether and that the drums were being beaten at a village—until he remembered there was no village near enough and no drums in any case.

It was the behavior of the horse he rode, and of the led one and the mules, that announced at last beyond all question that a horse was coming down the Khyber in a hurry. One of the mules brayed until the whole gorge echoed with the insult, and a man hit him hard on the nose to silence him.

King legged his horse into the shadow of a great rock. And after shepherding the men and mules into another shadow, Ismail came and held his stirrup, with the leather bag in the other hand. The bag fascinated him, because he did not know what was in it, and it was plain that he meant to cling to it until death or King should put an end to curiosity.

King drew his pistol. Ismail drew in his breath with a hissing sound, as if he and not King were the marksman. King notched the foresight against the corner of a crag, at a height that ought to be an inch or two above an oncoming horse's ears, and Ismail nodded sagely. Whoever now should gallop round that rock would be obliged to cross the line of fire. Such are the vagaries of the Khyber's night echoes that it was a long five minutes yet before a man appeared at last, riding like the night wind, on a horse that seemed to be very nearly on his last legs. The beast was going wildly, sobbing, with straggled ears.

Instead of speaking, King spurred out of the shadow and blocked the oncoming horseman's way, making his own horse meet the other shoulder to breast, knocking most of the remaining wind out of him. At risk of his own life, Ismail seized the man's reins. The sparks flew, and there was a growled oath; but the long and the short of it was that the rider squinted uncomfortably down the barrel of King's repeating pistol.

"Give an account of yourself!" commanded King.

The man did not answer. He was a jezailchi of the Khyber Rifles—hook-nosed as an osprey—black-bearded—with white teeth glistening out of a gap in the darkness of his lower face. And he was armed with a British government rifle, although that is no criterion in that borderland of professional thieves, where many a man has offered himself for enlistment with a stolen government rifle in his grasp.

The waler he rode was an officer's charger. The poor brute sobbed and heaved and sweated in his tracks as his rightful owner surely had never made him do.

"Whither?" King demanded.

"Jamrud!"

The jezailchi growled the one-word answer with one eye on King, but the other eye still squinted down the pistol barrel warily.

"Have you a letter?"

The man did not answer.

"You may speak to me. I am of your regiment. I am Captain King."

"That is a lie, and a poor one!" the fellow answered. "But a very little while ago I spoke with King sahib in Ali Masjid Fort; and he is no cappitin, he is leftnant. Therefore thou art a liar twice over—nay, three times! Thou art no arrficer of Khyber Rifles! I am a jezailchi, and I know them all!"

"None the less," said King, "I am an officer of the Khyber Rifles, newly appointed. I asked you, have you a letter?"

"Aye!"

"Let me see it."

"Nay!"

"I order you!"

"Nay! I am a true man! I will eat the letter rather!"

"Tell me who wrote it, then."

But the fellow shook his head, still eying the pistol as if it were a snake about to strike.

"I have eaten the salt!" he said. "May dogs eat me if I break faith! Who art thou, to ask me to break faith? An arrficer? That *must* be a lie! The letter is from him who wrote it, to whom I bear it—and thac is my answer if I die this minute!"

King let his reins fall and raised his left wrist untii the moonlight glinted on the gold of his bracelet under the jezailchi's very eyes.

"May God be with thee!" said the man at once.

"From whom is your letter, and to whom?" asked King, wondering what the men in the clubs at home would say if they knew that a woman's bracelet could outweigh authority on British sod; for the Khyber Pass is as much British as the air is an eagle's or Korea Japanese, or Panama United States American, and the Khyber jezailchis are paid to help keep it so.

"From the karnal sahib (colonel) at Landi Kotal, whose horse I ride," said the jezailchi slowly, "to the arrficer at Jamrud. To King sahib, the arrficer at Ali Masjid I bore a letter also, and left it as I passed."

"Had they no spare horse at Ali Masjid? That beast is foundered."

"There are two horses there, and both lame. The man who thou sayest is thy brother is heavy on horses."

King nodded. "What is in the letter?" he asked.

"Nay! Have I eyes that can see through paper?"

OF THE KHYBER RIFLES   123

"Thou hast ears that can listen!" answered King.

"In the letter that I left at Ali Masjid there is news of the lashkar that is gathering in the 'Hills,' above Ali Masjid and beyond Khinjan. King sahib is ordered to be awake and wary."

"And to lame no more horses jumping them over rocks!"

"Nay, the karnal sahib said he is to ride after no more jackals with a spear!"

"Same old game!" said King to himself. "What knowest thou of the lashkar that is gathering?"

"I? Oh, a little. An uncle of mine, and three half-brothers, and a brother are of its number! One came at night to tempt me to join—but I have eaten the salt. It was I who first warned our karnal sahib. Now, let me by!"

"Nay, wait!" ordered King. But he lowered his pistol point.

To hold up a despatch rider was about as irregular as any proceeding could be; but it was within his province to find out how far the Khyber jezailchis could be trusted and within his power more than to make up the lost time. So that the irregularity did not trouble him much.

"Does this other letter tell of the lashkar, too?"

"Am I God, that I should know? But of what else should the karnal sahib write?"

"What is the object of the rising?" King asked him next; and the man threw his head back to laugh like a wolf. Laughter, at night in the Khyber, is an insult. Ismail chattered into his beard; but King sat still.

"Object? What but to force the Khyber and burst through into India and loot? What but to plunder, now that English backs are turned the other way?"

"Who said their backs are turned?" demanded King.

"Ha-ha-ha-ha-ha-ho! Hear him!"

The Khyber echoed the mockery away and away into the distance.

"Their backs are this way and their faces that! The kites know it! The vultures know it! The little jackals know it! The little butchas in the valley villages all know it! Ask the rocks, and the grass—the very water running from the 'Hills'! They all know that the English fight for life!"

"And the Khyber jezailchis? What of them?" King asked.

"They know it better than any!"

"And?"

"They make ready, even as I."

"For what?"

"For what Allah shall decide! We ate the salt, we jezailchis. We chose, and we ate of our own free will. We have been paid the price we named, in silver and rifles and clothing. The arrficers the sirkar sent us are men of faith who have made no trouble with our women. What, then, should the Khyber jezailchis do? For a little while there will be fighting—or, if we be very brave and our arrficers skilful, and Allah would fain see sport, then for a longer while. Then we shall be overridden. Then the Khyber will be a roaring river of men pouring into India, as my father's father told me it has often been! India shall bleed in these days—but there will be fighting in the Khyber first!"

"And what of her? Of Yasmini?" King asked.

"Thou wearest that—and askest what of her? Nay —tell!"

"Should she order the jezailchis to be false to the salt—?"

"Such a question!"

The man clucked into his beard and began to fidget in the saddle. King gave him another view of the bracelet, and again he found a civil answer.

"We of the Rifles have *her* leave to be loyal to the salt, for, said she, otherwise how could we be true men; and she loves no liars. From the first, when she first won our hearts in the 'Hills,' she gave us of the Rifles leave to be true men first and her servants afterward! We may love her—as we do!—and yet fight against her, if so Allah wills—and she will yet love us!"

"Where is she?" King asked him suddenly, and the man began to laugh again.

"Let me by!" he shouted truculently. "Who am I to sit a horse and gossip in the Khyber? Let me by, I say!"

"I will let you by when you have told me where she is!"

"Then I die here, and very likely thou, too!" the man answered, bringing his rifle to the port in front of him so quickly that he almost had King at a disadvantage. As it was, King was quick enough to balance matters by covering him with the pistol again. The horses sensed excitement and began to stir. With a laugh the jezailchi let the rifle fall across his lap, and at that King put the pistol out of sight.

"Fool!" hissed Ismail in his ear; but King knows the "Hills" better in some ways than the savages who live in them; they, for instance, never seem able to judge whether there will be a fight presently or not.

"Why won't you tell me where she is?" he asked in his friendliest voice, and that would wheedle secrets from the Sphynx.

"Her secrets are her own, and may Allah help her guard them! I will tear my tongue out first!"

"Enviable woman!" murmured King. "Pass, friend!" he ordered, reining aside. "Take my spare horse and leave me that weary one, so you will recover the lost time and more into the bargain."

The man changed horses gladly, saying nothing. When he had shifted the saddle and mounted, he began to ride off with a great air, not so much as deigning to scowl at Ismail. But he had not ridden a dozen paces when he sat round in the saddle and drew rein.

"Sahib!" he called. "Sahib!"

King waited. He had waited for this very thing and could afford to wait a minute longer.

"Hast thou—is there—does the sahib—I have not tasted—"

He made a sign with his hand that men recognize in pretty nearly every land under the sun.

"So-ho!" laughed King, patting his hip pocket, from which the cap of a silver-topped flask had been protruding ever since he put the pistol out of sight. "So our copper's hot, eh?"

"May Allah do more to me if my throat is not lined with the fires of Eblis!"

"But the Kalamullah!" King objected. "What saith the Prophet?"

"The Prophet forbade the faithful to drink wine," said the jezailchi. "He said nothing about whisky, that I ever heard!"

"Mine is brandy," said King.

"May Allah bless the sahib's sons and grandsons to the seventh generation! May Allah—"

"Tell me about Yasmini first! Where is she?"

"Nay!"

King tapped the flask in his pocket.

"Nay! My throat is dry, but it shall parch! I know not! As to where she is, I know not!"

"Remember, and I will give you the whole of it!"

He drew the flask out of his pocket and rode a little way toward the man.

"None can overhear. Tell me now."

"Nay, sahib! I am silent!"

"Have you passed her on your way?"

The man shook his head—shook it until the whites of his eyes were a streak in the middle of his dark face; and when a Hillman is as vehement as that he is surely lying.

King set the flask to his own lips and drank a few drops.

"Salaam, sahib!" said the jezailchi, wheeling his horse to ride away.

King let him ride twenty paces before calling to him to halt.

"Come back!" he ordered, and rode part of the way to meet him.

"I but tried thee, friend!" he said, holding out the flask.

"Allah then preserve me from a second test!"

The jezailchi seized the flask, clapped it to his lips and drained it to the last drop while King sat still in the moonlight and smiled at him.

"God grant the giver peace!" he prayed, handing the flask back. The kindly East possesses no word for "Thank you." Then he wheeled the horse in a sudden eddy, as polo ponies turn on the Indian plains, and rode away down the wind as if the Pass were full of devils in pursuit of him.

King watched him out of sight and then listened

until the hoof-beats died away and the Pass grew still again.

"The jezailchis'll stand!" he said, lighting a new cheroot. "Good men and good luck to 'em!"

Then he rode back to his own men.

"Where starts the trail to Khinjan?" he asked; not that he had forgotten it, but to learn who knew.

"This side of Ali Masjid!" they answered all together.

"Two miles this side. More than a mile from here," said Ismail. "What next? Shall we camp here? Here is fuel and a little water. Give the word—"

"Nay—forward!" ordered King.

"Forward?" growled Ismail. "With this man it is ever 'forward!' Is there neither rest nor fear? Has *she* bewitched him? *Hai!* Ye lazy ones! Ho! Sons of sloth! Urge the mules faster! Beat the led horse!"

So in weird wan moonlight, King led them forward, straight up the narrowing gorge, between cliffs that seemed to fray the very bosom of the sky. He smoked a cigar and stared at the view, as if he were off to the mountains for a month's sport with dependable shikarris whom he knew. Nobody could have looked at him and guessed he was not enjoying himself.

"That man," mumbled Ismail behind him, "is not as other sahibs I have known. He is a man, this one! He will do unexpected things!"

"Forward!" King called to them, thinking they were grumbling. "Forward, men of the 'Hills'!"

The owl he has eyes that are big for his size,
And the night like a book he deciphers;
"Too-woop!" he asserts, and "Hoo-woo-ip!" he cries,
And he means to remark he is awfully wise;
But he lags behind us, who are "on" to the lies
Of the hairy Himalayan knifers!

> *For eyes we be, of Empire, we,*
> *Skinned and puckered and quick to see,*
> *And nobody guesses how wise we be,*
> *Nor hidden in what disguise we be,*
> *A-cooking a sudden surprise we be*
> *For hairy Himahlyan knifers!*

CHAPTER VII

AFTER a time King urged his horse to a jog-trot, and the five Hillmen pattered in his wake, huddled so close together that the horse could easily have kicked more than one of them. The night was cold enough to make flesh creep; but it was imagination that herded them until they touched the horse's rump and kept the whites of their eyes ever showing as they glanced to left and right. The Khyber, fouled by memory, looks like the very birthplace of the ghosts when the moon is fitful and a mist begins to flow.

"*Cheloh!*" King called merrily enough; but his horse shied at nothing, because horses have an uncanny way of knowing how their riders really feel. The led mules and the spare horse, instead of dragging at their bridles, pressed forward to have their heads among the men, and every once and again there would sound the dull thump of a fist on a beast's nose—such being the attitude of men toward the lesser beasts.

They trotted forward until the bed of the Khyber began to grow very narrow, and Ali Masjid Fort could not be much more than a mile away, at the widest

131

guess. Then King drew rein and dismounted, for he would have been challenged had he ridden much farther. A challenge in the Khyber after dark consists invariably of a volley at short range, with the mere words afterward, and the wise man takes precautions.

"Off with the mules' packs!" he ordered, and the men stood round and stared. Darya Khan, leaning on the only rifle in the party, grinned like a post-office letter box.

"Truly," growled Ismail, forgetting past expressions of a different opinion, "this man is as mad as all the other Englishmen."

"Were you ever bitten by one?" wondered King aloud.

"God forbid!"

"Then, off with the packs—and hurry!"

Ismail began to obey.

"Thou! Lord of the Rivers! (For that is what Darya Khan means.) What is thy calling?"

"*Badragga*" (guide), he answered. "Did *she* not send me back down the Pass to be a guide?"

"And before that what wast thou?"

"Is that thy business?" he snarled, shifting his rifle-barrel to the other hand. "I am what she says I am! She used to call me '*Chikki*'—the Lifter!—and I was! There are those who were made to know it! If she says now I am *badragga*, shall any say she lies?"

"I say thou art unpacker of mules' burdens!" answered King. "Begin!"

For answer the fellow grinned from ear to ear and thrust the rifle-barrel forward insolently. King, with the movement of determination that a man makes when about to force conclusions, drew up his sleeves above the wrist. At that instant the moon shone through the mist and the gold bracelet glittered in the moonlight.

"May God be with thee!" said "Lord of the Rivers" at once. And without another word he laid down his rifle and went to help off-load the mules.

King stepped aside and cursed softly. To a man who knows how to enforce his own authority, it is worse than galling to be obeyed because he wears a woman's favor. But for a vein of wisdom that underlay his pride he would have pocketed the bracelet there and then and have refused to wear it again. But as he sweated his pride he overheard Ismail growl:

"Good for thee! He had *taught* thee obedience in another bat of the eye!"

"I obey *her!*" muttered Darya Khan.

"I, too," said Ismail. "So shall he before the week dies! But now it is good to obey him. He is an ugly man to disobey!"

"I obey him until she sets me free, then," grumbled Darya Khan.

"Better for thee!" said Ismail.

The packs were laid on the ground, and the mules shook themselves, while the jackals that haunt the Khyber came closer, to sit in a ring and watch. King dug a flashlight out of one of the packs, gave it to Ismail to hold, sat on the other pack and began to write on a memorandum pad. It was a minute before he could persuade Ismail that the flashlight was harmless, and another minute before he could get him to hold it still. Then, however, he wrote swiftly.

"In the Khyber, a mile below you.

"Dear Old Man—I would like to run in and see you, but circumstances don't permit. Several people sent

you their regards by me. Herewith go two mules and
their packs. Make any use of the mules you like, but
store the loads where I can draw on them in case of
need. I would like to have a talk with you before
taking the rather desperate step I intend, but I don't
want to be seen entering or leaving Ali Masjid. Can
you come down the Pass without making your intention known? It is growing misty now. It ought to
be easy. My men will tell you where I am and show
you the way. Why not destroy this letter?

"ATHELSTAN."

He folded the note and stuck a postage stamp on it
in lieu of seal. Then he examined the packs with the
aid of the flash-light, sorted them and ordered two of
the mules reloaded.

"You three!" he ordered then. "Take the loaded
mules into Ali Masjid Fort. Take this chit, you. Give
it to the sahib in command there."

They stood and gaped at him, wide-eyed—then came
closer to see his eyes and to catch any whisper that
Ismail might have for them. But Ismail and Darya
Khan seemed full of having been chosen to stay behind; they offered no suggestions—certainly no encouragement to mutiny.

"To hear is to obey!" said the nearest man, seizing
the note, for at all events that was the easiest task. His
action decided the other two. They took the mules'
leading-reins and followed him. Before they had gone
ten paces they were all swallowed in the mist that had
begun to flow southeastward; it closed on them like a
blanket, and in a minute more the clink of shod hooves
had ceased. The night grew still, except for the whimpering of jackals. Ismail came nearer and squatted at
King's feet.

"Why, sahib?" he asked: and Darya Khan came

closer, too. King had tied the reins of the two horses and the one remaining mule together in a knot and was sitting on the pack.

"Why not?" he countered.

Solemn, almost motionless, squatted on their hunkers, they looked like two great vultures watching an animal die.

"What have they done that they should be sent away?" asked Ismail. "What have they done that they should be sent to the fort, where the arrficer will put them in irons?"

"Why should he put them in irons?" asked King.

"Why not? Here in the Khyber there is often a price on men's heads!"

"And not in Delhi?"

"In Delhi these were not known. There were no witnesses in Delhi. In the fort at Ali Masjid there will be a dozen ready to swear to them!"

"Then, why did they obey?" asked King.

"What is that on the sahib's wrist?"

"You mean—?"

"Sahib—if she said, 'Walk into the fire or over that cliff!' there be many in these 'Hills' who would obey without murmuring!"

"I have nothing against them," said King. "As long as they are my men I will not send them into a trap."

"Good!" nodded Ismail and Darya Khan together, but they did not seem really satisfied.

"It is good," said Ismail, "that she should have nothing against thee, sahib! Those three men are in thy keeping!"

"And I in thine?" King asked, but neither man answered him.

They sat in silence for five minutes. Then suddenly

the two Hillmen shuddered, although King did not bat an eyelid. Din burst into being. A volley ripped out of the night and thundered down the Pass.

"*How-utt! Hukkums dar?*" came the insolent challenge half a minute after it—the proof positive that Ali Masjid's guards neither slept nor were afraid.

A weird wail answered the challenge, and there began a tossing to and fro of words, that was prelude to a shouted invitation:

"Ud-vance-frrrennen-orsss-werrul !"

English can be as weirdly distorted as wire, or any other supple medium, and native levies advance distortion to the point of art; but the language sounds no less good in the chilly gloom of a Khyber night.

Followed another wait, this time of half an hour. Then a man's footsteps—a booted, leather-heeled man, striding carelessly. Not far behind him was the softer noise of sandals. The man began to whistle *Annie Laurie*.

"Charles? That you?" called King.

"That you, old man?"

A man in khaki stepped into the moonlight. He was so nearly the image of Athelstan King that Ismail and Darya Khan stood up and stared. Athelstan strode to meet him. Their walk was the same. Angle for angle, line for line, they might have been one man and his shadow, except for three-quarters of an inch of stature.

"Glad to see you, old man," said Athelstan.

"Sure, old chap!" said Charles; and they shook hands.

"What's the desperate proposal?" asked the younger,

"I'll tell you when we are alone."

His brother nodded and stood a step aside. The three who had taken the note to the fort came closer—partly to call attention to themselves, partly to claim credit, partly because the outer silence frightened them. They elbowed Ismail and Darya Khan, and one of them received a savage blow in the stomach by way of retort from Ismail. Before that spark could start an explosion Athelstan interfered.

"Ismail! Take two men. Go down the Pass out of ear-shot, and keep watch! Come back when I whistle thus—but no sooner!"

He put fingers between his teeth and blew until the night shrilled back at him. Ismail seized the leather bag and started to obey.

"Leave that bag. Leave it, I say!"

"But some man may steal it, sahib. How shall a thief know there is no money in it?"

"Leave it and go!"

Ismail departed, grumbling, and King turned on Darya Khan.

"Take the remaining man, and go up the Pass!" he ordered. "Stand out of ear-shot and keep watch. Come when I whistle!"

"But this one has a belly ache where Ismail smote him! Can a man with a belly ache stand guard? His moaning will betray both him and me!" objected "Lord of the Rivers."

"Take him and go!" commanded King.

"But—"

King was careful now not to show his bracelet. But there was something in his eye and in his attitude—a subtle suggestive something-or-other about him—that was rather more convincing than a pistol

or a stick. Darya Khan thrust his rifle-end into the
hurt man's stomach for encouragement and started
off into the mist.

"Come and ache out of the sahibs' sight!" he
snarled.

In a minute King and his brother stood unseen, un-
heard in the shadow by a patch of silver moonlight.
Athelstan sat down on the mule's pack.

"Well?" said the younger. "Tell me. I shall have
to hurry. You see I'm in charge back there. They
saw me come out, but I hope to teach 'em a lesson
going back."

Athelstan nodded. "Good!" he said. "I've a roving
commission. I'm ordered to enter Khinjan Caves."

His brother whistled. "Tall order! What's your
plan?"

"Haven't one—yet. Know more when I'm nearer
Khinjan. You can help no end."

"How? Name it!"

"I shall go up in disguise. Nobody can put the
stain on as well as you. But tell me something first.
Any news of a holy war yet?"

His brother nodded. "Plenty of talk about one to
come," he said. "We keep hearing of that lashkar
that we can't locate, under a mullah whose name seems
to change with the day of the week. And there are
everlasting tales about the 'Heart of the Hills.' "

"No explanation of 'em?" Athelstan asked him.

"None! Not a thing!"

"D'you know of Yasmini?"

"Heard of her of course," said his brother.

"Has she come up the Pass?"

His brother laughed. "No, neither she nor a coach
and four."

"I have heard the contrary," said Athelstan.

"Heard what, exactly?"

"She's up the Pass ahead of me."

"She hasn't passed Ali Masjid!" said his brother, and Athelstan nodded.

"Are the Turks in the show yet?" asked Charles.

"Not yet. But I know they're expected in."

"You bet they're expected in!" The younger man grinned from ear to ear. "They're working both tides under to prepare the tribes for it. They flatter themselves they can set alight a holy war that will put Timour Ilang to shame. You should hear my jezailchies talk at night when they think I'm not listening!"

"The jezailchies'll stand though," said Athelstan.

"Stake my life on it!" said his brother. "They'll stick to the last man!"

"I can't tell you," said Athelstan, "why we're not attacking brother Turk before he's ready. I imagine Whitehall has its hands full. But it's likely enough that the Turk will throw in his lot with the Prussians the minute he's ready to begin. Meanwhile my job is to help make the holy war seem unprofitable to the tribes, so that they'll let the Turk down hard when he calls on 'em. Every day that I can point to forts held strongly in the Khyber is a day in my favor. There are sure to be raids. In fact, the more the merrier, provided they're spasmodic. We must keep 'em separated—keep 'em from swarming too fast—while I sow other seeds among 'em."

His brother nodded. Sowing seeds was almost that family's hereditary job. Athelstan continued:

"Hang on to Ali Masjid like a leech, old man! The day one raiding lashkar gets command of the Khyber's

throat, the others'll all believe they've won the game.
Nothing'll stop 'em then! Look out for traps. Smash
'em on sight. But don't follow up too far!"

"Sure," said Charles.

"Help me with the stain now, will you?"

With his flash-light burning as if its battery provided
current by the week instead of by the minute, Athelstan
dragged open the mule's pack and produced a host of
things. He propped a mirror against the pack and
squatted in front of it. Then he passed a little bottle
to his brother, and Charles attended to the chin-strap
mark that would have betrayed him a British officer
in any light brighter than dusk. In a few minutes his
whole face was darkened to one hue, and Charles
stepped back to look at it.

"Won't need to wash yourself for a month!" he
said. "The dirt won't show!" He sniffed at the bottle. "But that stain won't come off if you do wash—
never worry! You'll do finely."

"Not yet, I won't!" said Athelstan, picking up a little
safety razor and beginning on his mustache. In a
minute he had his upper lip bare. Then his brother
bent over him and rubbed in stain where the scrubby
mustache had been.

After that Athelstan unlocked the leather bag that
had caused Ismail so much concern and shook out
from it a pile of odds and ends at which his brother
nodded with perfect understanding. The principal
item was a piece of silk—forty or fifty yards of it—
that he proceeded to bind into a turban on his head,
his brother lending him a guiding, understanding finger
at every other turn. When that was done, the man
who had said he looked in the least like a British officer would have lied.

One after another he drew on native garments, picking them from the pile beside him. So, by rapid stages he developed into a native hakim—by creed a converted Hindu, like Rewa Gunga,—one of the men who practise *yunani*, or modern medicine, without a license and with a very great deal of added superstition, trickery and guesswork.

"I wouldn't trust you with a ha'penny!" announced his brother when he had done.

"Really? As good as all that?"

"The part to a T."

"Well—take these into the fort for me, will you?" His brother caught the bundle of discarded European clothes and tucked them under his arm. "Now, remember, old man! This is the biggest show there has ever been! We've *got* to hold the Khyber, and we can't do it by riding pell-mell into the first trap set for us! We must smash when the fighting starts—but we mayn't miss! We mayn't run past the mark! Be a coward, if that's the name you care to give it. You needn't tell me you've got orders to hunt skirmishers to a standstill, because I know better. I know you've just had your wig pulled for laming two horses!"

"How d'you know that?"

"Never mind! I've been seconded to your crowd. I'm your senior, and I'm giving you orders. This show isn't sport, but the real red thing, and I want to count on you to fight like a trained man, not like a natural-born fool. I want to know you're holding Ali Masjid like Fabius held Rome, by being slow and wily, just for the sake of the comfortable feeling it will give me when I'm alone among the 'Hills.' Hit hard when you have to, but for God's sake, old man, ware traps!"

"All right." said his brother.

"Then good-by, old man !"

"Good-by, Athelstan !"

They stood facing and shook hands. Where had
been a man and his reflection in the mist, there now
seemed to be the same man and a native. Athelstan
King had changed his very nature with his clothes.
He stood like a native—moved like one; even his voice
was changed, as if—like the actor who dyed himself
all over to act Othello—he could do nothing by halves.

"I'm going to try to get in without my men seeing
me !" said the younger.

"If they do see you, they'll shoot !"

"Yes, and miss ! Trust a Khyber jezailchi not to
hit much in the dark ! It'll do 'em good either way.
I'll have time to give 'em the password before they
fire a second volley. They're not really dangerous till
the third one. Good-by !"

" 'By, Charles !"

Officers in that force are not chosen for their clumsiness, or inability to move silently by night. His footsteps died in the mist almost as quickly as his shadow.
Before he had been gone a minute the Pass was silent
as death again, and though Athelstan listened with
trained ears, the only sound he could detect was of a
jackal cracking a bone fifty or sixty yards away.

He repacked the loads, putting everything back
carefully into the big leather envelopes and locking the
empty hand-bag, after throwing in a few stones for
Ismail's benefit. Then he went to sit in the moonlight,
with his back to a great rock and waited there cross-
legged to give his brother time to make good a retreat
through the mist. When there was no more doubt
that his own men, at all events, had failed to detect

the lieutenant, he put two fingers in his mouth and whistled.

Almost at once he heard sandals come pattering from both directions. As they emerged out of the mist he sat silent and still. It was Darya Khan who came first and stood gaping at him, but Ismail was a very close second, and the other three were only a little behind. For full two minutes after the man with the sore stomach had come they all stood holding one another's arms, astonished. Then—

"Where is he?" asked Ismail.

"Who?" said King, the hakim.

"Our sahib—King sahib—where is he?"

"Gone!"

Even his voice was so completely changed that men who had been reared amid mutual suspicion could not recognize it.

"But there are his loads! There is his mule!"

"Here is his bag!" said Ismail, pouncing on it, picking it up and shaking it. "It rattles not as formerly! There is more in it than there was!"

"His two horses and the mule are here," said Darya Khan.

"Did I say he took them with him?" asked the hakim, who sat still with his back to a rock. "He went because I came! He left me here in charge! Should he not leave the wherewithal to make me comfortable, since I must do his work? Hah! What do I see? A man bent nearly double? That means a belly ache! Who should have a belly ache when I have potions, lotions, balms to heal all ills, magic charms and talismans, big and little pills—and at *such* a little price! *So* small a price! Show me the belly and pay your money! Forget not the money, for nothing is free except air, water and the Word of God! I have paid money for water before now, and where is the mullah who will not take a fee? Nay, only air costs nothing! For a rupee, then—for one rupee I will heal the sore belly and forget to be ashamed for taking such a little fee!"

"Whither went the sahib? Nay—show us proof!" objected Darya Khan; and Ismail stood back a pace to scratch his flowing beard and think.

"The sahib left this with me!" said King, and held up his wrist. The gold bracelet Rewa Gunga had given him gleamed in the pale moonlight.

"May God be with thee!" boomed all five men together.

King jumped to his feet so suddenly that all five gave way in front of him, and Darya Khan brought his rifle to the port.

"Hast thou never seen me before?" he demanded, seizing Ismail by the shoulders and staring straight into his eyes.

"Nay, I never saw thee!"

"Look again!"

He turned his head, to show his face in profile.

"Nay, I never saw thee!"

"Thou, then! Thou with the belly! Thou! Thou!"
They all denied ever having seen him.

So he stepped back until the moon shone full in his face and pulled off his turban, changing his expression at the same time.

"Now look!"

"*Ma'uzbillah!* (May God protect us!)"

"Now ye know me?"

"Hee-yee-yee!" yelled Ismail, hugging himself by the elbows and beginning to dance from side to side.

"Hee-yee-yee! What said I? Said I not so? Said
I not this is a different man? Said I not this is a
good one—a man of unexpected things? Said I not
there was magic in the leather bag? I shook it often,
and the magic grew! Hee-yee-yee! Look at him!
See such cunning! Feel him! Smell of him! He is
a good one—good!"

Three of the others stood and grinned, now that
their first shock of surprise had died away. The
fourth man poked among the packs. There was little
to see except gleaming teeth and the whites of eyes,
set in hairy faces in the mist. But Ismail danced all
by himself among the stones of Khyber road and he
looked like a bearded ghoul out for an airing.

"Hee-yee-yee! She smelt out a good one! Hee-
yee-yee! This is a man after my heart! Hee-yee-yee!
God preserve me! God preserve me to see the end of
this! This one will show sport! Oh-yee-yee-yee!"

Suddenly he closed with King and hugged him until
the stout ribs cracked and bent inward and King
sobbed for breath among the strands of the Afridi's
beard. He had to use knuckles and knees and feet to
win freedom, and though he used them with all his
might and hurt the old savage fiercely, he made no
impression on his good will.

"After my own heart, thou art! Spirit of a cunning
one! Worker of spells! Allah! That was a good
day when she bade me wait for thee!"

King sat down again, panting. He wanted time to
get his breath back and a little of the ache out of his
ribs, but he did not care to waste any more minutes,
and his eyes watched the faces of the other four men.
He saw them slowly waken to understanding of what
Ismail meant by "worker of spells" and "magic in

the bag" and knew that he had even greater hold on them now than Yasmini's bracelet gave him.

"*Ma'uzbillah!*" they murmured as Ismail's meaning dawned and they recognized a magician in their midst. "May God protect us!"

"May God protect me! I have need of it!" said King. "What shall my new name be? Give ye me a name!"

"Nay, choose thou!" urged Ismail, drawing nearer. "We have seen one miracle; now let us hear another!"

"Very well. Khan is a title of respect. Since I wish for respect, I will call myself Khan. Name me a village the first name you can think of—quick!"

"Kurram," said Ismail, at a hazard.

"Kurram is good. Kurram I am! Kurram Khan is my name henceforward! Kurram Khan the dakitar!"

"But where is the sahib who came from the fort to talk?" asked the man whose stomach ached yet from Ismail and Darya Khan's attentions to it.

"Gone!" announced King. "He went with the other one!"

"Went whither? Did any see him go?"

"Is that thy affair?" asked King, and the man collapsed. It is not considered wise to the north of Jamrud to argue with a wizard, or even with a man who only claims to be one. This was a man who had changed his very nature almost under their eyes.

"Even his other clothes have gone!" murmured one man, he who had poked about among the packs.

"And now, Ismail, Darya Khan, ye two dunderheads!—ye bellies without brains!—when was there ever a dakitar—a hakim, who had not two assistants at the least? Have ye never seen, ye blinder-than-

bats—how one man holds a patient while his boils are
lanced, and yet another makes the hot iron ready?"

"Aye! Aye!"

They had both seen that often.

"Then, what are ye?"

They gaped at him. Were they to work wonders
too? Were they to be part and parcel of the miracle?
Watching them, King saw understanding dawn behind
Ismail's eyes and knew he was winning more than a
mere admirer. He knew it might be days yet, might
be weeks before the truth was out, but it seemed to
him that Ismail was at heart his friend. And there
are no friendships stronger than those formed in the
Khyber and beyond—no more loyal partnerships. The
"Hills" are the home of contrasts, of blood-feuds that
last until the last-but-one man dies, and of friendships
that no crime or need or slander can efface. If the
feuds are to be avoided like the devil, the friendships
are worth having.

"There is another thing ye might do," he suggested,
"if ye two grown men are afraid to see a boil slit open.
Always there are timid patients who hang back and
refuse to drink the medicines. There should be one or
two among the crowd who will come forward and
swallow the draughts eagerly, in proof that no harm
results. Be ye two they!"

Ismail spat savagely.

"Nay! *Bismillah!* Nay, nay! I will hold them
who have boils, sitting firmly on their bellies—so—or
between their shoulders—thus—when the boils are
behind! Nay, I will drink no draughts! I am a man,
not a cess-pool!"

"And I will study how to heat hot irons!" said
Darya Khan, with grim conviction. "It is likely that,

having worked for a blacksmith once, I may learn quickly! *Phaughghgh!* I have tasted physic! I have drunk Apsin Saats! (Epsom Salts.)"

He spat, too, in a very fury of reminiscence.

"Good!" said King. "Henceforward, then, I am Kurram Khan, the dakitar, and ye two are my assistants, Ismail to hold the men with boils, and Darya Khan to heat the irons—both of ye to be my men and support me with words when need be!"

"Aye!" said Ismail, quick to think of details, "and these others shall be the tasters! They have big bellies, that will hold many potions without crowding. Let them swallow a little of each medicine in the chest now, for the sake of practise! Let them learn not to make a wry face when the taste of cess-pools rests on the tongue—"

"Aye, and the breath comes sobbing through the nose!" said Darya Khan, remembering fragments of an adventurous career. "Let them learn to drink Apsin Saats without coughing!"

"We will not drink the medicines!" announced the man who had a stomach ache. "Nay, nay!"

But Ismail hit him with the back of his hand in the stomach again and danced away, hugging himself and shouting "Hee-yee-yee!" until the jackals joined him in discontented chorus and the Khyber Pass became full of weird howling. Then suddenly the old Afridi thought of something else and came back to thrust his face close to King's.

"Why be a Rangar? Why be a Rajput, sahib? *She* loves us Hillmen better!"

"Do I *look* like a Hillman of the 'Hills'?" asked King.

"Nay, not now. But he who can work one miracle

can work another. Change thy skin once more and be a true Hillman!"

"Aye!" King laughed. "And fall heir to a blood-feud with every second man I chance upon! A Hillman is cousin to a hundred others, and what say they in the 'Hills'?—'to hate like cousins,' eh? All cousins are at war. As a Rangar I have left my cousins down in India. Better be a converted Hindu and be despised by some than have cousins in the 'Hills'! Besides—do I speak like a Hillman?"

"Aye! Never an Afridi spake his own tongue better!"

"Yet—does a Hillman slip? Would a Hillman use Punjabi words in a careless moment?"

"God forbid!"

"Therefore, thou dunderhead, I will be a Rangar Rajput,—a stranger in a strange land, traveling by *her* favor to visit her in Khinjan! Thus, should I happen to make mistakes in speech or action, it may be overlooked, and each man will unwittingly be my advocate, explaining away my errors to himself and others instead of my enemy denouncing me to all and sundry! Is that clear, thou oaf?"

"Aye! Thou art more cunning than any *man* I ever met!"

The great Afridi began to rub the tips of his fingers through his straggly beard in a way that might mean anything, and King seemed to draw considerable satisfaction from it, as if it were a sign language that he understood. More than any one thing in the world just then he needed a friend, and he certainly did not propose to refuse such a useful one.

"And," he added, as if it were an afterthought, instead of his chief reason. "if her special man Rewa

Gunga is a Rangar, and is known as a Rangar throughout the 'Hills,' shall I not the more likely win favor
by being a Rangar too? If I wear her bracelet and
at the same time am a Rangar, who will not trust me?"

"True!" agreed Ismail. "True! Thou art a
magician!"

But the moon was getting low and Khyber would be
dark again in half an hour, for the great crags in the
distance to either hand shut off more light than do the
Khyber walls. The mist, too, was growing thicker.
It was time to make a move.

King rose. "Pack the mule and bring my horse!"
he ordered and they hurried to obey with alacrity born
of new respect, Darya Khan attending to the trimming
of the mule's load in person instead of snarling at another man. It was a very different little escort from
the one that had come thus far. Like King himself,
it had changed its very nature in fifteen minutes!

They brought the horse, and King laughed at them,
calling them idiots—men without eyes.

"I am Kurram Khan, the dakitar, but who in the
'Hills' would believe it? Look now—look ye and tell
me what is wrong?"

He pointed to the horse, and they stood in a row
and stared.

"The saddle?" Ismail suggested. "It is a government arrficer's saddle."

"Stolen!" said King, and they nodded. "Stolen
along with the horse!"

"Then the bridle?"

"Stolen too, ye men without eyes! Ye insects! A
stolen horse and saddle and bridle, are they not a
passport of gentility this side of the border?"

"Aye!"

"Shorten those stirrups, then, six holes at the least!
Men will laugh at me if I ride like a British arrficer!"
"Aye!" said Ismail, hurrying to obey.
"Aye! Aye! Aye!" agreed the others.
"Now," he said, gathering the reins and swinging
into the saddle, "who knows the way to Khinjan?"
"Which of us does not!"
"Ye all know it? Then ye all are border thieves and
worse! No honest man knows that road! Lead on,
Darya Khan, thou Lord of Rivers! Do thy duty as
badragga and beware lest we get our knees wet at the
fords! Ismail, you march next. Now I. You other
two and the mule follow me. Let the man with the
belly ache ride last on the other horse. So! Forward
march!"

So Darya Khan led the way with his rifle, and King's
face glowed in cigarette light not very far behind him
as he legged his horse up the narrow track that led
northward out of the Khyber bed.

It would be a long time before he would dare smoke
a cigar again, and his supply of cigarettes was destined
to dwindle down to nothing before that day. But he
did not seem to mind.

"*Cheloh!*" he called. "Forward, men of the mountains! *Kuch dar nahin hai!*"

"Thy mother and the spirit of a fight were one!"
swore Ismail just in front of him, stepping out like a
boy going to a picnic. "She will love thee! Allah!
She will love thee! Allah! Allah!"

The thought seemed to appal him. For hours after
that he climbed ahead in silence.

Dear is the swagger that takes a man in
  Helmeted, clattering, proud.
Sweet are the honors the arrogant win,
  Hot from the breath of a crowd.
Precious the spirit that never will bend—
  Hot challenge for insolent stare!
But—talk when you've tried it!—to win in the
    end,
  Go ahsti!* Be meek! And beware!

_____
* Slowly.

CHAPTER VIII

EVEN with the man with the stomach ache mounted on the spare horse for the sake of extra speed (and he was not suffering one-fifth so much as he pretended); with Ismail to urge, and King to coax, and the fear of mountain death on every side of them, they were the part of a night and a day and a night and a part of another day in reaching Khinjan.

Darya Khan, with the rifle held in both hands, led the way swiftly, but warily; and the last man's eyes looked ever backward, for many a sneaking enemy might have seen them and have judged a stern chase worth while.

In the "Hills" the hunter has all the best of it, and the hunted needs must run. The accepted rule is to stalk one's enemy relentlessly and get him first. King happened to be hunting, although not for human life, and he felt bold, but the men with him dreaded each upstanding crag, that might conceal a rifleman. Armed men behind corners mean only one thing in the "Hills."

The animals grew weary to the verge of dropping, for the "road" had been made for the most part by mountain freshets, and where that was not the case it was imaginary altogether. They traveled upward, along ledges that were age-worn in the limestone— downward where the "hell-stones" slid from under them to almost bottomless ravines, and a false step would have been instant death—up again between big edged boulders, that nipped the mule's pack and let the mule between—past many and many a lonely cairn that hid the bones of a murdered man (buried to keep his ghost from making trouble)—ever with a tortured ridge of rock for sky-line and generally leaning against a wind, that chilled them to the bone, while the fierce sun burned them.

At night and at noon they slept fitfully at the chance-met shrine of some holy man. The "Hills" are full of them, marked by fluttering rags that can be seen for miles away; and though the Quran's meaning must be stretched to find excuse, the Hillmen are adept at stretching things and hold those shrines as sacred as the Book itself. Men who would almost rather cut throats than gamble regard them as sanctuaries.

When a man says he is holy he can find few in the "Hills" to believe him; but when he dies or is tortured to death or shot, even the men who murdered him will come and revere his grave.

Whole villages leave their preciousest possessions at a shrine before wandering in search of summer pasture. They find them safe on their return, although the "Hills" are the home of the lightest-fingered thieves on earth, who are prouder of villainy than of virtue. A man with a blood-feud, and his foe hard after him, may sleep in safety at a faquir's grave. His foe will wait within range, but he will not draw trigger until the grave is left behind.

So a man may rest in temporary peace even on the

road to Khinjan, although Khinjan and peace have nothing whatever in common.

It was at such a shrine, surrounded by tattered rags tied to sticks, that fluttered in the wind three or four thousand feet above Khyber level, that King drew Ismail into conversation, and deftly forced on him the rôle of questioner.

"How can'st thou see the Caves!" he asked, for King had hinted at his intention; and for answer King gave him a glimpse of the gold bracelet.

"Aye! Well and good! But even she dare not disobey the rule. Khinjan was there before she came, and the rule was there from the beginning, when the first men found the Caves! Some—hundreds—have gained admission, lacking the right. But who ever saw them again? Allah! I, for one, would not chance it!"

"Thou and I are two men!" answered King. "Allah gave thee qualities I lack. He gave thee the strength of a bull and a mountain goat in one, and *her* for a mistress. To me he gave other qualities. I shall see the Caves. I am not afraid."

"Aye! He gave thee other gifts indeed! But listen! How many Indian servants of the British Raj have set out to see the Caves? Many, many—aye, very many! Again and again the sirkar sent its loyal ones. Did any return? Not one! Some were crucified before they reached the place. One died slowly on the very rock whereon we sit, with his eyelids missing and his eyes turned to the sun! Some entered Khinjan, and the women of the place made sport with them. Those would rather have been crucified outside had they but known. Some, having got by Khinjan, entered the Caves. None ever came out again!"

"Then, what is my case to thee?" King asked him.
"If I can not come out again and there is a secret,
then the secret will be kept, and what is the trouble?"

"I love thee," the Afridi answered simply. "Thou
art a man after mine own heart. Turn! Go back
before it is too late!"

King shook his head.

"Be warned!"

Ismail reached out a hairy-backed hand that shook
with half-suppressed emotion.

"When we reach Khinjan, and I come within reach
of *her* orders again, then I am *her* man, not thine!"

King smiled, glancing again at the gold bracelet on
his arm.

"I look like *her* man, too!"

"Thou!" Ismail's scorn was well feigned if it was
not real. "Thou chicken running to the hand that will
pluck thy breast-feathers! Listen! Abdurrahman—
he of Khabul—and may Allah give his ugly bones no
peace!—Abdurrahman of Khabul sought the secret of
the Caves. He sent his men to set an ambush. They
caught twenty coming out of Khinjan on a raid. The
twenty were carried to Khabul and put to torture
there. How many, think you, told the secret under
torture? They died cursing Abdurrahman to his face,
and *he* died without the secret! May God recompense
him with the fire that burns forever and scalding water
and ashes to eat! May rats eat his bones!"

"Had Abdurrahman this?" asked King, touching
the bracelet.

"Nay! He would have given one eye for it, but
none would trade with him! He knew of it, but never
saw it."

"I am more favored. I have it. It is *hers,* is it not?"
Does not *she* know the secret?"

"She knows all that any man knows and more!"

"Was she seen to slay a man in the teeth of written
law?" asked King, and Ismail stared so hard at him
that he laughed.

"I was in Khinjan once before, my friend! I know
the rule! I failed to reach the Caves that other time
because I had no witnesses to swear they had seen *me*
slay a man in the teeth of written law. I know!"

"Who saw thee this time?" Ismail asked, and began
to cackle with the cruel humor of the "Hills," that
sees amusement in a man's undoing, or in the destruction of his plans. His humor forced him to explain.

"The price of an entrance has come of late to be the
life of an English arrficer! Many an one the English
have dubbed Ghazi, because he crossed the border and
buried his knife in a man on church parade! They
hang and burn them, knowing our Muslim law, that
denies Heaven to him who is hanged and burned. Yet
the man they miscall ghazi sought but the key to
Khinjan Caves, with no thought at all about Heaven!
Thou art a British arrficer. It may be they will let
thee enter the Caves at *her* bidding. It may be, too,
that they will keep thee in a cage there for some chief's
son to try his knife on when the time comes to win
admission! Listen—man o' my heart!—so strict is
the rule that boys born in the Caves, when they come
to manhood, must go and slay an Englishman and
earn outlawry before they may come back; and lest
they prove fearful and betray the secret, ten men follow each. They die by the hand of one or other of the
ten unless they have slain their man within two weeks.

So the secret has been kept more years than ten men
can remember!" (That estimate was doubtless due
to a respect for figures and bore no relation to the
length of a human generation.)

"Whom did *she* kill to gain admission?" King
asked him unexpectedly.

"Ask her!" said Ismail. "It is her business."

"And thou? Was the life of a British officer the
price paid?"

"Nay. I slew a mullah."

The calmness of the admission, and the satisfaction
that its memory seemed to bring the owner made King
laugh. He found lawless satisfaction for himself in
that Ismail's blood-price should have been a priest, not
one of his brother officers. A man does not follow
King's profession for health, profit or sentiment's
sake, but healthy sentiment remains. The loyalty that
drives him, and is its own most great reward, makes
him a man to the middle. He liked Ismail. He could
not have liked him in the same way if he had known
him guilty of English blood, which is only proof, of
course, that sentiment and common justice are not one.
But sentiment remains. Justice is an ideal.

"Be warned and go back!" urged Ismail.

"Come with me, then."

"Nay, I am *her* man. She waits for me!"

"I imagine she waits for me!" laughed King. "Forward! We have rested in this place long enough!"

So on they went, climbing and descending the naked
ramparts that lead eastward and upward and northward to the Roof of Mother Earth—Ismail ever grumbling into his long beard, and King consumed by a
fiercer enthusiasm than ever had yet burned in him.

"Forward! Forward! Cast hounds forward! For-

ward in any event!" says Cocker. It is only regular
generals in command of troops in the field who must
keep their rear open for retreat. The Secret Service
thinks only of the goal ahead.

It was ten of a blazing forenoon, and the sun had
heated up the rocks until it was pain to walk on them
and agony to sit, when they topped the last escarpment
and came in sight of Khinjan's walls, across a mile-
wide rock ravine—Khinjan the unregenerate, that has
no other human habitation within a march because
none dare build.

They stood on a ridge and leaned against the wind.
Beneath them a path like a rope ladder descended in
zigzags to the valley that is Khinjan's dry moat;
it needed courage as well as imagination to believe that
the animals could be guided down it.

"Is there no other way?" asked King. He knew well
of one other, but one does not tell all one knows in the
"Hills," and there might have been a third way.

"None from this side," said Ismail.

"And on the other side?"

"There is a rather better path—that by which the
sirkar's troops once came—although it has been greatly
obstructed since. It is two days' march from here to
reach it. Be warned a last time, sahib—little hakim—
be warned and go back!"

"Thou bird of ill omen!" laughed King. "Must thou
croak from every rock we rest on?"

"If I were a bird I would fly away back with thee!"
said Ismail.

"Forward, since we can not fly—forward and downward!" King answered. "She must have crossed this
valley. Therefore there are things worth while beyond! Forward!"

The animals, weary to death anyhow, fell rather than walked down the track. The men sat and scrambled. And the heat rose up to meet them from the waterless ravine as if its floor were Tophet's lid and the devils busy under it, stoking.

It was midday when at last they stood on bottom and swayed like men in a dream fingering their bruises and scarcely able for the heat haze to see the tangled mass of stone towers and mud-and-stone walls that faced them, a mile away. Nobody challenged them yet. Khinjan itself seemed dead, crackled in the heat.

"Sahib, let us mount the hill again and wait for night and a cool breeze!" urged Darya Khan.

Ismail clucked into his beard and spat to wet his lips.

"This glare makes my eyes ache!" he grumbled.

"Wait, sahib! Wait a while!" urged the others.

"Forward!" ordered King. "This must be Tophet. Know ye not that none come out of Tophet by the way they entered in? Forward! The exit is beyond!"

They staggered after him, sheltering their eyes and faces from the glare with turban-ends and odds and ends of clothing. The animals swayed behind them, with hung heads and drooping ears, and neither man nor beast had sense enough left to have detected an ambush. They were more than half-way across the valley, hunting for shadow where none was to be found, when a shotted salute brought them up all-standing in a cluster. Six or eight nickel-coated bullets spattered on the rocks close by, and one so narrowly missed King that he could feel its wind.

Up went all their hands together, and they held them so until they ached. Nothing whatever happened. Their arms ceased aching and grew numb.

"Forward!" ordered King.

After another quarter of a mile of stumbling among
hot boulders, not one of which was big enough to
afford cover, or shelter from the sun, another volley
whistled over them. Their hands went up again, and
this time King could see turbaned heads above a parapet in front. But nothing further happened.

"Forward!" he ordered.

They advanced another two hundred yards and a
third volley rattled among the rocks on either hand,
frightening one of the mules so that it stumbled and
fell and had to be helped up again. When that was
done, and the mule stood trembling, they all faced the
wall. But they were too weary to hold their hands up
any more. Thirst had begun to exercise its sway. One
of the men was half delirious.

"Who are ye?" howled a human being, whose voice
was so like a wolf's that the words at first had no
meaning. He peered over the parapet, a hundred feet
above, with his head so swathed in dirty linen that he
looked like a bandaged corpse.

"What will ye? Who comes uninvited into Khinjan?"

King bethought him of Yasmini's talisman. He held
it up, and the gold band glinted in the sun. Yet, although a Hillman's eyes are keener than an eagle's,
he did not believe the thing could be recognized at
that angle, and from that distance. Another thought
suggested itself to him. He turned his head and
caught Ismail in the act of signaling with both hands.

"Ye may come!" howled the watchman on the parapet, disappearing instantly.

King trembled—perhaps as a racehorse trembles at
the starting gate, though he was weary enough to

tremble from fatigue. The "Hills," that numb the
hearts of many men, had not cowed him, for he loved
them and in love there is no fear. Heat and cold and
hunger were all in the day's work; thirst was an incident; and the whistle of lead in the wind had never
meant more to him than work ahead to do.

But a greyhound trembles in the leash. A boiler
trembles when word goes down the speaking-tube from
the bridge for "all she's got." And so the mild-look-
ing hakim Kurram Khan, walking gingerly across hot
rocks, donning cheap, imitation shell-rimmed spectacles
to help him look the part, trembled even more than the
leg-weary horse he led.

But that passed. He was all in hand when he led his
men up over a rough stone causeway to a door in the
bottom of a high battlemented wall and waited for
somebody to open it.

The great teak door looked as if it had been stolen
from some Hindu temple, and he wondered how and
when they could have brought it there across those
savage intervening miles. With its six-inch teak
planks and bronze bolts its weight must be guessed at
in tons—yet a horse can hardly carry a man along any
of the trails that lead to Khinjan!

The wood bore the marks of seige and fracture and
repair. The walls were new-built, of age-old stone.
The last expedition out of India had leveled every bit
of those defenses flat with the valley, but Khinjan's
devils had re-erected them, as ants rebuild a rifled
nest.

The door was swung open after a time, pulled by a
rope, manipulated from above by unseen hands. Inside was another blind wall, twenty feet behind the
first. To the right a low barricade blocked the passage

and provided a safe vantage point from which it could
be swept by a hail of lead; but to the left a path ran
unobstructed for more than a hundred yards between
the walls, to where the way was blocked by another
teak door, set in unscalable black rock. High above the
door was a ledge of rock that crossed like a bridge
from wall to wall, with a parapet of stone built upon it,
pierced for rifle-fire.

As they approached this second door a Rangar turban, not unlike King's own, appeared above the parapet on the ledge and a voice he recognized hailed him
good-humoredly.

"*Salaam aleikoum!*"

"And upon thee be peace!" King answered in the
Pashtu tongue, for the "Hills" are polite, whatever
the other principles.

Rewa Gunga's face beamed down on him, wreathed
in smiles that seemed to include mockery as well
as triumph.   Looking up at him at an angle that
made his neck ache and dazzled his eyes, King could
not be sure, but it seemed to him that the smile said,
"Here you are, my man, and aren't you in for it?" He
more than half suspected he was intended to understand that. But the Rangar's conversation took another line.

"By jove!" he chuckled. "*She* expected you. She
guessed you are a hound who can hunt well on a dry
scent, and she dared bet you will come in spite of all
odds! But she didn't expect you in Rangar dress!
No, by jove! You jolly well *will* take the wind out
of her sails!"

King made no answer. For one thing, the word
"hound," even in English, is not essentially a compliment. But he had a better reason than that.

"Did you find the way easily?" the Rangar asked; but King kept silence.

"Is he parched? Have they cut his tongue out on the road?"

That question was in Pashtu, directed at Ismail and the others, but King answered it.

"Oh, as for that," he said, salaaming again in the fastidious manner of a native gentleman, "I know no other tongue than Pashtu and my own Rajasthani. My name is Kurram Khan. I ask admittance."

He held up his wrist to show the gold bracelet, and high over his head the Rangar laughed like a bell.

"*Shabash!*" he laughed. "Well done! Enter, Kurram Khan, and be welcome, thou and thy men. Be welcome in *her* name!"

Somebody pulled a rope and the door yawned wide, giving on a kind of courtyard whose high walls allowed no view of anything but hot blue sky. King hurried under the arch and looked up, but on the courtyard side of the door the wall rose sheer and blank, and there was no sign of window or stairs, or of any means of reaching the ledge from which the Rangar had addressed him. What he did see, as he faced that way, was that each of his men salaamed low and covered his face with both hands as he entered.

"Whom do ye salute?" he asked.

Ismail stared back at him almost insolently, as one who would rebuke a fool.

"Is this not *her* nest these days?" he answered. "It is well to bow low. She is not as other women. She is *she!* See yonder!"

Through a gap under an arch in a far corner of the courtyard came a one-eyed, lean-looking villain in Afridi dress who leaned on a long gun and stared at them under his hand. After a leisurely consideration of them he rubbed his nose slowly with one finger, spat contemptuously, and then used the finger to beckon them, crooking it queerly and turning on his heel. He did not say one word.

King led the way after him on foot, for even in the "Hills" where cruelty is a virtue, a man may be excused, on economic grounds, for showing mercy to his beast. His men tugged the weary animals along behind him, through the gap under the arch and along an almost interminable, smelly maze of alleys whose sides were the walls of square stone towers, or sometimes of mud-and-stone-walled compounds, and here and there of sheer, slab-sided cliff.

At intervals they came to bolted narrow doors, that probably led up to overhead defenses. Not fifty yards of any alley was straight; not a yard but what was commanded from overhead. Khinjan had been rebuilt since its last destruction by some expert who knew all about street fighting. Like Old Jerusalem, the place could have contained a civil war of a hundred factions, and still have opposed stout resistance to an outside army.

Alley gave on to courtyard, and filthy square to alley, until unexpectedly at last a seemingly blind passage turned sharply and opened on a straight street, of fair width, and more than half a mile long. It is marked "Street of the Dwellings" on the secret army maps, and it has been burned so often by Khinjan rioters, as well as by expeditions out of India, that a man who goes on a long journey never expects to find it the same on his return.

It was lined on either hand with motley dwellings, out of which a motlier crowd of people swarmed to

stare at King and his men. There were houses built
of stolen corrugated iron—that cursed, hot, hideous
stuff that the West has inflicted on an all-too-willing
East; others of wood—of stone—of mud—of mats—
of skins—even of tent-cloth. Most of them were
filthy. A row of kites sat on the roof of one, and in
the gutter near it three gorged vultures sat on the remains of a mule. Scarcely a house was fit to be defended, for Khinjan's fighting men all possess towers,
that are plastered about the overfrowning mountain
like wasp nests on a wall. These were the sweepers,
the traders, the loose women, the mere penniless and
the more or less useful men—not Khinjan's inner
guard by any means.

There were Hindus—sycophants, keepers of ac-
counts and writers to the chiefs (since literacy is at a
premium in these parts). In proof of Khinjan's cath-
olic taste and indiscriminate villainy, there were women
of nearly every Indian breed and caste, many of them
stolen into shameful slavery, but some of them there
from choice. And there were little children—little
naked brats with round drum tummies, who squealed
and shrilled and stared with bold eyes; some of them
were pretending to be bandits on their own account already, and one flung a stone that missed King by an
inch. The stone fell in the gutter on the far side and
started a fight among the mangy street curs, which
proved a diversion and probably saved King's party
from more accurate attentions.

Perhaps a thousand souls came out to watch, all told.
Not an eye of them all missed the government marks
on King's trappings, or the government brand on the
mules, and after a minute or two, when the procession

was half-way down the street, a man reproved the child who had thrown a stone, and he was backed up by the others. They classified King correctly, exactly as he meant they should. As a hakim—a man of medicine—he could fill a long-felt want; but by the brand on his accouterments he walked an openly avowed robber, and that made him a brother in crime. Somebody cuffed the next child who picked up a stone.

He knew the street of old, although it had changed perhaps a dozen times since he had seen it. It was a cul-de-sac, and at the end of it, just as on his previous visit, there stood a stone mosque, whose roof leaned back at a steep angle against the mountain-side. The fact that it was a mosque, and that it was the only building used as such in Khinjan, had saved it from being leveled to the ground by the last British expedition.

It was a famous mosque in its way, for the bed-sheet of the Prophet is known to hang in it, preserved against the ravages of time and the touch of infidels by priceless Afghan rugs before and behind, so that it hangs like a great thin sandwich before the rear stone wall. King had seen it. Very vividly he recalled his almost exposure by a suspicious mullah, when he had crept nearer to examine it at close range. For the Secret Service must probe all things.

There had been an attempt since his last visit to make the mosque's exterior look more in keeping with the building's use. It was cleaner. It had been smeared with whitewash. A platform had been built on the roof for the muezzin. But it still looked more like a fort than a place of worship.

Toward it the one-eyed ruffian led the way, with the

long, leisurely-seeming gait of a mountaineer. At the
door, in the middle of the end of the street, he paused
and struck on the lintel three times with his gun-butt.
And that was a strange proceeding, to say the least, in a
land where the mosque is public resting place for home-
less ones, and all the "faithful" have a right to enter.

A mullah, shaven like a mummy for some unac-
countable reason—even his eyebrows and eyelashes
had been removed—pushed his bare head through the
door and blinked at them. There was some whispering and more staring, and at last the mullah turned his
back.

The door slammed. The one-eyed guide grounded
his gun-butt on the stone, and the procession waited,
watched by the crowd that had lost its interest suffi-
ciently to talk and joke.

In two minutes the mullah returned and threw a mat
over the threshold. It turned out to be the end of a
long narrow strip that he kicked and unrolled in front
of him all across the floor of the mosque. After that it
was not so astonishing that the horses and mules were
allowed to enter.

"Which proves I was right after all!" murmured
King to himself.

In a steel box at Simla is a memorandum, made
after his former visit to the place, to the effect that the
entrance into Khinjan Caves might possibly be inside
the mosque. Nobody had believed it likely, and he had
not more than half favored it himself; but it is good,
even when the next step may lead into a death-trap, to
see one's first opinions confirmed.

He nodded to himself as the outer door slammed
shut behind them, for that was another most unusual
circumstance.

A faint light shone through slit-like windows, changing darkness into gloom, and little more than vaguely hinting at the Prophet's bed-sheet. But for a section of white wall to either side of it, the relic might have seemed part of the shadows. The mullah stood with his back to it and beckoned King nearer. He approached until he could see the pattern on the covering rugs, and the pink rims round the mullah's lashless eyes.

"What is thy desire?" the mullah asked—as a wolf might ask what a lamb wants.

Supposing Yasmini to be jealous of invasion of her realm, King did not doubt she would be glad to have him break down at this point. Until he had actually gained access to her, nobody could reasonably charge her with his safety. If he had been done to death in the Khyber, the sirkar would have known it in a matter of hours. If he were killed here they might never know it.

"Answer!" said the mullah. "What is thy desire?"

"Audience with *her!*" he answered, and showed the gold bracelet on his wrist.

The red eye-rims of the mullah blinked a time or two, and though he did not salute the bracelet, as others had invariably done, his manner underwent a perceptible change.

"That is proof that she knows thee. What is thy name?"

"Kurram Khan."

"And thy business?"

"Hakim."

"We need thee in Khinjan Caves! But none enter who have not earned right to enter! There is but one key. Name it!"

King drew in his breath. He had hoped Yasmini's talisman would prove to be key enough. The nails of his left hand nearly pierced the palm, but he smiled pleasantly.

"He who would enter must slay a man before witnesses in the teeth of written law!" he said.

"And thou?"

"I slew an Englishman!" The boast made his blood run cold, but his expression was one of sinful pride.

"Whom? When? Where?"

"Athelstan King—a British arrficer—sent on his way to these 'Hills' to spy!"

It was like having spells cast on himself to order!

"Where is his body?"

"Ask the vultures! Ask the kites!"

"And thy witnesses?"

Hoping against hope, King turned and waved his hand. As he did so, being quick-eyed, he saw Ismail drive an elbow home into Darya Khan's ribs, and caught a quick interchange of whispers.

"These men are all known to me," said the mullah. "They all have right to enter here. They have right to testify. Did ye see him slay his man?"

"Aye!" lied Ismail, prompt as friend can be.

"Aye!" lied Darya Khan, fearful of Ismail's elbow.

"Then, enter!" said the priest resignedly, as one who admits a communicant against his better judgment.

He turned his back on them so as to face the Prophet's bed-sheet and the rear wall, and in that minute a hairy hand gripped King's arm from behind, and Ismail's voice hissed hot-breathed in his ear.

"Ready of tongue! Ready of wit! Who told thee I would lie to save thy skin? Be thy kismet as thy

courage, then—but I am *hers,* not thy man! *Hers,*
thou light of life—though God knows I love thee!"

The mullah seized the Prophet's bed-sheet and its
covering rugs in both hands, with about as much reverence as salesmen show for what they keep in stock.
The whole lot slid to one side by means of noisy rings
on a rod, and a wall lay bare, built of crudely cut but
very well laid stone blocks. It appeared to reach unbroken across the whole width of the mosque's interior.

On the floor lay a mallet, a peculiar thing of bronze,
cast in one piece, handle and all. The mullah took it in
his hand and struck the stone floor sharply once—then
twice again—then three times—then a dozen times in
quick succession. The floor rang hollow at that spot.

After about a minute there came one answering
hammer-stroke from beyond the wall. Then the mullah laid the mallet down and though King ached to
pick it up and examine it he did not dare.

Excitement now was probably the least of his emotions. It had been swallowed in interest. But in his
guise of hakim he had to beware of that superficial
western carelessness, that permits folk to acknowledge
themselves frightened or excited or amused. His business was to attract as little attention to himself as possible; and to that end he folded his hands and looked
reverent, as if entering some Mecca of his dreams.
Through his horn-rimmed spectacles his eyes looked
far-away and dreamy. But it would have been a mistake to suppose that a detail was escaping him.

The irregular lines in the masonry began to be more
pronounced. All at once the wall shook and they
gaped by an inch or two, as happens when an earth-
quake has shaken buildings without bringing anything

down. Then an irregular section of wall began to move quite smoothly away in front of him, leaving a gap through which eight men abreast could have marched.

As it receded he observed that the lowest course of stones was laid on a bronze foundation, that keyed into wide bronze grooves. There was oil enough in the grooves to have greased a ship's ways and there was neither squeak nor tremor as the tons of masonry slid back.

At the end of perhaps three minutes that section of the wall had become the fourth side of a twenty-foot-wide island that stood fair in the middle of a tunnel, splitting it in two to right and left. Judging by the angle of the two divisions they became one again before going very far.

The mullah stood aside and motioned King to enter. But the one-eyed guide who had led them to the mosque thrust himself between Darya Khan and Ismail, pushed King aside and took the lead.

"Nay!" he said, "I am responsible to *her*."

It was the first time he had spoken and he appeared to resent the waste of words.

The tunnel that led to the left was pierced in twenty places in the roof for rifle-fire; a score of men with enough ammunition could have held it forever against an army. But the right-hand way looked undefended. Nevertheless, the guide led to the left, and King followed him, filled with curiosity.

"Many have entered!" sang the lashless mullah in a sing-song chant. "More have sought to enter! Some who remained without were wisest! I count them! I keep count! Many went in! Not all came out again by this road!"

"Then there is another road?" King wondered, but he held his tongue and followed the guide.

It proved to be fifty yards through part natural, part hand-hewn, tunnel to the neck of the fork where the left- and right-hand passages became one again. He stopped at the fork and looked back, for none of his men was following.

He caught the sound of scuffling—of clattering hoofs, and grunts and shouted oaths—and started to run back, since even a native hakim may protect his own, should he care to, even in the "Hills."

For the sake of principle he chose the other passage, for Cocker says, "Look! Look! Look!" But the guide seized him by the arm from behind and swung him back again.

"Not that way!" he growled. But he offered no explanation.

In the "Hills" it is not good to ask "why" of strangers. It is good to be glad one was not knifed, and to be deferent until more suitable occasion. King started to run again, but this time along the same defended passage down which they had come. And now the guide made no objection but leaned on his long gun and waited.

The charger proved to be making the trouble—the horse that King had exchanged with the jezailchi in the Khyber. The terrified brute was refusing to enter the passage, and all the men, including Ismail and the mullah, were shoving, or else tugging at the reins.

At the moment King appeared the united strength of six men was beginning to prevail. The mullah let go the reins, and in that instant the horse saw King advance toward him out of the tunnel; so, after the manner of horses, he chose the other passage. King ran

at full speed round the corner after him, remembering
that the guide had admitted responsibility, and therefore that the chances were he would be rescued should
he run into a trap.

Suddenly, ten yards in the lead down the dark tunnel
the horse threw his weight back with a clatter of sparks
and screamed as only a horse can. After that there
was neither sight nor sound of him.

Creeping forward with both arms outstretched
against the left-hand wall, he reached the spot where
the horse had been, and shuddered on the smooth dark
edge of a hole that went the full width of the floor.
There came whispering up out of it, and a dank wet
smell, as if there were running water a mile away below. He could feel that a little air flowed downward
into it. Twenty yards away on the far side the path
resumed, but there was neither hand nor foothold on
the smooth damp walls between. He went back to his
men with a shiver between his shoulder-blades, and the
mullah, standing in the gap of the mosque wall, blinked
at him with lashless eyes.

"Many have entered," he chanted maliciously.
"Some went out by a different road !"

"Come !" Ismail growled at the other men, seizing
the mule's bridle himself and leading to the left. "The
ghosts will have a charger now for their captain to
ride ! Lead on, hakim sahib !"

"Come !" called the one-eyed guide from the neck of
the fork ahead. And as they all pressed forward after
King the hairless mullah gave a signal and the great
stone door slid slowly into place. It was like a tomb-
stone. It was as if the world that mortals know were
a thing of the forgotten past and the underworld lay
ahead.

"Lead along, Charon!" King grinned. He needed some sort of pleasantry to steady his nerves. But even so he wondered what the nerves of India would be like if her millions knew of this place.

Oh, Abdul trod with a martial tread,
Swinging his scimiter's weight.
"I am overlord here," he said,
"And he who wishes may chance his head,
"For my blade is long, and my arm is strong,
"And the goods of the world to the bold belong!"
So Abdul guarded the gate.

Many a head did Abdul cleave,
Turban and crown and chin,
For all the 'venturers sought to know
What it could be he guarded so.
And since none give but eke receive,
A thrust in his ribs made Abdul grieve
For good blood outpourin'.

His men wept, watching Abdul bleed
And life's light waning dim,
Till he cursed them. "Open the fort gate wide!
To saddle, and scour the countryside
For a leech!" he swore. "God rot ye, ride!"
'Twas thus, in the guise of a friend in need,
His enemy came to him.

CHAPTER IX

THE second gap closed up behind them and the tunnel began to echo weirdly. The mule was the next to be panic-stricken. The noise of his plunging increased the echoes a thousand times and multiplied his fright, until the poor brute collapsed into meek obedience at last. But the guide strode on unconcerned with his easy Hillman gait, neither deigning to glance back nor making any verbal comment.

Over their heads, at irregular intervals, there were holes that if they led as King presumed into caves above, left not an inch of all the long passage that could not have been swept by rifle-fire. It was impregnable; for no artillery heavy enough to pound the mountain into pieces could ever be dragged within range. Whatever hiding place this entrance guarded could be held forever, given food and cartridges!

The tunnel wound to right and left like a snake, growing lighter and lighter after each bend; and soon their own din began to be swallowed in a greater one that entered from the farther end. After two sharp turns they came out unexpectedly into the blaze of

177

blue day, nearly stunned by light and sound. A roar
came up from below like that of an ocean in the grip of
a typhoon.

When his wits recovered from the shock, King
struggled with a wild desire to yell, for before him
was what no servant of British India had ever seen
and lived to tell about, and that is an experience more
potent than unbroken rum.

They had emerged from a round-mouthed tunnel—
it looked already like a rabbit-hole, so huge was the
cliff behind—on to a ledge of rock that formed a
sort of road along one side of a mile-wide chasm.
Above him, it seemed a mile up, was blue sky, to which
limestone walls ran sheer, with scarcely a foothold that
could be seen. Beneath, so deep that eyes could not
guess how deep, yawned the stained gorge of the underworld, many-colored, smooth and wet.

And out of a great, jagged slit in the side of the
cliff, perhaps a thousand feet below them, there poured
down into thunderous dimness a waterfall whose
breadth seemed not less than half a mile. It spouted
seventy or eighty yards before it began to curve, and its
din was like the voice of all creation.

Ismail came and stood by King in silence, taking his
hand, as a little child might. Presently he stooped and
picked up a stone and tossed it over.

"Gone!" he said simply. "That down there is
Earth's Drink!"

"And this is the 'Heart of the Hills' men boast
about?"

"Nay! It is not!" snapped Ismail.

"Then, where—"

But the one-eyed guide beckoned impatiently, and
King led the way after him, staring as hakim or pris-

oner or any man had right to do on first admission to
such wonders. Not to have stared would have been
to proclaim himself an idiot.

The least of all the wonders was that the secret of
the place should have been kept all down the centuries;
for it was the hollow middle of a limestone mountain,
that could neither be looked down into from above,
because the heights were not scalable, nor guessed at
from the conformation of the country. The river, that
flowed out of rock and went plunging down into the
chasm, must be snow from the Himalayan peaks, on
its way to swell the sea. There was no other way to
account for that; but that explanation did explain why
at least one Indian river is no greater than it is.

The road they followed was a fold in the natural
rock, rising and falling and curving like a ribbon, but
tending on the average downward. It looked to be
about two miles to the point where it curved at the
chasm's end and swept round and downward, to be lost
in a fissure in the cliff.

They soon began to pass the mouths of caves. Some
were above the road, now and then at crazy heights
above it, reached by artificial steps hewn out of the
stone. Others were below, reached from the road by
means of ladders, that trembled and swayed over the
dizzying waterfall. Most of the caves were inhabited,
for armed men and sullen women came to their en-
trances to stare.

Ears grow accustomed to the sound of water sooner
than to almost anything. It was not long before King's
ears could catch the patter of his men's feet following,
and the shod clink of the mule. He could hear when
Ismail whispered:

"Be brave, little hakim! She loves fearless men:"

As the track descended caves became more numerous. In one there were horses, for as they passed there came a whiff of unclean stables, and the litter of fodder and dung was all about the entrance. The mouths of other caves were sealed, with great wax disks, strangely stamped, affixed to stout wooden doors. One cave smelt as if oil were stored in it, and King wondered whence the oil was brought—for the sirkar knows to a pint and an ounce what products travel up and down the Khyber.

At last the guide halted, in the middle of a short steep slope where the path was less than six feet wide and a narrow cave mouth gave directly on to it.

"Be content to rest here!" he said, pointing.

"Thy cave?" asked King.

"Nay. God's! I am the caretaker!"

(The "Hills" are very pious and polite, between the acts of robbing and shedding blood.)

"Allah, then, reward thee, brother!" answered King. "Allah give sight to thy blind eye! Allah give thee children! Allah give thee peace, and to all thy house!"

The guide salaamed, half-mockingly, half-wondering at such eloquence, pausing in the passage to point into the side-caves that debouched to either hand. There was a niche of a place, where a man might lie on guard near the entrance; another cave in which horses could be stabled, with plenty of fodder piled up ready; another beyond that for servants and baggage, with a fireplace and cooking pots; and at the last at the rear of all a great cavern full of eerie gloom, that opened out from the end of the passage like a bottle at the end of a long neck.

Peering about him into vastness, King became aware of frame beds, placed at intervals in a row, each with a mat beside it. And there were several brass basins and ewers for water. Also there were some little bronze lamps; the guide lit three of them, and King took up one to examine it. As he did so, involuntarily his hand almost went to his bosom, where the strange knife still reposed that he had taken from the would-be murderer in the train to Delhi.

There was no gold on the lamp; but the handle by which he lifted it had been cast, the devils of the Himalayas only knew how many centuries ago, in the form of a woman dancing; her size, and her shape, and the art with which she had been fashioned, were the same as the handle of the knife.

Watching him as a wolf eyes another one, the strange guide found his tongue.

"How many such hast thou ever seen?" he asked.

"None!" answered King, and the guide cackled at him, like a hen that has laid an egg.

"There be many strange things in Khinjan, but few strangers!" he remarked; and then, as if that were enough for any man to say on any occasion, he turned on his heel and stalked out of the cavern. It was the last King ever saw of him. He followed him down the passage to the entrance and watched him until his back disappeared round the first bend, but the man never turned his head once. He did not even look over the edge of the road, down into the amazing waterfall, nor up to the round disk of sky.

King turned back and looked into the other caves— saw the weary horse and mule fed, watered and bedded down—took note of the running water that rushed out of a rock fissure and gurgled out of sight down another one—examined the servants' cave and saw that they had been amply provided with blankets. There was

nothing lacking that the most exacting traveler could
have demanded at such a distance from civilization.
There was more than the most exacting would have
dared expect.

"Why isn't it damp in here?" he wondered, returning to his own cave. And then he noticed long fissures
in the cavern walls, and that the smoke from the lamps
drifted toward them. He could not guess what made it
do that, unless it were the suction of the enormous
river hurrying underground; and then he remembered
that at the entrance air had rushed downward into the
hole down which the horse had disappeared, which
partly confirmed his guess.

"Ismail!" he shouted, and jumped at the revolver-
crack-like echo of his voice.

Ismail came running.

"Make the men carry the mule's packs into this cave.
You and Darya Khan stay here and help me open
them. Remember, ye are both assistants of Kurram
Khan, the hakim!"

"They will laugh at us! They will laugh at us!"
clucked Ismail, but he hurried to obey, while King
wondered who would laugh.

Within an hour a delegation came from no less a
person than Yasmini herself, bearing her compliments,
and hot food savory enough to make a brass idol's
mouth water. By that time King had his sets of sur-
gical instruments and drugs and bandages all laid out
on one of the beds and covered from view by a blanket.

It was only one more proof of the British army's
everlasting luck that one of the men, who set the great
brass dish of food on the floor near King, had a swollen
cheek, and that he should touch the swelling clumsily

as he lifted his hand to shake back a lock of greasy
hair.

There followed an oath like flint struck on steel ten
times in rapid succession.

"Does it pain thee, brother?" asked Kurram Khan
the hakim.

"Are there devils in Tophet! Fire and my veins are
one!"

The man did not notice the eagerness beaming out of
King's horn-rimmed spectacles, but Ismail did; it
seemed to him time to prove his virtues as assistant.

"This is the famous hakim Kurram Khan," he
boasted. "He can cure anything, and for a very little
fee!"

"Nay, for no fee at all in this case!" said King.

The man looked incredulous, but King drew the covering from his row of instruments and bottles.

"Take a chance!" he advised. "None but the brave
wins anything!"

The man sat down, as if he would argue the point at
length, but Ismail and Darya Khan were new to the
business and enthusiastic. They had him down, held
tight on the floor to the huge amusement of the rest,
before the man could even protest; and his howls of
rage did him no good, for Ismail drove the hilt of a
knife between his open jaws to keep them open.

A very large proportion of King's stores consisted of
morphia and cocaine. He injected enough cocaine to
deaden the man's nerves, and allowed it time to work.
Then he drew out three back teeth in quick succession,
to make sure he had the right one.

Ismail let the victim up, and Darya Khan gave him
water in a brass cup. Utterly without pain for the

first time for days, the man was as grateful as a wolf freed from a trap.

"Allah reward thee, since the service was free!" he smirked.

"Are there any others in pain in Khinjan?" King asked him.

"Listen to him! What *is* Khinjan? Is there one man without a wound or a sore or a scar or a sickness?"

"Then, tell them," said King.

The man laughed.

"When I show my jaw, there will be a fight to be first! Make ready, hakim! I go!"

He was true to his word and left the cave like a gust of wind, followed by the three who had come with him. King sat down to eat, but he had not finished his meal —he had made the last little heap of rice into a ball with his fingers, native style, and was mopping up the last of the curried gravy with it—when the advance guard of the lame and the halt and the sick made its appearance. The cave's entrance became jammed with them, and no riot ever made more noise.

"Hakim! Ho, hakim! Where is the hakim who draws teeth? Where is the man who knows yunani?"

Ten men burst down the passage all together, all clamoring, and one man wasted no time at all but began to tear away bloody bandages to show his wound. The hardest thing now was to get and keep some kind of order, and for ten minutes Ismail and Darya Khan labored, using threats where argument failed, and brute force when they dared. It was like beating mad hounds from off their worry. What established order at last was that King rolled up his sleeves and began, so that eagerness gave place to wonder.

The "Hills" are not squeamish in any one particular;
so that the fact that the cave became a shambles upset
nobody. The surgeon's thrill that makes even half-
amateurs oblivious of all but the work in hand, coupled
with the desperate need of winning this first trick,
made King horror-proof; and nobody waiting for the
next turn was troubled because the man under the
knife screamed a little or bled more than usual.

When they died—and more than one did die—men
carried them out and flung them over the precipice into
the waterfall below.

Ismail and Darya Khan became choosers of the victims. They seized a man, laid him on the bed, tore off
his disgusting bandages and held their breath until
the awful resulting stench had more or less dispersed.
Then King would probe or lance or bandage as he saw
fit, using anæsthetics when he must, but managing
mostly without them.

They almost flung money at him. Few of them
asked what his fee would be. Those who had no
money brought him shawls, and swords, and even
clothing. Two or three brought old-fashioned firearms; but they were men who did not expect to live.
And King accepted every gift without comment, because that was in keeping with the part he played. He
tossed money and clothes and every other thing they
gave him into a corner at the back of the cave, and
nobody tried to steal them back, although a man suspected of honesty in that company would have been
tortured to death as an heretic and would have had
no sympathy.

For hour after gruesome hour he toiled over wounds
and sores such as only battles and evil living can pro-
duce, until men began to come at last with fresh

wounds, all caused by bullets, wrapped in bandages
on which the blood had caked but had not grown foul.

"There has been fighting in the Khyber," somebody
informed him, and he stopped with lancet in mid-air to
listen, scanning a hundred faces swiftly in the smoky
lamplight. There were ten men who held lamps for
him, one of them a newcomer, and it was he who
spoke.

"Fighting in the Khyber! Aye! We were a little
lashkar, but we drove them back into their fort! Aye!
we slew many!"

"Not a jihad yet?" King asked, as if the world might
be coming to an end. The words were startled out of
him. Under other circumstances he would never have
asked that question so directly; but he had lost reckoning of everything but these poor devils' dreadful
need of doctoring, and he was like a man roused out of
a dream. If a holy war had been proclaimed already,
then he was engaged on a forlorn hope. But the man
laughed at him.

"Nay, not yet. Bull-with-a-beard holds back yet.
This was a little fight. The jihad shall come later!"

"And who is 'Bull-with-a-beard'?" King wondered;
but he did not ask that question because his wits were
awake again. It pays not to be in too much of a hurry
to know things in the "Hills."

As it happened, he asked no more questions, for
there came a shout at the cave entrance whose purport
he did not catch, and within five minutes after that,
without a word of explanation, the cave was left empty
of all except his own five men. They carried away the
men too sick to walk and vanished, snatching the last
man away almost before King's fingers had finished
tying the bandage on his wound.

"Why is that?" he asked Ismail. "Why did they go? Who shouted?"

"It is night," Ismail answered. "It was time."

King stared about him. He had not realized until then that without aid of the lamps he could not see his own hand held out in front of him; his eyes had grown used to the gloom, like those of the surgeons in the sick-bays below the water line in Nelson's fleet.

"But who shouted?"

"Who knows? There is only one here who gives orders. We be many who obey," said Ismail.

"Whose men were the last ones?" King asked him, trying a new line.

"Bull-with-a-beard's."

"And whose man art thou, Ismail?"

The Afridi hesitated, and when he spoke at last there was not quite the same assurance in his voice as once there had been.

"I am *hers!* Be thou hers, too! But it is night. Sleep against the toil to-morrow. There be many sick in Khinjan."

King made a little effort to clean the cave, but the task was hopeless. For one thing he was so weary that his very bones were water; for another, Ismail pretended to be equally tired, and when the suggestion that they should help was put to the others they claimed their izzat indignantly. Izzat and sharm (honor and shame) are the two scarcely distinguishable enemies of honest work, into whose teeth it takes both nerve and resolution to drive a Hillman at the best of times. Nerve King had, but his resolution was asleep. He was too tired to care.

He appointed them to two-hour watches, to relieve one another until dawn, and flung himself on a clean bed. He was asleep before his head had met the pillow; and for all he knew to the contrary he dreamed of Yasmini all night long.

It seemed to him that she came into the cave—she, the woman of the faded photograph the general had given him in Peshawur—and that the cave became filled with the strange intoxicating scent that had first wooed his senses in her reception room in Delhi.

He dreamed that she called him by name. First, "King sahib!" Then, "Kurram Khan!" And her voice was surprisingly familiar. But dreams are strange things.

"He sleeps!" said the same voice presently. "It is good that he sleeps!" And in his sleep he thought that a shadowy Ismail grunted an answer.

After that he was very sure in his dream that it was good to sleep, although a voice he did not recognize and that he was quite sure was a dream-voice, kept whispering to him to wake up and protect himself.

But the scent grew stronger, and he began to dream of cobras, that danced with a woman and struck at her so swiftly that she had to become two women in order to avoid them; and Rewa Gunga came and laughed at both and called them amateurs, so that the woman became enraged and drew a bronze-bladed dagger with a golden hilt.

Then intelligible dreams ceased altogether, and he slept like a dead man, but with a vague suggestion ever with him that Yasmini was not very far away, and that she was interested in him to a point that was actually embarrassing. It was like the ether-dream he once dreamt in a hospital.

When he awoke at last it was after dawn, and light shone down the passage into his cave.

"Ismail !" he shouted, for he was thirsty. But there was no answer.

"Darya Khan !"

Again there was no answer. He called each of the other men by name with the same result.

He got up and realized then for the first time that he had not undressed himself the night before. His head felt heavy, and although he did not believe he had been drugged, there was a scent he half-recognized that permeated the cave, and even overcame the dreadful atmosphere that the sick of yesterday had left behind. He decided to go to the cave mouth, summon his men, who were no doubt sleeping as he had done, sniff the fresh air outside and come back to try the scent again; he would know then whether his nose were deceiving him.

But there was no Ismail near the entrance—no Darya Khan—nor any of the other men. The horse was gone. So was the mule. So was the harness, and everything he had, except the drugs and instruments and the presents the sick had given him; he had noticed all those still lying about in confusion when he woke.

"Ismail !" he shouted at the top of his lungs, thinking they might all be outside.

He heard a man hawk and spit, close to the entrance, and went out to see. A man whom he had never seen before leaned on a magazine rifle and eyed him as a tiger eyes its prey.

"No farther !" he growled, bringing his rifle to the port.

"Why not ?" King asked him.

"Allah ! When a camel dies in the Khyber do the kites ask why? Go in !"

He thought then of Yasmini's bracelet, that had

always gained him at least civility from every man who saw it. He held up his left wrist and knew that instant why it felt uncomfortable. The bracelet had disappeared!

He turned back into the cave to hunt for it, and the strange scent greeted him again. In spite of the surrounding stench of drugs and filthy wounds, there was no mistaking it. If it had been her special scent in Delhi, as Saunders swore it was, and her special scent on the note Darya Khan had carried down the Khyber, then it was hers now, and she had been in the cave.

He hunted high and low and found no bracelet. His pistol was gone, too, and his cartridges, but not the dagger, wrapped in a handkerchief, under his shirt. The money, that his patients had brought him, lay on the floor untouched. It was an unusual robber who had robbed him.

At least once in his life (or he were not human, but an angel) it dawns on a man that he has done the unforgivable. It dawns on most men oftener than once a week. So men learn sympathy.

"I should have been awake to change the guard every two hours!" he admitted, sitting on the bed. "I wouldn't hesitate to shoot another man for that—or for less!"

He let the thought sink in, until the very lees of shame tasted like ashes in his mouth. Then, being what he was,—and there are not very many men good enough to shoulder what lay ahead of him—he set the whole affair behind him as part of the past and looked forward.

"Who's 'Bull-with-a-beard'?" he wondered. "Nobody interfered with me until I doctored his men. He's in opposition. That's a fair guess. Now, who is

thunder—by the fat lord Harry—can 'Bull-with-a-
beard' be? And why fighting in the Khyber so early
as all this? And why does 'Bull-with-a-beard,' whoever he is, hang back?"

Are jackalls a tiger's friends because they flatter him and eat his leavings?

Choose, ye with stripes and proud whiskers, choose between friend and enemy.—NATIVE PROVERB.

CHAPTER X

THEY came and changed the guard two hours after dawn, to the accompaniment of a lot of hawking and spitting, orders growled through the mist, and the crash of rifle-butts grounding on the rock path. King went to the cave entrance, to look the new man over; but because he was in Khinjan, and Khinjan in the "Hills," where indirectness is the key to information, he stood for a while at gaze, listening to the thunder of tumbling water and looking at the cliff-edge six feet away that was laid like a knife in the ascending mist.

Out of the corner of his eye he noticed that the new man was a Mahsudi—no sweeter to look at and no less treacherous for the fact. Also, that he had boils all over the back of his neck. He was not likely to be better tempered because of that fact, either. But it is an ill wind that blows no good to the Secret Service.

"There is an end to everything," he remarked presently, addressing the world at large, or as much as he could see of it through the cave mouth. "A hill is so high, a pool so deep, a river so wide. How long, for instance, must thy watch be?"

"What is that to thee?" the fellow growled.

193

"There is an end to pain!" said King, adjusting his horn-rimmed spectacles. "I lanced a man's boils last night, and it hurt him, but he must be well to-day."

"Get in!" growled the guard. "*She* says it is sorcery! *She* says none are to let thee touch them!"

Plainly, he was in no receptive mood; orders had been spat into his hairy ear too recently.

"Get in!" he growled, lifting his rifle-butt as if to enforce the order.

"I can heal boils!" said King, retiring into the cave. Then, from a safe distance down the passage, he added a word or two to sink in as the hours went by.

"It is good to be able to bend the neck without pain and to rest easily at night! It is good not to flinch at another's touch. Boils are bad! Healing is easy and good!"

Then, since a quarrel was the very last thing he was looking for, he retired into his own gloomy quarters at the rear, taking care to sit so that he could see and overhear what passed at the entrance. Among other things in the course of the day he noticed that the watch was changed every four hours and that there were only three men in the guard, for the same man was back again that evening.

At intervals throughout the day Yasmini sent him food by silent messengers; so he ate, for "the thing to do," says Cocker, "is the first that comes to hand, and the thing not to do is worry." It is not easy to worry and eat heartily at one and the same time. Having eaten, he rolled up his sleeves and native-made cotton trousers and proceeded to clean the cave. After that he overhauled his stock of drugs and instruments, repacking them and making ready against opportunity.

"As I told that heathen with a gun out there, there's an end to everything!" he reflected. "May this come soon!"

When they changed the guard that afternoon he had grown weary of his own company and of fruitless speculation and was pacing up and down. The second guard proved even less communicative than the first, up to the point when, to lessen his ennui, King began to whistle. Because a Secret Service man must be consistent, the tune was not English, but a weird minor one to which the "Hills" have set their favorite love song (that is, all about hate in the concrete!).

The echo of the waterfall within the cave was like the roaring in a shell held to the ear, but each time he came near the entrance the new guard could catch a few bars of the tune. After a little while the hook-nosed ruffian began to sing the words to it, in a voice like a forgotten dog's.

So he stopped at the entrance and changed the tune. And the guard sang the words of the new tune, too. After that he came out into the light of day (direct sunlight was cut off by the huge height of the cliffs all around) and leaned in the entrance, smiling.

"Allah preserve thee, brother!" he remarked. "Thine is a voice like a warrior's—bold and big! Thou art a true son of the Prophet!"

"Aye!" said the fellow, "that I am! Allah preserve *thee,* for thou hast more need of it than I, although I guard thee just at present. Whistle me another one!"

So King whistled the refrain of a song that boasts of an Afghan invasion of India, and of the loot that came of it, and the prisoners, and the women—particularly the women, mentioning more than a few of them by name, and their charms in detail. It was a

song to warm the very cockles of a Hillman's heart.
Nothing could have been better chosen for that setting,
of a cave mouth half-way down the side of a gash in
earth's wildest mountains, with the blue sky resting on
a jagged rim a mile above.

"Good!" said the bearded jailer. "Now begin
again and I will sing!"

He threw his head back and howled until the mountain walls rang with the song, and other men in far-off
caves took it up and howled it back at him. When he
left off singing at last, to drink from a water-bottle,
that surely had been looted from a British soldier, King
decided to be done with overtures and make the next
move in the game.

"Didst thou ever sing for *her?*" he asked, and the
man turned round to stare at him as if he were mad.
King saw then a blood-soaked bandage on the right of
his neck, not very far from the jugular.

"When *she* sings we are silent! When she is silent
it is good to wait a while and see!" he answered.

"Hah!" said King. "Was that wound got in the
Khyber the other day?"

"Nay. Here in Khinjan. I had my thumb in a
man's eye, and the bastard bit me! May devils do
worse to him where he has gone! I threw him into
Earth's Drink!"

"A good place for one's enemies!" laughed King.

"Aye!"

"A man told me last night," said King, drawing on
imagination without any compunction at all, "that the
fight in the Khyber was because a jihad is launched
already."

"That man lied!" said the guard, shifting position
uneasily, as if afraid to talk too much.

"So I told him!" answered King. "I told him there never will be another jihad."

"Then art thou a greater liar than he!" the guard answered hotly. "There will be a jihad when *she* is ready, such an one as never yet was! India shall bleed for all the fat years she has lain unplundered! Not a throat of an unbeliever in the world shall be left unslit! No jihad? Thou liar! Get in out of my sight!"

So King retired into the cave, with something new to think about. Was *she* planning the jihad! Or pretending to plan one? Every once in a while the guard leaned far into the cave mouth and hurled adjectives at him, the mildest of which was a well of information. If his temper was the temper of the "Hills," it was easy to read disappointment for a jihad that should have been already but had been postponed.

When they changed the guard again the new man proved surly. There was no getting a word out of him. He showed dirty yellow teeth in a wolfish snarl, and his only answer was a lifted rifle and a crooked forefinger. King let him alone and paced the cave for hours.

He was squatting on his bed-end in the dark, like a spectacled image of Buddha, when the first of the three men came on guard again and at last Ismail came for him holding a pitchy torch that filled the dim passage full of acrid smoke and made both of them cough. Ismail was red-eyed with it.

"Come!" he growled. "Come, little hakim!" Then he turned on his heel at once, as if afraid of being twitted with desertion. He seemed to want to get outside, where he could keep out of range of words, yet not to wish to seem unfriendly.

But King made no effort to speak to him, following
in silence out on to the dark ledge above the waterfall and noticing that the guard with the boils was
back again on duty. He grinned evilly out of a shadow
as King passed.

"Make an end!" he advised, spitting over the cliff
into thunderous darkness to illustrate the suggestion.
"Jump, hakim, before a worse thing happens!"

To add further point he kicked a loose stone over
the edge, and the movement caused him to bend his
neck and so inadvertently to hurt his boils. He cursed,
and there was pity in King's voice when he spoke next.

"Do they hurt thee?"

"Aye, like the devil! Khinjan is a place of plagues!"

"I could heal them," King said, passing on, and the
man stared hard.

"Come!" boomed Ismail through the darkness, shaking the torch to make it burn better and beckoning impatiently, and King hurried after him, leaving behind
a savage at the cave mouth who fingered his sores and
wondered, muttering, leaning on a rifle, muttering and
muttering again as if he had seen a new light.

Instead of waiting for King to catch up, Ismail began to lead the way at great speed along a path that
descended gradually until it curved round the end of
the chasm and plunged into a tunnel where the darkness grew opaque. In the tunnel the torch's smoke cast
weird shadows on walls and roof, and the fitful light
only confused, so that Ismail slowed down and let
him come up close.

Then for thirty minutes he led swiftly down a crazy
devil's stairway of uneven boulders, stopping to lend
a hand at the worst places, but everlastingly urging
him to hurry. They were both breathless, and King

was bruised in a dozen places when they reached level going at least six or seven hundred feet below the cave from which they started.

Then the hell-mouth gloom began to grow faintly luminous, and the waterfall's thunder burst on their ears from close at hand. They emerged into fresh wet air and a sea of sound, on a rock ledge like the one above. Ismail raised the torch and waved it. The fire and smoke wandered up, until they flattened on a moving opal dome, that prisoned all the noises in the world.

"Earth's Drink!" he announced, waving the torch and then shutting his mouth tight, as if afraid to voice sacrilege.

It was the river, million-colored in the torch-light, pouring from a half-mile-long slash in the cliff above them and plunging past them through the gloom toward the very middle of the world. Its width was a matter of memory, and its depth unguessable, for although dim moonlight filtered through it, he did not know where the moon was, nor how far such light could penetrate through moving water. Somewhere it met rock-bottom and boiled there, for a roar like the sea's came up from deeps unimaginable.

He watched the overturning dome until his senses reeled. Then he crawled on hands and knees to the ledge's brink and tried to peer over. But Ismail dragged him back.

"Come!" he howled; but in all that din his shout was like a whisper.

"How deep is it?" King bellowed back.

"Allah! Ask Him who made it!"

The fear of the falls was on the Afridi, and he tugged at King's arm in a frenzy of impatience. Sud-

denly he let go and broke into a run. King trotted
after him, afraid, too, to look to right or left, lest the
fear should make him throw himself over the brink.
The thunder and the hugeness had their grip on him
and had begun to numb his power to think and his will
to be a man. Suddenly when they had run a hundred
yards, Ismail turned sharp to the right into a tunnel
that led straight back into the cliff and sloped up-hill.
As the din of the falls grew less behind him and his
power to think returned, King calculated that they
must be following the main direction of the river bed,
but edging away gradually to the right of it. After
ten minutes' hurrying up-hill he guessed they must be
level with the river, in a tunnel running nearly parallel.

He proved to be right, for they came to a gap in the
wall, and Ismail thrust the torch through it. The light
shone on swift black water, and a wind rushed through
the gap that nearly blew the torch out. It accounted
altogether for the dryness of the rock and the fresh
air in the tunnel. The river's weight seemed to suck
a hurricane along with it—air enough for a million
men to breathe.

After that there was no more need to stop at intervals and beat the torch against the wall to make it
burn brightly, for the wind fanned it until the flame
was nearly white. Ismail kept looking back to bid
King hurry and never paused once to rest.

"Come!" he urged fiercely. "This leads to the 'Heart
of the Hills'!" And after that King had to do his
best to keep the Afridi's back in sight.

They began after a time to hear voices and to see
the smoky glare made by other torches. Then Ismail
set the pace yet faster, and they became the last two
of a procession of turbaned men, who tramped along

a winding tunnel into a great mountain's womb. The sound of slippers clicking and rutching on the rock floor swelled and died and swelled again as the tunnel led from cavern into cavern.

In one great cave they came to every man beat out his torch and tossed it on a heap. The heap was more than shoulder high, and three parts covered the floor of the cave. After that there was a ledge above the height of a man's head on either side of the tunnel, and along the ledge little oil-burning lamps were spaced at measured intervals. They looked ancient enough to have been there when the mountain itself was born, and although all the brass ones suggested Indian and Hindu origin, there were others among them of earthenware that looked like plunder from ancient Greece.

It was like a transposition of epochs. King felt already as if the twentieth century had never existed, just as he seemed to have left life behind for good and all when the mosque door had closed on him.

A quarter of a mile farther along the tunnel opened into another, yet greater cave, and there every man kicked off his slippers, without seeming to trouble how they lay; they littered the floor unarranged and uncared for, looking like the cast-off wing-cases of gigantic beetles.

After that cave there were two sharp turns in the tunnel, and then at last a sea of noise and a veritable blaze of light.

Part of the noise made King feel homesick, for out of the mountain's very womb brayed a music-box, such as the old-time carousels made use of before the days of electricity and steam. It was being worked by inexpert hands, for the time was something jerky; but it was robbed of its tinny meanness and even lent

majesty by the hugeness of a cavern's roof, as well as
by the crashing, swinging march it played—wild—wonderful—invented for lawless hours and a kingless
people.

"Marchons!—Citoyens!—"

The procession began to tramp in time to it, and the
rock shook. They deployed to left and right into a
space so vast that the eye at first refused to try to
measure it. It was the hollow core of a mountain, filled
by the sea-sound of a human crowd and hung with
huge stalactites that danced and shifted and flung back
a thousand colors at the flickering light below.

There was an undertone to the clangor of the music-
box and the human hum, for across the cavern's
farther end for a space of two hundred yards the great
river rushed, penned here into a deep trough of less
than a tenth its normal width—plunging out of a great
fanged gap and hurrying out of view down another
one, licking smooth banks on its way with a hungry
sucking sound. Its depth where it crossed the cavern's
end could only be guessed by remembering the half-
mile breadth of the waterfall.

There were little lamps everywhere, perched on
ledges amid the stalactites, and they suffused the whole
cavern in golden glow, made the crowd's faces look
golden and cast golden shimmers on the cold, black
river bed. There was scarcely any smoke, for the
wind that went like a storm down the tunnel seemed
to have its birth here; the air was fresh and cool and
never still. No doubt fresh air was pouring in con-
tinually through some shaft in the rock, but the shaft
was invisible.

In the midst of the cavern a great arena had been
left bare, and thousands of turbaned men squatted

round it in rings. At the end where the river formed
a tangent to them the rings were flattened, and at that
point they were cut into by the ramp of a bridge, and
by a lane left to connect the bridge with the arena.
The bridge was almost the most wonderful of all.

So delicately formed that fairies might have made
it with a guttered candle, it spanned the river in one
splendid sweep, twenty feet above water, like a suspen-
sion bridge. Then, so light and graceful that it scarcely seemed to touch anything at all, it swept on in
irregular arches downward to the arena and ceased
abruptly as if shorn off by a giant ax, at a point less
than half-way to it.

Its end formed a nearly square platform, about
fourteen feet above the floor, and the broad track
thence to the arena, as well as all the arena's boundary,
had been marked off by great earthenware lamps,
whose greasy smoke streaked up and was lost by the
wind among the stalactites.

"Greek lamps, every one of 'em!" King whispered
to himself, but he wasted no time just then on trying
to explain how Greek lamps had ever got there. There
was too much else to watch and wonder at.

No steps led down from the bridge end to the floor;
toward the arena it was blind. But from the bridge's
farther end across the hurrying water stairs had been
hewn out of the rock wall and led up to a hole of twice
a man's height, more than fifty feet above water level.

On either side of the bridge end a passage had
been left clear to the river edge, and nobody seemed
to care to invade it, although it was not marked off
in any way. Each passage was about fifty feet wide
and quite straight. But the space between the bridge
end and the arena, and the arena itself, had to be kept

free from trespassers by fifty swaggering ruffians, armed to the teeth.

Every man of the thousands there had a knife in evidence, but the arena guards had magazine rifles as well as Khyber tulwars. Nobody else wore firearms openly. Some of the arena guards bore huge round shields of prehistoric pattern of a size and sort he had never seen before, even in museums. But there was very little that he was seeing that night of a kind that he had seen before anywhere!

The guards lolled insolently, conscious of brute strength and special favor. When any man trespassed with so much as a toe beyond the ring of lamps, a guard would slap his rifle-butt until the swivels rattled, and the offender would scurry into bounds amid the jeers of any who had seen.

Shoving, kicking and elbowing with set purpose, Ismail forced a way through the already seated crowd and drew King down into the cramped space beside him, close enough to the arena to be able to catch the guards' low laughter. But he was restless. He wished to get nearer yet, only there seemed no room anywhere in front.

The music-box was hidden. King could see it nowhere. Five minutes after he and Ismail were seated it stopped playing. The hum of the crowd died too.

Then a guard threw his shield down with a clang and deliberately fired his rifle at the roof. The ricochetting bullet brought down a shower of splintered stone and stalactite, and he grinned as he watched the crowd dodge to avoid it.

Before they had done dodging and while he yet grinned, a chant began—ghastly—tuneless—so out of time that the words were not intelligible—yet so ob-

vious in general meaning that nobody could hear it
and not understand.

It was a devils' anthem, glorifying hellishness—suggestive of the gnashing of a million teeth, and the
whicker of drawn blades—more shuddersome and
mean than the wind of a winter's night. And it ceased
as suddenly as it had begun.

Another ruffian fired at the roof, and while the
crack of the shot yet echoed seven other of the arena
guards stepped forward with long horns and blew a
blast. That was greeted by a yell that made the cavern tremble.

Instantly a hundred men rose from different directions and raced for the arena, each with a curved
sword in either hand. The yelling changed back into
the chant, only louder than before, and by that much
more terrible. Cymbals crashed. The music-box resumed its measured grinding of *The Marseillaise.* And
the hundred began an Afridi sword dance, than which
there is nothing wilder in all the world. Its like can
only be seen under the shadow of the "Hills."

Ismail put his hands together and howled through
them like a wolf on the war-path, nudging King with
an elbow. So King imitated him, although one extra
shout in all that din seemed thrown away.

The dancers pranced in a circle, each man whirl-
ing both swords around his head and the head of the
man in front of him at a speed that passed belief.
Their long black hair shook and swayed. The sweat
began to pour from them until their arms and shoulders glistened. The speed increased. Another hundred men leaped in, forming a new ring outside the
first, only facing the other way. Another hundred
and fifty formed a ring outside them again, with the

direction again reversed; and two hundred and fifty
more formed an outer circle—all careering at the limit
of their power, gasping as the beasts do in the fury
of fighting to the death, slitting the air until it whistled, with swords that missed human heads by immeasurable fractions of an inch.

Ismail seemed obsessed by the spirit of hell let
loose—drawn by it, as by a magnet, although subsequent events proved him not to have been altogether
without a plan. He got up, with his eyes fixed on
the dance, and dragged King with him to a place ten
rows nearer the arena, that had been vacated by a
dancer. There—two, where there was only rightly
room for one—he thrust himself and King next to
some Orakzai Pathans, elbowing savagely to right and
left to make room. And patience proved scarce. The
instant oaths of anything but greeting were like the
overture to a dog fight.

"Bismillah!" swore the nearest man, deigning to use
intelligible sentences at last. "Shall a dog of an
Afridi hustle me?"

He reached for the ever-ready Pathan knife, and
Ismail, with both eyes on the dancing, neither heard
nor saw. The Pathan leaned past King to stab, but
paused in the instant that his knife licked clear. From
a swift side-glance at King's face he changed to a
full stare, his scowl slowly giving place to a grin as
he recognized him.

"Allah!"

He drove the long blade back again, fidgeting about
to make more room and kicking out at his next neigh-
bor to the same end, so that presently King sat on
the rock floor instead of on other men's hip-bones.

"Well met, hakim! See—the wound heals finely!"
Baring his shoulder under the smelly sheepskin coat,
he lifted a bandage gingerly to show the clean opening out of which King had coaxed a bullet the day
before. It looked wholesome and ready to heal.

"Name thy reward, hakim! We Orakzai Pathans
forget no favors!" (Now that boast was a true one.)

King glanced to his left and saw that there was
no risk of being overheard or interrupted by Ismail;
the Afridi was beating his fists together, rocking from
side to side in frenzy, and letting out about one yell
a minute that would have curdled a wolf's heart.

"Nay, I have all I need!" he answered, and the
Pathan laughed.

"In thine own time, hakim! Need forgets none of
us!"

"True!" said King.

He nodded more to himself than to the other man.
He needed, for instance, very much to know who was
planning a jihad, and who "Bull-with-a-beard" might
be; but it was not safe to confide just yet in a chance-
made acquaintance. A very fair acquaintance with
some phases of the East had taught him that names
such as Bull-with-a-beard are often almost photograph-
ically descriptive. He rose to his feet to look. A
blind man can talk, but it takes trained eyes to gather
information.

The din had increased, and it was safe to stand up
and stare, because all eyes were on the madness in the
middle. There were plenty besides himself who stood
to get a better view, and he had to dodge from side
to side to see between them.

"I'm not to doctor his men. Therefore it's a fair

guess that he and I are to be kept apart. Therefore
he'll be as far away from me now as possible, supposing he's here."

Reasoning along that line, he tried to see the faces
on the far side, but the problem was to see over the
dancers' heads. He succeeded presently, for the Orakzai Pathan saw what he wanted, and in his anxiety
to be agreeable, reached forward to pull back a box
from between the ranks in front.

Its owners offered instant fight, but made no further objection when they saw who wanted it and why.
King wondered at their sudden change of mind, and
the Pathan looked actually grieved that a fight should
have been spared him. He tried, with a few barbed
insults, to rearouse a spark of enmity, but failed, to
his own great discontent.

The box was a commonplace affair, built square, of
pine, and had probably contained somebody's new helmet at one stage of its career. The stenciled marks
on its sides and top had long ago become obliterated
by wear and dirt.

King got up on it and gazed long at the rows of
spectators on the far side, and having no least notion
what to look for, he studied the faces one by one.

"If he's important enough for her to have it in for
him, he'll not be far from the front," he reasoned;
and with that in mind he picked out several bull-
necked, bearded men, any one of whom could easily
have answered to the description. There were too
many of them to give him any comfort, until the
thought occurred to him that a man with brains enough
to be a leader would not be so obsessed and excited
by mere prancing athleticism as those men were. Then
he looked farther along the line.

He found a man soon who was not interested in the dancing, but who had eyes and ears apparently for everything and everybody else. He watched him for ten minutes, until at last their eyes met. Then he sat down and kicked the box back to its owners.

He looked again at Ismail. With teeth clenched and eyes ablaze, the Afridi was smashing his knuckles together and rocking to and fro. There was no need to fear him. He turned and touched the Pathan's broad shoulder. The man smiled and bent his turbaned head to listen.

"Opposite," said King, "nearly exactly opposite— three rows back from the front, counting the front row as one—there sits a man with his arm in a sling and a bandage over his eye."

The Pathan nodded and touched his knife-hilt.

"One-and-twenty men from him, counting him as one, sits a man with a big black beard, whose shoulders are like a bull's. As he sits he hangs his head between them—thus."

"And you want him killed? Nay, I think you mean Muhammad Anim. His time is not yet."

The suggestion was as good-naturedly prompt as if the hakim's need had been water, and the other's flask were empty. He was sorry he could not offer to oblige.

"Who am I that I should want him killed?" King answered with mild reproof. "My trade is to heal, not slay. I am a hakim."

The other nodded.

"Yet, to enter Khinjan Caves you had to slay a man, hakim or no!"

"He was an unbeliever," King answered modestly, and the other nodded again with friendly understanding.

"What about the man yonder, then?" the Pathan
asked. "What will you have of him?"

"Look! See! Tell me truly what his name is!"

The Pathan got up and strode forward to stand on
the box, kicking aside the elbows that leaned on it and
laughing when the owners cursed him. He stood on
it and stared for five minutes, counting deliberately
three times over, striking a finger on the palm of his
hand to check himself.

"Bull-with-a-beard!" he announced at last, dropping
back into place beside King. "Muhammad Anim. The
mullah Muhammad Anim."

"An Afghan?" King asked.

"He says he is an Afghan. But unless he lies he is
from Ishtainboul (Constantinople)."

Itching to ask more questions, King sat still and held
his peace. The direr the need of information in the
"Hills," and in all the East for that matter, the greater
the wisdom, as a rule, of seeming uninquisitive. And
wisdom was rewarded now, for the Pathan, who would
have dried up under eager questioning, grew talkative.
Civility and volubility are sometimes one, and not
always only among the civilized. King—the hakim
Kurram Khan—blinked mildly behind his spectacles
and looked like one to whom a savage might safely ease
his mind.

"He bade me go to Sikaram where my village is
and bring him a hundred men for his lashkar. He says
he has *her* special favor. Wait and watch, I say!"

"Has he money?" asked King, apparently drawing a
bow at a venture for conversation's sake. But there is
an art in asking artless questions.

"Aye! The liar says the Germans gave it to him.
He swears they will send more. Who are the Ger-

mans? Who is a man who talks of a jihad that is to
be, that he should have gold coin given him by unbelievers? I saw a German once, at Nuklao. He ate pig-
meat and washed it down with wine. Are such men
sons of the Prophet? Wait and watch, say I!"

"Money?" said King. "He admits it? And none
dare kill him for it? You say his time is not yet
come?"

More than ever it was obvious that the hakim was a
very simple man. The Pathan made a gesture of con-
tempt.

"I dare what I will, hakim! But he says there is
more money on the way! When he has it all—why—
we are all in Allah's keeping—He decides!"

"And should no more money come?"

This was courteous conversation and received as
such—many a long league removed from curiosity.

"Who am I to foretell a man's kismet? I know what
I know, and I think what I think! I know thee, hakim,
for a gentle fellow, who hurt me almost not at all in
the drawing of a bullet out of my flesh. What knowest
thou about me?"

"That I will dress the wound for thee again!"

Artless statements are as useful in their way as
artless questions. Let the guile lie deep, that is all.

"Nay, nay! For *she* said nay! Shall I fall foul of
her, for the sake of a new bandage?"

The temptation was terrific to ask why *she* had given
that order, but King resisted it; and presently it occurred to the Pathan that his own theories on the subject might be of interest.

"She will use thee for a reward," he said. "He who
shall win and keep her favor may have his hurts
dressed and his belly dosed. Her enemies may rot."

"Who is fool enough to be her enemy?" asked King, the altogether mild and guileless.

The Pathan stuck out his tongue and squeezed his nose with one finger until it nearly disappeared into his face.

"If she calls a man enemy, how shall he prove otherwise?" he answered. Then he rolled off center, to pull out his great snuff-box from the leather bag at his waist.

"Does she call the mullah Muhammad Anim enemy?" King asked him.

"Nay, she never mentions him by name."

"Art thou a man of thy word?" King asked.

"When it suits me."

"There was a promise regarding my reward."

"Name it, hakim! We will see."

"Go tell the mullah Muhammad Anim where I sit!"

The fellow laughed. He considered himself tricked; one could read that plainly enough; for taking polite messages does not come within the Hills' elastic code of izzat, although carrying a challenge is another matter. Yet he felt grateful for the hakim's service and was ready to seize the first cheap means of squaring the indebtedness.

"Keep my place!" he ordered, getting up. He growled it, as some men speak to dogs, because growling soothed his ruffled vanity.

He helped himself noisily to snuff then and began to clear a passage, kicking out to right and left and laughing when his victims protested. Before he had traversed fifty yards he had made himself more enemies than most men dare aspire to in a lifetime, and he seemed well pleased with the fruit of his effort.

The dance went on for fifteen minutes yet, but then

—quite unexpectedly—all the arena guards together fired a volley at the roof, and the dance stopped as if every dancer had been hit. The spectators were set surging by the showers of stone splinters, that hurt whom they struck, and their snarl was like a wolf-pack's when a tiger interferes. But the guards thought it all a prodigious joke and the more the crowd swore the more they laughed.

Panting—foaming at the mouth, some of them—the dancers ran to their seats and set the crowd surging again, leaving the arena empty of all but the guards. The man whose seat Ismail had taken came staggering, slippery with sweat, and squeezed himself where he belonged, forcing King into the Pathan's empty place. Ismail threw his arms round the man and patted him, calling him "mighty dancer," "son of the wind," "prince of prancers," "prince of swordsmen," "war-horse," and a dozen more endearing epithets. The fellow lay back across Ismail's knees, breathless but well enough contented.

And after a few more minutes the Orakzai Pathan came back, and King tried to make room for him to sit.

"I bade thee keep my place!" he growled, towering over King and plucking at his knife-belt irresolutely. He made it clear without troubling to use words that any other man would have had to fight, and the hakim might think himself lucky.

"Take my seat," said King, struggling to get up.

"Nay, nay—sit still, thou. I can kick room for myself. So! So! So!"

There was an answering snarl of hate that seemed like a song to him, amid which he sat down.

"The mullah Muhammad Anim answered he knows nothing of thee and cares less! He said—and he said

it with vehemence—it is no more to him where a hakim
sits than where the rats hide !"

He watched King's face and seeing that, King
allowed his facial muscles to express chagrin.

"Between us, it is a poor time for messages to him.
He is too full of pride that his lashkar should have
beaten the British."

"Did they beat the British greatly ?" King asked him,
with only vague interest on his face and a prayer inside
him that his heart might flutter less violently against
his ribs. His voice was as non-committal as the mullah's message.

"Who knows, when so many men would rather lie
than kill? Each one who returned swears he slew a
hundred. But some did not return. Wait and watch,
say I !"

Now a man stood up near the edge of the crowd
whom King recognized; and recognition brought no
joy with it. The mullah without hair or eyelashes, who
had admitted him and his party through the mosque
into the Caves, strode out to the middle of the arena
all alone, strutting and swaggering. He recalled the
man's last words and drew no consolation from them,
either.

"Many have entered ! Some went out by a different
road !"

Cold chills went down his back. All at once Ismail's
manner became unencouraging. He ceased to make a
fuss over the dancer and began to eye King sidewise,
until at last he seemed unable to contain the malice that
would well forth.

"At the gate there were only words !" he whispered.
"Here in this cavern men wait for proof !"

He licked his teeth suggestively, as a wolf does when

he contemplates a meal. Then, as an afterthought, as though ashamed, "I love thee! Thou art a man after my own heart! But I am *her* man! Wait and see!"

The mullah in the arena, blinking with his lashless eyes, held both arms up for silence in the attitude of a Christian priest blessing a congregation. The guards backed his silent demand with threatening rifles. The din died to a hiss of a thousand whispers, and then the great cavern grew still, and only the river could be heard sucking hungrily between the smooth stone banks.

"*God is great!*" the mullah howled.

"*God is great!*" the crowd thundered in echo to him; and then the vault took up the echoes. "God is great— is great—is great—ea—ea—eat!"

"*And Muhammad is His prophet!*" howled the mullah. Instantly they answered him again.

"*And Muhammad is His prophet!*"

"His prophet—is His prophet—is His prophet!" said the stalactites, in loud barks—then in murmurs— then in awe-struck whispers.

That seemed to be all the religious ritual Khinjan remembered or could tolerate. Considering that the mullah, too, must have killed his man in cold blood before earning the right to be there, perhaps it was enough—too much. There were men not far from King who shuddered.

"There are strangers!" announced the mullah, as a man might say, "I smell a rat!" But he did not look at anybody in particular; he blinked at the crowd.

"Strangers!" said the stalactites, in an awe-struck whisper.

"*Show them! Show them! Let them stand forth!*"

"*Oh-h-h-h-h!* Let them stand forth!" said the roof.

The mullah bowed as if that idea were a new one and he thought it better than his own; for all crowds love flattery.

"Bring them!" he shouted, and King suppressed a shudder—for what proof had he of right to be there, beyond Ismail's verbal corroboration of a lie? Would Ismail lie for him again? he wondered. And if so, would the lie be any use?

Not far from where King sat there was an immediate disturbance in the crowd, and a wretched-looking Baluchi was thrust forward at a run, with arms lashed to his sides and a pitiful look of terror on his face. Two more Baluchis were hustled along after him, protesting a little, but looking almost as hopeless.

Once in the arena, the guards took charge of all three of them and lined them up facing the mullah, clubbing them with their rifle-butts to get quicker obedience. The crowd began to be noisy again, but the mullah signed for silence.

"These are traitors!" he howled, with a gesture such as Ajax might have used when he defied the lightning.

The roof said "Traitors!"

"Slay them, then!" howled the crowd, delighted. And blinking behind the horn-rimmed spectacles, King began to look about busily for hope, where there did not seem to be any.

"Nay, hear me first!" the mullah howled, and his voice was like a wolf's at hunting time. "Hear, and be warned!"

The crowd grew very still, but King saw that some men licked their lips, as if they well knew what was coming.

"These three men came, and one was a new man!" the mullah howled. "The other two were his witnesses! All three swore that the first man came from slaying an unbeliever in the teeth of written law. They said he ran from the law. So, as the custom is, I let all three enter!"

"Good!" said the crowd. "Good!" They might have been five thousand judges, judging in equity, so grave they were. Yet they licked their lips.

"But later, word came to me saying they are liars. So—again as the custom is—I ordered them bound and held!"

"Slay them! Slay them!" the crowd yelped, gleeful as a wolf-pack on a scent and abandoning solemnity as suddenly as it had been assumed. "Slay them!"

They were like the wind, whipping in and out among Khinjan's rocks, savage and then still for a minute, savage and then still.

"Nay, there is a custom yet!" the mullah howled, holding up both arms. And there was silence again like the lull before a hurricane, with only the great black river talking to itself.

"Who speaks for them? Does any speak for them?"

"Speak for them?" said the roof.

There was silence. Then there was a murmur of astonishment. Over opposite to where King sat the mullah stood up, who the Pathan had said was "Bull-with-a-beard"—Muhammad Anim.

"The men are mine!" he growled. His voice was like a bear's at bay; it was low, but it carried strangely. And as he spoke he swung his great head between his shoulders, like a bear that means to charge. "The proof they brought has been stolen! They had good proof! I speak for them! The men are mine!"

The Pathan nudged King in the ribs with an elbow like a club and tickled his ear with hot breath.

"Bull-with-a-beard speaks truth!" he grinned.
"Truth and a lie together! Good may it do him and
them! They die, they three Baluchis!"

"Proof!" howled the mullah who had no hair or
eyelashes.

"Proof—oof—oof!" said the stalactites.

"Proof! Show us proof!" yelled the crowd.

"Words at the gate—proof in the cavern!" howled
the lashless one.

The Pathan next King leaned over to whisper to him
again, but stiffened in the act. There was a great gasp
the same instant, as the whole crowd caught its breath
all together. The mullah in the middle froze into im-
mobility. Bull-with-a-beard stood mumbling, swaying
his great head from side to side, no longer suggestive
of a bear about to charge, but of one who hesitates.

The crowd was staring at the end of the bridge.
King stared, too, and caught his own breath. For Yasmini stood there, smiling on them all as the new moon
smiles down on the Khyber! She had come among
them like a spirit, all unheralded.

So much more beautiful than the one likeness King
had seen of her that for a second he doubted who
she was—more lovely than he had imagined her even
in his dreams—she stood there, human and warm and
real, who had begun to seem a myth, clad in gauzy silk
transparent stuff that made no secret of sylph-like
shapeliness and looking nearly light enough to blow
away. Her feet—and they were the most marvelously
molded things he had ever seen—were naked and
played restlessly on the naked stone. Not one part of
her was still for a fraction of a second; yet the whole
effect was of insolently lazy ease.

Her eyes blazed brighter than the little jewels

stitched to her gossamer dress, and when a man once
looked at them he did not find it easy to look away
again. Even mullah Muhammad Anim seemed transfixed, like a great foolish animal.

But King was staring very hard indeed at something
else—mentally cursing the plain glass spectacles he
wore, that had begun to film over and dim his vision.
There were two bracelets on her arm, both barbaric
things of solid gold. The smaller of the two was on
her wrist and the larger on her upper arm, but they
were so alike, except for size, and so exactly like the
one Rewa Gunga had given him in her name and that
had been stolen from him in the night, that he ran the
risk of removing the glasses a moment to stare with
unimpeded eyes. Even then the distance was too
great. He could not quite see.

But her eyes began to search the crowd in his direction, and then he knew two things absolutely. He
was sitting where she had ordered Ismail to place him;
for she picked him out almost instantly, and laughed
as if somebody had struck a silver bell. And one of
those bracelets was the one that he had worn; for
she flaunted it at him, moving her arm so that the light
should make the gold glitter.

Then, perhaps because the crowd had begun to whisper, and she wanted all attention, she raised both arms
to toss back the golden hair that came cascading nearly
to her knees. And as if the crowd knew that symptom
well, it drew its breath in sharply and grew very still.

"Muhammad Anim!" she said, and she might have
been wooing him. "That was a devil's trick!"

It was rather an astounding statement, coming
from lovely lips in such a setting. It was rather suggestive of a driver's whiplash, flicked through the air

for a beginning. Muhammad Anim continued glaring
and did not answer her, so in her own good time, when
she had tossed her golden hair back once or twice
again, she developed her meaning.

"We who are free of Khinjan Caves do not send
men out to bring recruits. We know better than to bid
our men tell lies for others at the gate. Nor, seeking
proof for our new recruit, do we send men to hunt a
head for him—not even those of us who have a lashkar that we call our own, mullah Muhammad Anim!
Each of us earns his own way in!"

The mullah Muhammad Anim began to stroke his
beard, but he made no answer.

"And—mullah Muhammad Anim, thou wandering
man of God—when that lashkar has foolishly been
sent and has failed, is it written in the Kalamullah
saying we should pretend there was a head, and that
the head was stolen? A lie is a lie, Muhammad Anim!
Wandering perhaps is good, if in search of the *way*.
Is it good to lose the *way*, and to lie, thou true follower
of the Prophet?"

She smiled, tossing her hair back. Her eyes challenged, her lips mocked him and her chin scorned.
The crowd breathed hard and watched. The mullah
muttered something in his beard, and sat down, and
the crowd began to roar applause at her. But she
checked it with a regal gesture, and a glance of con-
tempt at the mullah that was alone worth a journey
across the "Hills" to see.

"Guards!" she said quietly. And the crowd's sigh
then was like the night wind in a forest.

"Away with those three of Muhammad Anim's
men !"

Twelve of the arena guards threw down their shields

with a sudden clatter and seized the prisoners, four
to each. The crowd shivered with delicious anticipa-
tion. The doomed men neither struggled nor cried,
for fatalism is an anodyne as well as an explosive.
King set his teeth. Yasmini, with both hands behind
her head, continued to smile down on them all as
sweetly as the stars shine on a battle-field.

She nodded once; and then all was over in a minute. With a ringing "Ho!" and a run, the guards
lifted their victims shoulder high and bore them forward. At the river bank they paused for a second to
swing them. Then, with another "Ho!" they threw
them like dead rubbish into the swift black water.

There was only one wild scream that went echoing
and re-echoing to the roof. There was scarcely a
splash, and no extra ripple at all. No heads came up
again to gasp. No fingers clutched at the surface.
The fearful speed of the river sucked them under, to
grind and churn and pound them through long caverns
underground and hurl them at last over the great cata-
ract toward the middle of the world.

"Ah-h-h-h-h!" sighed the crowd in ecstasy.

"Is there no other stranger?" asked Yasmini, search-
ing for King again with her amazing eyes. The skin
all down his back turned there and then into gooseflesh.
And as her eyes met his she laughed like a bell at him.
She knew! She knew who he was, how he had entered, and how he felt. Not a doubt of it!

Long slept the Heart o' the Hills, oh, long!
(Ye who have watched, ye know!)
As sap sleeps in the deodars
When winter shrieks and steely stars
Blink over frozen snow.
Ye haste? The sap stirs now, ye say?
Ye feel the pulse of spring?
But sap must rise ere buds may break,
Or cubs fare forth, or bees awake,
Or lean buck spurn the ling!

CHAPTER XI

"KURRAM KHAN!" the lashless mullah howled, like a lone wolf in the moonlight, and King stood up.

It is one of the laws of Cocker, who wrote the S. S. Code, that a man is alive until he is proved dead, and where there is life there is opportunity. In that grim minute King felt heretical; but a man's feelings are his own affair provided he can prove it, and he managed to seem about as much at ease as a native hakim ought to feel at such an initiation.

"Come forward!" the mullah howled, and he obeyed, treading gingerly between men who were at no pains to let him by, and silently blessing them, because he was not really in any hurry at all. Yasmini looked lovely from a distance, and life was sweet.

"Who are his witnesses?"

"Witnesses?" the roof hissed.

"I!" shouted Ismail, jumping up.

"I!" cracked the roof. "I! I!" So that for a second King almost believed he had a crowd of men to

223

swear for him and did not hear Darya Khan at all, who rose from a place not very far behind where he had sat.

Ismail followed him in a hurry, like a man wading a river with loose clothes gathered in one arm and the other arm ready in case of falling. He took much less trouble than King not to tread on people, and oaths marked his wake.

Darya Khan did not go so fast. As he forced his way forward a man passed him up the wooden box that King had used to stand on; he seized it in both hands with a grin and a jest and went to stand behind King and Ismail, in line with the lashless mullah, facing Yasmini. Yasmini smiled at them all as if they were actors in her comedy, and she well pleased with them.

"Look ye!" howled the mullah. "Look ye and look well, for this is to be one of us!"

King felt ten thousand eyes burn holes in his back, but the one pair of eyes that mocked him from the bridge was more disconcerting.

"Turn, Kurram Khan! Turn that all may see!"

Feeling like a man on a spit, he revolved slowly. By the time he had turned once completely around, besides knowing positively that one of the two bracelets on her right arm was the one he had worn, or else its exact copy, he knew that he was not meant to die yet; for his eyes could work much more swiftly than the horn-rimmed spectacles made believe. He decided that Yasmini meant he should be frightened, but not much hurt just yet.

So he ceased altogether to feel frightened and took care to look more scared than ever.

"Who paid the price of thy admission?" the mullah howled, and King cleared his throat, for he was not quite sure yet what that might mean.

"Speak, Kurram Khan!" Yasmini purred, smiling her loveliest. "Tell them whom you slew."

King turned and faced the crowd, raising himself on the balls of his feet to shout, like a man facing thousands of troops on parade. He nearly gave himself away, for habit had him unawares. A native hakim, given the stoutest lungs in all India, would not have shouted in that way.

"Cappitin Attleystan King!" he roared. And he nearly jumped out of his skin when his own voice came rattling back at him from the roof overhead.

"Cappitin Attleystan King!" it answered.

Yasmini chuckled as a little rill will sometimes chuckle among ferns. It was devilish. It seemed to say there were traps not far ahead.

"Where was he slain?" asked the mullah.

"In the Khyber Pass," said King.

"In the Khyber Pass!" the roof whispered hoarsely, as if aghast at such cold-bloodedness.

"Now give proof!" said the mullah. "Words at the gate—proof in the cavern! Without good proof, there is only one way out of here!"

"Proof!" the crowd thundered. "Proof!"

"Proof! Proof! Proof!" the roof echoed.

There was no need for Darya Khan to whisper. King's hands were behind him, and he had seen what he had seen and guessed what he had guessed while he was turning to let the crowd look at him. His fingers closed on human hair.

"Nay, it is short!" hissed Darya Khan. "Take the two ears, or hold it by the jawbone! Hold it high in both hands!"

King obeyed, without looking at the thing, and Ismail, turning to face the crowd, rose on tiptoe and
filled his lungs for the effort of his life.

"The head of Cappitin Attleystan King—infidel—
kaffir—British arrficer!" he howled.

"Good!" the crowd bellowed. "Good! Throw it!"

The crowd's roar and the roof's echoes combined in
pandemonium.

"Throw it to them, Kurram Khan!" Yasmini purred
from the bridge end, speaking as softly and as sweetly
as if she coaxed a child. Yet her voice carried.

He lowered the head, but instead of looking at it he
looked up at her. He thought she was enjoying herself and his predicament as he had never seen any one
enjoy anything.

"Throw it to them, Kurram Khan!" she purred. "It
is the custom!"

"Throw it! Throw it!" the crowd thundered.

He turned the ghastly thing until it lay face-upward
in his hands, and so at last he saw it. He caught his
breath, and only the horn-rimmed spectacles, that he
had cursed twice that night, saved him from self-be-
trayal. The cavern seemed to sway, but he recovered,
and his wits worked swiftly. If Yasmini detected his
nervousness she gave no sign.

"Throw it! Throw it! Throw it!"

The crowd was growing impatient. Many men were
standing, waving their arms to draw attention to themselves, and he wondered what the ultimate end of the
head would be, if he obeyed and threw it to them.
Watching Yasmini's eyes, he knew it had not entered
her head that he might disobey.

He looked past her toward the river. There were
no guards near enough to prevent what he intended;

but he had to bear in mind that the guards had rifles,
and if he acted too suddenly one of them might shoot
at him unbidden. They were wondrous free with their
cartridges, those guards, in a land where ammunition
is worth its weight in silver coin.

Holding the head before him with both hands, he
began to walk toward the river, edging all the while a
little toward the crowd as if meaning to get nearer before he threw.

He was much more than half-way to the river's edge
before Yasmini or anybody else divined his true intention. The mullah grew suspicious first and yelled.
Then King hurried, for he did not believe Yasmini
would need many seconds in which to regain command
of any situation. But she saw fit to stand still and
watch.

He reached the river and stood there. Now he was
in no hurry at all, for it stood to reason that unless
Yasmini very much desired him to be kept alive he
would have been shot dead already. For a moment
the crowd was so interested that it forgot to bark and
snarl.

His next move was as deliberate as he could make
it, although he was careful to avoid the least suggestion
of mummery (for then the crowd would have suspected
disloyalty to Islam, and the "Hills" are very, very
pious, and very suspicious of all foreign ritual).

He did a thoughtful simple thing that made every
savage who watched him gasp because of its very unexpectedness. He held the head in both hands, threw
it far out into the river and stood to watch it sink.
Then, without visible emotion of any kind, he walked
back stolidly to face Yasmini at the bridge end, with
shoulders a little more stubborn now than they ought

to be, and chin a shade too high, for there never was a man who could act quite perfectly.

"Thou fool!" Yasmini whispered through lips that did not move.

She betrayed a flash of temper like a trapped she-tiger's, but followed it instantly with her loveliest smile. Like to like, however, the crowd saw the flash of temper and took its cue from that.

"Slay him!" yelled a lone voice, that was greeted by an approving murmur.

"Slay him!" advised the roof in a whisper, in one of its phonetic tricks.

"This is a darbar!" Yasmini announced in a rising, ringing voice. "My darbar, for *I* summoned it! Did I invite any man to speak?"

There was silence, as a whipped unwilling pack is silent.

"Speak, *thou*, Kurram Khan!" she said. "Knowing the custom—having heard the order to throw that trophy to them—why act otherwise? Explain!"

Nothing in the wide world could be fairer! She left him to extricate himself from a mess of his own making! It was more than fair, for she went out of her way to offer him an opening to jump through. And she paid him the compliment of suggesting he must be clever enough to take it, for she seemed to expect a satisfying answer.

"Tell them why!" she said, smiling. No man could have guessed by the tone of her voice whether she was for him or against him, and the crowd, beginning again to whisper, watched to see which way the cat would jump.

He bowed low to her three times—very low indeed

and very slowly, for he had to think. Then he turned
his back and repeated the obeisance to the crowd. Still
he could think of no excuse, except Cocker's Rule No.
1 for Tight Places, and all the world knows that because Solomon said much the same thing first:
"A soft answer is better than a sword!"
But Cocker adds, "Never excuse. Explain! And
blame no man."
"My brothers," he said, and paused, since a man
must make a beginning, even when he can not see the
end. And as he spoke the answer came to him. He
stood upright, and his voice became that of a man
whose advice has been asked, and who gives it freely.
"These be stirring times! Ye need take care, my
brothers! Ye saw this night how one man entered
here on the strength of an oath and a promise. All
he lacked was proof. And I had proof. Ye saw!
Who am I that I should deny you a custom? Yet—
think ye, my brothers!—how easy would it not have
been, had I thrown that head to you, for a traitor to
catch it and hide it in his clothes, and make away with
it! He could have used it to admit to these caves—
why—even an Englishman, my brothers! If that had
happened, ye would have blamed me!"
Yasmini smiled. Taking its cue from her, the crowd
murmured, scarcely assent, but rather recognition of
the hakim's adroitness. The game was not won; there
lacked a touch to tip the scales in his favor, and Yasmini supplied it with ready genius.
"The hakim speaks truth!" she laughed.
King turned about instantly to face her, but he
salaamed so low that she could not have seen his expression had she tried.

"If ye wish it, I will order him tossed into Earth's
Drink after those other three."

Muhammed Anim rose, stroking his beard and rock ,
ing where he stood.

"It is the law!" he growled, and King shuddered.

"It is the law," Yasmini answered in a voice that
rang with pride and insolence, "that none interrupt me
while I speak! For such ill-mannered ones Earth's
Drink hungers! Will you test my authority, Muhammad Anim?"

The mullah sat down, and hundreds of men laughed
at him, but not all of the men by any means.

"It is the law that none goes out of Khinjan Caves
alive who breaks the law of the Caves. But he broke no
very big law. And he spoke truth. Think ye! If that
head had only fallen into Muhammad Anim's lap, the
mullah might have smuggled in another man with it!"

A roar of laughter greeted that thrust. Many men
who had not laughed at the mullah's first discomfiture
joined in now. Muhammad Anim sat and fidgeted,
meeting nobody's eye and answering nothing.

"So it seems to me good," Yasmini said, in a voice
that did not echo any more but rang very clear and true
(she seemed to know the trick of the roof, and to use
the echo or not as she chose), "to let this hakim live!
He shall meditate in his cave a while, and perhaps he
shall be beaten, lest he dare offend again. He can no
more escape from Khinjan Caves than the women who
are prisoners here. He may therefore live!"

There was utter silence. Men looked at one another
and at her, and her blazing eyes searched the crowd
swiftly. It was plain enough that there were at least
two parties there, and that none dared oppose Yasmini's will for fear of the others.

"To thy seat, Kurram Khan!" she ordered, when she had waited a full minute and no man spoke.

He wasted no time. He hurried out of the arena as fast as he could walk, with Ismail and Darya Khan close at his heels. It was like a run out of danger in a dream. He stumbled over the legs of the front-rank men in his hurry to get back to his place, and Ismail overtook him, seized him by the shoulders, hugged him, and dragged him to the empty seat next to the Orakzai Pathan. There he hugged him until his ribs cracked.

"Ready o' wit!" he crowed. "Ready o' tongue! Light o' life! Man after mine own heart! Hey, I love thee! Readily I would be thy man, but for being *hers!* Would I had a son like thee! Fool—fool— fool not to throw the head to them! Squeamish one! Man like a child! What is the head but earth when the life has left it? What would *thy* head be without the nimble wit? Fool—fool—fool! And clever! Turned the joke on Muhammad Anim! Turned it on Bull-with-a-beard in a twinkling—in the bat of an eye —in a breath! Turned it against her enemy and raised a laugh against him from his own men! Ready o' wit! Shameless one! Lucky one! Allah was surely good to thee!"

Still exulting, he let go, but none too soon for comfort. King's ribs were sore from his hugging for days.

"What is it?" he asked. For King seemed to be shaping words with his lips. He bent a great hairy ear to listen.

"Have they taken Ali Masjid Fort?" King whispered.

"How should I know? Why?"

"Tell me, man, if you love me! Have they taken it?"

"Nay, how should I know? Ask *her!* She knows more than any man knows!"

King turned to ask the same question of his friend the Orakzai Pathan; but the Pathan would have none of his questions, he was busy listening for whispers from the crowd, watching with both eyes, and he shoved King aside.

The crowd was very far from being satisfied. An angry murmur had begun to fill the cavern as a hive is filled with the song of bees at swarming time. But even so, surmise what one might, it was not easy to persuade the eye that Yasmini's careless smile and easy poise were assumed. If she recognized indignation and feared it, she disguised her fear amazingly.

King saw her whisper to a guard. The fellow nodded and passed his shield to another man. He began to make his way in no great hurry toward the edge of the arena. She whispered again and standing forward with their trumpets seven of the guards blew a blast that split across the cavern like the trump of doom; and as its hundred thousand echoes died in the roof, the hum of voices died, too, and the very sound of breathing. The gurgling of water became as if the river flowed in solitude.

Leisurely then, languidly, she raised both arms until she looked like an angel poised for flight. The little jewels stitched to her gauzy dress twinkled like fireflies as she moved. The crowd gasped sharply. She had it by the heart-strings.

She called, and four guards got under one shield, bowing their heads and resting the great rim on their shoulders. They carried it beneath her and stood still. With a low delicious laugh, sweet and true, she sprang on it, and the shield scarcely trembled; she seemed lighter than the silk her dress was woven from!

They carried her so, looking as if she and the shield were carved of a piece, and by a master such as has not often been. And in the midst of the arena before they had ceased moving she began to sing, with her head thrown back and bosom swelling like a bird's.

The East would ever rather draw its own conclusions from a hint let fall than be puzzled by what the West believes are facts. And parables are not good evidence in courts of law, which is always a consideration. So her song took the form of a parable.

And to say that she took hold of them and played rhapsodies of her own making on their heart-strings would be to undervalue what she did. They were dumb while she sang, but they rose at her. Not a force in the world could have kept them down, for she was deftly touching cords that stirred other forces—subtle, mysterious, mesmeric, which the old East understands —which Muhammad the Prophet understood when he harnessed evil in the shafts with men and wrote rules for their driving in a book. They rose in silence and stood tense.

While she sang, the guard to whom she had whispered forced a way through the ranks of the standing crowd, and came behind Ismail. He tweaked the Afridi's ear to draw attention, for like all the others —like King, too—Ismail was listening with dropped jaw and watching with burning eyes. For a minute they whispered, so low that King did not hear what they said; and then the guard forced his way back by the shortest route to the arena, knocking down half a dozen men and gaining safety beyond the lamps before his victims could draw knife and follow him.

Yasmini's song went on, verse after verse, telling never one fact, yet hinting unutterable things in a language that was made for hint and metaphor and parable and innuendo. What tongue did not hint at was conveyed by subtle gesture and a smile and flashing eyes. It was perfectly evident that she knew more than King—more than the general at Peshawur—more than the viceroy at Simla—probably more than the British government—concerning what was about to happen in Islam. The others might guess. She knew. It was just as evident that she would not tell. The whole of her song, and it took her twenty minutes by the count of King's pulse, to sing it, was a warning to wait and a promise of amazing things to come.

She sang of a wolf-pack gathering from the valleys in the winter snow—a very hungry wolf-pack. Then of a stalled ox, grown very fat from being cared for. Of the "Heart of the Hills" that awoke in the womb of the "Hills," and that listened and watched.

"Now, is *she* the 'Heart of the Hills'?" King wondered. The rumors men had heard and told again in India, about the "Heart of the Hills" in Khinjan seemed to have foundation.

He thought of the strange knife, wrapped in a handkerchief under his shirt, with its bronze blade and gold hilt in the shape of a woman dancing. The woman dancing was astonishingly like Yasmini, standing on the shield!

She sang about the owners of the stalled ox, who were busy at bay, defending themselves and their ox from another wolf-pack in another direction "far beyond."

She urged them to wait a little while. The ox was big enough and fat enough to nourish all the wolves in

the world for many seasons. Let them wait, then, until
another, greater wolf-pack joined them, that they
might go hunting all together, overwhelm its present
owners and devour the ox! So urged the "Heart of
the Hills," speaking to the mountain wolves, according
to Yasmini's song.

> "The little cubs in the burrows know.
> Are ye grown wolves, who hurry so?"

She paused, for effect; but they gave tongue then
because they could not help it, and the cavern shook to
their terrific worship.

"Allah! Allah!"

They summoned God to come and see the height and
depth and weight of their allegiance to her! And because for their thunder there was no more chance of
being heard, she dropped from the shield like a blossom. No sound of falling could have been heard in
all that din, but one could see she made no sound. The
shield-bearers ran back to the bridge and stood below
it, eyes agape.

Rewa Gunga spoke truth in Delhi when he assured
King he should some day wonder at Yasmini's dancing.

She became joy and bravery and youth! She danced
a story for them of the things they knew. She was the
dawn light, touching the distant peaks. She was the
wind that follows it, sweeping among the junipers and
kissing each as she came. She was laughter, as the
little children laugh when the cattle are loosed from
the byres at last to feed in the valleys. She was the
scent of spring uprising. She was blossom. She was
fruit! Very daughter of the sparkle of warm sun on
snow. she was the "Heart of the Hills" herself!

Never was such dancing! Never such an audience!
Never such mad applause! She danced until the great
rough guards had to run round the arena with clubbed
butts and beat back trespassers who would have
mobbed her. And every movement—every gracious
wonder-curve and step with which she told her tale
was as purely Greek as the handle on King's knife and
the figures on the lamp-bowls and as the bracelets on
her arm. Greek!

And she half-modern-Russian, ex-girl-wife of a
semi-civilized Hill-rajah! Who taught her? There
is nothing new, even in Khinjan, in the "Hills"!

And when the crowd defeated the arena guards at
last and burst through the swinging butts to seize her
and fling her high and worship her with mad barbaric
rite, she ran toward the shield. The four men raised
it shoulder-high again. She went to it like a leaf in
the wind—sprang on it as if wings had lifted her,
scarce touching it with naked toes—and leapt to the
bridge with a laugh.

She went over the bridge on tiptoes, like nothing else
under heaven but Yasmini at her bewitchingest. And
without pausing on the far side she danced up the
hewn stone stairs, dived into the dark hole and was
gone!

"Come!" yelled Ismail in King's ear. He could have
heard nothing less, for the cavern was like to burst
apart from the tumult.

"Whither?" the Afridi shouted in disgust. "Does
the wind ask whither? Come like the wind and see!
They will remember next that they have a bone to
pick with thee! Come away!"

That seemed good enough advice. He followed as

fast as Ismail could shoulder a way out between the frantic Hillmen, deafened, stupefied, numbed, almost cowed by the ovation they were giving the "Heart of their Hills."

A scorpion in a corner stings himself to death.
A coward blames the gods. They laugh and let him die.
A man goes forward—NATIVE PROVERB.

CHAPTER XII

AS THEY disappeared after a scramble through the mouth of the same tunnel they had entered by, a roar went up behind them like the birth of earthquakes. Looking back over his shoulder, King saw Yasmini come back into the hole's mouth, to stand framed in it and bow acknowledgment. She looked so ravishing in contrast to the huge grim wall, and the black river, and the darkness at her back, that Khinjan's thousands tried to storm the bridge and drag her down to them. The guards were hard put to it, with their backs to the bridge end, for two or three minutes.

But Ismail would not let him wait and watch from there. He dragged him down the tunnel and pushed him up on to a ledge where they could both see without being seen, through a fissure in the rock.

For the space of five minutes Yasmini stood in the great hole, smiling and watching the struggle below. Then she went, and the guards began to get the best of it, because the crowd's enthusiasm waned when they could see her no more. Then suddenly the guards began to loose random volleys at the roof and brought down hundredweights of splintered stalactite.

239

Within a minute there were a hundred men busy sweeping up the splinters. In another minute twenty Zakka Khels had begun a sword dance, yelling like the damned. A hundred joined them. In three minutes more the whole arena was a dinning whirlpool, and the river's voice was drowned in shouting and the stamping of naked feet on stone.

"Come!" urged Ismail, and led the way.

King's last impression was of earth's womb on fire and of hellions brewing wrath. The stalactites and the hurrying river multiplied the dancing lights into a million, and the great roof hurled the din down again to make confusion with the new din coming up.

Ismail went like a rat down a run, and King failed to overtake him until he found him in the cave of the slippers kicking to right and left at random.

"Choose a good pair!" he growled. "Let late-comers fight for what is left! Nay, I have thine! Choose thou the next best!"

The statement being one of fact, and that no time or place for a quarrel with the only friend in sight, King picked out the best slippers he could see. The instant he had them on Ismail was off again, running like the wind.

They had no torch. They left the little tunnel lamps behind. It became so dark that King had to follow by ear, and so it happened that he missed seeing where the tunnel forked. He imagined they were running back toward the ledge under the waterfall; yet, when Ismail called a halt at last, panting, groped behind a great rock for a lamp and lit the wick with a common safety match, they were in a cave he had never seen before.

"Where are we?" King asked.

"Where none dare seek us."

Ismail held the lamp high, shielding its wick with a hollowed palm and peering about him as if in doubt, his ragged beard looking like smoke in the wind; for a wind blew down all the passages in Khinjan.

King examined the lamp. It was of bronze and almost as surely ancient Greek as it surely was not Indian. There were figures graven on the bowl representing a woman dancing, who looked not unlike Yasmini; but before he had time to look very closely Ismail blew the lamp out and was off again, like a shadow shot into its mother night.

Confused by the sudden darkness King crashed into a rock as he tried to follow. Ismail turned back and gave him the end of a cotton girdle that he unwound from his waist; then he plunged ahead again into Cimmerian blackness, down a passage so narrow that they could touch a wall with either hand.

Once he shouted back to duck, and they passed under a low roof where water dripped on them, and the rock underfoot was the bed of a shallow stream. After that the track began to rise, and the grade grew so steep that even Ismail, the furious, had to slacken pace.

They began to climb up titanic stairways all in the dark, feeling their way through fissures in a mountain's framework, up zigzag ledges, and over great broken lumps of rock from one cave to another; until at last in one great cave Ismail stopped and relit the lamp. Hunting about with its aid he found an imported "hurricane" lantern and lit that, leaving the bronze lamp in its place.

Soon after that they lost sight of walls to their left for a time, although there were no stars, nor any light

to suggest the outer world—nothing but wind. The
wind blew a hurricane.

Their path now was a very narrow ledge formed by
a crack that ran diagonally down the face of a black
cliff on their right. They hugged the stone because of
a sense of fathomless space above—below—on every
side but one. The rock wall was the one thing tangible, and the footing the crack in it afforded was
the gift of God.

The moaning wind rose to a shriek at intervals and
made their clothes flutter like ghosts' shrouds, and in
spite of it King's shirt was drenched with sweat, and
his fingers ached from clinging as if they were on fire.

Crawling against the wind along a wider ledge at
the top, they came to a chasm, crossed by a foot-wide
causeway. The wind howled and moaned in it, and
the futile lantern rays only suggested unimaginable
things—death the least of them.

"Art thou afraid?" asked Ismail, holding the lantern
to King's face.

"*Kuch dar nahin hai!*" he answered. "There is no
such thing as fear!"

It was a bold answer, and Ismail laughed, knowing
well that neither of them believed a word of it at that
moment. Only, each thought better of the other, that
the one should have cared to ask, and that the other
should be willing to give the lie to a fear that crawled
and could be felt. Too many men are willing to admit
they are afraid. Too many would rather condemn and
despise than ask and laugh. But it is on the edges of
eternity that men find each other out, and sympathize.

Ismail went down on his hands and knees, lifting
the lantern along a foot at a time in front of him
and carrying it in his teeth by the bail the last part

of the way. It seemed like an hour before he stood up, nearly a hundred yards away on the far side, and yelled for King to follow.

The wind snatched the yells away, but the waving lantern beckoned him, and King knelt down in the dark. It happened that he laid his hand on a loose stone, the size of his head, near the edge. He shoved it over and listened.

He listened for a minute but did not hear it strike anything, and the shudder, that he could not repress, came from the middle of his backbone and spread outward through each fiber of his being. If he had delayed another second his courage would have failed; he began at once to crawl to where Ismail stood swinging the light.

There was room on the ledge for his knees and no more. Toes and fingers were overside. He sat down as on horseback, and transferred both slippers to his pockets, and then went forward again with bare feet, waiting whenever the wind snatched at him with redoubled fury, to lean against it and grip the rock with numb fingers. Ismail swung the lamp, for reasons best known to himself, and half-way over King sat astride the ridge again to shout to him to hold it still. But Ismail did not understand him.

"Khinjan graves are deep!" he howled back. "Fear and the shadow of death are one!"

He swung the lamp even more violently, as if it were a charm that could exorcise fear and bring a man over safely. The shadows danced until his brain reeled, and King swore he would thrash the fool as soon as he could reach him. He lay belly-downward on the rock and crawled like an insect the remainder of the way.

And as if aware of his intention Ismail started to hurry on while there was yet a yard or two to crawl, and anger not being a load worth carrying, nor revenge a thing permitted to interfere with the sirkar's business, King let both die.

Hunted by the wind, they ran round a bold shoulder of cliff into another black-dark tunnel. There the wind died, swallowed in a hundred fissures, but the track grew worse and steeper until they had to cling with both hands and climb and now and then Ismail set the lantern on a ledge and lowered his girdle to help King up. Sometimes he stood on King's shoulder in order to reach a higher level. They climbed for an hour and dropped at last panting, on a ledge, after squeezing themselves under the corner of a boulder.

The lantern light shone on a tiny trickle of cold water, and there Ismail drank deep, like a bull, before signing to King to imitate him.

"A thirsty throat and a crazy head are one!" he counseled. "A man needs wit and a wet tongue who would talk with *her!*"

"Where is *she?*" asked King, when he had finished drinking.

"Go and look!"

Ismail gave him a sudden shove, that sent him feet first forward over the edge. He fell a distance rather greater than his own height, to another ledge and stood there looking up. He could see Ismail's redrimmed eyes blinking down at him in the lantern light, but suddenly the Afridi blew the lamp out, and then the darkness became solid. Thought itself left off less than a yard away.

"Ismail!" he whispered. But Ismail did not answer him.

He faced about, leaning against the rock, with the
flat of both hands pressed tight against it for the sake
of its company; and almost at once he saw a little
bright red light glowing in the distance. It might
have been a hundred yards, and it might have been a
mile away below him; it was perfectly impossible to
judge, for the darkness was not measurable.

"Flowers turn to the light!" droned Ismail's voice
above sententiously, and turning, he thought he could
see red eyes peering over the rock. He jumped, and
made a grab for the flowing beard that surely must
be below them, but he missed.

"Little fish swim to the light!" droned Ismail.
"Moths fly to the light! Who is a man that he should
know less than they?"

He turned again and stared at the light. Dimly,
very vaguely he could make out that a causeway led
downward from almost where he stood. He was con-
vinced that should he try to climb back Ismail would
merely reach out a hand and shove him down again,
and there was no sense in being put to that indignity.
He decided to go forward, for there was even less sense
in standing still.

"Come with me! Come along, Ismail!" he called.

"Allah! Hear him! Nay, nay, nay! Who was it
said a little while ago, 'There is no such thing as fear!'
I am afraid, but thou and I are two men! Go thou
alone!"

Reason is a man's only dependable faculty. Reason
told him that at a word from Yasmini he would have
been flung into "Earth's Drink" hours ago. Therefore, added reason, why should she forego that spec-
tacular opportunity when his death would have amused
Khinjan's thousands, only to kill him now in the dark

alone? He had treated a few dozen sick men, but surely she had not been afraid to offend them. Had she not dared forbid the sick coming to him altogether? "Forward!" says Cocker, in at least a dozen places. "Go forward and find out! Better a bed in hell than a seat on the horns of a dilemma! Forward!"

There was no sound now anywhere. He stretched a leg downward and felt a rock two or three feet lower down, and the sound of his slipper sole touching it, being the only noise, made the short hair rise on the back of his neck. Then he took himself, so to speak, by the hand and went forward and downward, for action is the only curb imagination knows.

He forgot to count his pulse and judge how long it took him to descend that causeway in the dark. It was not so very rough, nor so very dangerous, but of course he only knew that fact afterward. He had to grope his way inch by inch, trusting to sense of touch and the British army's everlasting luck, with an eye all the while on a red light that was something like the glow through hell's keyhole.

When he reached bottom, after perhaps twenty minutes, and stood at last on comparatively level rock, his legs were trembling from tension, and he had to sit down while he stretched them out and rested. The light still looked a quarter of a mile away, although that was guesswork. It made scarcely more impression on the surrounding darkness than one coal glowing in a cellar. The silence began to make his head ache.

He got up and started forward, but just as he did that he thought he heard a footstep. He suspected Ismail might be following after all.

"Ismail!" he called, trying to peer through the dark.

But all the darkness had its home there. He could not even see his own hand stretched out. His own voice made him jump; after a second's pause it began to crack and rattle from wall to wall and from roof to floor, until at last the echoing word became one again and died with a hiss somewhere in the bowels of the world—Mbisssss!—like the sound of hot iron being plunged into a blacksmith's trough with a little after-murmur of complaining water.

But then he was sure he heard a footstep! He faced about; and now there were two red lights where there had been only one. They seemed rather nearer, perhaps because there were two of them.

"Hullo, King sahib!" said a voice he recognized; and he choked. He felt that if he had coughed his heart would have lain on the floor!

"Are you afraid, King sahib?" said the Rangar Rewa Gunga's voice, and he took a step forward to be closer to his questioner. He found himself beside a rock, looking up at the Rangar's turban, that peered over the top of it. He could dimly make out the Rangar's dark eyes.

"I would be afraid if I were you!"

Rewa Gunga flashed a little electric torch into his eyes, but after a few seconds he shifted it so that both their faces could be seen, although the Rangar's only very faintly.

"I have come to warn you!"

"Very good of you, I'm sure!" said King.

"If *she* knew I were here, she would jolly well have my liver nailed to a wall! I come to advise you to go back!"

Have they taken Ali Masjid Fort?" King asked him.

"Never mind, sahib, but listen! I have brought
her bracelet! I stole it! She stole it from you, and I
stole it back! Take it! Put it on and wear it! Use
it as a passport out of Khinjan Caves—for no man
dare touch you while you wear it—and as a passport
down the Khyber into India! Go back to India and
stay there! Take it and go! Quick! Take it!"

"No, thanks!" said King.

The Rangar laughed mirthlessly, shifting the light
a little as King stepped aside to get a better view of
him. He held the torch more cunningly than a Span-
ish lady holds a fan.

"All Englishmen are fools—most of them stiff-
necked fools," he asserted. "Bah! Do you think I do
not know? Do you think anything is hidden from
her? I know—and she knows—that you think you
have a surprise in store for her! You think you will
go to her, and she will say, 'King sahib, why did you
throw that head into the river, and put me in danger
from my men?' And you will say, will you not,
'Princess, that was my brother's head!'? Was that
not what you intended? Is it not true? Does she
not know it? She knows more than you know, King
sahib! Because you showed me certain little courtesies,
I have come to warn you to run away!"

"Do you suppose she knows you are here?" King
asked, and the Rangar laughed.

"If she knows so much, and is able to read my mind
from a distance, where does she suppose you are?"
King insisted.

The Rangar laughed again, leaning his chin on both
fists and switching out the light.

"Perhaps she sent me to warn you!"

"Well," said King, "my brother commanded at Ali

Masjid Fort. There are things I must ask her. How did she know that head was my brother's? What part had she in taking it from his shoulders? What did she mean by that song of hers?"

The Rangar chuckled softly.

"There are no fools in the world like Englishmen! Listen! You are being offered life and liberty! Here is the key to both!"

He made the gold bracelet ring on the rock by way of explanation.

"Take the key and go!"

"No!" said King.

"Very well, sahib! Hear the other side of it! Beyond those two red lights there is a curtain. This side of that curtain you are Athelstan King of the Khyber Rifles, or Kurram Khan, or whatever you care to call yourself. Beyond it, you are what *she* calls you! Choose!"

King did not answer, so he continued after a pause.

"You shall pass behind that curtain, if you insist. Beyond it you shall know what she knows about Ali Masjid and your brother's head! You shall know all that she knows! There shall be no secrets between you and her! She shall translate the meaning of her song to you! But you shall never come out again King of the Khyber Rifles, or Kurram Khan! If you ever come out again, it shall be as you never dreamed, bearing arms you never saw yet, and you shall cut with your own hand the ties that bind you to England! Choose!"

"I chose long ago," said King.

"Are the gentle English never serious?" the Rangar asked. "Will you not understand that if you pass that curtain you shall know all things that Yasmini knows,

but that you shall cease to be yourself? Cease—to—
be—yourself! Is my meaning clear?"

"Not in the least," said King, "but I hope mine is!"

"You will go forward?"

"Yes," said King.

Rewa Gunga made no answer to that, although King
waited for an answer. For about a minute there was
no sound at all, except the beating of King's heart.
Then he moved, to try and see the Rangar's turban
above the rock. He could not see it. He found a
niche in the rock, set his foot in it and mounted three
or four feet, until his head was level with the top.
The Rangar was gone!

He listened for two or three minutes, but the silence
began to make his head ache again; so he stooped to
feel the floor with his hand before deciding to go forward. There was no mistaking the finish given by
the tread of countless feet. He was on a highway,
and there are not often pitfalls where so many feet
have been.

For all that he went forward as a certain Agag
once did, and it was many minutes before he could
see a curtain glowing blood-red in the light behind
the two lamps, at the top of a flight of ten stone steps.
It was peculiar to him and to his service that he
counted the steps before going nearer.

When he went quite close he saw carpet down the
middle of the steps, so ancient that the stone showed
through in places; all the pattern, supposing it ever
had any, was worn or faded away. Carpet and steps
glowed red too. His own face, and the hands he held
in front of him were red-hot-poker color. Yet outside the little ellipse of light the darkness looked like

ᴀ thing to lean against, and the silence was so intense
that he could hear the arteries singing by his ears.

He saw the curtains move slightly, apparently in
a little puff of wind that made the lamps waver. He
was very nearly sure he heard a footfall beyond the
curtains and a tinkle—as of a tiny silver bell, or a jewel
striking against another one.

He kicked his slippers off, because there are no
conditions under which bad manners ever are good
policy. Vide history and Cocker's famous code. Then
he walked up the steps without treading on the carpet,
because living scorpions have been known to be placed
under carpets on purpose on occasion. And at the
top, being a Secret Service man, he stooped to examine
the lamps.

They were bronze, cast, polished and graved. All
round the circumference of each bowl were figures in
half-relief, representing a woman dancing. She was
the woman of the knife-hilt, and of the lamps in the
arena! She looked like Yasmini! Only she could not
be Yasmini because these lamps were so ancient and
so rare that he had never seen any in the least like
them, although he had visited most of the museums
of the East.

Both lamps were alike, for he crossed over to make
sure and took each in his hands in turn. But no two
figures of the dance were alike on either. It was the
same woman dancing, but the artist had chosen twenty
different poses with which to immortalize his skill, and
hers. Both lamps burned sweet oil with a wick, and
each had a chimney of horn, not at all unlike a modern lamp-chimney. The horn was stained red.

As he set the second lamp down he became aware

of a subtle interesting smell, and memory took him
back at once to Yasmini's room in the Chandni Chowk
in Delhi where he had smelled it first. It was the
peculiar scent he had been told was Yasmini's own—a
blend of scents, like a chord of music, in which musk
did not predominate.

He took three strides and touched the curtains, discovering now for the first time that there were two
of them, divided down the middle. They were about
eight feet high, and each three feet wide, of leather,
and though they looked old as the "Hills" themselves
the leather was supple as good cloth. They had once
been decorated with figures in gold leaf, but only a
little patch of yellow here and there remained to him
at faded glories.

He decided to remember his manners again, and at
least to make opportunity for an invitation.

"Kurram Khan hai!" he announced, forgetting the
echo. But the echo was the only answer. It cackled
at him, cracking back and forth down the cavern to
die with a groan in illimitable darkness.

"Kurram-urram-urram-urram-urram-ahn-hai! Ur-
ram-urram-urram-urram-ahn-hai! Urram-urram-ur-
ram—ah-hh-ough-ah!"

There was no sound beyond the curtains. No answer. Only he thought the strange scent grew stronger.
He decided to go forward. With his heart in his
mouth he parted the curtains with both hands, startled
by the sharp jangle of metal rings on a rod.

So he stood, with arms outstretched, staring—staring—staring—with eyes skilled swiftly to take in details, but with a brain that tried to explain—formed
a hundred wild suggestions—and then reeled. He was
face to face with the unexplainable—the riddle of
Khinjan Caves.

Grand was thy goal!   Thy vision new!
          Ave, Cæsar!
Conquest?   Ends of Earth thy view?
          Ave, Cæsar!
To sow—to reap—to play God's game?
How many Cæsars did that same
Until the great, grim Reaper came!
Who ploughs with death shall garner rue,
And under all skies is nothing new.
          Vale, Cæsar!

CHAPTER XIII

TELLING the story afterward King never made any effort to describe his own sensations. It was surely enough to state what he saw, after a breathless climb among the rat-runs of a mountain with his imagination fired already by what had happened in the Cavern of Earth's Drink.

The leather curtains slipped through his fingers and closed behind him with the clash of rings on a rod. But he was beyond being startled. He was not really sure he was in the world. He knew he was awake, and he knew he was glad he had left his shoes outside. But he was not certain whether it was the twentieth century, or fifty-five B. C., or earlier yet; or whether time had ceased. Very vividly in that minute there flashed before his mind Mark Twain's suggestion of the *Transposition of Epochs*.

The place where he was did not look like a cave, but a palace chamber, for the rock walls had been trimmed square and polished smooth; then they had been painted pure white, except for a wide blue frieze, with a line of gold-leaf drawn underneath it. And on the frieze, done in gold-leaf too, was the Grecian

255

lady of the lamps, always dancing. There were fifty
or sixty figures of her, no two the same.

A dozen lamps were burning, set in niches cut in
the walls at measured intervals. They were exactly
like the two outside, except that their horn chim-
neys were stained yellow instead of red, suffusing
everything in a golden glow.

Opposite him was a curtain, rather like that through
which he had entered. Near to the curtain was a bed,
whose great wooden posts were cracked with age. And
it was at the bed he stared, with eyes that took in
every detail but refused to believe.

In spite of its age it was spread with fine new linen.
Richly embroidered, not very ancient Indian draperies
hung down from it to the floor on either side. On it,
above the linen, a man and a woman lay hand-in-hand;
and the woman was so exactly like Yasmini, even to
her clothing, and her naked feet, that it was not possible for a man to be self-possessed.

They both seemed asleep. It was as if Yasmini,
weary from the dancing, had laid herself to sleep beside her lord. But who was he? And why did he
wear Roman armor? And why was there no guard
to keep intruders out?

It was minutes before he satisfied himself that the
man's breast did not rise and fall under the bronze
armor and that the woman's jeweled gauzy stuff was
still. Imagination played such tricks with him that
in the stillness he imagined he heard breathing.

After he was sure they were both dead, he went
nearer, but it was a minute yet before he knew the
woman was not *she*. At first a wild thought possessed
him that she had killed herself.

The only thing to show who he had been were the

letters S. P. Q. R. on a great plumed helmet, on a little table by the bed. But she was the woman of the lamp-bowls and the frieze. A life-size stone statue in a corner was so like her, and like Yasmini too, that it was difficult to decide which of the two it represented.

She had lived when he did, for her fingers were locked in his. And he had lived two thousand years ago, because his armor was about as old as that, and for proof that he had died in it part of his breast had turned to powder inside the breastplate. The rest of his body was whole and perfectly preserved.

Stern, handsome in a high-beaked Roman way, gray on the temples, firm-lipped, he lay like an emperor in harness. But the pride and resolution on his face were outdone by the serenity of hers. Very surely those two had been lovers.

Something—he could not decide what—about the man's appearance kept him staring for ten minutes, holding his breath unconsciously and letting it out in little silent gasps. It annoyed him that he could not pin down the elusive thing; and when he went on presently to be curious about more tangible things, it was only to be faced with the unexplainable at every turn.

How had the bodies been preserved, for instance? They were perfect, except for that one detail of the man's breast. The air was full of the perfume he had learned to recognize as Yasmini's, but there was no sniff about the bodies of pitch or bitumen, or of any other chemical. Nor was there any sign of violence about them, or means of telling how they died, or when, except for the probable date of the man's armor.

Both of them looked young and healthy—the woman younger than thirty—twenty-five at a guess—and the man perhaps forty, perhaps forty-five.

He bent over them. Every stitch of the man's clothing had decayed in the course of centuries, so that his armor rested on the naked skin, except for a dressed leather kilt about his middle. The leather was as old as the curtains at the entrance, and as well preserved.

But the woman's silken clothing was as new as the bedding; and that was so new that it had been woven in Belfast, Ireland, by machinery and bore the mark of the firm that made it!

Yet, they both died at about the same time, or how could their fingers have been interlaced? And some of the jewelry on the woman's clothes was very ancient as well as priceless.

He looked closer at the fingers for signs of force and suddenly caught his breath. Under the woman's flimsy sleeve was a wrought gold bracelet, smaller than that one he himself had worn in Delhi and up the Khyber— exactly like the little one that Yasmini wore on her wrist in the Cavern of Earth's Drink! He raised the loose sleeve to look more closely at it.

The sleeve overlay the man's forearm, and the movement laid bare another bracelet, on the man's right wrist. Size for size, this was the same as the one that had been stolen from himself.

Memory prompted him. He felt its outer edge with a finger-nail. There was the little nick that he had made in the soft gold when he struck it against the cell bars in the jail at the Mir Khan Palace!

That put another thought in his head. It was less than two hours since Yasmini danced in the arena.

It might well be much less than that since she had
taken off her bracelets. He laid a finger on the dead
man's stone-cold hand and let it rest so for a minute.
Then, running it slowly up the wrist, he touched the
gold. It was warm. He repeated the test on the woman's wrist. Hers was warm, too. Both bracelets had
been worn by a living being within an hour—

"Probably within minutes!"

He muttered and frowned in thought, and then suddenly jumped backward. The leather curtain near
the bed had moved on its bronze rod.

"Aren't they dears?" a voice said in English behind
him. "Aren't they sweet?"

He had jumped so as to face about, and somebody
laughed at him. Yasmini stood not two arms' lengths
away, lovelier than the dead woman because of the
merry life in her, young and warm, aglow, but looking
like the dead woman and the woman of the frieze—the
woman of the lamp-bowls—the statue—come to life,
speaking to him in English more sweetly than if it had
been her mother tongue. The English abuse their
language. Yasmini caressed it and made it do its work
twice over.

Being dressed as a native, he salaamed low. Knowing him for what he was, she gave him the senna-
stained tips of her warm fingers to kiss, and he thought
she trembled when he touched them. But a second
later she had snatched them away and was treating
him to raillery.

"Man of pills and blisters!" she said, "tell me how
those bodies are preserved! Spill knowledge from
that learned skull of thine!"

He did not answer. He never shone in conversation
at any time, having made as many friends as enemies

by saying nothing until the spirit moves him. But she did not know that yet.

"If I knew for certain why those two did not turn to worms," she went on, "almost I would choose to die now, while I am beautiful! Think of the fogy museum men! (She called them by a far less edifying name, really, for the East is frank in that way, especially in its use of other tongues.) "What would they say, think you, King sahib, if they found us two dead beside those two? Would not that be a mystery? Don't you love mysteries? Speak, man, speak! Has Khinjan struck you dumb?"

But he did not speak. He was staring at her arm, where two whitish marks on the skin betrayed that bracelets had been.

"Oh, those! They are theirs. I would not rob the dead, or the gods would turn on me. I robbed you, instead, while you slept. Fie, King sahib, while you slept!"

But her steel did not strike on flint. It was her eyes that flashed. He would have done better to have seemed ashamed, for then he might have fooled her, at least for a while. But having judged himself, he did not care a fig for her judgment of him. She realized that instantly and having found a tool that would not work, discarded it for a better one. She grew confidential.

"I borrow them," she explained, "but I put them back. I take them for so many days, and when the day comes—the gods like us to be exact! Once there was an Englishman to whom I lent the larger one, and he refused to return it. He wanted it to wear, to bring him luck. Collins, of the Gurkhas. A cobra bit him."

King's eyes changed, for Collins of the Gurkhas had

died in his two arms, saying never a word. He had
always wondered why the native who ran in to kill the
cobra had run away again and left Collins lying there
after seeming to shake hands with him. Yasmini,
watching his eyes and reading his memory, missed
nothing.

"You saw?" she said excitedly. "You remember?
Then you understand! You yourself were near death
when I took the bracelet last night. The time was up.
I would have stabbed you if you had tried to prevent
me!"

Now he spoke at last and gave her a first glimpse of
an angle of his mind she had not suspected.

"Princess," he said. He used the word with the
deference some men can combine with effrontery, so
that very tenderness has barbs. "You might have had
that thing back if you had sent a messenger for it at
any time. A word by a servant would have been
enough."

"You could never have reached Khinjan then!" she
retorted. Her eyes flashed again, but his did not
waver.

"Princess," he said, "why speak of what you don't
know?"

He thought she would strike like a snake, but she
smiled at him instead. And when Yasmini has smiled
on a man he has never been just the same man afterward. He knows more, for one thing. He has had a
lesson in one of the finer arts.

"I will speak of what I do know," she said. "No,
there is no need. Look! Look!"

She pointed at the bed—at the man on the bed—
fingers locked in those of a woman who looked so
like herself.

"You see—yet you do not see! Men are blind!
Men look into a mirror, and see only whiskers they
forgot to shave the day before. Women look once and
then remember! Look again!"

He looked, knowing well there was something to be
understood, that stared him in the face. But for the
life of him he could not determine question or answer.

"What is in your bosom?" she asked him.

He put his hand to his shirt.

"Draw it out!" she said, as a teacher drills a child.

He drew out the gold-hilted knife with the bronze
blade, with which a man had meant to murder him.
He let it lie on the palm of his hand and looked from
it to her and back again. The hilt might have been
a portrait of her modeled from the life.

"Here is another like it," she said, stepping to the
bedside. She drew back the woman's dress at the
bosom and showed a knife exactly like that in King's
hand. "One lay on her bosom and one on his when
I found them!" she said. "Now, think again!"

He did think, of thirty thousand possibilities, and
of one impossible idea that stood up prominent among
them all and insisted on seeming the only likely one.

"I saw the knife in your bosom last night," she
said, "and laughed so that I nearly wakened you.
Man! Are you stupid? Will that ready wit of yours
not work? Have I bewildered you? Is it my perfume? My eyes? My jewels? What is it? Think,
man! Think!"

But if she wanted to make him guess aloud for
her amusement she was wasting time. Had he known
the answer he would have held his tongue. As he
did not know it, he had all the more reason to wait
—indefinitely, if need be. But interminable waiting

was no part of her plan. Words were welling out of her.

"I gave a fool that knife to use, because he was afraid. It gave him courage. When he failed I knew it by telegram, and I sent another fool before the wires were cold, to kill him in the police-station cell for having failed. One fool has been stabbed and the English will hang the other. Then I sent twenty men to turn India inside out and find the knife again, for like the bracelets it has its place. And that is why I laughed. They are hunting. They will hunt until I call them off!"

"Why didn't you take it with the bracelet?" King asked her, holding it out. "Take it now. I don't want it."

She accepted it and laid it on the man's bronze armor. Then, however, she resumed it and played with it.

"Look again!" she said. "Think and look again!"

He looked, and he knew now. But he still preferred that she should tell him, and his lips shut tight.

"Why, having ordered your death, did I countermand the order when your life had been attempted once? Why, as soon as Rewa Gunga had seen you, did I order you to be aided in every way?"

Still he did not answer, although the solution to that riddle, too, was beginning to dawn on his consciousness. He suspected she would be annoyed if he deprived her of the fun of telling him, so that by being silent he played both her game and his own.

"Why did I order your death in the first place?"

The answer to that was obvious, but she answered it for him.

"Because, since the sirkar insisted that one man must

come with me to Khinjan, I preferred a fool, whc
could be lost on the way. I knew your reputation. I
never heard any man call you a fool."

She laughed. He nodded. She was obviously telling truth.

"Can you guess why I changed my mind about you
—wise man?"

She looked from him to the man on the bed and
back to him again. Having solved her riddle, King
had leisure to be interested in her eyes, and watched
them analytically, like a jeweler appraising diamonds.
They were strangely reminiscent, but much more
changeable and colorful than any he had ever seen.
They had the baffling trick of changing while he
watched them.

"Having sent a man to kill you, why did I cease
to want you killed? Instead of losing you on the way
to Khinjan, why did I run risks to protect you after
you reached here? Why did I save your life in the
Cavern of Earth's Drink to-night? You do not know
yet? Then I will tell you something else you do not
know. I was in Delhi when you were! I watched
and listened while you and Rewa Gunga talked in my
house! I was in Rewa Gunga's carriage on the train
that he took and you did not! I have learned at first
hand that you are not a fool. But that was not
enough! You had to be three things—clever and brave
and one other. The one other you are! Brave you
have proved yourself to be! Clever you must be, to
trick your way into Khinjan Caves, even with Ismail at your elbow! That is why I saved your life
—because you are those two things and—and—one
other!"

She snatched a mirror from a little ivory table—a

modern mirror—bad glass, bad art, bad workmanship, but silver warranted.

"Look in it and then at him!" she ordered.

But he did not need to look. The man on the bed was not so much like himself as the woman was like her, but the resemblance seemed to grow under his eyes, as such things do. It was helped out by the stain his brother had applied to his face in the Khyber. King was the taller and the younger by several years, but the noses were the same, and the wrinkled foreheads; both men had the same firm mouth; both looked like Romans.

"How did you get that scar?"

She came closer and took his hand, holding it in both hers, and he felt the same thrill Samson knew. He steeled himself as Samson did not.

"A Mahsudi got me with a martini at long range in the blockade of 1902," he said dryly.

"Look! Did he get his from a spear or from an arrow?"

· Almost in the same spot, also on the dead man's left hand, was a scar so nearly like it that it needed a third and a fourth glance to tell the difference. They both bent over the bed to see it, and she laid a hand on his shoulder. Touch and scent and confidence, all three were bewitching; all three were calculated, too! He could have killed her, and she knew he could have killed her, just as she knew he would not. Yet what right had she to know it!

"Athelstan!"

She pronounced his given name as if she loved the word, standing straight again and looking into his eyes. There were high lights in hers that outgleamed the diamonds on her dress.

"Your gods and mine have done this, Athelstan. When the gods combine they lay plans well indeed!"

"I only know one God," he answered simply, as a man speaks of the deep things in his heart.

"I know of many! They love me! They shall love you, too! Many are better than one! You shall learn to know my gods, for we are to be partners, you and I!"

She laughed at him, looking like a goddess herself, but he frowned. And the more he frowned the better she seemed to like him.

"Partners in what, Princess?"

"Thou—Ismail dubbed thee Ready o' wit!—answer thine own question!"

She took his hand again, her eyes burning with excitement and mysticism and ambition like a fever. She seemed to take more than physical possession of him.

"What brought *them* here? Tell me that!" she demanded, pointing to the bed. "You think he brought her? I tell you she was the spur that drove him! Is it a wonder that men called her the 'Heart of the Hills'? I found them ten years ago and clothed her and put new linen on their bed, for the old was all rags and dust. There have always been hundreds— and sometimes thousands—who knew the secret of Khinjan Caves, but this has been a secret within a secret. Some one, who knew the secret before I, sawed those bracelets through and fitted hinges and clasps. The men you saw in the Cavern of Earth's Drink have no doubt I am the 'Heart of the Hills' come to life! They shall know thee as Him within a little while!"

She held his hand a little tighter and pressed closer

to him, laughing softly. He stood as if made of iron,
and that only made her laugh the more.

"Tales of the 'Heart of the Hills' have puzzled the
Raj, haven't they, these many years? They sent me
to find the source of them. Me! They chose well!
There are not many like me! I have found this one
dead woman who was like me. And in ten years, until you came, I have found no man like Him!"

She tried to look into his eyes, but he frowned
straight in front of him. His native costume and
Rangar turban did not make him seem any less a man.
His jowl, that was beginning to need shaving, was
as grim and as satisfying as the dead Roman's. She
stroked his left hand with soft fingers.

"I used to think I knew how to dance!" she laughed.
"For ten years I have taken those pictures of her for
my model and have striven to learn what she knew.
I have surpassed her! I used to think I knew how
to amuse myself with men's dreams—until I found
this! Then I dreamed on my own account! My
dream was true, my warrior! You have come! Our
hour has come!"

She tugged at his hand. He was hers, soul and
harness, if outward signs could prove it.

"Come!" she said. "Is this my hospitality? You
are weary and hungry. Come!"

She led him by the hand, for it would have needed
brute force to pry her fingers loose. She drew aside
the leather curtain that hung on a bronze rod near the
bed, led him through it, and let it clash to again behind them.

Now they were in the dark together, and it was not
comprehended in her scheme of things to let circumstance lie fallow. She pressed his hand, and sighed,

and then hurried, whispering tender words he could scarcely catch. When they burst together through a curtain at the other end of a passage in the rock, his skin was red under the tan and for the first time her eyes refused to meet his.

"Why did they choose that cave to sleep in?" she asked him. "Is not this a better one? Who laid them there?"

He stared about. They were in a great room far more splendid than the first. There was a fountain in the center splashing in the midst of flowers. They were cut flowers. The "Hills" must have been scoured for them within a day.

There were great cushioned couches all about and two thrones made of ivory and gold. Between two couches was a table, laden with golden plates and a golden jug, on pure white linen. There were two goblets of beaten gold and knives with golden handles and bronze blades. The whole room seemed to be drenched in the scent Yasmini favored, and there was the same frieze running round all four walls, with the woman depicted on it dancing.

"Come, we shall eat!" she said, leading him by the hand to a couch. She took the one facing him, and they lay like two Romans of the Empire with the table in between.

She struck a golden gong then, and a native woman came in who stared at King as if she had seen him before and did not like him. Except for the jewels, she was dressed exactly like Yasmini, which is to say that her gauzy stuff was all but transparent. But Yasmini uses raiment as she does her eyes; it is part of her, and of her art. The maid, who would have shone among many women, looked stiff and dull by contrast.

"I trust no Hill woman—they are cattle with human tongues," Yasmini said, frowning at the maid. "Even in Delhi there was only this one woman whom I dared bring here with me. *You* brought my men-servants! They are loyal, but as clumsy as the bears in their cold 'Hills'! Rewa Gunga brought me this one disguised as a man—you remember?"

She nodded to the servant, who clapped her hands. At once came a stream of Hillmen, robed in white, who carried sherbet in bottles cooled in snow and dishes fragrant with hot food. He recognized his own prisoners from the Mir Khan Palace jail, and nodded to them as they set the things down under the maid's direction. When they had done the woman chased them out and came and stood behind Yasmini with a fan, for though it was not too hot, she liked to have her golden hair blown into movement.

"My cook was a viceroy's," she said, beginning to eat. "He killed an officer who said the curry had pig's fat in it. That made him free of Khinjan but of not many other places! I have promised him a swim in Earth's Drink when he ever forgets his art!"

King ate, because a man can not talk and eat at once. It was true that he was hungry, that hunger is a piquant sauce, and that artist was an adjective too mild to apply to the cook. But the other reason was his chief one. Yasmini ate daintily, as if only to keep him company.

"You would rather have wine?" she asked suddenly. "All sahibs drink wine. Bring wine!" she ordered.

But King shook his head, and she looked pleased.

He had thought she would be disappointed. When he had finished eating she drove the maid away with a sharp word; and when King jumped to his feet she led him toward the gold-and-ivory thrones, taking her seat on one of them and bidding him adjust the footstool.

"Would I might offer you the other!" she said, merrily enough, "but you must sit at my feet until our hearts are one!"

It was clear that she took no delight in easy victories, for she laughed aloud at the quizzical expression on his face. He guessed that if she could have conquered him at the first attempt a day would have found her weary of him; there was deliberate wisdom in his plan for the present to seem to let her win by little inches at a time. He reasoned that so she would tell him more than if he defied her outright.

He brought an ivory footstool and set it about a yard away from her waxen toes. And she, watching him with burning eyes, wound tresses of her hair around the golden dagger handle, making her jewels glitter with each movement.

"You pleased me by refusing wine," she said. "You please me—oh, you please me! Christians drink wine and eat beef and pig-meat. Ugh! Hindu and Muslim both despise them, having each a little understanding of his own. The gods of India, who are the only real gods, what do they think of it all! They have been good to the English, but they have had no thanks. They will stand aside now and watch a greater jihad than the world has ever seen! And the Hindu, who holds the cow sacred, will not support Christians who hold nothing sacred, against Muhammadans who loathe

the pig! Christianity has failed! The English must go down with it—just as Rome went down when she dabbled in Christianity. Oh, I know all about Rome!"

"And the gods of India?" he asked, to keep her to the point now that she seemed well started.

He was there to learn, not to teach.

"I know them, too! I know them as nobody else does! They are neither Hindu, nor Muhammadan, but are older by a thousand ages than either foolishness! I love them, and they love me—as you shall love me, too! If they did not love both of us, we would not both be here! We must obey them!"

None of the East's amazing ways of courtship are ever tedious. Love springs into being on an instant and lives a thousand years inside an hour. She left no doubt as to her meaning. She and King were to love, as the East knows love, and then the world might have just what they two did not care to take from it.

His only possible course as yet was the defensive, and there is no defense like silence. He was still.

"The sirkar," she went on, "the silly sirkar fears that *perhaps* Turkey may enter the war. *Perhaps* a jihad may be proclaimed. So much for fear! I know! I have known for a very long time! And I have not let fear trouble me at all!"

Her eyes were on his steadily, and she read no fear in his, either, for none was there. In hers he saw ambition—triumph already—excitement—the gambler's love of all the hugest risks. Behind them burned genius and the devilry that would stop at nothing. As the general had told him in Peshawur, she would dare open Hell's gate and ride the devil down the Khyber for the fun of it.

"*Au diable, diable et demie!*" the French say; and

like most French proverbs it is a wise one. But
whence the devil and a half should come to thwart
her was not obvious.

"I must be a devil and a half," he told himself, and
very nearly laughed aloud at the idea. She mistook the
sudden humor in his eyes for admiration of herself,
being used to that from men.

"Listen, while I tell you all from the beginning!
The sirkar sent me to discover what may be this
'Heart of the Hills' men talk about. I found these
caves—and this! I told the sirkar a little about the
Caves, and nothing at all about the Sleepers. But
even at that they only believed the third of what I
said. And I—back in Delhi I bought books—borrowed
books—sent to Europe for more books—and hired
babu Sita Ram to read them to me, until his tongue
grew dry and swollen and he used to fall asleep in a
corner. I know *all* about Rome! Days I spent—
weeks!—months!—listening to the history of their
great Cæsar, and their little Cæsars—of their conquests and their games! It was good, and I understood it all! Rome should have been true to the old
gods, and they would have been true to her! She fell
when she fooled with Christianity!"

She was speaking dreamily now, with her chin resting on a hand and an elbow on the ivory arm of the
throne, remembering as she told her story. And it
meant so much to her, she was so in earnest, that her
voice conjured up pictures for King to see.

"When I had read enough I came back here to think.
I knew enough now to be sure that the Sleeper is a
Roman, and the 'Heart of the Hills' a Grecian maid.
She is like me. That is why I know she drove him
to make an empire, choosing for a beginning these

'Hills' where Rome had never penetrated. He found her in Greece. He plunged through Persia to build a throne for her! I have seen it all in dreams, and again in the crystal! And because I was all alone, I saw that I would need all the skill I could learn, and much patience. So I began to learn to dance as she danced, using those pictures of her as a model. I have surpassed her! I can dance better than she ever did!

"Between times I would go to Delhi and dance there a little, and a little in other places—once indeed before a viceroy, and once for the king of England—and all men—the king, too!—told me that none in the world can dance as I can! And all the while I kept looking for the man—the man who should be like the Sleeper, even as I am like her whom he loved!

"Many a man—many and many a man I have tried and found wanting! For I was impatient in spite of resolutions. I burned to find him at once, and begin! But you are the first of all the men I have tested who answered all the tests! Languages—he must speak the native tongues. Brave he must be—and clever—resembling the Sleeper in appearance. I began to think long ago that I must forego that last test, for there was none like the Sleeper until you came. And when this world war broke—for it is a world war, a world war I tell you!—I thought at last that I must manage all alone. And then you came!

"But there were many I tried—many—especially after I abandoned the thought that the man must resemble the Sleeper. There was a Prince of Germany who came to India on a hunting trip. You remember?"

King pricked his ears and allowed himself to grin, for in common with many hundred other men who had been lieutenants at the time, he would once have given an ear and an eye to know the truth of that affair. The grin transformed his whole appearance, until Yasmini beamed on him,

"I'm listening, Princess!" he reminded her.

"Well—he came—the Prince of Germany—the borrower!"

"Borrower of what, Princess?"

"Of wit! Of brains! Of platitudes! Of reputation! There came a crowd with him of such clumsy plunderers, asking such rude questions, that even the sirkar could not shut its ears and eyes!

"I did not know all about sahibs in those days. I thought that, although this man is what he is, yet he is a prince, and perhaps I can fire him with my genius. I could have taught him the native tongues. I thought he had ambition, but I learned that he is only greedy. You see, I was foolish, not knowing yet that in good time if I am patient my man will come to me! But I learned all about Germans—all!

"I offered him India first, then Asia, then the world —even as I now offer them to you. The sirkar sent him to see me dance, and he stayed to hear me talk. When I saw at last that he has the head and heart of a hyena I told him lies. But he, being drunk, told me truths that I have remembered.

"Later he sent two of his officers to ask me questions, and they were little better than he, although a little better mannered. I told them lies, too, and they told me lies, but they told me much that was true.

"Then the prince came again, a last time. And I was weary of him. The sirkar was very weary of him, too. He offered me money to go to Germany and dance for the kaiser in Berlin. He said I will be shown there much that will be to my advantage. I refused. He made me other offers. So I spat in his face and threw food at him.

"He complained to the sirkar against me, sending one of his high officers to demand that I be whipped. So I told the sirkar some—not much, indeed, but enough—of the things he and his officers had told me. And the sirkar said at once that there was both cholera and bubonic plague, and he must go home!

"I have heard—three men told me—that he said he will never rest until I have been whipped! But I have heard that his officers laughed behind his back. And ever since that time there have always been Germans in communication with me. I have had more money from Berlin than would bribe the viceroy's council, and I have not once been in the dark about Germany's plans—although they have always thought I am in the dark.

"I went on looking for my man—studying all, Germans, English, Turks, French—and there was a Frenchman whom I nearly chose—and an American, a man who used the strangest words, who laughed at me. I studied Hindu, Muslim, Christian, every good-looking fighting man who came my way, knowing well that all creeds are one when the gods have named their choice.

"There came that old Bull-with-a-beard, Muhammad Anim, and for a time I thought he is the man, for he is a man whatever else he is. But I tired of him. I called him Bull-with-a-beard, and the 'Hills' took it up and mocked him, until the new name stuck. He still thinks he is the man, having more strength to hope and more will to will wrongly than any man I ever met, except a German. I have even been sur

sometimes that Muhammad Anim is a German; yet
now I am not sure.

"From all the men I met and watched l have learned
all they knew! And I have never neglected to tell
the sirkar sufficient of what men have told me, to keep
the sirkar pleased with me!

"Nor have I ever played Germany's game—no, no!
I have talked with a prince of Germany, and I understand too well! Who sups with a boar may get
good roots to eat, but must endure pigs' feet in the
trough! Pigs' hides make good saddles; I have used
the Germans, as they *think* they have used me! I
have used them ruthlessly.

"Knowing all I knew, and being ready except that
I had not found my man yet, I dallied in India on
the eve of war, watching a certain Sikh to discover
whether he is the man or not. But he lacked imagination, and I was caught in Delhi when war broke and
the English closed the Khyber Pass. Yet I had to
come up the Khyber, to reach Khinjan.

"So it was fortunate that I knew of a German plot
that I could spoil at the last minute. I fooled the
Germans by letting the Sikh whom I had watched
discover it. The Germans still believe me their accomplice. And the sirkar was so pleased that I think if
I had asked for an English peerage they would have
answered me soberly. A million dynamite bombs was
a big haul for the sirkar! My offer to go to Khinjan
and keep the 'Hills' quiet was accepted that same day!

"But what are a million dynamite bombs! Dynamite bombs have been coming into Khinjan month by
month these three years! Bombs and rifles and cartridges! Muhammad Anim's men, whom he trusts because he must, hid it all in a cave I showed them,

that they think, and he thinks, has only one entrance
to it. Muhammad Anim sealed it, and he has the key.
But I have the ammunition!

"There was another way out of that cave, although
there is none now, for I have blocked it. My men,
whom I trust because I know them, carried everything
out by the back way, and I have it all. I will show it
to you presently.

"I know all Muhammad Anim's plans. Bull-with-
a-beard believes himself a statesman, yet he told me
all he knows! He has told me how Germany plans
to draw Turkey in and to force Turkey to proclaim a
jihad. As if I did not know it first, almost before the
Germans knew it! Fools! The jihad will recoil on
them! It will be like a cobra, striking whoever stirs
it! A typhoon, smiting right and left! Christianity is
doomed, and the Germans call themselves Christians!
Fools! Rome called herself Christian—and where is
Rome?

"But we, my warrior, when Muhammad Anim gets
the word from Germany and gives the sign, and the
'Hills' are afire, and the whole East roars in the flame
of the jihad—we will put ourselves at the head of that
jihad, and the East and the world is ours!"

King smiled at her.

"The East isn't very well armed," he objected.
"Mere numbers—"

"Numbers?" She laughed at him. "The West has
the West by the throat! It is tearing itself! They will
drag in America! There will be no armed nation with
its hands free—and while those wolves fight, other
wolves shall come and steal the meat! The old gods,
who built these caverns in the 'Hills,' are laughing!
They are getting ready! Thou and I—"

As she coupled him and herself together in one plan she read the changed expression of his face—the very quickly passing cloud that even the best-trained man can not control.

"I know!" she asserted, sitting upright and coming out of her dream to face facts as their master. She looked more lovely now than ever, although twice as dangerous. "You are thinking of your brother—of his head! That I am a murderess who can never be your friend! Is that not so?"

He did not answer, but his eyes may have betrayed something, for she looked as if he had struck her. Leaning forward, she held the gold-hilted dagger out to him, hilt first.

"Take it and stab me!" she ordered. "Stab—if you blame me for your brother's death! I should have known him for your brother if I had come on him in the dark!—His head might have come from your shoulders!—You were like a man holding up his own head, as I have seen in pictures in a book! I would never have killed him!"

Her golden hair fell all about his shoulders, and its scent was not intended to be sobering. She ran warm fingers through his hair while she held the knife toward him with the other hand.

"Take it and stab!"

"No," he said.

"No!" she laughed. "No! You are my warrior—my man—my well-beloved! You have come to me alone out of all the world! You would no more stab me than the gods would forget me!"

Their eyes were on each other's—deep looking into deep.

"Strength!" she said, flinging him away and leaning

back to look at him, almost as a fed cat stretches in
the sunlight. "Courage! Simplicity! Directness!
Strength I have, too, and courage never failed me,
but my mind is a river winding in and out, gathering
as it goes. I have no directness—no simplicity! You
go straight from point to point, my sending from the
gods! I have needed you! Oh, I have needed you
so much, these many years! And now that you have
come you want to hate me because you think I killed
your brother! Listen—I will tell you all I know about
your brother."

Without a scrap of proof of any kind he knew she
was telling truth unadorned—or at least the truth as
she saw it. Eye to eye, there are times when no proof
is needed.

"Without my leave, Muhammad Anim sent five hundred men on a foray toward the Khyber. Bull-with-
a-beard needed an Englishman's head, for proof for
a spy of his who could not enter Khinjan Caves.
They trapped your brother outside Ali Masjid with
fifty of his men. They took his head after a long
fight, leaving more than a hundred of their own in
payment.

"Bull-with-a-beard was pleased. But he was careless, and I sent my men to steal the head from his
men. I needed evidence for you. And I swear to you
—I swear to you by my gods who have brought us
two together—that I first knew it was your brother's
head when you held it up in the Cavern of Earth's
Drink! Then I knew it could not be anybody else's
head!"

"Why bid me throw it to them, then?" he asked her,
and he was aware of her scorn before the words had
left his lips.

She leaned back again and looked at him through lowered eyes, as if she must study him all anew. She seemed to find it hard to believe that he really thought so in the commonplace.

"What is a head to me, or to you—a head with no life in it—carrion!—compared to what shall be? Would you have known it was his head if you had thrown it to them when I ordered you?"

He understood. Some of her blood was Russian. some Indian.

"A friend is a friend, but a brother is a rival," says the East, out of world-old experience, and in some ways Russia is more eastern than the East itself.

"Muhammad Anim shall answer to you for your brother's head!" she said with a little nod, as if she were making concessions to a child. "At present we need him. Let him preach his jihad, and loose it at the right time. After that he will be in the way! You shall name his death—Earth's Drink—slow torture —fire! Will that content you?"

"No," he said, with a dry laugh.

"What more can you ask?"

"Less! My brother died at the head of his men. He couldn't ask more. Let Bull-with-a-beard alone."

She set both elbows on her knees and laid her chin on both hands to stare at him again. He began to remember long-forgotten schoolboy lore about chemical reagents, that dissolve materials into their component parts, such was the magic of her eyes. There were no eyes like hers that he had ever seen, although Rewa Gunga's had been something like them. Only Rewa Gunga's had not changed so. Thought of the Rangar no sooner crossed his mind than she was speaking of him.

"Rewa Gunga met you in the dark, beyond those outer curtains, did he not?" she asked.

He nodded.

"Did he tell you that if you pass the curtains you shall be told *all* I know?"

He nodded again, and she laughed.

"It would take time to tell you *all* I know! First, I think I will show you things. Afterward you shall ask me questions, and I will answer them."

She stood up, and of course he stood up, too. So, she on the footstool of the throne, her eyes and his were on a level. She laid hands on his shoulders and looked into his eyes until he could see his own twin portraits in hers that were glowing sunset pools. Heart of the Hills? The Heart of all the East seemed to burn in her, rebellious!

"Are you believing me?" she asked him.

He nodded, for no man could have helped believing her. As she knew the truth, she was telling it to him, as surely as she was doing her skilful best to mesmerize him. But the Secret Service is made up of men trained against that.

"Come!" she said, and stepping down she took his arm.

She led him past the thrones to other leather curtains in a wall, and through them into long hewn passages from cavern into cavern, until even the Rock of Gibraltar seemed like a doll's house in comparison.

In one cave there were piles of javelins that had been stacked there by the Sleeper and his men. In another were sheaves of arrows; and in one were spears in racks against a wall. There were empty stables, with rings made fast into the rock where a hundred horses could have stood in line.

She showed him a cave containing great forges,
where the bronze had been worked, with charcoal still
piled up against the wall at one end. There were copper and tin ingots in there of a shape he had never
seen.

"I know where *they* came from," she told him. "I
have made it my business to know *all* the 'Hills.' I
know things the Hillmen's great-great-great-grand-
fathers forgot! I know old workings that would make
a modern nation rich! We shall have money when we
need it, never fear! We shall conquer India while the
English backs are turned and the best troops are oversea. We will bring a hundred thousand slaves back
here to work our mines! With what they dig from the
mines, copper and gold and tin, we will make ready to
buy the English off when they are free to turn this way
again. The English will do anything for money! They
will be in debt when this war is over, and their price
will be less then than now!"

She laughed merrily at him because his face showed
that he did not appreciate that stricture. Then she
called him her Warrior and her Well-beloved and took
him down a long passage, holding his hand all the way,
to show him slots cut in the floor for the use of archers.

"You entered Khinjan Caves by a tunnel under this
floor, Well-beloved. There is no other entrance!"

By this time Well-beloved was her name for him,
although there was no air of finality about it. It was
as if she paved the way for use of Athelstan and that
was a sacred name. It was amazing how she conveyed
that impression without using words.

"The Sleeper cut these slots for his archers. Then
he had another thought and set these cauldrons in

place, to boil oil to pour down. Could any army force a way through by the route by which you entered?"

"No," he said, marveling at the ton-weight copper cauldrons, one to each hole.

"Even without rifles for the defense?"

"No," he said.

"And I have more than a thousand Mauser rifles here, and more than a million rounds of ammunition!"

"How did you get them?"

"I shall tell you that later. Come and see some other things. See and believe!"

She showed him a cave in which boxes were stacked in high square piles.

"Dynamite bombs!" she boasted. "How many boxes? I forget! Too many to count! Women brought them all the way from the sea, for even Muhammad Anim could not make Afridi riflemen carry loads. I have wondered what Bull-with-a-beard will say when he misses his precious dynamite!"

"You've enough in there to blow the mountain up!" King advised her. "If somebody fired a pistol in here, the least would be the collapse of this floor into the tunnel below with a hundred thousand tons of rock on top of it. There is no other way out?"

"Earth's Drink!" she said, and he made a grimace that set her to laughing.

But she looked at him darkly after that and he got the impression that the thought was not new to her, and that she did not thank him for the advice. He began to wonder whether there was anything she had not thought of—any loophole she had left him for escape —any issue she had not foreseen.

"Kill her!" a secret voice urged him. But that was

the voice of the "Hills," that are violent first and
regretful afterward. He did not listen to it. And
then the wisdom of the West came to him, as epito-
mized by Cocker along the lines laid down by Solomon.

"It isn't possible to make a puzzle that has no solution to it. The fact that it's a puzzle is the proof that
there's a key! Go ahead!"

It was the "Go ahead!" that Solomon omitted, and
that makes Cocker such cheerful reading. King ceased
conjecturing and gave full attention to his guide.

She showed him where eleven hundred Mauser rifles
stood in racks in another cave, with boxes of ammunition piled beside them—each rifle and cartridge worth
its weight in silver coin—a very rajah's ransom!

"The Germans are generous in some things—only in
some things—very mean in others!" she told him.
"They sent no medical stores, and no blankets!"

Past caves where provisions of every imaginable
kind were stored, sufficient for an army, she led him
to where her guards slept together with the thirty
special men whom King had brought with him up the
Khyber.

"I have five hundred others whom I dare trust to
come in here," she said, "but they shall stay outside
until I want them. A mystery is a good thing! It is
good for them all to wonder what I keep in here! It
is good to keep this sanctuary; it makes for power!"

Pressing very close to him, she guided him down another dark tunnel until he and she stood together in
the jaws of the round hole above the river, looking
down into the cavern of Earth's Drink.

Nobody looked up at them. The thousands were too
busy working up a frenzy for the great jihad that was
to come.

Stacks of wood had been piled up, six-man high in the middle, and then fired. The heat came upward like a furnace blast, and the smoke was a great red cloud among the stalactites. Round and round that holocaust the thousands did their sword-dance, yelling as the devils yelled at Khinjan's birth. They needed no wine to craze them. They were drunk with fanaticism, frenzy, lust!

"The women brought that wood from fifty miles away!" Yasmini shouted in his ear; for the din, mingling with the river's voice, made a volcano chord. "It is a week's supply of wood! But so they are—so they will be! They will lay waste India! They will butcher and plunder and burn! It will be what they leave of India that we shall build anew and govern, for India herself will rise to help them lay her own cities waste! It is always so! Conquests always are so! Come!"

She tugged at him and led him back along the tunnel and through other tunnels to the throne room, where she made him sit at her feet again.

The food had been cleared away in their absence. Instead, on the ebony table there were pens and ink and paper.

She leaned back on her throne, with bare feet pressed tight against the footstool, staring, staring at the table and the pens, and then at King, as if she would compose an ultimatum to the world and send King to deliver it.

"I said I will tell you," she said slowly. "Listen!"

Nothing new!   Nothing new!
Nowhere to hide when a reckoning's due,
But right earns right, and wrong gets rue,
With nothing deducted or given in lieu;
And neither the War God, I, nor you
Ever could make one lie come true!
          Vale, Cæsar!

CHAPTER XIV

AS YASMINI herself had admitted, she headed from point to point after a manner of her own.

"You know where is Dar es Salaam?" she asked.

"East Africa," said King.

"How far is that from here?"

"Two or three thousand miles."

"And English war-ships watch the Persian Gulf and all the seas from India to Aden?"

King nodded.

"Have the English any ships that dive under water?"

He nodded again.

"In these waters?"

"I think not. I'm not sure, but I think not."

"The grenades you have seen, and the rifles and cartridges were sent by the Germans to Dar es Salaam, to suppress a rising of African natives. Does it begin to grow clear to you, my friend?"

He smiled as well as nodded this time.

"Muhammad Anim used to wait with a hundred women at a certain place on the seashore. What he found on the beach there he made the women carry on their heads to Khinjan. And by the time he had hidden what he found and returned from Khinjan to the beach, there were more things to find and bring. So they worked, he and the Germans, for I know not how long—with the English watching the seas as on land lean wolves comb the valleys.

"Did you ever hear of the big whale in the Gulf?"

"No," said King. That was natural. There are as a rule about as many whales as salmon in the Persian Gulf.

"A German who came to me in Delhi—he who first showed me pictures of an underwater ship—said that at that time the officers and crew of one such ship were getting great practise. Do you suppose their practise made whales take refuge in the Gulf?"

"How should I know, Princess?"

"Because I heard a story later, of an English cruiser on its way up the Gulf, that collided with a whale. The shock of hitting it bent many steel plates, and the cruiser had to put back for repair. It must have been a very big whale, for there was much oil on the sea for a long time afterward. So I heard.

"And no more dynamite came—nor rifles—nor cartridges, although the Germans had promised more. And orders for Muhammad Anim that had been said to come by sea came now by way of Bagdad, carried by pilgrims returning from the holy places. I know that because I intercepted a letter and threw its bearer into Earth's Drink to save Muhammad Anim the trouble of asking questions."

"What were the terms of the German bargain?" King asked her. "What stipulations did they make?"

"With the tribes? None! They were too wise. A jihad was decided on in Germany's good time; and when that time should come ten rifles in the 'Hills' and a thousand cartridges would mean not only a hun-

dred dead Englishmen, but ten times that number
busily engaged. Why bargain when there was no
need? A rifle is what it is. The 'Hills' are the
'Hills'!"

"Tell me about your lamp oil, then," he said. "You
burn enough oil in Khinjan Caves to light Bombay!
That does not come by submarine. The sirkar knows
how much of everything goes up the Khyber. I have
seen the printed lists myself—a few hundred cans
of kerosene—a few score gallons of vegetable oil, and
all bound for farther north. There isn't enough oil
pressed among the 'Hills' to keep these caves going for
a day. Where does it all come from?"

She laughed, as a mother laughs at a child's questions, finding delicious enjoyment in instructing him.

"There are three villages, not two days' march from
Khabul, where men have lived for centuries by pressing oil for Khinjan Caves," she said. "The Sleeper
fetched his oil thence. There are the bones of a camel
in a cave I did not show you, and beside the camel are
the leather bags still in which the oil was carried.
Nowadays it comes in second-hand cans and drums.
The Sleeper left gold in here. Those who kept the
Sleeper's secret paid for the oil in gold. No Afghan
troubled why oil was needed, so long as gold paid for
it, until Abdurrahman heard the story. He made a ten-
year-long effort to learn the secret, but he failed.
When he cut off the supply of oil for a time, there was
a rebellion so close to Khabul gates that he thought
better of it. Of gold and Abdurrahman, gold was the
stronger. And I know where the Sleeper dug his gold!"

They sat in silence for a long while after that, she
looking at the table, with its ink and pens and paper,
and he thinking, with hands clasped round one knee;

for it is wiser to think than to talk, even when a woman is near who can read thoughts that are not guarded.

"Most disillusionments come simply," King said at last. "D'you know, Princess, what has kept the sirkar from really believing in Khinjan Caves?"

She shook her head. "The gods!" she said. "The gods can blindfold governments and whole peoples as easily as they can make *us* see!"

"It was the fact that they knew what provisions and what oil and what necessities of life went up the Khyber and came down it. They knew a place such as this was said to be could not be. They knew it! They could prove it!"

Yasmini nodded.

"Let it be a lesson to you, Princess!"

She stared, and her fiery-opal eyes began to change and glow. She began to twist her golden hair round the dagger hilt again. But always her feet were still on the footstool of the throne, as if she knew—knew—knew that she stood on firm foundations. No sirkar ever doubted less than she, and the suggestions in King's little homily did not please her. She looked toward the table again—then again into his eyes.

"Athelstan!" she said. "It sounds like a king's name! What was the Sleeper's name? I have often wondered! I found no name in all the books about Rome that seemed to fit him. None of the names I mouthed could make me dream as the sight of him could. But, Athelstan! That is a name like a king's! It seems to fit him, too! Was there such a name in Rome?"

"No," he said.

"What does it mean?" she asked him.

"Slow of resolution!"

She clapped her hands.

"Another sign!" she laughed. "The gods love me! There always is a sign when I need one! Slow of resolution, art thou? I will speed thy resolution, Well-beloved! You were quick to change from King, of the Khyber Rifle Regiment, to Kurram Khan. Change now into my warrior—my dear lord—my King again!"

She rose, with arms outstretched to him. All her dancer's art, her untamed poetry, her witchery, were expressed in a movement. Her eyes melted as they met his. And since he stood up, too, for manner's sake, they were eye to eye again—almost lip to lip. Her sweet breath was in his nostrils.

In another moment she was in his arms, clinging to him, kissing him. And if any man has felt on his lips the kiss of all the scented glamour of the East, let him tell what King's sensations were. Let Cæsar, who was kissed by Cleopatra, come to life and talk of it!

King's arm is strong, and he did not stand like an idol. His head might swim, but she, too, tasted the delirium of human passion loosed and given for a mad swift minute. If his heart swelled to bursting, so must hers have done.

"I have needed you!" she whispered. "I have been all alone! I have needed you!"

Then her lips sought his again, and neither spoke.

Neither knew how long it was before she began to understand that he, not she, was winning. The human answer to her appeal was full. He gave her all she asked of admiration, kiss for kiss. And then—her arms did not cling so tightly, although his strong right arm was like a stanchion. Because he knew that he, not she, was winning, he picked her up in his arms and kissed her as if she were a child. And then, because he knew he had won, he set her on her feet on the footstool of the throne, and even pitied her.

She felt the pity. As she tossed the hair back over her shoulder her eyes glowed with another meaning—dangerous—like a tiger's glare.

"You pity me? You think because I love you, you can feed my love on a plate to the Indian government? You think my love is a weapon to use against me? Your love for me may wait for a better time? You are not so wise as I thought you, Athelstan!"

But he knew he had won. His heart was singing down inside him as it had not sung since he left India behind. But he stood quite humbly before her, for had he not kissed her?

"You think a kiss is the bond between us? You mistake! You forget! The kiss, my Athelstan, was the fruit, not the seed! The seed came first! If I loosed you—if I set you free—you would never dare go back to India!"

He scarcely heard her. He knew he had won. His heart was like a bird, fluttering wildly. He knew that the next step would be shown him, and for the present he had time and grace to pity her, knowing how he would have felt if she had won. Besides, he had kissed her, and he had not lied. Each kiss had been a tribute of admiration, for was she not splendid—amazing—more to be desired than wine? He stood with bowed head, lest the triumph in his eyes offend her. Yet if any one had asked him how he knew that he had won, he never could have told.

"If you were to go back to India except as its conqueror, they would strip the buttons from your uniform and tear your medals off and shoot you in the back against a wall! My signature is known in India and I am known. What I write will be believed. Rewa Gunga shall take a letter. He shall take two—four—witnesses. He shall see them on their way and shall give them the letter when they reach the Khyber and shall send them into India with it. Have no fear. Bull-with-a-beard shall not intercept them, as I have intercepted his men. When Rewa Gunga shall return and tell me he saw my letter on its way down the Khyber, then we shall talk again about pity—you and I! Come!"

She took his arm, as if her threats had been caresses. Triumph shone from her eyes. She tossed her brave chin and laughed at him, only encouraged to greater daring by his attitude.

"Why don't you kill me?" she asked, and though his answer surprised her, it did not make her angry.

"It would do no good," he said simply.

"Would you kill me if you thought it would do good?"

"Certainly!" he said.

She laughed at that as if it were the greatest joke she had ever heard. It set her in the best humor possible, and by the time they reached the ebony table and she had taken the pen and dipped it in the ink, she was chuckling to herself as if the one good joke had grown into a hundred.

She wrote in Urdu. It is likely that for all her knowledge of the spoken English tongue she was not so swift or ready with the trick of writing it. She had said herself that a babu read English books to her aloud. But she wrote in Urdu with an easy flowing hand, and in two minutes she had thrown sand on the letter and had given it to King to read. It was not like a woman's letter. It did not waste a word.

"Your Captain King has been too much trouble. He has taken money from the Germans. He adopted native dress. He called himself Kurram Khan. He slew his own brother at night in the Khyber Pass. These men will say that he carried the head to Khinjan, and their word is true, for I, Yasmini, saw. He used the head for a passport, to obtain admittance. He proclaims a jihad! He urges invasion of India! He held up his brother's head before five thousand men and boasted of the murder. The next you shall hear of your Captain King of the Khyber Rifles, he will be leading a jihad into India. You would have better trusted me. Yasmini."

He read it and passed it back to her.

"They will not disbelieve me," she said, triumphant as the very devil over a brandered soul all hot. "They will be sure you are mad, and they will believe the witnesses!"

He bowed. She sealed the letter and addressed it with only a scrawled mark on its outer cover. That, by the way, was utter insolence, for the mark would be understood at any frontier post by the officer commanding.

"Rewa Gunga shall start with this to-day!" she said, with more amusement than malice. After that she was still for a moment, watching his eyes, at a loss to understand his carelessness. He seemed strangely unabased. His folded arms were not defiant, but neither were they yielding.

"I love you, Athelstan!" she said. "Do you love me?"

"I think you are very beautiful, Princess!"

"Beautiful? I know I am beautiful. But is that all?"

"Clever!" he added.

She began to drum with the golden dagger hilt on the

table, and to look dangerous, which is not to infer by any means that she looked less lovely.

"Do you love me?" she asked.

"Forgive me, Princess, but you forget. I was born east of Mecca, but my folk were from the West. We are slower to love than some other nations. With us love is more often growth, less often surrender at first sight. I think you are wonderful."

She nodded and tucked the sealed letter in her bosom.

"It shall go," she said darkly, "and another letter with it. They looted your brother's body. In his pocket they found the note you wrote him, and that you asked him to destroy! That will be evidence. That will convince! Come!"

He followed her through leather curtains again and down the dark passage into the outer chamber; and the illusion was of walking behind a golden-haired Madonna to some shrine of Innocence. Her perfume was like incense; her manner perfect reverence. She passed into the cave where the two dead bodies lay like a high priestess performing a rite.

Walking to the bed, she stood for minutes, gazing at the Sleeper and his queen. And from the new angle from which King saw him the Sleeper's likeness to himself was actually startling. Startling—weird—like an incantation were Yasmini's words when at last she spoke.

"Muhammad lied! He lied in his teeth! His sons have multiplied his lie! Siddhattha, whom men have called Gotama, the Buddha, was before Muhammad and he knew more! He told of the wheel of things, and there is a wheel! Yet, what knew the Buddha of the wheel? He who spoke of Dharma (the customs

of the law) not knowing Dharma! This is true—
Of old there was a wish of the gods—of the old gods.
And so these two were. There is a wish again now of
the old gods. So, are we two not as they two were?
It is the same wish, and lo! We are ready, this man
and I. We will obey, ye gods—ye old gods!"

She raised her arms and, going closer to the bed,
stood there in an attitude of mystic reverence, giving
and receiving blessings.

"Dear gods!" she prayed. "Dear *old* gods—older
than these 'Hills'—show me in a vision what their
fault was—why these two were ended before the end!

"I know all the other things ye have shown me. I
know the world's silly creeds have made it mad, and it
must rend itself, and this man and I shall reap where
the nations sowed—if only we obey! Wherein, ye old
dear gods, who love me, did these two disobey? I
pray you, tell me in a vision!"

She shook her head and sighed. Sadness seemed to
have crept over her, like a cold mist from the night. It
was as if she could dimly see her plans foredoomed,
and yet hoped on in spite of it. The fatalism that she
scorned as Muhammad's lie held her in its grip, and
her natural courage fought with it. Womanlike, she
turned to King in that minute and confided to him her
very inmost thoughts. And he, without an inkling as
to how she must fail, yet knew that she must, and
pitied her.

"Have you seen that breast under the armor?" she
asked suddenly. "Come nearer! Come and look!
Why did his breast decay and his body stay whole like
hers? Did she kill him? Was that a dagger-stab in his
breast? I found perfume in these caves—great jars of
it, and I use it always. It is better than temple incense

and all the breath of gardens in the spring! I have
put it on slaughtered animals. Where the knife has
touched them, they decay—as that man's breast did—
but the rest of them remains undecaying year after
year. It was a knife, I think, that pierced his breast.
I think that scent is the preservative. Did she kill him?
Was she jealous of him? How did she die? There is
no mark on her! Athelstan—listen! I think he would
have failed her! I think she stabbed him rather than
see him fail, and then swallowed poison! Afterward
their servants laid them there. She smiles in death
because she knew the wheel will turn and that death
dies too! He looks grim because he knew less than
she. It is always woman who understands and man
who fails! I think she stabbed him. She should have
loved him better, and then there would have been no
need. I will love you better than she loved him!"

She turned and devoured him with her eyes, so that
it needed all his manhood to hold him back from being
her slave that minute. For in that minute she left no
charm   unexercised—sex—mesmerism—beauty—flattery (her eyes could flatter as a dumb dog's flatter a
huntsman!)—grace unutterable—mystery—she used
every art on him she knew. Yet he stood the test.

"Even if you fail me, Well-beloved, I will love you!
The gods who gave you to me will know how to make
you love; and lessons are to learn. If you fail me I
will forgive, knowing that in the end the gods will
never let you fail me! You are mine, and Earth is
ours, for the old gods intend it so!"

She seemed to expect him to take her in his arms
again; but he stood respectfully and made no answer,
nor any move. Grim and strong his jowl was, like the
Sleeper's, and the dark hair three days old on it soft-

ened nothing of its lines. His Roman nose and steady, dark, full eyes suggested no compromise. Yet he was good to look at. She had not lied when she said she loved him, and he understood her and was sorry. But he did not look sorry, nor did he offer any argument to quench her love. He was a servant of the raj; his life and his love had been India's since the day he first buckled on his spurs, and Yasmini would not have understood that.

Nor did she understand that, even supposing he had loved her with all his heart, not on any conditions would he have admitted it until absolutely free, any more than that if she crucified him he would love her the same, supposing that he loved her at all. Nor did she trust the "old gods" too well, or let them work unaided.

"Come with me, Athelstan!" she said. She took his arm—found little jeweled slippers in a closet hewn in the wall—put them on and led him to the curtains he had entered by. She led him through them, and, red as cardinals in lamplight on the other side, they stood hand-in-hand, back to the leather, facing the unfathomable dark. Her fingers were so strong that he could not have wrenched his own away without using the other hand to help.

"Where are your shoes?" she asked him.

"At the foot of these steps, Princess."

"Can you see them yonder in the dark?"

"No."

"Can you guess where the darkness leads to?"

"No."

He shuddered and she chuckled.

"Could you return alone by the way Ismail brought you?"

"I think not."

"Will you try?"

"If I must. I am not afraid."

"You have heard the echo? Yes, I know you heard the echo. Hear it again!"

She raised her head and howled like a wolf—like a lone wolf that has found no quarry—melancholy, mean, grown reckless with his hunger. There was a pause of nearly a minute. Then in the hideous darkness a phantom wolf-pack took up the howl in chorus, and for three long minutes there was din beside which the voice of living wolves at war would be a slumber song. Ten times ghastlier than if it had been real, the chorus wailed and ululated back and forth along immeasurable distances—became one yell again—and went howling down into earth's bowels as if the last of a phantom pack were left behind and yelling to be waited for.

When it ceased at last King was sweating.

"Nor am I afraid," she laughed, squeezing his hand yet tighter.

She led him down the steps, and at the foot told him to put on his slippers, as if he were a child. Then, hurrying as if those opal eyes of hers were indifferent to dark or daylight, she picked her way among boulders that he could feel but not see, along a floor that was only smooth in places, for a distance that was long enough by two or three times to lose him altogether. When he looked back there was no sign of red lights behind him. And when he looked forward, there was a dim outer light in front and a whiff of the cool fresh air that presages the dawn!

She led him through a gap on to a ledge of rock that hung thousands of feet above the home of thunder,

a ledge less than six feet wide, less than twenty long,
tilted back toward the cliff. There they sat, watching
the stars. And there they saw the dawn come.

Morning looks down into Khinjan hours after the
sun has risen, because the precipices shut it out. But
the peaks on every side are very beacons of the range
at the earliest peep of dawn. In silence they watched
day's herald touch the peaks with rosy jeweled fingers—she waiting as if she expected the marvel of it
all to make King speak.

It was cold. She came and snuggled close to him,
and it was so they watched the sparkle of dawn's jewels die and the peaks grow gray again, she with an arm
on his shoulder and strands of her golden hair blown
past his face.

"Of what are you thinking?" she asked him at last.

"Of India, Princess."

"What of India?"

"She lies helpless."

"Ah! You love India?"

"Yes."

"You shall love me better! You shall love me better than your life! Then, for love of me, you shall
own the India you think you love! This letter shall
go!" She tapped her bosom. "It is best to cut you off
from India first. You shall lose that you may win!"

She got up and stood in the gap, smiling mockingly,
framed in the darkness of the cave behind.

"I understand!" she said. "You think you are my
enemy. Love and hate never lived side by side. You
shall see!"

Then in an instant she was gone, backward into the
dark. He sat and waited for her, cross-legged on the
ledge. As daylight began to filter downward he could

dimly make out the waterfall, thundering like the whelming of a world; he sat staring at it, trying to formulate a plan, until it dawned on him that he was nearly chilled to the bone. Then he got up and stepped through the gap, too.

"Princess!" he called. Then louder, "Princess!"

When the echo of his own voice died, it was as if the ghoul who made the echoes had taken shape. A beard —red eye-rims—and a hook nose came out of the dark, and Ismail bared yellow teeth.

"Come!" he said. "Come, little hakim!"

Private preserves? New Notions?
Measure me a quart of honesty,
And I will trade it for a pound weight of my thoughts;
Then you and I shall go and dream together
A brand-new dream of things that never happened,
Nor ever can be. Come, trade with me!

CHAPTER XV

WHAT Yasmini had been doing in the minutes
while King stared from the ledge in the dawn
was unguessable. Perhaps she had been praying to her
old gods. At least she had given Ismail strict orders,
for he said nothing, but seized King's hand and led him
through the dark as a rat leads a blind one—swiftly,
surely, unhesitating. King had no means whatever
of guessing their direction. They did not pass the two
lights again with the curtain and the steps all glowing
red.

They came instead to other steps, narrow and steep,
that led upward in a semicircle to a rough hole in a
rock wall. At the top there was a little yellow light,
so dim and small that its rays scarcely sufficed to show
the opening.

"Go up!" said Ismail, giving King a shove and disappearing at once. One side-step into blackness and
he might have been a mile away.

So King went up, stooping to feel each next footing
with a cautious hand. He was beginning to be sleepy,

303

and to suspect that Yasmini had taken him to view the
dawn with just that end in view. Nothing can make
tired eyes so long for sleep as a glimpse of waking day.
Sleepy eyes are easiest to trick.

It was not many minutes before he was sure his
guess was right.

The opening at the head of the stairs led into a tunnel. He followed it with a hand on either wall and
reached another of Khinjan's strange leather curtains.
His face struck the leather unexpectedly, and at that
instant, as if his touch were electric, the curtain sprang
aside and his eyes were dazzled by the light of diamonds.

It was Aladdin's Cave, with *her* acting spirit of the
lamp! It needed effort of self-control to know that
the huge, white, cut crystals that sparkled all about
the hewn cell could not be diamonds. They were as
big as his head, and bigger—at least a hundred of
them, and they multiplied the light of half a dozen little oil lamps until the cave seemed the home of light.

Yasmini had not a jewel on her. She was in a new
mood and new garments to suit it. Her feet were still
bare, but she was robed from head to heel in pure white
linen, on which her long hair shone as if it were truly
strands of gold. She received him with an air of mystic
calm, gracious and dignified as the high-priestess of
Grecian temple. She seemed devout—to have forgotten that she ever killed a man, or made a threat
or plotted for a kingdom.

"Be still," she said, raising a finger. "The old gods
talk to us in here. It is not for us to answer them in
words, but in deeds. Let us listen and do!"

There were two cushions—great billowy modern
ones, covered in gold brocade—on the floor in the

midst of the cave. Between them was a stand of ivory,
some two feet high, whose top was a disk, cut from
the largest tusk that ever could have been. On the disk
resting in a little hollow in the ivory, was a pure, perfect crystal sphere of a foot diameter. He could see
his reflection in it, and Yasmini's, too, the moment he
entered the cave, and whichever way they moved both
images remained undistorted. He suspected that the
lighting and the crystal reflectors had not been arranged at random.

In each corner of the four-square cave there was a
brazier of bronze, and from each rose incense smoke,
straight upward. The four streams of smoke met at
the ceiling and converged into a cloud that hung almost
motionless.

Yasmini stepped very reverently to a cushion by the
crystal in the middle, and signed to King to imitate
her. They stood facing. She seemed to pray, for her
eyes were hidden under the long lashes. Then she
knelt, and King did the same, his knees sinking deep
into another cushion. So they knelt eye to eye above
the crystal for many minutes without either saying a
word. It was Yasmini who spoke first.

"The old gods have showed me the past many and
many a time in this," she said. "It is their way of
speaking to me. Now, to-day, I have prayed to them
to show me the future. Look! Look, Athelstan! Do
as I do—so!"

There seemed nothing to be gained by disobeying her.
To obey her might be to win new insight into the rami-
fications of her plans. Men who have experience of
the East are the last to deny that there is method in
Eastern magic; they glimpse the knowledge that belonged to Pharaoh's men, although unlike Moses they

are not always able to confound it. The East forgets
nothing. The West ignores. But there are men from
the West who are willing to look and to listen and to
try to understand; like King, they go high in the Service. There are others who look on at the magic with an
understanding eye and are caught by it. Their end is
not good to contemplate. The East is fettered in her
own mesmeric spell and must suffer until she wakes.

Yasmini held the upright column of the ivory stand
with both hands, close under the disk at the top. He
copied her, placing his hands below hers. Hers slipped
down and covered his, soft and warm; and so they
stayed.

"Look!" she said. "Look!"

Her own eyes were grown big and round, and she
gazed at the crystal ball as she had looked into King's
eyes that night, with the very hunger of her soul. Her
lips were parted. Watching her, King grew expectant,
too. His eyes followed hers, to stare into the middle
of the crystal, no longer feeling sleepy, and in less
than a minute he could not have withdrawn them had
he tried.

The crystal clouded over. Yasmini's breath came
steadily, with a little hissing sound between her teeth,
and the crystal, or else the whole world, seemed to
sway in time to it. Then the man in Roman armor
strode out of a mist, and all was steady again and easy
to understand. When the man in armor opened his
lips to speak, one knew what he had said. When he
frowned, one knew why he frowned. When he smiled,
one knew that *she* was coming.

And she did come, dancing out of the mist behind
him, to fling soft arms round his neck and whisper
praises in his ear. He stood like a king who has come

into his own, with an arm round her and his chin held high. She kissed him on his proud chin, and laughed into his face.

There were troubles—difficulties, all in the mist behind, but he stood and despised them then while she caressed him!

Just as spoken words had no part in the vision, yet the whole was understood, so time did not enter into it. There was no connecting link between each scene; each dissolved into the other, and all were one.

She faded into mist, in a swirl of graceful drapery, and he frowned again. A long line of men-at-arms stood before him, grim as he and as discontented. They leaned on spears, at ease, and that seemed to annoy him most of all. A spokesman stood out from the ranks and addressed him, with gesticulations and a head so far thrown back that his helmet-plume stood out like a secretary's pen behind him. He was not a Roman, although there was something Roman about his attitude and armor. None of the men-at-arms was a Roman.

They demanded to be led home, wherever home was. (It was as plain as if their spokesman had shouted it into King's ear aloud.) And he refused them bluntly, proudly.

Two men brought him a native woman, each holding an arm and thrusting her forward between them. She was not at all unlike a native woman of to-day, either in dress or sullenness; she had the beak and the keen eyes and the cruel lips of the "Hills." They showed her to him, and it was quite clear that they compared her to their own women, left behind; the comparison was plainly to her disadvantage.

He wasted no argument on them, but his scorn made

the two men fade away, and the woman with them.
Yet he had no scorn for his lined-up fighting men,
and so could act none. He ordered the spokesman
back to the ranks, and the man obeyed. He gave another order, and the long lines stood at attention,
spears straight up and down, and their round shields
like great medallions on a wall. He ordered them
away, but they stood still.

Then he did a truly Roman thing. He got his harness off—unbuckled and took off the great bronze corselet, in which he lay dead in another cave. He threw
it down—tore open the white shirt underneath—and
held his arms out. He bade them come and kill him.
He bade them drive their spears into his unprotected
breast.

There was not a movement down the line of men.
They stood as a cliff looks at the tide. He dared them.
He called them cowards—women—weaklings afraid
of blood. But they stood still. He strode up and down
the line, seeking a man with heart enough to plunge
a spear into him, and no man moved.

Then he stood still before them all again and wept,
because they loved him and he loved them. And then
she came, not dancing this time, but barefooted and
walking like a poem of the early days of Greece. She
picked up his corselet and buckled it on him, making
him hold up his arms and kneel while she slipped it
over his head. And the grim men-at-arms hove their
long spears up into the air and roared her an ovation,
bringing down their right feet with a thunder all together.

"*Ave!*"

But the mist closed up and then the crystal was
clear again. It was Yasmini's voice that spoke. King

looked up into her eyes, and they made him shudder, for he had never seen eyes like them. Her hands still clasped his own, burning hot. She was more terrible than Khinjan.

"I never saw that before," she said. "It is because you are here! We shall see it all now! We shall know it all! We shall know whether it was she who killed him, or whether his own men took him at his word. We shall know! Look again! Look again!"

His eyes seemed unable to obey his own will any longer. They obeyed her voice. He gazed again into the crystal, and it clouded over. But although he obeyed her, the crystal obeyed him and answered at least in part the questions his imagination asked. He was not conscious of asking anything, but being a soldier his curiosity followed a more or less definite line.

Yasmini's breath began to come and go again with the little hissing sound. Her hot hands pressed his own. The mist suddenly dissolved. There was a road—a long white road, across a plain, and the men-at-arms fought their way along it. They were facing east.

Archers opposed them—archers on foot, and cavalry—Parthians. The Parthians were wild, but the drill of the men-at-arms was a thing to marvel at. When the flights of arrows came they knelt behind their shields. When the horsemen charged they closed in solid phalanx, and the inner ranks hurled javelins at ten-yard range. When the fury of the onslaught died they formed in column and went forward, gaining furlongs at a time while their enemy watched them and wondered.

It was plain that the enemy expected them to re-

treat sooner or later, for the archers and cavalry were
at great pains to get behind them, so that before long
the road ahead was less well defended than that behind. It did not seem to occur to the enemy that
they were pressing toward the distant line of hills and
did not seek to return at all.

They had no baggage to impede them. It was ab-
surd to suppose they would not try to fight a way back
soon. They must be a Roman raiding party, out to
teach Parthians a lesson. Yet they pressed ever forward, and the hills grew ever nearer; while he sat
a great brown charger calmly in their midst and gave
them not too many orders, but here and there a word
of praise, and once or twice a trumpet shout of encouragement. He seemed to own the knack of being
wherever the fight was fiercest. His mere presence
seemed better than a hundred men when the phalanx
bent before charging cavalry.

She rode a little white horse, beside him always and
utterly scornful of the risk. She wore no armor—
carried no shield. Her bare feet showed through the
sandal straps, and the outlines of her lissom body
were quite visible through the muslin stuff she wore.
She might have just come from the dancing. She
had a flower in her hand, and a wreath of flowers in
her hair. She shouted more encouragement than he.
She shouted too much. Once he laid a strong brown
hand across her mouth, and she held it there and
kissed it.

They lost men—five or six or ten or twenty at each
onslaught. Perhaps they had been a thousand strong
in the beginning. Their own men—the regimental surgeons probably—cut the throats of the badly wounded,
to save them from the enemy's attentions; and by this

time they were not more than seven or eight hundred strong.

But they went forward—ever forward—and the line of hills drew near. Then he began to stir himself, and she with him. He shouted to them to charge, and she echoed him, leaving his side at last to take command of a wing and sting the tired-out men-at-arms into new enthusiasm. In a minute they were a roaring tide that swept forward to the foot of the hills and surged upward without a check. In a little while they were hurling boulders down on an enemy that seemed inclined to parley.

Then, like a shadow of the incense cloud above, the mist closed up in the crystal again, and in a moment more King and Yasmini were looking into each other's eyes again above it.

"I have seen that before," she said, shaking her head. "I am weary of their battles. They won; that is enough! I must know how they failed, so that we make no such mistakes!"

Her face was flushed, and her eyes glowed with the fire that is not lit by ordinary passion. She was being eaten by ambition—burned by her own fire—by ambition not totally selfish, for she yearned to shepherd King as she seemed to think this woman of the vision had not shepherded the man in armor.

"Look again!" she said. "Look again! And oh, ye old gods, show—show me wherein she failed!"

They stared again, and once more the crystal clouded. Out of the cloud came a city in the middle of a plain, and the city was besieged. It was not a very great city, but from the outside it looked rich, for domes and roofs and towers showed above the wall, all well built and well preserved. He and she,

sitting their horses out of arrow range from the main
gate seemed confident of taking it and eager to get it
over with.

They no longer had only six or seven hundred men,
but men by the thousand. Their veterans in Roman
armor were in command of others now, and they had
a human pack-train with them, heavily burdened cap-
tives who sulked in chains under a guard.

The mist cleared further, and the gate gave in under the blows of an improvised battering-ram, covered by showers of arrows from short range. Then,
like a river breaking down a dam, the thousands
stormed in, howling. Smoke rose. There were screams
of women. A great tower near the gate, that was
half wood, half stone, crackled and curled up in yellow
and crimson flame. He and she rode in together as
modern men and women ride through a gate to the
covert side at a fox-hunt. They chatted and laughed
together, and their horses pranced, responding to the
humor of their riders.

King would have liked to tear his eyes away from
the scenes that followed in the tree-lined streets, but
the crystal ball held him as if in a trance—that and
Yasmini's hands that clasped his own like hot torture
chamber clamps. Animals fighting to the death are
not so vile, nor so inhuman as men can be in the hour
of what they call victory. Even the little children of
that city paid the penalty for having closed the gate.

Time was no measure to the crystal ball. In minutes it showed the devil's work of hours. The city
went up in smoke and flame, and from the far side
through a great breach in the wall the conquerors
went out, with their plunder and such prisoners as
had been saved to drag and carry it.

Now there were wagons and camels and horses.
Now there were tents and furniture. Now each man
of the fighting force had as much as he himself could
carry, as well as what was loaded on the prisoners.
Only *he* and *she* seemed to care nothing for the loot
and rode as if each was all the other needed. Still
he wore nothing but his armor, and she no more than
her dancing dress and sandals. But now she had
eight prisoners to hold a panoply above her horse and
keep the sun from her.

She had flowers woven in her hair, and others in her
hand, as if she rode from a bridal feast and were not
in mourning for a plundered, butchered city. They
were headed northward now, toward distant mountains, and the dust of their long column went up like
a river of smoke, flowing from the holocaust behind.

Yasmini shook her head impatiently. The crystal
clouded over, and King's eyes were free.

"I am tired of it," she said. "I have seen that so
many times. I know they won. I know they found
their way to Khinjan. I know they began to build an
empire here. I have seen all that a hundred times.
What I must know is what mistake they made. What
did they do wrong? How did they come to fail?
Look again! Let us look again!"

She never once let King's hands go, but pressed
them tighter and tighter until the circulation nearly
stopped and they grew numb. Her own strength
seemed endless—to grow rather than to wane in proportion as her yearning to look into the past grew.
Her attitude would have been more understandable
if she had believed herself and King to be reincarna-
tions of those forgotten conquerors; but she was too
original for that. She had said the old gods wished,

and the man and the woman were; the old gods wished the same wish again, and she and King were. Why, then, if the old gods were contriving it all, should she seek to steady the ark for them? But down at bottom there is no logic connected with gods many. She clutched King's fingers as if to hold him there, and to make him see and understand the distant past, were the only way to save him from mistakes.

"Look!" she insisted. "Look again!" And he obeyed her. By this time obedience was much the easiest course. Between times his eyes were so weary he could hardly hold them open, and it was only when he gazed into the crystal that he could rest them and feel easy. He knew well that she was winning control over him in some sort, and he fought against it grimly. Soon he became weirdly conscious of being two men—one, whom she had grasped and overcome, a physical man who did not matter much, and another, mental man who was free from her, who could understand her, whom she could not reach or touch.

"Look!" she insisted. "Look!" And the crystal clouded over.

He strode out of the mist again, frowning, with his chin hung low and fists clenched tight at his sides. Four of his own men came out of the mist to him and greeted him respectfully, yet not without a touch of irony.

They spoke to him and pointed westward. One laid a hand on his shoulder, but he shook it off and the man reeled back as if he had been struck. Another man took up the argument, but he shook his head. They all spoke together, gesticulating and growing angry; but he stood calm among them, as a rock stands in a storm. He folded his arms across his breast after a while and listened, saying nothing.

Then as if to end the argument for good and all, he drew his sword and held it out toward them, hilt first, telling them again to kill him and have done with it. They refused. He laughed at them, but they still refused; so he put his sword back in the sheath.

One of the men stepped into the mist and disappeared. Presently he came again, with two others, helping a wounded man along between them. Whoever the wounded man might be he was treated with respect. Prouder than Lucifer, he who had struck another man's hand from off his shoulder knelt to give this wounded man a knee and seemed pained when the man refused him.

The wounded man pointed to the westward too and argued in short clipped-off sentences. He had a day or two to live—certainly not longer, for the blood flowed slowly from a wound that would not stanch; yet he argued as a man who has lost no interest in life, but rather sees its problems truly now that his own are near an end.

He demanded something almost truculently. *He* took his helmet off and passed it down to him. With fingers that were growing feeble the wounded man held it and traced out the letters S. P. Q. R. on the front.

"Go home!" he said, passing it back to him. "Fight your way back home!" What he said was as distinct as if a voice in the cave had spoken it.

Then, vision within a vision—dream within a dream —there was a view of the Via Appia, with gaunt grim gallows set along it in a row and on them a regi-

ment's commander crucified along with the remnant
of his men.

"So Rome treats traitors!" said a voice, that might
have been either man's.

But instantly there was another vision, of ten thousand wolves baying down a Himalayan gorge in win-
ter-time, the sleet frozen stiff on their fur and their
tongues hanging. Eye and fang flashed altogether
and made one gleam.

"Choose!" said a voice.

So he chose. He nodded. The men saluted him
and the wounded man was helped away to die. And
then *she* came, angry as a flash of lightning, to spring
at him and cling to him and call him names—begging,
demanding, ordering, crying—abusing him and prais-
ing him in turn. He shook his head. She sobbed, but
he shook his head again and pointed westward. Then
she took him by the hand and led him away, not looking at his face again.

The crystal ball grew clouded. Yasmini's breath
came and went as if she were running in a race, and
her pressure on King's fingers was actually painful.
The mist dissolved, and King forgot the pressure—
forgot everything. The man in armor lay dead on his
back in the cave on the wooden bed, and *she* bent over
him, dagger in hand.

"Ah!" said Yasmini, her teeth chattering. "But
what else could she do?" The mist closed in again
and the crystal grew opaque. "The future!" she
begged. "It is the future I must know! Ye old gods,
tell me! Show me!"

The mist turned red. The crystal ball became as
it were a ball of fire revolving within itself. The fire
turned to blood, and the blood to fire again. The very

cavern that they knelt in seemed to sway. Yasmini screamed and moaned. She loosed King's hands to cover her own eyes.

And as she did that King sank, like a sack half-empty and toppled over sidewise on the floor asleep.

He neither dreamed nor was conscious of anything, but slept like a dead man, having fought against her mesmerism harder than he knew.

Statesmen, generals, outlaws, all make their big mistakes and manage to recover. Very nearly always it is an apparently little mistake that does most damage in the end, something unnoticeable at the time, that grows in geometrical proportion, minus instead of plus.

Yasmini made her little mistake that minute in believing King was utterly mesmerized at last and utterly in her power. Whereas in truth he was only weary. It may be that she gave him orders in his sleep, after the accepted manner of mesmerists; but if she did, they never reached him; he was far too fast asleep. He slept so deep and long that he was not conscious of men's voices, nor of being carried, nor of time, nor of anxiety, nor of anything.

Wolf met wolf in the dawning day
Where scent hung sweet over trodden clay,
And square each stood in the jungle way
Eyeing the other with ears laid back.
Still were the watchers. When foe greets foe
The wisest are quietest. Better to go—
Who stays to watch trouble woos trouble!

But lo!

They trotted together to hunt one doe,
Eyeing each other with ears laid back.

CHAPTER XVI

WHEN King awoke he lay on a comfortable bed in a cave he had never yet seen, but there was no trace of Yasmini, nor of the men who must have carried him to it. Barbaric splendor and splendor that was not by any means barbaric lay all about—tiger skins, ivory-legged chairs, graven bronze vases, and a yak-hair shawl worth a rajah's ransom.

The cave was spacious and not gloomy, for there was a wide door, apparently unguarded, and another square opening cut in the rock to serve as a window. Through both openings light streamed in like taut threads of Yasmini's golden hair—strings of a golden zither, on which his own heart's promptings played a tune.

He had no idea how long he had slept, but judged from memory of his former need of sleep and recognition of his present freshness—and from the fact that it was a morning sun that shone through the openings —that he must have slept the clock round.

319

It did not matter. He knew it did not matter in the least. He had no more plan than a mathematician has who starts to solve a problem, knowing that twice two is four in infinite combination. Like the mathematician, he knew that he must win.

No man ever won a battle or conceived a stroke of statesmanship, no great deed was ever accomplished without a first taste of the triumphant foreknowledge, such as comes only to men who have digged hard, hewing to the line, loyal to first principles. King had been loyal all his life.

The difference between first principles and the other thing could hardly be better illustrated than by comparing Yasmini's position with his. From her point of view he had no ground to stand on, unless he should choose to come and stand on hers. She had men, ammunition, information. He had what he stood in, and his only information had been poured into his ears for her ends.

Yet his heart sang inside him now; and he trusted it because that singing never had deceived him. He did not believe she would have left him alone at that stage of affairs unless through over-confidence. It is one of the absolute laws that over-confidence begets blindness and mistakes.

She had staked on what seemed to her the certainty of India's rising at the first signal of a holy war. She believed from close acquaintance that India was utterly disloyal, having made a study of disloyalty. And having read history she knew that many a conqueror has staked on such cards as hers, to win for lack of a better man to take the other side.

But King had studied loyalty all his life, and he knew that besides being the home of money-lenders,

thugs and murderers, India is the very motherland of
chivalry; that besides sedition she breeds gentlemen
with stout hearts; that in addition to what one Christian Book calls "whoring after strange gods" India
strives after purity. He knew that India's ideals are
all imperishable, and her crimes but a kaleidoscopic
phase.

Not that he was analyzing thoughts just then. He
was listening to the still small voice that told him half
of his purpose was accomplished. He had probed
Khinjan Caves, and knew the whole purpose for which
the lawless thousands had been gathering and were
gathering still. Remained, to thwart that purpose.
And he had no more doubt of there being a means to
thwart it than a mathematician has of the result of
two times two, applied.

Like a mathematician, he did not waste time and
confuse issues by casting too far ahead, but began to
devote himself steadily to the figures nearest. Knots
are not untied by wholesale, but are conquered strand
by strand. He began at the beginning, where he
stood.

He became conscious of human life near by and tip-
toed to the door to look. A six-foot ledge of smooth
rock ended just at the door and sloped in the other
direction sharply downward toward another opening
in the cliff side, three or four hundred yards away and
two hundred feet lower down.

Behind him in a corner at the back of the cave was
a narrow fissure, hung with a leather curtain, that was
doubtless the door into Khinjan's heart; but the only
way to the outer air was along that ledge above a dizzying precipice, so high that the huge waterfall looked
like a little stream below. He was in a very eagle's

aerie; the upper rim of Khinjan's gorge seemed not
more than a quarter of a mile above him.

Round the corner, ten feet from the entrance, stood
a guard, armed to the teeth, with a rifle, a sword, two
pistols and a long curved Khyber knife stuck handy
in his girdle. He spoke to the man and received no
answer. He picked up a splinter of rock and threw
it. The fellow looked at him then. He spoke again.
The man transferred his rifle to the other hand and
made signs with his free fingers. King looked puzzled.
The man opened his mouth and showed that his tongue
was missing. He had been made dumb, as pegs are
made to fit square holes. King went in again, to wait
on events and shudder.

Nor did he have long to wait. There came a sound
of grunting, up the rock path. Then footsteps. Then
a hoarse voice, growling orders. He went out again
to look, and beheld a little procession of women, led
by a man. The man was armed, but the women were
burdened with his own belongings — the medicine
chest—his saddle and bridle—his unrifled mule-pack
—and, wonder of wonders! the presents Khinjan's
sick had given him, including money and weapons.
They came past the dumb man on guard and laid them
all at King's feet just inside the cave.

He smiled, with that genial, face-transforming smile
of his that has so often melted a road for him through
sullen crowds. But the man in charge of the women
did not grin. He was suffering. He growled at the
women, and they went away like obedient animals, to
sit half-way down the ledge and await further orders.
He himself made as if to follow them, and the dumb
man on guard did not pay much attention; he let
women and man pass behind him, stepping one pace

forward toward the edge to make more room. That was his last entirely voluntary act in this world.

With a suddenness that disarmed all opposition the other humped himself against the wall and bucked into the dumb man's back, sending him, weapons and all, hurtling over the precipice. With a wild effort to recover, and avenge himself, and do his duty, the victim fired his rifle, that was ready cocked. The bullet struck the rock above and either split or shook a great fragment loose, that hurtled down after him, so that he and the stone made a race of it for the waterfall and the caverns into which the water tumbled thousands of feet away. The other ruffian spat after him, and then walked back to where King stood.

"Now heal me my boils!" he said, grinning at last, doubtless from pleasure at the prospect. He was the same man who had stood on guard at the "guest-cave" when Ismail led King out to see the Cavern of Earth's Drink.

The temptation was to fling the brute after his victim. The temptation always is to do the wrong thing —to cap wrath with wrath, injustice with vengeance. That way wars begin and are never ended. King beckoned him into the cave, and bent over the chest of medical supplies. Then, finding the light better for his purpose at the entrance, he called the man back and made him sit down on the box.

The business of lancing boils is not especially edifying in itself; but that particular minor operation probably saved India. But for hope of it the man with boils would never have stood two turns on guard hand running and let the relief sleep on; so he would not have been on duty when the message came to carry King's belongings to his new cave of residence. There would have been no object in killing the dumb man, and so there would have been an expert with a loaded rifle to keep Muhammad Anim lurking down the trail.

Muhammad Anim came—like the devil, to scotch King's faith. He had followed the women with the loads. He stood now, like a big bear on a mountain track, swaying his head from side to side six feet away from King, watching the boils succumb to treatment. He grunted when the job was finished, and King jumped, nearly driving the lance into a new place in his patient's neck.

"Let him go!" growled Muhammad Anim. "Go, thou! Stand guard over the women until I come!"

The mullah turned a rifle this way and that in his paws, like a great bear dancing. The Mahsudi with a sore neck could have shot him, perhaps, but there are men with whom only the bravest dare try conclusions. In cold gray dawn it would have needed a martinet to make a firing squad do execution on Muhammad Anim, even with his hands tied and his back against a wall. A man whose boils had just been lanced was no match for him at all, even in broad daylight. The Hillman slunk away and did as he was told.

"What meant thy message?" growled the mullah. "There came a Pathan to me in the Cavern of Earth's Drink with word that yonder sits a hakim. What of it?"

King had almost forgotten the message he had sent to Muhammad Anim in the Cavern of Earth's Drink. But that was not why his eyes looked past the mullah's now, nor why he did not answer. The mullah did not look round, for he knew what was happening.

The very Orakzai Pathan who had sat next King in

the Cavern of Earth's Drink, and who had carried the message for him, was creeping up behind the women and already had his rifle leveled at the man with boils. "Aye!" said the mullah, watching King's eyes. "He has done well, and the road is clear!"

The man with boils offered no fight. He dropped his rifle and threw his hands up. In a moment the Orakzai Pathan was in command of two rifles, holding them in one hand and nodding and making signs to King from among the women, whom he seemed to regard as his plunder too. The women appeared supremely indifferent in any event. King nodded back to him. A friend is a friend in the "Hills," and rare is the man who spares his enemy.

"Why send that message to me?" asked Muhammad Anim.

"Why not?" asked King. "If none know where the hakim is, how shall the hakim earn a living?"

"None comes to earn a living in the Hills," growled the mullah, swaying his head slowly and devouring King with cruel calculating eyes. "Why art thou here?"

"I slew a man," said King.

"Thou liest! It was my men who got the head that let thee in! Speak! Why art thou here?"

But King did not answer. The mullah resumed.

"He who brought me the message yesterday says he has it from another, who had it from a third, that thou art here because *she* plans a simultaneous rising in India, and thou art from the Punjab where the Sikhs all wait to rise. Is that true?"

"Thy man said it," answered King.

"What sayest thou?" the mullah asked.

"I say nothing," said King.

"Then hear me!" said the mullah. "Listen, thou."
But he did not begin to speak yet. He tried to see past
King into the cave and to peer about into the shadows.
"Where is she?" he asked. "Her man Rewa Gunga
went yesterday, with three men and a letter to carry
down the Khyber. But where is she?"

So he *had* slept the clock round! King did not
answer. He blocked the way into the cave and looked
past the mullah at a sight that fascinated, as a ser-
pent's eyes are said to fascinate a bird. But the mullah, who knew perfectly well what must be happening,
did not trouble to turn his head.

The Orakzai Pathan crouched among the women,
and the women grinned. The Mahsudi, having sur-
rendered and considering himself therefore absolved
from further responsibility at least for the present,
spat over the precipice and fingered gingerly the sore
place where his boils had been. He yawned and
dropped both hands to his side; and it was at that
instant that the Pathan sprang at him.

With arms like the jaws of a vise he pinned the
Mahsudi's to his side, and lifted him from off his feet.
The fellow screamed, and the Pathan shouted "Ho!"
But he did no murder yet. He let his victim grow
fully conscious of the fate in store for him, holding
him so that his frantic kicks were squandered on thin
air. He turned him slowly, until he was upside-down;
and so, perpendicular, face-outward, he hove him forward like a dead log. He stood and watched his victim fall two or three thousand feet before troubling to
turn and resume both rifles; and it was not until then,
as if he had been mentally conscious of each move,
that the mullah turned to look, and seeing only one
man nodded.

"Good!" he grunted. "*Shabash!*" (Well done!)

Then he turned his head to stare into King's face, with the scrutiny of a trader appraising loot. Fire leaped up behind his calculating eyes. And without a word passing between them, King knew that this man as well as Yasmini was in possession of the secret of the Sleeper. Perhaps he knew it first; perhaps she snatched the keeping of the secret from him. At all events he knew it and recognized King's likeness to the Sleeper, for his eyes betrayed him. He began to stroke his beard monotonously with one hand. The rifle, that he pretended to be holding, really leaned against his back and with the free hand he was making signals.

King knew well he was making signals. But he knew too that in Yasmini's power, her prisoner, he had no chance at all of interfering with her plans. Having grounded on the bottom of impotence, so to speak, any tide that would take him off must be a good tide. He pretended to be aware of nothing, and to be particularly unaware that the Pathan, with a rifle in each hand, was pretending to come casually up the path.

In a minute he was covered by a rifle. In another minute the mullah had lashed his hands. In five minutes more the women were loaded again with his belongings and they were all half-way down the track in single file, the mullah bringing up the rear, descending backward with rifle ready against surprise, as if he expected Yasmini and her men to pounce out any minute to the rescue.

They entered a tunnel and wound along it, stepping at short intervals over the bodies of three stabbed sentries. The Pathan spurned them with his heel as he passed. In the glare at the tunnel's mouth King tripped over the body of a fourth man and fell with his chin beyond the edge of a sheer precipice.

They were on a ledge above the waterfall again, having come through a projection on the cliff's side, for Khinjan is all rat-runs and projections, like a sponge or a hornet's nest on a titanic scale.

The Pathan laughed and came back to gather him like a sheaf of corn. The great smelly ruffian hugged him to himself as he set him on his feet.

"Ah! Thou hakim!" he grinned. "There is no pain in my shoulder at all! Ask of me another favor when the time comes! Hey, but I am sick of Khinjan!"

He gave King a shove along the path in the general direction of the mullah. Then he seized the dead body by the legs, and hurled it like a slung shot, watching it with a grin as it fell in a wide parabola. After that he took the dead man's rifle, and those of the three other dead men, that he had hidden in a crevice in the rock, and loaded them all on a woman in addition to King's saddle that she carried already.

"Come!" he said. "Hurry, or Bull-with-a-beard yonder will remember us again. I love him best when he forgets!"

They soon reached another cave, at which the mullah stopped. It was a dark ill-smelling hole, but he ordered King into it and the Pathan after him on guard, after first seeing the women pile all their loads inside. Then he took the women away and went off muttering to himself, swaggering, swinging his right arm as he strode, in a way few natives do.

"Let us hope he has forgotten these!" the Pathan grinned, touching the pile of rifles. "Weight for weight in silver they will bring me a fine price! He may forget. He dreams. For a mullah he cares less

for meat and money than any I ever saw. He is
mad, I think. It is my opinion Allah touched him."

"What is that, under thy shirt?" King asked.

The Pathan grinned, and undid the button. There
was a second shirt underneath, and to that on the left
breast were pinned two British medals.

"Oh, yes!" he laughed. "I served the raj! I was
in the army eleven years."

"Why did you leave it?" King asked, remembering
that this man loved to hear his own voice.

"Oh, I had furlough, and the bastard who stood next
me in the ranks was the son of a dog with whom my
father had a blood-feud. The blind fool did not know
me. He received his furlough on the same day as I. I
would not lay finger on him that side of the border,
for we ate the same salt. I knifed him this side the
border. It was no affair of the British. But I was
seen, and I fled. And having slain a man, and having
no doubt a report had gone back to the regiment, I
entered this place. Except for a raid now and then
to cool my blood I have been here ever since. It is
a devil of a place."

Now the art of ruling India consists not in treading
barefooted on scorpions—not in virtuous indignation at
men who know no better—but in seeking for and making much of the gold that lies ever amid the dross.
There is gold in the character of any man who once
passed the grilling tests before enlistment in a British-
Indian regiment. It may need experience to lay a finger on it, but it is surely there.

"I heard," said King, "as I came toward the Khyber
in great haste (for the police were at my heels)—"

"Ah, the police!" the Pathan grinned pleasantly.

The inference was that at some time or other he had left his mark on the police.

"I heard," said King, "that men are flocking back to their old regiments."

"Aye, but not men with a price on their heads, little hakim!"

"I could not say," said King. To seem to know too much is as bad as to drink too much. "But I heard say that the sirkar has offered pardons to all deserters who return."

"Hah! The sirkar must be afraid. The sirkar needs men!"

"For myself," said King, "a whole skin in the 'Hills' seems better than one full of bullet holes in India."

"Hah! But thou art a hakim, not a soldier!"

"True!" said King.

"Tell me that again! Free pardons? Free pardons for all deserters?"

"So I heard."

"Ah! But I was seen to slay a man of my own regiment."

"On this side the border or that?" asked King artfully.

"On this side."

"Ah, but you were seen."

"Ay! But that is no man's business. In India I earned my salt. I obeyed the law. There is no law here in the 'Hills.' I am minded to go back and seek that pardon! It would feel good to stand in the ranks again, with a stiff-backed sahib out in front of me, and the thunder of the gun-wheels going by. The salt was good! Come thou with me!"

"The pardon is for deserters," King objected, "not for political offenders."

"Haugh!" said the Pathan, bringing down his flat hand hard on the hakim's thigh. "I will attend to that for thee. I will obtain my pardon first. Then will I lead thee by the hand to the karnal sahib and lie to him and say, 'This is the one who persuaded me against my will to come back to the regiment!'"

"And he will believe? Nay, I would be afraid!" said King.

"Would a pardon not be good?" the Pathan asked him. "A pardon and leave to swagger through the bazaars again and make trouble with the daughters and wives of fat traders—a pardon—Allah! It would be good to salute the karnal sahib again and see him raise a finger, thus; and to have the captain sahib call me a scoundrel—or some worse name if he loves me very much, for the English are a strange race—"

"Thou art a dreamer!" said King. "Untie my hands; the thong cuts me."

The Pathan obeyed.

"Dreamer, am I? It is good to dream such dreams. By Allah, I've a mind to see that dream come true! I never slew a man on Indian soil, only in these 'Hills.' I will go to them and say 'Here I am! I am a deserter. I seek that pardon!' Truly I will go! Come thou with me, little hakim!"

"Nay," said King, "I have another thought."

"What then?"

"You, who were seen to slay a man a yard this side of the border—"

"Nay; half a mile this side!"

"Half a mile, then. You who were seen to slay a fellow soldier of your regiment, and I who am a political offender, do not win pardons so easily as that."

"Would they hang us?"

That was the first squeamishness the Pathan had
shown of any kind, but men of his race would rather
be tortured to death than hanged in a merciful hempen
noose.

"They would hang us," said King, "unless we came
bearing gifts."

"Gifts? Has Allah touched thee? What gifts should
we bring? A dozen stolen rifles? A bag of silver?
And I am the dreamer, am I?"

"Nay," said King. "I am the dreamer. I have seen
a good vision."

"Well?"

"There are others in these 'Hills'—others in Khinjan
who wear British medals?"

The Pathan nodded.

"How many?" asked King.

"Hundreds. Men fight first on one side, then on
the other, being true to either side while the contract
lasts. In all there must be the makings of many regiments among the 'Hills.' "

King nodded. He himself had seen the chieftains
come to parley after the Tirah war. Most of them
had worn British medals and had worn them proudly.

"If we two," he said, speaking slowly, "could speak
with some of those men and stir the spirit in them
and persuade them to feel as thou dost, mentioning
the pardon for deserters and the probability of bonuses
to the time-expired for reenlistment; if we could
march down the Khyber with a hundred such, or even
with fifty or with twenty-five or with a dozen men—
we would receive our pardon for the sake of service
rendered."

"Good!"

The Pathan thumped him on the back so hard that his eyes watered.

"We would have to use much caution," King advised him, when he was able to speak again.

"Aye! If Bull-with-a-beard got wind of it he would have us crucified. And if *she* heard of it—"

He was silent. Apparently there were no words in his tongue that could compass his dread of her revenge. He was silent for ten minutes, and King sat still beside him, letting memory of other days do its work—memory of the long, clean regimental lines, and of order and decency and of justice handed out to all and sundry by gentlemen who did not think themselves too good to wear a native regiment's uniform.

"In two days I could do the drill again as well as ever," he said at last. Then there was silence again for fifteen minutes more. "I could always shoot," he murmured; "I could always shoot."

When Muhammad Anim came back they had both forgotten to replace the lashing on King's wrists, but the mullah seemed not to notice it.

"Come!" he ordered, with a sidewise jerk of his great ugly head, and then stood muttering impatiently while they obeyed.

He had twice the number of women with him, but none of them the same; and he had brought five ruffians to guard them, who pounced on the captured rifles and claimed one apiece, to the Pathan's loud-growled disgust. Then the women were made to gather up King's belongings, and at a word from the mullah they started in single file—the mullah leading, then two men, then King, then the Orakzai Pathan.

and then the other three. The Pathan began to whisper busily to the man next behind and noticing that King looked straight forward and contented himself; his heart was singing within him unexplainedly; he wanted to sing and dance, as once David did before the ark. He did not feel in the least like a prisoner.

They marched downward through interminable tunnels and along ledges poised between earth and heaven, until they came at last to the tunnel leading to the one entrance into Khinjan Caves. Just before they entered it two more of the mullah's men came up with them, leading horses. One horse was for the mullah, and they helped King mount the other, showing him more respect than is usually shown a prisoner in the "Hills."

Then the mullah led the way into the tunnel, and he seemed in deadly fear. The echo of the hoof-beats irritated him. He eyed each hole in the roof as if Yasmini might be expected to shoot down at him or drench him with boiling oil and hurried past each of them at a trot, only to draw rein immediately afterward because the noise was too great.

It became evident that his men had been at work here too, for at intervals along the passage lay dead bodies. Yasmini must have posted the men there, but where was she? Each of them lay dead with a knife wound in his back, and the mullah's men possessed themselves of rifles and knives and cartridges, wiping off blood that had scarcely cooled yet.

When they came to the end of the tunnel it was to find the door into the mosque open in front of them, and twenty more of Muhammad Anim's men standing guard over the eyelashless mullah. They had bound and gagged him. At a word from Muhammad Anim they loosed him; and at a threat the hairless one gave a signal that brought the great stone door sliding forward on its oiled bronze grooves.

Then, with a dozen jests thrown to the hairless one for consolation, and an utter indifference to the sacredness of the mosque floor, they sought outer air, and Muhammad Anim led them up the Street of the Dwellings toward Khinjan's outer ramparts. They reached the outer gate without incident and hurried into the great dry valley beyond it. As they rode across the valley the mullah thumbed a long string of beads. Unlike Yasmini, he was praying to one god; but he seemed to have many prayers. His back was a picture of determined treachery—the backs of his men were expressions of the creed that "He shall keep who can!" King rode all but last now and had a good view of their unconsciously vaunted blackguardism. There was not a hint of honor or tenderness among the lot, man, woman or mullah. Yet his heart sang within him as if he were riding to his own marriage feast!

Last of all, close behind him, marched his friend, the Orakzai Pathan, and as they picked their way among the boulders across the mile-wide moat the two contrived to fall a little to the rear. The Pathan began speaking in a whisper and King, riding with lowered head as if he were studying the dangerous track, listened with both ears.

"She sent her man Rewa Gunga toward the Khyber with a message," he whispered. "He took a few men with him, and he is to send them with the message when they reach the Khyber, but he is to come back. All he went for is to make sure the message is not intercepted, for Bull-with-a-beard is growing reckless these days. He knew what was doing and said at once that she is treating with the British, but there were few who believed that. There are more who wonder where she hides while the message is on its way. None has seen her. Men have swarmed into the Cavern of Earth's Drink and howled for her, but she did not come. Then the mullah went to look for his ammunition that he stored and sealed in a cave. And it was gone. It was all gone. And there was no proof of who had taken it!

"Hakim, there be some who say—and Bull-with-a-beard is one of them—that she is afraid and hides. Men say she fears vengeance for the stolen ammunition, because it was plenty for a conquest of India. So men say. So say these here, for I have asked them."

"And thou?" asked King, struggling to keep the note of exultation from his voice. He did not believe she was hiding. She might be staring into a crystal in some secret cave—she might be planning new mischief of any kind. But afraid she was surely not. And just as surely he could vow she was working out her own undoing.

"I?" said the Pathan. "I swear she is afraid of nothing. If she has taken all the ammunition, then we shall hear from it again and from her too!"

"And what of me?" asked King. "What will the mullah do with me?"

"His men say he is desperate. His own are losing faith in him. He snatched thee to be a bait for her, having it in mind that a man whom she hides in her private part of Khinjan must be of great value to her.

He has sworn to have thee skinned alive on a hot rock should she fail to come to terms!"

That being not such a comforting reflection, King rode in silence for a while, with the Pathan trudging solemnly beside his stirrup keeping semblance of guard over him. When they reached the steep escarpment he had to dismount, although the mullah in the lead tried to make his own beast carry him up the lower spur and was mad-angry with his men for laughing when the horse fell back with him.

Far in the rear King and the Pathan shoved and hauled and nearly lost their horse a dozen times at that. But once at the top the mullah set a furious pace and the laden women panted in their efforts to keep up, the men taking less notice of them than if they had been animals.

The march went on in single file until the sun died down in splendid fury. Then there began to be a wind that they had to lean against, but the women were allowed no rest.

At last at a place where the trail began to widen, the mullah beckoned King to ride beside him. It was not that he wished to be communicative, but there were things King knew that he did not know, and he had his own way of asking questions.

"Damned hakim!" he growled. "Pill-man! Poulticer! That is a sweeper's trade of thine! Thou shalt apply it at my camp! I have some wounded and some sick."

King did not answer, but buttoned his coat closer against the keen wind. The mullah mistook the shudder for one of another kind.

"Did she choose thee only for thy face?" he asked.

"Did she not consider thy courage? Does she love thee well enough to ransom thee?"

Again King did not answer, but he watched the mullah's face keenly in the dark and missed nothing of its expression. He decided the man was in doubt— even racked by indecision.

"Should she not ransom thee, hakim, thou shalt have a chance to show my men how a man out of India can die! By and by I will lend thee a messenger to send to her. Better make the message clear and urgent! Thou shalt state my terms to her and plead thine own cause in the same letter. My camp lies yonder."

He motioned with one sweep of his arm toward a valley that lay in shadow far below them. As far as the slope leading down to it was visible in the moonlight it was littered with what the "Hills" call "hellstones," that will neither lie flat nor keep on rolling, and are dangerous to man and beast alike. Nothing else could be made out through the darkness but a few twisted tamarisk trees, that served to make the savagery yet more savage and the loneliness more desolate. The gloom below the trees was that of the very underdepths of hell itself.

The mullah pointed to a rock that rose like a shadow from the deeper blackness.

"Yes," said King, "I have seen." And the mullah stared at him. Then he shouted, and the top of the rock turned into a man, who gave them leave to advance, leaning on his rifle as one who had assured himself of their identity long minutes ago.

As they approached it the rock clove in two and became two great pillars, with a man on each. And between the pillars they looked down into a valley lit by fires that burned before a thousand hide tents, with shadows by the hundred flitting back and forth between them. A dull roar, like the voice of an army, rose out of the gorge.

"More than four thousand men!" said the mullah proudly.

"What are four thousand for a raid into India?" sneered King, greatly daring.

"Wait and see!" growled the mullah; but he seemed depressed.

He led the way downward, getting off his horse and giving the reins to a man. King copied him, and partway sliding, part stumbling down they found their way along the dry bed of a water-course between two spurs of a hillside, until they stood at last in the midst of a cluster of a dozen sentries, close to a tamarisk to which a man's body hung spiked. That the man had been spiked to it alive was suggested by the body's attitude.

Without a word to the sentries the mullah led on down a lane through the midst of the camp, toward a great open cave at the far side, in which a bonfire cast fitful light and shadow. Watchers sitting by the thousand tents yawned at them, but took no particular notice.

The mouth of the cave was like a lion's, fringed with teeth. There were men in it, ten or eleven of them, all armed, squatting round the fire.

"Get out!" growled the mullah. But they did not obey. They sat and stared at him.

"Have ye tents?" the mullah asked, in a voice like thunder.

"Aye!" But they did not go yet.

One of the men, he nearest the mullah, got on his feet, but he had to step back a pace, for the mullah would not give ground and their breath was in each other's faces.

"Where are the bombs? And the rifles? And the many cartridges?" he demanded. "We have waited long, Muhammad Anim. Where are they now?"

The others got up, to lend the first man encouragement. They leaned on rifles and surrounded the mullah, so that King could only get a glimpse of him between them. They seemed in no mood to be treated cavalierly—in no mood to be argued with. And the mullah did not argue.

"Ye dogs!" he growled at them, and he strode through them to the fire and chose himself a good, thick burning brand. "Ye sons of nameless mothers!"

Then he charged them suddenly, beating them over head and face and shoulders, driving them in front of him, utterly reckless of their rifles. His own rifle lay on the ground behind him, and King kicked its stock clear of the fire.

"Oh, I shall pray for you this night!" Muhammad Anim snarled. "What a curse I shall beg for you! Oh, what a burning of the bowels ye shall have! What a sickness! What running of the eyes! What sores! What boils! What sleepless nights and faithless women shall be yours! What a prayer I will pray to Allah!"

They scattered into outer gloom before his rage, and then came back to kneel to him and beg him withdraw his curse. He kicked them as they knelt and drove them away again. Then, silhouetted in the cave mouth, with the glow of the fire behind him, he stood with folded arms and dared them shoot. He lacked little in that minute of being a full-grown brute at bay. King admired him, with reservations.

After five minutes of angry contemplation of the camp he turned on a contemptuous heel and came back to the fire, throwing on more fuel from a great pile in a corner. There was an iron pot in the embers. He seized a stick and stirred the contents furiously, then set the pot between his knees and ate like an animal. He passed the pot to King when he had finished, but fingers had passed too many times through what was left in it and the very thought of eating the mess made his gorge rise; so King thanked him and set the pot aside.

Then, "That is thy place!" Muhammad Anim growled, pointing over his shoulder to a ledge of rock, like a shelf in the far wall. There was a bed upon it, of cotton blankets stuffed with dry grass. King walked over and felt the blankets and found them warm from the last man who had lain there. They smelt of him too. He lifted them and laughed. Taking the whole in both hands he carried it to the fire and threw it in, and the sudden blaze made the mullah draw away a yard; but it did not make him speak.

"Bugs!" King explained, but the mullah showed no interest. He watched, however, as King went back to the bed, and subsequent proceedings seemed to fascinate him.

Out of the chest that one of the women had set down King took soap. There was a pitcher of water between him and the fire; he carried it nearer. With an improvised scrubbing brush of twigs he proceeded to scrub

every inch of the rock-shelf, and when he had done and
had dried it more or less, he stripped and began to
scrub himself.

"Who taught thee thy squeamishness?" the mullah
asked at last, getting up and coming nearer. It was
well that King's skin was dark (although it was many
shades lighter than his face, that had been stained so
carefully). The mullah eyed him from head to foot
and looked awfully suspicious, but something prompted
King and he answered without an instant's hesitation.

"Why ask a woman's questions?" he retorted. "Only
women ask when they know the answer. When I
watched thee with the firebrand a short while ago, oh,
mullah, I mistook thee for a man."

The mullah grunted and began to tug his beard. But
King said no more and went on washing himself.

"I forgot," said the mullah then, "that thou art her
pet. She would not love thee unless thy smell was
sweet."

"No," said King quite cheerfully—going it blind, for
he did not know what had possessed him to take that
line, but knew he might as well be hanged for a sheep
as for a lamb—"No, if I stank like thee she would not
love me."

The mullah snorted and went back to the fire, but he
took King's cake of soap with him and sat examining
it.

"*Tauba!*" he swore suddenly as if he had made a
gruesome discovery. "Such filthy stuff is made from
the fat of pigs!"

"Doubtless!" said King. "That is why *she* uses it,
and why I use it. She is a better Muhammadan than

thou. She would surely cleanse her skin with the fat
of pigs!"

"Thou art a shameless one!" said the mullah, shaking his head like a bear.

"I am what Allah made me!" answered King, and
then, for the sake of the impression, he went through
the outward form of muslim prayer, spreading a mat
and omitting none of the genuflections. When he had
finished he unfolded his own blankets that a woman
had thrown down beside the chest and spread them
carefully on the rock-shelf. But though he was allowed to climb up and lie there, he was not allowed
to sleep—nor did he want to sleep—for more than an
hour to come.

The mullah came over from the fire again and stood
beside him, glaring like a great animal and grumbling
in his beard.

"Does she surely love thee?" he asked at last, and
King nodded, because he knew he was on the trail of
information.

"So thou art to ape the Sleeper in his bronze mail,
eh? Thou art to come to life, as she was said to come
to life, and the two of you are to plunder India? Is
that it?"

King nodded again, for a nod is less committal than
a word; and the nod was enough to start the mullah off
again.

"I saw the Sleeper and his bride before she knew of
either! It was I who let her into Khinjan! It was
I who told the men she is the 'Heart of the Hills' come
to life! She tricked me! But this is no hour for
bearing grudges. She has a plan and I am minded to
help."

King lay still and looked up at him, sure that treachery was the ultimate end of any plan the mullah Muhammad Anim had. India has been saved by the treachery of her enemies more often than ruined by false friends. So has the world, for that matter.

"A jihad when the right hour comes will raise the tribes," the mullah growled. "She and thou, as the Sleeper and his mate, could work wonders. But who can trust her? She stole that head! She stole all the ammunition! Does she *surely* love thee?"

King nodded again, for modesty could not help him at that juncture. Love and boastfulness go together in the "Hills."

"She shall have thee back, then, at a price!"

King did not answer. His brown eyes watched the mullah's, and he drew his breath in little jerks, lest by breathing aloud he should miss one word of what was coming.

"She shall have thee back against Khinjan and the ammunition! She and thou shall have India, but I shall be the power behind you! She must give me Khinjan and the ammunition! She must admit me to the inner caves, whence her damned guards expelled me. I must have the reins in my two hands, so! Then, thou and she shall have the pomp and glitter while I guide!"

King did not answer.

"Dost understand?"

King murmured something unintelligible.

"Otherwise, I and my men will storm Khinjan, and she and thou shall go down into Earth's Drink lashed together!"

King shuddered, not because he felt afraid, but be-

cause some instinct told him to make the mullah think
him afraid. He was far too interested to be fearful.

"Ye shall both be tortured before the plunge into
the river! She shall be tortured in the Cavern of
Earth's Drink before the men!"

King shuddered again, this time without an effort.
He could imagine the thousands watching grimly while
the flayer used his knife.

"I have men in Khinjan! I have as many as she!
On the day I march there will be a revolt within. She
would better agree to terms!"

King lay looking at him, like a prisoner on the rack
undergoing examination. He did not answer.

"Write thou a letter. Since she loves thee, state
thine own case to her. Tell her that I hold thee hostage, and that Khinjan is mine already for a little fighting. In a month she can not pick out my men from
among her own. Her position is undermined. Tell
her that. Tell her that if she obeys she shall have India and be queen. If she disobeys, she shall die in the
Cavern of Earth's Drink!"

"She is a proud woman, mullah," answered King.
"Threats to such as she—?"

The mullah mumbled and strode back and forth
three times between King's bed and the fire, with his
fists knotted together behind him and his head bent,
as Napoleon used to walk. When he stood beside the
bed again at last it was with his mind made up, as his
clenched fists and his eyes indicated.

"Make thine own terms with her!" he growled.
"Write the letter and send it! I hold thee; she holds
Khinjan and the ammunition. I am between her and
India. So be it. She shall starve in there! She shall

lie in there until the war is over and take what terms
are offered her in the end! Write thine own letter!
State the case, and bid her answer!"

"Very well," said King. He began to see now defi-
nitely how India was to be saved. It was none of his
business to plan yet, but to help others' plans destroy
themselves and to sow such seed in the broken ground
as might bear fruit in time.

The mullah left him, to squat and gaze into the fire,
and mutter, and King lay still. After a while the mullah went and carried a great water bowl nearer to the
fire and, as King had done, stripped himself. Then he
heaped great fagots on the fire—wasteful fagots, each
of which had cost some woman hours of mountain
climbing. And in the glow of the leaping flame he
scrubbed himself from head to foot with King's soap.
Finally, with a feat of strength that nearly forced an
exclamation out of King, he lifted the great water
bowl in both hands and emptied the whole contents
over himself. Then he resumed his smelly garments
without troubling to dry his body, and got out a Quran
from a corner and began to read it in a nasal singsong
that would have kept dead men awake. King lay and
watched and listened.

Reading scripture only seemed to fire the mullah's
veins. For him sleep was either out of reach or despi-
cable, perhaps both. He seemed in a mood to despise
anything but conquest and strode back and forth up
and down the cave like a caged bear, muttering to himself.

After a time he went to the mouth of the cave, to
stand and stare out at the camp where the thousand
fires were dying fitfully and wood smoke purged the

air of human nastiness. The stars looked down on him, and he seemed to try to read them, standing with fists knotted together at his back.

And as he stood so, six other mullahs came to him and began to argue with him in low tones, he browbeating them all with furious words hissed between half-closed teeth. They were whispering still when King fell asleep. It was courage, not carelessness, that let him sleep—courage and a great hope born of the mullah's perplexity.

He dreamed that he was writing, writing, writing, while the torturers made a hot fire ready in the Cavern of Earth's Drink and whetted knives on the bridge end while the organ played *The Marseillaise*. He dreamed Yasmini came to him and whispered the solution to it all, but what she whispered he could not catch, although she whispered the same words again and again and seemed to be angry with him for not listening.

And when he awoke at last he had fragments of his blanket in either hand, and the sun was already shining into the jaws of the cave. The camp was alive and reeked of cooking food. But the mullah was gone, and so was all the money the women had brought, together with his medicines and things from Khinjan.

When the last evil jest has been made, and the rest
Of the ink of hypocrisy spilt,
When the awfully right have elected to fight
Lest their own should discover their guilt;
When the door has been shut on the "if" and the "but"
And it's up to the men with the guns,
On their knees in that day let diplomatists pray
For forgiveness from prodigal sons.

CHAPTER XVII

INSTEAD of the mullah, growling texts out of a Quran on his lap, the Orakzai Pathan sat and sunned himself in the cave mouth, emitting worldlier wisdom unadulterated with divinity. As King went toward him to see to whom he spoke he grinned and pointed with his thumb, and King looked down on some sick and wounded men who sat in a crowd together on the ramp, ten feet or so below the cave.

They seemed stout soldierly fellows. Men of another type were being kept at a distance by dint of argument and threats. Away in the distance was Muhammad Anim with his broad back turned to the cave, in altercation with a dozen other mullahs. For the time he was out of the reckoning.

"Some of these are wounded," the Pathan explained. "Some have sores. Some have the belly ache. Then again, some are sick of words, hot and cold by day and night. All have served in the army. All have medals. All are deserters, some for one reason, some for another and some for no reason at all. Bull-with-a-beard

349

looks the other way. Speak thou to them about the
pardon that is offered!"

So King went down among them, taking some of the
tools of his supposed trade with him and trying to
crowd down the triumph that would well up. The seed
he had sown had multiplied by fifty in a night. He
wanted to shout, as men once did before the walls of
Jericho.

A man bared a sword cut. He bent over him, and
if the mullah had turned to look there would have been
no ground for suspicion. So in a voice just loud
enough to reach them all, he repeated what he had told
the Pathan the day before.

"But who art thou?" asked one of them suspiciously.
Perhaps there had been a shade too much cocksureness
in the hakim's voice, but he acted faultlessly when he
answered. Voice, accent, mannerism, guilty pride,
were each perfect.

"Political offender. My brother yonder in the cave
mouth"—(The Pathan smirked. He liked the imputa-
tion)—"suggested I seek pardon, too. He thinks if
I persuade many to apply for pardon then the sirkar
may forgive me for service rendered."

The Pathan's smirk grew to a grin. He liked
grandly to have the notion fathered on himself; and
his complacency of course was suggestive of the hakim's trustworthiness. But the East is ever cautious.

"Some say thou art a very great liar," remarked a
man with half a nose.

"Nay," answered King. "Liar I may be, but I am
one against many. Which of you would dare stand
alone and lie to all the others? Nay, sahibs, I am a
political offender, not a soldier!"

They all laughed at that and seizing the moment when they were in a pliant mood the Orakzai Pathan proceeded to bring proposals to a head.

"Are we agreed?" he asked. "Or have we waggled our beards all night long in vain? Take him with us, say I. Then, if pardons are refused us he at least will gain nothing by it. We can plunge our knives in him first, whatever else happens."

"Aye!"

That was reasonable and they approved in chorus. Possibility of pardon and reinstatement, though only heard of at second hand, had brought unity into being. And unity brought eagerness.

"Let us start to-night!" urged one man, and nobody hung back.

"Aye! Aye! Aye!" they chorused. And eagerness, as always in the "Hills," brought wilder counsel in its wake.

"Who dare stab Bull-with-a-beard? He has sought blood and has let blood. Let him drink his own!"

"Aye!"

"Nay! He is too well guarded."

"Not he!"

"Let us stab him and take his head with us; there well may be a price on it."

They took a vote on it and were agreed; but that did not suit King at all, whatever Muhammad Anim's personal deserts might be. To let him be stabbed would be to leave Yasmini without a check on her of any kind, and then might India defend herself! Yet to leave the mullah and Yasmini both at large would be almost equally dangerous, for they might form an alliance. There must be some other way, and he set out to gain time.

"Nay, nay, sahibs!" he urged. "Nay, nay!"

"Why not?"

"Sahibs, I have wife and children in Lahore. Same are most dear to me and I to them. I find it expedient to make great effort for my pardon. Ye are but fifty. Ye are less than fifty. Nay, let us gather a hundred men."

"Who shall find a hundred?" somebody demanded, and there was a chorus of denial. "We be all in this camp who ate the salt."

It was plain, though, that his daring to hold out only gave them the more confidence in him.

"But Khinjan," he objected. The crimes of the Khinjan men were not to the point. Time had to be gained.

"Aye," they agreed. "There be many in Khinjan!" Mere mention of the place made them regard Orakzai Pathan and hakim with new respect, as having right of entry through the forbidden gate.

"Then I have it!" the Pathan announced at once, for he was awake to opportunity. "Many of you can hardly march. Rest ye here and let the hakim treat your belly aches. Bull-with-a-beard bade me wait here for a letter that must go to Khinjan to-day. Good. I will take his letter. And in Khinjan I will spread news about pardons. It is likely there are fifty there who will dare follow me back, and then we shall march down the Khyber like a full company of the old days! Who says that is not a good plan?"

There were several who said it was not, but they happened to have nothing the matter with them and

could have marched at once. The rest were of the
other way of thinking and agreed in asserting that
Khinjan men were a higher caste of extra-ultra murderers whose presence doubtless would bring good
luck to the venture. These prevailed after considerable argument.

Strangely enough, none of them deemed the propo-
sition beneath Khinjan men's consideration. Pardon
and leave to march again behind British officers loomed
bigger in their eyes than the green banner of the
Prophet, which could only lead to more outrageous
outlawry. They knew Khinjan men were flesh and
blood—humans with hearts—as well as they. But caution had a voice yet.

"*She* will catch thee in Khinjan Caves," suggested
the man with part of his nose missing. "She will have
thee flayed alive!"

"Take note then, I bequeath all the women in the
world to thee! Be thou heir to my whole nose, too,
and a blessing!" laughed the Pathan, and the butt of
the jest spat savagely. In the "Hills" there is only
one explanation given as to how one lost his nose,
and they all laughed like hyenas until the mullah Muhammad Anim came rolling and striding back.

By that time King had got busy with his lancet,
but the mullah called him off and drove the crowd
away to a distance; then he drove King into the cave
in front of him, his mouth working as if he were bit-
ing bits of vengeance off for future use.

"Write thy letter, thou! Write thy letter! Here
is paper. There is a pen—take it! Sit! Yonder is
ink—ttutt-ttutt!—Write, now, write!"

King sat at a box and waited, as if to take dictation, but the mullah, tugging at his beard, grew furious.

"Write thine own letter! Invent thine own argument! Persuade her, or die in a new way! I will invent a new way for thee!"

So King began to write, in Urdu, for reasons of his own. He had spoken once or twice in Urdu to the mullah and had received no answer. At the end of ten minutes he handed up what he had written, and Muhammad Anim made as if to read it, trying to seem deliberate, and contriving to look irresolute. It was a fair guess that he hated to admit ignorance of the scholars' language.

"Are there any alterations you suggest?" King asked him.

"Nay, what care I what the words are? If she be not persuaded, the worse for thee!"

He held it out, and as he took it King contrived to tear it; he also contrived to seem ashamed of his own clumsiness.

"I will copy it out again," he said.

The mullah swore at him, and conceiving that some extra show of authority was needful, growled out:

"Remember all I said. Set down she must surrender Khinjan Caves or I swear by Allah I will have thee tortured with fire and thorns—and her, too, when the time comes!"

Now he had said that, or something very like it, in the first letter. There was no doubt left that the mullah was trying to hide ignorance, as men of that fanatic ambitious mold so often will at the expense of better judgment. If fanatics were all-wise, it would be a poor world for the rest.

"Very well," King said quietly. And with great pretense of copying the other letter out on fresh paper he now wrote what he wished to say, taking so long about it (for he had to weigh each word), that the mullah strode up and down the cave swearing and kicking things over.

"Greeting," he wrote, "to the most beautiful and very wise Princess Yasmini, in her palace in the Caves in Khinjan, from her servant Kurram Khan the hakim, in the camp of the mullah Muhammad Anim, a night's march distant in the hills.

"The mullah Muhammad Anim makes his stand and demands now surrender to himself of Khinjan Caves and of all his ammunition. Further, he demands full control of you and of me and of all your men. He is ready to fight for his demands and already—as you must well know—he has considerable following in Khinjan Caves. He has at least as many men as you have, and he has four thousand more here.

"He threatens as a preliminary to blockade Khinjan Caves, unless the answer to this prove favorable, letting none enter, but calling his own men out to join him. This would suit the Indian government, because while the 'Hills' fight among themselves they can not raid India, and while he blockades Khinjan Caves there will be time to move against him.

"Knowing that he dares begin and can accomplish what he threatens, I am sorry; because I know it is said how many services you have rendered of old to the government I serve. We who serve one raj are one—one to remember—one to forget—one to help each other in good time.

"I have not been idle. Some of Muhammad Anim's men are already mine. With them I can return to India, taking information with me that will serve my government. My men are eager to be off.

"It may be that vengeance against me would seem

sweeter to you than return to your former allegiance.
In that case, Princess, you only need betray me to
the mullah, and be sure my death would leave nothing
to be desired by the spectators. At present he does
not suspect me.

"Be assured, however, that not to betray me to him
is to leave me free to serve my government and well
able to do so.

"I invite you to return to India with me, bearing
news that the mullah Muhammad Anim and his men
are bottled in Khinjan Caves, and to plan with me
to that end.

"If you will, then write an answer to Muhammad
'Anim, not in Urdu, but in a language he can understand; seem to surrender to him. But to me send
a verbal message, either by the bearer of this or by
some trustier messenger.

"India can profit yet by your service if you will.
And in that case I pledge my word to direct the government's attention only to your good service in the
matter. It is not yet too late to choose. It is not
impertinent in me to urge you.

"Nor can I say how gladly I would subscribe myself
your grateful and loyal servant."

The mullah pounced on the finished letter, pretended
to read it, and watched him seal it up, smudging the
hot wax with his own great gnarled thumb. Then
he shouted for the Orakzai Pathan, who came striding in, all grins and swagger.

"There—take it! Make speed!" he ordered, and
with his rifle at the "ready" and the letter tucked inside his shirt, the Pathan favored King with a fare-
well grin and obeyed.

"Get out!" the mullah snarled then immediately.
"See to the sick. Tell them I sent thee. Bid them
be grateful!"

King went. He recognized the almost madness that constituted the mullah's driving power. It is contagious, that madness, until it destroys itself. It had made several thousand men follow him and believe in him, but it had once given Yasmini a chance to fool him and defeat him, and now it gave King his chance. He let the mullah think himself obeyed implicitly.

He became the busiest man in all the "Hills." While the mullah glowered over the camp from the cave mouth or fulminated from the Quran or fought with other mullahs with words for weapons and abuse for argument, he bandaged and lanced and poulticed and physicked until his head swam with weariness.

The sick swarmed so around him that he had to have a body-guard to keep them at bay; so he chose twenty of the least sick from among those who had talked with him after sunrise.

And because each of those men had friends, and it is only human to wish one's friend in the same boat, especially when the sea, so to speak, is rough, the progress through the camp became a current of missionary zeal and the virtues of the Anglo-Indian raj were better spoken of than the "Hills" had heard for years.

Not that there was any effort made to convert the camp en masse. Far from it. But the likely few were pounced on and were told of a chance to enlist for a bounty in India. And what with winter not so far ahead, and what with experience of former fighting against the British army, the choosing was none so difficult. From the day when the lad first feels soft down upon his face until the old man's beard turns white and his teeth shake out, the Hillman would rather fight than eat; but he prefers to fight on the winning side if he may, and he likes good treatment.

Before it was dark that night there were thirty men sworn to hold their tongues and to wait for the word to hurry down the Khyber for the purpose of enlisting in some British-Indian regiment. Some even began to urge the hakim not to wait for the Orakzai Pathan, but to start with what he had.

"Shall I leave my brother in the lurch?" the hakim asked them; and though they murmured, they thought better of him for it.

Well for him that he had plenty of Epsom salts in his kit, for in the "Hills" physic should taste evil and show very quick results to be believed in. He found a dozen diseases of which he did not so much as know the name, but half of the sufferers swore they were cured after the first dose. They would have dubbed him faquir and have foisted him to a pillar of holiness had he cared to let them.

Muhammad Anim slept most of the day, like a great animal that scorns to live by rule. But at evening he came to the cave mouth and fulminated such a sermon as set the whole camp to roaring. He showed his power then. The jihad he preached would have tempted dead men from their graves to come and share the plunder, and the curses he called down on cowards and laggards and unbelievers were enough to have frightened the dead away again.

In twenty minutes he had undone all King's missionary work. And then in ten more, feeling his power and their response, and being at heart a fool as all rogues are, he built it up again.

He began to make promises too definite. He wanted

Khinjan Caves. More, he needed them. So he promised them they should all be free of Khinjan Caves
within a day or two, to come and go and live there
at their pleasure. He promised them they should leave
their wives and children and belongings safe in the
Caves while they themselves went down to plunder
India. He overlooked the fact that Khinjan Caves
for centuries had been a secret to be spoken of in
whispers, and that prospect of its violation came to
them as a shock.

Half of them did not believe him. Such a thing
was impossible, and if he were lying as to one point,
why not as to all the others, too?

And the army veterans, who had been converted
by King's talk of pardons, and almost reconverted by
the sermon, shook their heads at the talk of taking
Khinjan. Why waste time trying to do what never
had been done, with *her* to reckon against, when a
place in the sun was waiting for them down in India,
to say nothing of the hope of pardons and clean living for a while? They shook their heads and combed
their beards and eyed one another sidewise in a way
the "Hills" understand.

That night, while the mullah glowered over the
camp like a great old owl, with leaping firelight reflected in his eyes, the thousands under the skin tents
argued, so that the night was all noise. But King
slept.

All of another day and part of another night he
toiled among the sick, wondering when a message
would come back. It was nearly midnight when he
bandaged his last patient and came out into the star-
light to bend his back straight and yawn and pick his

way reeling with weariness back to the mullah's cave.
He had given his bag of medicines and implements to
a man to carry ahead of him and had gone perhaps
ten paces into the dark when a strong hand gripped
him by the wrist.

"Hush!" said a voice that seemed familiar.

He turned swiftly and looked straight into the eyes
of the Rangar Rewa Gunga!

"How did you get here?" he asked in English.

"Any fool could learn the password into this camp!
Come over here, sahib. I bring word from her."

The ground was criss-crossed like a man's palm by
the shadows of tent-ropes. The Rangar led him to
where the tents were forty feet apart and none was
likely to overhear them. There he turned like a flash.

"She sends you this!" he hissed.

In that same instant King was fighting for his life.
In another second they were down together among
the tent-pegs, King holding the Rangar's wrist with
both hands and struggling to break it, and the Rangar
striving for another stroke. The dagger he held had
missed King's ribs by so little that his skin yet tingled
from its touch. It was a dagger with bronze blade
and a gold hilt—her dagger. It was her perfume in
the air.

They rolled over and over, breathing hard. King
wanted to think before he gave an alarm, and he could
not think with that scent in his nostrils and creeping
into his lungs. Even in the stress of fighting he wondered how the Rangar's clothes and turban had come
to be drenched in it. He admitted to himself afterward that it was nothing else than jealousy that sug-

gested to him to make the Rangar prisoner and hand
him over to the mullah.

That would have been a ridiculous thing to do, for
it would have forced his own betrayal to the mullah.
But as if the Rangar had read his mind he suddenly
redoubled his efforts and King, weary to the point
of sickness, had to redouble his own or die. Perhaps
the jealousy helped put venom in his effort, for his
strength came back to him as a madman's does. The
Rangar gave a moan and let the knife fall.

And because jealousy is poison King did the wrong
thing then. He pounced on the knife instead of on
the Rangar. He could have questioned him—knelt
on him and perhaps forced explanations from him.
But with a sudden swift effort like a snake's the Rangar freed himself and was up and gone before King
could struggle to his feet—gone like a shadow among
shadows.

King got up and felt himself all over, for they had
fought on stony ground and he was bruised. But
bruises faded into nothing, and weariness as well, as
his mind began to dwell on the new complication to
his problem.

It was plain that the moment he had returned from
his message to the Khyber the Rangar had been sent
on this new murderous mission. If Yasmini had told
the truth a letter had gone into India describing him,
King, as a traitor, and from her point of view that
might be supposed to cut the very ground away from
under his feet.

Then why so much trouble to have him killed?
Either Rewa Gunga had never taken the first letter,

or—and this seemed more probable—Yasmini had
never believed the letter would be treated seriously
by the authorities, and had only sent it in the hope
of fooling him and undermining his determination.
In that case, especially supposing her to have received
his ultimatum on the mullah's behalf before sending
Rewa Gunga with the dagger, she must consider him
at least dangerous. Could she be afraid? If so her
game was lost already!

Perhaps she saw her own peril. Perhaps she contemplated—gosh! what a contingency!—perhaps she
contemplated bolting into India with a story of her
own, and leaving the mullah to his own devices! In
such a case, before going she would very likely try
to have the one man stabbed who could give her away
most completely. In fact, would she dare escape into
India and leave himself alive behind her?

He rather thought she would dare do anything.
And that thought brought reassurance. She would
dare, and being what she was she almost surely would
seek vengeance on the mullah before doing anything
else.

Then why the dagger for himself? She must believe him in league with the mullah against her. She
might believe that with him out of the way the mullah would prove an easier prey for her. And that
belief might be justifiable, but as an explanation it
failed to satisfy.

There was an alternative, the very thought of
which made him fearfully uneasy, and yet brought a
thrill with it. In all eastern lands, love scorned takes
to the dagger. He had half believed her when she
swore she loved him! The man who could imagine

himself loved by Yasmini and not be thrilled to his core would be inhuman, whatever reason and caution and caste and creed might whisper in imagination's wake.

Reeling from fatigue (he felt like a man who had been racked, for the Rangar's strength was nearly unbelievable), he started toward where the mullah sat glowering in the cave mouth. He found the man who had carried his bag asleep at the foot of the ramp, and taking the bag away from him, let him lie there. And it took him five minutes to drag his hurt weary bones up the ramp, for the fight had taken more out of him than he had guessed at first.

The mullah glared at him but let him by without a word. It was by the fire at the back of the cave, where he stooped to dip water from the mullah's enormous crock that the next disturbing factor came to light. He kicked a brand into the fire and the flame leaped. Its light shone on a yard and a half of exquisitely fine hair, like spun gold, that caressed his shoulder and descended down one arm. One thread of hair that conjured up a million thoughts, and in a second upset every argument!

If Rewa Gunga had been near enough to her and intimate enough with her not only to become scented with her unmistakable perfume but even to get her hair on his person, then gone was all imagination of her love for himself! Then she had lied from first to last! Then she had tried to make him love her that she might use him, and finding she had failed, she had sent her true love with the dagger to make an end!

In a moment he imagined a whole picture, as it

might have been in a crystal, of himself trapped and
made to don the Roman's armor and forced to pose
to the savage "Hills"—or fooled into posing to them
—as her lover, while Rewa Gunga lurked behind the
scenes and waited for the harvest in the end. And
what kind of harvest?

And what kind of man must Rewa Gunga be who
could lightly let go all the prejudices of the East and
submit to what only the West has endured hitherto
with any complacency—a "tertium quid"?

Yet what a fool he, King, had been not to appreciate at once that Rewa Gunga *must* be her lover.
Why should he not be? Were they not alike as cousins? And the East does not love its contrary, but its
complement, being older in love than the West, and
wiser in its ways in all but the material. He had been
blind. He had overlooked the obvious—that from
first to last her plan had been to set herself and this
Rewa Gunga on the throne of India!

He washed and went through the mummery of muslim prayers for the watchful mullah's sake, and
climbed on to his bed. But sleep seemed out of the
question. He lay and tossed for an hour, his mind
as busy as a terrier in hay. And when he did fall
asleep at last it was so to dream and mutter that the
mullah came and shook him and preached him a half-
hour sermon against the mortal sins that rob men of
peaceful slumber by giving them a foretaste of the
hell to come.

All that seemed kinder and more refreshing than
King's own thoughts had been, for when the mullah
had done at last and had gone striding back to the
cave mouth, he really did fall sound asleep, and it was

after dawn when he awoke. The mullah's voice, not
untuneful was rousing all the valley echoes in the call
to prayer.

Allah is Almighty! Allah is Almighty!
I declare there is no God but Allah!
I declare Muhammad is his prophet!
Hie ye to prayer!
Hie ye to salvation!
Prayer is better than sleep!
Prayer is better than sleep!
There is no God but Allah!

And while King knelt behind the mullah and the
whole camp faced Mecca in forehead-in-the-dust
abasement there came a strange procession down the
midst—not strange to the "Hills," where such sights
are common, but strange to that camp and hour.
Somebody rose and struck them, and they knelt like
the rest; but when prayer was over and cooking had
begun and the camp became a place of savory smell,
they came on again—seven blind men.

They were weary, ragged, lean—seven very tatter-
demalions—and the front man led them, tapping the
ground with a long stick. The others clung to him
in line, one behind the other. He was the only clean-
shaven one, and he was the tallest. He looked as if
he had not been blind so long, for his physical health
was better. All seven men yelled at the utmost of
their lungs, but he yelled the loudest.

"Oh, the hakim—the good hakim!" they wailed.
"Where is the famous hakim? We be blind men—
blind we be—blind—blind! Oh, pity us! Is any kismet worse than ours? Oh, show us to the hakim!

Show us the way to him! Lead us to him! Oh, the famous, great, good hakim who can heal men's eyes!"

The mullah looked down on them like a vulture waiting to see them die, and seeing they did not die, turned his back and went into his cave. Close to the ramp they stopped, and the front man, cocking his head to one side as only birds and the newly blind do, gave voice again in nasal singsong.

"Will none tell me where is the great, good, wise hakim Kurram Khan?"

"I am he," said King, and he stepped down toward him, calling to an assistant to come and bring him water and a sponge. The blind man's face looked strangely familiar, though it was partly disguised by some gummy stuff stuck all about the eyes. Taking it in both hands he tilted the eyes to the light and opened one eye with his thumb. There was nothing whatever the matter with it. He opened the other.

"Rub me an ointment on!" the man urged him, and he stared at the face again.

"Ismail!" he said. "You?"

"Aye! Father of cleverness! Make play of healing my eyes!"

So King dipped a sponge in water and sent back for his bag and made a great show of rubbing on ointment. In a minute Ismail, looking almost like a young man without his great beard, was dancing like a lunatic with both fists in the air, and yelling as if wasps had stung him.

"Aieee-aieee-aieee!" he yelled. "I see again! I see! My eyes have light in them! Allah! Oh, Allah heap riches on the great wise hakim who can heal men's eyes! Allah reward him richly, for I am a beggar and have no goods!"

The other six blind men came struggling to be next, and while King rubbed ointment on their eyes and saw that there was nothing there he could cure the whole camp began to surge toward him to see the miracle, and his chosen body-guard rushed up to drive them back.

"Find your way down the Khyber and ask for the Wilayti dakitar. He will finish the cure."

The six blind men, half-resentful, half-believing, turned away, mainly because Ismail drove them with words and blows. And as they went a tall Afridi came striding down the camp with a letter for the mullah held out in a cleft stick in front of him.

"Her answer!" said Ismail with a wicked grin.

"What is her word? Where is the Orakzai Pathan?"

But Ismail laughed and would not answer him. It seemed to King that he scented climax. So did his near-fifty and their thirty friends. He chose to take the arrival of the blind men as a hint from Providence and to "go it blind" on the strength of what he had hoped might happen. Also he chose in that instant to force the mullah's hand, on the principle that hurried buffaloes will blunder.

"To Khinjan!" he shouted to the nearest man. "The mullah will march on Khinjan!"

They murmured and wondered and backed away from him to give him room. Ismail watched him with dropped jaw and wild eye.

"Spread it through the camp that we march on Khinjan! Shout it! Bid them strike the tents!"

Somebody behind took up the shout and it went across the camp in leaps, as men toss a ball. There was a surge toward the tents, but King called to his deserters. and they clustered back to him. He had to cement their allegiance now or fail altogether, and he would not be able to do it by ordinary argument or by pleading; he had to fire their imagination. And he did.

"*She* is on our side!" That was a sheer guess. "*She* has kept our man and sent another as hostage for him in token of good faith! Listen! Ye saw this man's eyes healed. Let that be a token! Be ye the men with new eyes! Give it out! Claim the title and be true to it and see me guide you down the Khyber in good time like a regiment, many more than a hundred strong!"

They jumped at the idea. The "Hills"—the whole East, for that matter—are ever ready to form a new sect or join a new band or a new blood-feud. Witness the Nikalseyns, who worship a long-since dead Englishman.

"We see!" yelled one of them.

"We see!" they chorused, and the idea took charge. From that minute they were a new band, with a war-cry of their own.

"To Khinjan!" they howled, scattering through the camp, and the mullah came out to glare at them and tug his beard and wonder what possessed them.

"To Khinjan!" they roared at him. "Lead us to Khinjan!"

"To Khinjan, then!" he thundered, throwing up both arms in a sort of double apostolic blessing, and then motioning as if he threw them the reins and leave to

gallop. They roared back at him like the sea under
the whip of a gaining wind. And Ismail disappeared
among them, leaving King alone. Then the mullah's
eyes fell on King and he beckoned him.

King went up with an effort, for he ached yet from
his struggle of the night before. Up there by the
ashes of the fire the mullah showed him a letter he
had crumpled in his fist. There were only a few lines,
written in Arabic, which all mullahs are supposed to
be able to read, and they were signed with a strange
scrawl that might have meant anything. But the paper smelt strongly of her perfume.

"Come, then. Bring all your men, and I will let
you and them enter Khinjan Caves. We will strike
a bargain in the Cavern of Earth's Drink."

That was all, but the fire in the mullah's eyes
showed that he thought it was enough. He did not
doubt that once he should have his extra four thousand
in the caves Khinjan would be his; and he said so.

"Khinjan is mine!" he growled. "India is mine!"

And King did not answer him. He did not believe
Yasmini would be fool enough to trust herself in any
bargain with Muhammad Anim. Yet he could see no
alternative as yet. He could only be still and be glad
he had set the camp moving and so had forced the
mullah's hand.

"The old fatalist would have suspected her answer
otherwise!" he told himself, for he knew that he himself suspected it.

While he and the mullah watched the tents began to
fall and the women labored to roll them. The men

began firing their rifles, and within the hour enough
ammunition had been squandered to have fought a
good-sized skirmish; but the mullah did not mind, for
he had Khinjan Caves in view, and none knew better
than he what vast store of cartridges and dynamite
was piled in there. He let them waste.

Watching his opportunity, King slipped down the
ramp and into the crowd, while the mullah was busy
with personal belongings in the cave. King left his
own belongings to the fates, or to any thief who should
care to steal them. He was safe from the mullah in
the midst of his nearly eighty men, who half believed
him a sending from the skies.

"We see! We see!" they yelled and danced around
him.

Before ever the mullah gave an order they got under
way and started climbing the steep valley wall. The
mullah on his brown mule thrust forward, trying to
get in the lead, and King and his men hung back, to
keep at a distance from him. It was when the mullah had reached the top of the slope and was not far
from being in the lead that Ismail appeared again,
leading King's horse, that he had found in possession
of another man. That did not look like enmity or
treachery. King mounted and thanked him. Ismail
wiped his knife, that had blood on it, and stuck his
tongue through his teeth, which did not look quite like
treachery either. Yet the Afridi could not be got to
say a word.

Two or three miles along the top of the escarpment
the mullah sent back word that he wanted the hakim
to be beside him. Doubtless he had looked back and

had seen King on the horse, head and shoulders above the baggage.

But King's men treated the messenger to open scorn and sent him packing.

"Bid the mullah hunt himself another hakim! Be thou his hakim! Stay, we will give thee a lesson in how to use a knife!"

The man ran, lest they carry out their threat, for men joke grimly in the "Hills."

Ismail came and held King's stirrup, striding beside him with the easy Hillman gait.

"Art thou my man at last?" King asked him, but Ismail laughed and shook his head.

"I am *her* man."

"Where is *she?*" King asked.

"Nay, who am I that I should know?"

"But *she* sent thee?"

"Aye, *she* sent me."

"To what purpose?"

"To *her* purpose!" the Afridi answered, and King could not get another word out of him. He fell behind.

But out of the corner of his eye, and once or twice by looking back deliberately, King saw that Ismail was taking the members of his new band one by one and whispering to them. What he said was a mystery, but as they talked each man looked at King. And the more they talked the better pleased they seemed. And as the day wore on the more deferential they grew. By midday if King wanted to dismount there were three at least to hold his stirrup and ten to help him mount again.

By the sweat of your brow; by the ache of your bones;
In the sun, in the wind, in the chill of the rains,
Ye sowed as ye knew. And ye know it was blown
To be trodden and burned—aye, and that by your own
Who sneered at lean furrows and mocked at the stones.
But ye stayed and sowed on. And a little remains.
Ye shall have for your faith. Ye shall reap for your
   pains.

CHAPTER XVIII

FOUR thousand men with women and children
and baggage do not move so swiftly as one man
or a dozen, especially in the "Hills," where discipline
is reckoned beneath a proud man's honor. There were
many miles to go before Khinjan when night fell and
the mullah bade them camp. He bade them camp
because they would have done it otherwise in any case.

"And we," said King to his all but eighty who
crowded around him, "being men with new eyes and
with a great new hope in us, will halt here and eat
the evening meal and watch for an opportunity."

"Opportunity for what?" they asked him.

"An opportunity to show how Allah loves the
brave!" said King, and they had to be content with
that, for he would say no more to them. Seeing he
would not talk, they made their little fires all around
him and watched while their women cooked the food.
The mullah would not let them eat until he and the
whole camp had prayed like the only righteous.

When the evening meal was eaten, and sentries had

been set at every vantage point, and the men all sat
about cleansing their beards. and fingers the mullah
sent for the hakim again. Only this time he sent
twenty men to fetch him.

There was so nearly a fight that the skin all down
King's back was gooseflesh, for a fight at that juncture would have ruined everything. At the least he
would have been made a hopeless helpless prisoner.
But in the end the mullah's men drew off snarling,
and before they could have time to receive new orders or reinforcements, King's die was cast.

There came another order from the mullah. The
women and children were to be left in camp next
dawn, and to remain there until sent for. There was
murmuring at that around the camp, and especially
among King's contingent. But King laughed.

"It is good!" he said.

"Why? How so?" they asked him.

"Bid your women make for the Khyber soon after
the mullah marches to-morrow. Bid them travel down
the Khyber until we and they meet!"

"But—"

"Please yourselves, sahibs!" The hakim's air was
one of supremest indifference. "As for me, I leave
no women behind me in the mountains. I am content."

They murmured a while, but they gave the orders
to their women, and King watched the women nod.
And all that while Ismail watched him with carefully
disguised concern, but undisguised interest. And King
understood. Enlightenment comes to a man swiftly,
when it does come, as a rule.

He recalled that Yasmini had not done much to
make his first entry into Khinjan easy. On the con-

trary, she had put him on his mettle and had set Rewa
Gunga to the task of frightening him and had tested
him and tried him before tempting him at last.

She must be watching him now, for even the East
repeats itself. She had sent Ismail for that purpose.
It might be Ismail's business to drive a knife in him
at the first opportunity, but he doubted that. It was
much more likely that, having failed in an attempt to
have him murdered, she was superstitiously remorse-
ful. Her course would depend on his. If he failed,
she was done with him. If he succeeded in establish-
ing a strong position of his own, she would yield.

All of which did not explain Ismail's whisperings
and noddings and chin strokings with King's contingent. But it explained enough for King's present
purpose, and he wasted no time on riders to the problem. With or without Ismail's aid, with or without
his enmity, he must control his eighty men and give
the slip to the mullah, and he went at once about the
best way to do both.

"We will go now," he said quietly. "That sentry
in yonder shadow has his back turned. He has over-
eaten. We will rush him and put good running between us and the mullah."

Surprised into obedience, and too delighted at the
prospect of action to wonder why they should obey
a hakim so, they slung on their bandoliers and made
ready. Ismail brought up King's horse and he
mounted. And then at King's word all eighty made
a sudden swoop on the drowsy sentry and took him
unawares. They tossed him over the cliff, too startled
to scream an alarm; and though sentries on either hand
heard them and shouted, they were gone into outer

darkness like wind-blown ghosts of dead men before the mullah even knew what was happening.

They did not halt until not one of them could run another yard, King trusting to his horse to find a footing along the cliff-tops, and to the men to find the way.

"Whither?" one whispered to him.

"To Khinjan!" he answered; and that was enough. Each whispered to the other, and they all became fired with curiosity more potent than money bribes.

When he halted at last and dismounted and sat down and the stragglers caught up, panting, they held a council of war all together, with Ismail sitting at King's back and leaning a chin on his shoulder in order to hear better. Bone pressed on bone, and the place grew numb; King shook him off a dozen times; but each time Ismail set his chin back on the same spot, as a dog will that listens to his master. Yet he insisted he was *her* man, and not King's.

"Now, ye men of the Hills," said King, "listen to me who am political-offender-with-reward-for-capture-offered!" That was a gem of a title. It fired their imaginations. "I know things that no soldier would find out in a thousand years, and I will tell you some of what I know."

Now he had to be careful. If he were to invent too much they might denounce him as a traitor to the "Hills" in general. If he were to tell them too little they would lose interest and might very well desert him at the first pinch. He must feel for the middle way and upset no prejudices.

"*She* has discovered that this mullah Muhammad Anim is no true muslim, but an unbelieving dog of a foreigner from Farangistan! *She* has discovered that he plans to make himself an emperor in these Hills, and to sell Hillmen into slavery!" Might as well serve the mullah up hot while about it! Beyond any doubt not much more than a mile away the mullah was getting even by condemning the lot of them to death. "An eye for the risk of an eye!" say the unforgiving Hills.

"If one of us should go back into his camp now he would be tortured. Be sure of that."

Breathing deeply in the darkness, they nodded, as if the dark had eyes. Ismail's chin drove a fraction deeper into his shoulder.

"Now ye know—for all men know—that the entrance into Khinjan Caves is free to any man who can tell a lie without flinching. It is the way out again that is not free. How many men do ye know that have entered and never returned?"

They all nodded again. It was common knowledge that Khinjan was a very graveyard of the presumptuous.

"She has set a trap for the mullah. She will let him and all his men enter and will never let them out again!"

"How knowest thou?" This from two men, one on either hand.

"Was I never in Khinjan Caves?" he retorted. "Whence came I? I am *her* man, sent to help trap the mullah! I would have trapped all you, but for being weary of these 'Hills' and wishful to go back to India and be pardoned! That is who I am! That is how I know!"

Their breath came and went sibilantly, and the darkness was alive with the excitement they thought themselves too warrior-like to utter.

"But what will *she* do then?" asked somebody.

King searched his memory, and in a moment there came back to him a picture of the hurrying jezailchi he had held up in the Khyber Pass, and recollection of the man's words.

"Know ye not," he said, "that long ago *she* gave leave to all who ate the salt to be true to the salt? She gave the Khyber jezailchis leave to fight against her. Be sure, whatever she does, she will stand between no man and his pardon!"

"But will *she* lead a jihad? We will not fight against *her!*"

"Nay," said King, drawing his breath in. Ismail's chin felt like a knife against his collar bone, and Ismail's iron fingers clutched his arm. It was time to give his hostage to dame Fortune. "She will go down into India and use her influence in the matter of the pardons!"

"I believe thou art a very great liar indeed!" said the man who lacked part of his nose. "The Pathan went, and he did not come back. What proof have we?"

"Ye have me!" said King. "If I show you no proof, how can I escape you?"

They all grunted agreement as to that. King used his elbow to hit Ismail in the ribs. He did not dare speak to him; but now was the time for Ismail to carry information to *her*, supposing that to be his job. And after a minute Ismail rolled into a shadow and was gone. King gave him twenty minutes' start, letting his men rest their legs and exercise their tongues.

Now that he was out of the mullah's clutches—and he suspected Yasmini would know of it within an hour or two, and before dawn in any event—he began to feel like a player in a game of chess who foresees his opponent mate in so many moves.

If Yasmini were to let the mullah and his men into the Caves and to join forces with him in there, he would at least have time to hurry back to India with his eighty men and give warning. He might have time to call up the Khyber jezailchis and blockade the Caves before the hive could swarm, and he chuckled to think of the hope of that.

On the other hand, if there was to be a battle royal between Yasmini and the mullah he would be there to watch it and to comfort India with the news.

"Now we will go on again, in order to be close to Khinjan at break of day," he said, and they all got up and obeyed him as if his word had been law to them for years. Of all of them he was the only man in doubt—he who seemed most confident of all.

They swung along into the darkness under low-hung stars, trailing behind King's horse, with only half a dozen of them a hundred yards or so ahead as an advance guard, and all of them expecting to see Khinjan loom above each next valley, for distances and darkness are deceptive in the "Hills," even to trained eyes. Suddenly the advance guard halted, but did not shoot. And as King caught up with them he saw they were talking with some one.

He had to ride up close before he recognized the Orakzai Pathan.

"Salaam!" said the fellow with a grin. "I bring one hundred and eleven!"

As he spoke graveyard shadows rose out of the darkness all around and leaned on rifles

"Be ye men all ex-soldiers of the raj?" King asked them.

"Aye!" they growled in chorus.

"What will ye?"

"Pardons!" They all said the word together.

"Who gave you leave to come?" King asked.

"None! He told us of the pardons and we came!"

"Aye!" said the Orakzai Pathan, drawing King aside. "But *she* gave me leave to seek them out and tempt them!"

"And what does *she* intend?" King asked him suddenly.

"*She?* Ask Allah, who put the spirit in her! How should I know?"

"We will march again, my brothers!" King shouted, and they streamed along behind him, now with no advance guard, but with the Orakzai Pathan striding beside King's horse, with a great hand on the saddle. Like the others, he seemed decided in his mind that the hakim ought not to be allowed much chance to escape.

Just as the dawn was tinting the surrounding peaks with softest rose they topped a ridge, and Khinjan lay below them across the mile-wide bone-dry valley. They all stood and stared at it, leaning on their guns. All the "Men with New Eyes" saw it now for the first time, and it held them speechless, for with its patchwork towers and high battlements it looked like a very city of the spirits that their tales around the fire on winter nights so linger on.

And while they watched, and the Khinjan men were

beginning to murmur (for they needed no last view
of the place to satisfy any longings!) none else than
Ismail rose from behind a rock and came to King's
stirrup. He tugged and King backed his horse until
they stood together apart.

"*She* sends this message," said Ismail, showing his
teeth in the most peculiar grin that surely the Hills
ever witnessed. And then, omitting the message, he
proceeded first to give some news. "Many of *her* men,
who have never been in the army, are none the less
true to *her*, and *she* will not leave them to the mullah's
mercy. They will leave the Caves in a little while,
and will come up here. They are to go down into
India and be made prisoners if the sirkar will not
enlist them. You are to wait for them here."

"Is that all her message?" King asked him.

"Nay. That is none of it! This is *her* message.
THOU SHALT KNOW THIS DAY, THOU ENG-
LISHMAN, WHETHER OR NOT SHE TRULY
LOVED THEE! THERE SHALL BE PROOF
SUCH AS EVEN THOU SHALT UNDER-
STAND!"

"What does that mean?"

"Nay, who am I that I should know?"

Ismail slipped away and lost himself among the
men, and none of them seemed to notice that he had
been away and had come again. On King's advice a
dozen men climbed near-by eminences and began to
watch for the mullah's coming. The Khinjan men
murmured openly; they wanted to be off.

"But no," said King. "Go if ye will, but *she* has
sent word that other men are coming. I wait for them
here."

After a great deal of resentful argument they consented to lie hidden for an hour or two "but no longer,"
and King hid his horse in a hollow and persuaded
three of them to gather grass for him. It was a little more than an hour after dawn and the chilled rocks
were beginning to grow warmer when the head of a
procession came out of Khinjan Gate and started toward them over the valley. In all more than five
hundred men emerged and about a hundred women
and children, and King's men were kept busy for half
an hour counting them and quarreling about the exact
number. Some of them were burdened heavily, and
there was much discussion as to whether to loot them
or not. Then:

"Muhammad Anim comes !" shouted a voice from
a crag top.

They snuggled into better hiding, and there was no
thought now of leaving before the mullah should go
by. There began to be wagers as to whether *her* men
would be hidden out of sight before the mullah could
top the rise; and then, when the last man was safe
across the valley and up the cliff and in hiding, there
was endless argument as to how much each had betted
and to whom he had lost. It needed an effort to quiet
them when the mullah rose into view at last above the
rise and paused for a minute to stare across at Khinjan before leading his four thousand down and onward. He was silent as an image, but his men roared
like a river in flood and he made no effort to check
them. He was like a man who has made up his mind
to victory in any event. He seemed to be speculating
three or four moves ahead of this one, and to hold
this one such a foregone conclusion in his mind that

it had ceased to interest. He was admirable, there
was no doubt of that. In his own way, like an old
boar sniffing up the wind for trouble, he could command a decent man's respect.

He dismounted, for he had to, and tossed his reins
to the nearest man with the air of an emperor. And
he led the way down the cliffside without hesitation,
striding like a mountaineer. His men followed him
noisily, holding hands to make human chains at the
difficult places and shouting a great deal; but not quite
naturally now. They were too impressed by the seri-
ousness of what they undertook, and in their hearts too
much afraid. The noise was bravado.

It was a weary long wait, watching from the crev-
ices until the last man's back departed down the cliff,
and the procession—Pied Piper of Hamelin and rats
(but no music!)—wound across the valley. At last
Khinjan Gate opened and the mullah led in. The gate
did not shut after the last man, King noted that.

"Let us go now!" shouted fifty voices, and every
man of King's party showed himself and stretched.
"Let us go! Why wait?"

But King would not go. Nor would he explain why
he would not go. Nor could he tell himself what held
him, gazing at Khinjan, except that he thought of Yasmini and ached to know what she was doing.

It was thirty minutes after the last of the mullah's
men had vanished through the gate, and his own men
in dozens and twenties were scattered along the cliff-
top arguing against delay with growing rancor, when
a lone horseman galloped out of Khinjan Gate and
started across the valley. He rode recklessly. He
was either panic-stricken or else bolder than the devil.

In a minute King had recognized the mare, and so
had the eyes of fifty men around him. No man with
half an eye for a horse could have failed to recognize
that black mare, having ever seen her once. She came
like a goat among the rocks, just as she had once dived
into darkness in the Khyber with King following. In
another two minutes King had recognized the Rangar's
silken turban. And now there was no need to restrain
the men; they all stood and watched, to know what
new turn affairs were taking.

Most of them were staring downward at the Rangar's head as he urged the mare up the cliff path,
when the explanation of Yasmini's message came. It
was only King, urged by some intuition, who had his
eyes fixed on Khinjan.

There came a shock that actually swayed the hill
they stood on. The mare on the path below missed
her footing and fell a dozen feet, only to get up again
and scramble as if a thousand devils were behind her,
the Rangar riding her grimly, like a jockey in a race.
Three more shocks followed. A great slice of Khinjan suddenly caved in with a roar, and smoke and dust
burst upward through the tumbling crust.

There was a pause after that, as if the waiting ele-
ments were gathering strength. For ten minutes they
watched and scarcely breathed. Rewa Gunga gained
the summit and, dismounting, stood by King with the
reins over his arm. The mare was too blown to do
anything but stand and tremble. And King was too
enthralled to do anything but stare.

"That is what a woman can do for a man!" said
Rewa Gunga grimly. "She set a fuse and exploded
all the dynamite. There were tons of it! The gal-

ieries must have fallen in, one on the other! A thousand men digging for a thousand years could never get into Khinjan now, and the only way out is down Earth's Drink! She bade me come and bid you goodby, sahib. I would have stayed in there, but she commanded me. She said, 'Tell King sahib my love was true. Tell him I give him India and all Asia that were at my mercy!' "

While the Rangar spoke there came three more earth tremors in swift succession, and a thunder out of Khinjan as if the very "Hills" were coming to an end. The mare grew frantic and the Rangar summoned six men to hold her.

Suddenly, right over the top of Khinjan's upper rim, where only the eagles ever perched, there burst a column of water, immeasurable, huge, that for a moment blotted out the sun. It rose sheer upward, curved on itself, and fell in a million-ton deluge on to Khinjan and into Khinjan valley, hissing and roaring and thundering.

Earth's Drink had been blocked by the explosion and had found a new way over the barrier before plunging down again into the bowels of the world. The one sky-flung leap it made as its weight burst down a mountain wall was enough to blot out Khinjan forever, and what had been a dry mile-wide moat was a shallow lake with death's rack and rubbish floating on the surface.

The earth rocked. The Hillmen prayed, and King stared, trying to memorize all that had been. Suddenly it flashed across his mind that the Rangar who had striven like a fiend to stab him only a matter of hours ago was now standing behind him, within a yard.

He was up on his feet in a second and faced about.
The Rangar laughed.

"So ends the 'Heart of the Hills!'" he said. "Think
kindly of her, sahib. She thought well enough of
you!"

He laughed again and sprang on the black mare,
and before King could speak or raise a hand to stop
him he was off, hell-bent-for-leather along the precipice in the direction of the Khyber Pass and India.
Two of the men who had come out of Khinjan
mounted and spurred after him.

King collected his men and the women and children. It was easy, for they were numb from what
they had witnessed and dazed by fear. In half an
hour he had them mustered and marching.

"Let us go back and loot the mullah's camp and
take the women!" urged a dozen men at least.

"Go then!" said King. "Go back! But I go on!"

"He is afraid! The hakim is afraid of what he
saw!"

King let them think so. He let them think anything
they chose, knowing well that what had unnerved him
had at least rendered them amenable to leading. They
would have no more dared go back without him, and
without at least a hundred others, than they would
have dared go and hunt in the ruins of Khinjan.

Even Ismail clung to his stirrup and would not
leave him, looking like a fledgling with his beard all
new-sprouted on his jaw, and eyes wider than any
bird's.

"Why art thou here?" King asked him. "Had she
no true men who would die with her?"

The Afridi scowled, but choked the answer back.

"Art thou my man now?" King asked him. But he shook his head.

So they marched without talking over the hideous boulder-strewn range that separates Khinjan from the Khyber, sleeping fitfully whenever King called a halt, and eating almost nothing at all, for only a few of them had thought of bringing food.

They reached the Khyber famished and were fed at Ali Masjid Fort, after King had given a certain password and had whispered to the officer commanding. But he did not change into European clothes yet, and none of his following suspected him of being an Englishman.

"A Rangar on a black mare has gone down the pass ahead of you in a hurry," they told him at Ali Masjid. "He had two men with him and food enough. Only stopped long enough to make his business known."

"What did he say his business is?" asked King.

"He gave a sign and said a word that satisfied us on that point!"

"Oh!" said King. "Can you signal down the Pass?"

"Surely."

"Courtenay still at Jamrud?"

"Yes. In charge there and growing tired of doing nothing."

"Signal down and ask him to have that bath ready for me that I spoke about. Good-by."

So he left Ali Masjid at the head of a motley procession that grew noisier and more confident every hour. Ismail still clung to his stirrup, but began to grow more lively and to have a good many orders to fling to the rest.

"You mourn like a dog," King told him. "Three

howls and a whine and a little sulking—and then forgetfulness!"

Ismail looked nasty at that but did not answer, although he seemed to have a hot word ready. And thenceforward he hung his head more, and at least tried to seem bereaved. But his manner was unconvincing none the less, and King found it food for thought.

The ex-soldiers and would-be soldiers marched in fours behind him, growing hourly more like drilled men, and talking, with each stride that brought them nearer India, more as men do who have an interest in law and order. Behind them tramped the women from Khinjan, carrying their babies and their husbands' loads; and behind them again were the other women, who had been told they would be overtaken in the Khyber, but who had actually had to run themselves raw-footed in order to catch up.

Down the Khyber have come conquerors, a dozen conquering kings, and as many beaten armies; but surely no stranger host than this ever trudged between the echoing walls. The very eagles screamed at them.

And as they neared Jamrud Fort the men who sought pardons began to grow sheepish. They began to remember that the hakim might after all be a trickster, and to realize how much too friendly— how almost intimate he had been with the sahibs at Ali Masjid. They began to cluster round him instead of letting him lead, and by the time they met the farthest outposts up the Khyber they were as nervous as raw recruits and ready to turn and bolt at a word —for no one can be more timid than your Hillman

when he is not sure of himself, just as no one can be
braver when he knows his ground.

Signals preceded them, and Courtenay himself rode
up the Pass to greet them. But of course he was not
very cordial to King, considering his disguise; and
he chose to keep the Hillmen in doubt yet as to their
eventual reception. But one of them, the Orakzai
Pathan (for nothing could completely unman him),
shouted to know whether it was true that pardons
had been offered for deserters, and Courtenay nodded.
They were less timid after that. Some of them pulled
medals out and pinned them outside their shirts.

At Jamrud they were given food and their rifles
were taken away from them and a guard was set to
watch them. But the guard only consisted of two
men, both of whom were Pathans, and they assured
them that, ridiculous though it sounded, the British
were actually willing to forgive their enemies and to
pardon all deserters who applied for pardon on con-
dition of good faith in the future.

That night they prayed to Allah like little children
lost and found. The women crooned love-songs to
their babies over the clear fires and the men talked
—and talked—and talked until the stars grew big as
moons to weary eyes and they slept at last, to dream
of khaki uniforms and karnel sahibs who knew neither
fear nor favor and who said things that were so. It
is a mad world to the Himalayan Hillman where men
in authority tell truth unadorned without shame and
without consideration—a mad, mad world, and perhaps
too exotic to be wholesome, but pleasant while the
dream lasts.

Over in the fort Courtenay placed a bath at King's disposal and lent him clean clothes and a razor. But he was not very cordial.

"Tell me all the war news!" said King, splashing in the tub. And Courtenay told him, passing him another cake of soap when the first was finished. After all there was not much to tell—butchery in Belgium —Huns and guns—and the everlastingly glorious stand that saved Paris and France and Europe.

"According to the cables our men are going the records one better. I think that's all," said Courtenay.

"Then why the stuffiness?" asked King. "Why am I talked to at the end of a tube, so to speak?"

"You're under arrest!" said Courtenay.

"The deuce I am!"

"I'm taking care of you myself to obviate the necessity of putting a sentry on guard over you."

"Good of you, I'm sure. What's it all about?"

"I don't mind telling you, but I'd rather you'd wait. The minute you were sighted word was wired down to headquarters, and the general himself will be up here by train any minute."

"Very well," said King. "Got a cigar? Got a black one? Blacker the better!"

He was out of his bath and remembered that minute that he had not smoked a cigar since leaving India. Naked, shaved, with some of the stain removed, he did not look like a man in trouble as he filled his lungs with the saltpeterish smoke of a fat Trichinopoli.

And then the general came and did not wait for King to get dressed but burst into the bathroom and shook hands with him while he was still naked and asked ten questions (like a gatling gun) while King was getting on his trousers, divining each answer after the third word and waving the rest aside.

"And why am I arrested, sir?" asked King the moment he could slip the question in edgewise.

"Oh, yes, of course. Try the case here as well as anywhere. What does this mean?"

Out of his pocket the general produced a letter that smelt strongly of a scent King recognized. He spread it out on a table, and King read. It was Yasmini's letter that she had sent down the Khyber to make India too hot to hold him.

"Your Captain King has been too much trouble. He has taken money from the Germans. He adopted native dress. He called himself Kurram Khan. He slew his own brother at night in the Khyber Pass. These men will say that he carried the head to Khinjan, and their word is true. I, Yasmini, saw. He used the head for a passport to obtain admittance. He proclaims a jihad! He urges invasion of India! He held up his brother's head before five thousand men and boasted of the murder. The next you shall hear of your Captain King of the Khyber Rifles he will be leading a jihad into India. You would have better trusted me. Yasmini."

"Too bad about your brother," said the general. "The body is buried. How much is true about the head?"

King told him.

"Where's *she?*" asked the general.

King did not answer. The general waited.

"I don't know, sir."

"Ask the Rangar," Courtenay suggested.

"Where is he?" asked King.

"Caught him coming down the Khyber on his black
mare and arrested him. He's in the next room! I
hope he's to be hanged. So that I can buy the mare,"
he added cheerfully.

King whistled softly to himself, and the general
looked at him through half-closed eyes.

"Go in and talk to him, King. Let me know the
result."

He had picked King to go up the Khyber on that
errand not for nothing. He knew King and he knew
the symptoms. Without answering him King obeyed.
He went out of the room into a dark corridor and
rapped on the door of the next room to the right.
There was a muffled answer from within. Courtenay
shouted something to the sentry outside the door and
he called another man who fitted a key in the lock.
King walked into a room in which one lamp was burning and the door slammed shut behind him.

He was in there an hour, and it never did transpire
just what passed, for he can hold his tongue on any
subject like a clam, and the general, if anything, can
go him one better. Courtenay was placed under orders not to talk, so those who say they know exactly
what happened in the room between the time when
the door was shut on King and the time when he
knocked to have it opened and called for the general,
are not telling the truth.

What is known is that finally the general hurried
through the door and ejaculated, "Well, I'm damned!"
before it could close again. The sentry (Punjabi Mus-
sulman) has sworn to that over a dozen camp-fires
since the day.

And it is known, too, for the sentry has taken oath

on it and has told the story so many times without much variation that no one who knows the man's record doubts any longer—it is known that when the door opened again King and the general walked out with the Rangar between them. And the Rangar had no turban on, but carried it unwound in his hand. And his golden hair fell nearly to his knees and changed his whole appearance. And he was weeping. And he was not a Rangar at all, but *she,* and how anybody can ever have mistaken her for a man, even in man's clothes and with her skin darkened, was beyond the sentry's power to guess. He for one, etc. . . . But nobody believed that part of his tale.

As Yussuf bin Ali said over the camp-fire up the Khyber later on, "When *she* sets out to disguise herself, she is what she will be, and he who says he thinks otherwise has two tongues and no conscience!"

What is surely true is that the four of them— Yasmini, the general, Courtenay and King sat up all night in a room in the fort, talking together, while a succession of sentries overstrained their ears endeavoring to hear through keyholes. And the sentries heard nothing and invented very much.

But Partan Singh, the Sikh, who carried in bread and cocoa to them at about five the next morning and found them still talking, heard King say, "So, in my opinion, sir, there'll be no jihad in these parts. There'll be sporadic raids, of course, but nothing a brigade can't deal with. The heart of the holy war's torn out and thrown away."

"Very well," said the general. "You can get up the Khyber again and join your regiment."

But by that time the Rangar's turban was on again

and the tears were dry, and it was Partan Singh who
threw most doubt on the sentry's tale about the golden
hair. But, as the sentry said, no doubt Partan Singh
was jealous.

There is no doubt whatever that the general went
back to Peshawur in the train at eight o'clock and
that the Rangar went with him in a separate compartment with about a dozen Hillmen chosen from
among those who had come down with King.

And it is certain that before they went King had
a talk with the Rangar in a room alone, of which conversation, however, the sentry reported afterward that
he did not overhear one word; and he had to go to
the doctor with a cold in his ear at that. He said he
was nearly sure he heard weeping. But on the other
hand, those who saw both of them come out were certain that both were smiling.

It is quite certain that Athelstan King went up the
Khyber again, for the official records say so, and they
never lie, especially in time of war. He rode a coal-
black mare, and Courtenay called him "Chikki"—a
"lifter."

Some say the Rangar went to Delhi. Some say
Yasmini is in Delhi. Some say no. But it is quite
certain that before he started up the Khyber King
showed Courtenay a great gold bracelet that he had
under his sleeve. Five men saw him do it.

And if that was really Rewa Gunga in the general's
train, why was the general so painfully polite to him?
And why did Ismail insist on riding in the train, instead of accepting King's offer to go up the Khyber
with him?

One thing is very certain. King was right about

the jihad. There has been none in spite of all Turkey's and Germany's efforts. There have been sporadic raids, much as usual, but nothing one brigade could not easily deal with, the paid press to the contrary notwithstanding.

King of the Khyber Rifles is now a major, for you can see that by turning up the army list.

But if you wish to know just what transpired in the room in Jamrud Fort while the general and Courtenay waited, you must ask King—if you dare; for only he knows, and one other. It is not likely you can find the other.

But it is likely that you may hear from both of them again, for "A woman and intrigue are one!" as India says. The war seems long, and the world is large, and the chances for intrigue are almost infinite, given such combination as King and Yasmini and a love affair.

And as King says on occasion: *"Kuch dar nahin hai!* There is no such thing as fear!" Another one might say, "The roof's the limit!"

And bear in mind, for this is important: King wrote to Yasmini a letter, in Urdu from the mullah's cave, in which he as good as gave her his word of honor to be her "loyal servant" should she choose to return to her allegiance. He is no splitter of hairs, no quibbler. His word is good on the darkest night or wherever he casts a shadow in the sun.

"A man and his promise—a woman and intrigue—are one!"

THE END

CPSIA information can be obtained
at www.ICGtesting.com
Printed in the USA
LVHW02*1830090718
583160LV00009B/106/P